JAIME
CASTLE

C000121293

BLACK TALON

**North
Lincolnshire**
Council
www.northlincs.gov.uk

Library items can be renewed online 24/7,
you will need your library card number
and PIN.

Avoid library overdue charges by signing
up to receive email preoverdue reminders.

To find out more about North Lincolnshire
Library and Information Services, visit
www.northlincs.gov.uk/libraries

www.northlincs.gov.uk/librarycatalogue

BLACK TALON
©2023 CASTLE/PELOQUIN

Aethon Books
www.aethonbooks.com

Print and eBook formatting, and cover design by Steve Beaulieu. Artwork provided by Antti Hakosaari.

Published by Aethon Books LLC.

Aethon Books is not responsible for websites (or their content) that are not owned by the publisher.

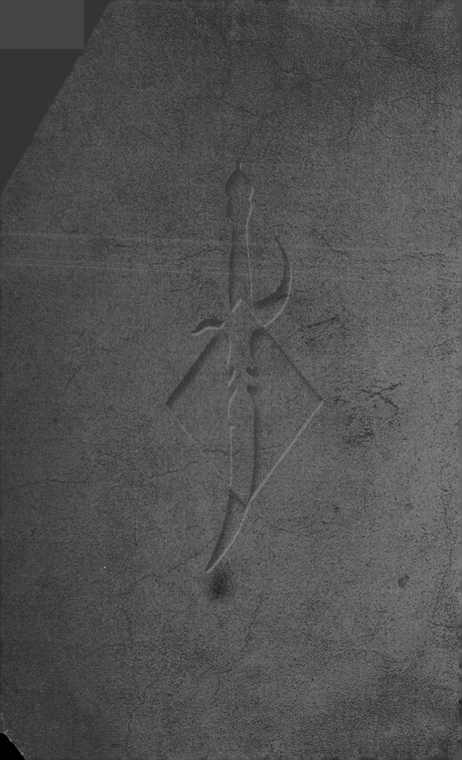

ALSO IN SERIES

BLACK TALON
RED CLAW
SILVER SPINES
GOLDEN FLAMES

I

KULLEN

Two men would die today.

One, the poor bastard screaming and thrashing on Arbiter Chuldok's bloody table atop the gallows. This one would die slowly. Painfully. Chuldok would stretch out the torture, savor each moment of the pitiful man's agony until even the crowd clustered around the hangman's scaffolding would lose their appetite for the kill.

Public executions were trite in Kullen's eyes. He preferred to bring death silently, swiftly, and without fanfare. The sycophants and sociopaths who chose to gather and watch while others' lives were drained away by degrees... it made Kullen sick to his stomach—and very little turned the assassin's insides.

Whatever the prisoner had done—stolen bread to feed his family? Gotten caught with his pecker in the wrong man's daughter?—his death would be just one more spectacle masked as "the Emperor's justice." When the time came to take his last tormented breath, the dying man would likely welcome Shekoth's cold embrace as surcease from his suffering.

But the second man—the pompous, self-important prick who wore the title of Magister Iltari like velvet robes of royalty—had not come prepared to die. Like the others, he'd come to watch the torture and public execution of the fool beneath Arbiter Chuldok's knives.

Kullen grinned. If only that overfed shit-stain knew he'd come to his own execution today.

The cobblestoned Court of Justice was packed to overflowing. There, amongst the rabble, Kullen was at home. He was a droplet of rain amidst a tumultuous typhoon. Just one thorn in the patch. A single blade on the battlefield. One of the thousands that comprised the jeering and shouting mass bearing witness to Chuldok's latest cruelty. Filthy, every single one of them. And not just their hearts. Their faces, too, were stained with soot, dirt, and worse. Coated in the stench that so enveloped this city —the reek of sewers and rotting, fetid flesh, but also like the roses the noblemen wore upon their lapels to mask the odor. Like the perfumes carried upon the powdered skin of their ladies.

The din of voices blended into a roar not even the nearby ocean could match. They shouted—chiefly from sheer joy that they were not the one strapped to the Arbiter's table, that they'd survived one more day in a city that treated life like a commodity, where blood was cheaper than gold.

So many wretched curs. All so desperate for an escape from the harshness of their cold reality.

To think, this was entertainment to these people. When this was over, and the prisoner's head had finally been separated from his neck, they would return to their miserable lives. To their hungry families and empty larders. To their squalid homes in the Embers, cast deep in the shadows of the Upper Crest—fine manors and grand estates belonging to the nobility of Dimvein, the Karmian Empire's capital city.

Kullen cast one last glance at the grisly exhibition atop the raised scaffolding. Dark carrion birds roosted on the gallows, cawing in eager anticipation of their next meal. They seemed to prefer the eyeballs as appetizers and intestines as dessert, seemingly unpicky in terms of anything else.

Arbiter Chuldok was a beast—and not just because of his Orken heritage. His arms must have been twice the size of Kullen's own. Two giant hands rested upon the pommel of his axe, blade pressed into the platform between his feet. Beside him, a headsman's block, bloodied and chipped, was on full display for the waiting crowd. The dry, splinter-laden wood of the platform, stained dark from years of use, was the center of attention.

And there, upon the Arbiter's table, the thrashing man—a distraction ideal for Kullen's purposes this night.

Sinking deeper into his hood, Kullen slithered through the crowd, heading away from the Court of Justice. No one took notice of his departure. Those he passed simply flowed forward to fill the space he'd vacated, jockeying for a position closer to the gallows as if they longed to be showered with the blood of the guilty. Finally, he broke free of the thinning throng and ducked down a narrow side street adjoining the broad avenue that led toward the main square—as all roads in Dimvein tended to do.

Night was nearing, twinkling stars already piercing the purpling skies. Cold shadows grew long, their emaciated fingers stretching from the city's tall towers, grasping, clawing for anything to swallow up. For Kullen, that made for a simple task, disappearing into obscurity, hidden, shrouded—the perfect place for an assassin.

Around him, tall, wooden structures rose, half a dozen on each side of the square, each bearing the varied colors of their respective houses. More scented flowers encircled them.

Kullen had one such tower in his sights.

Two guards stood beside a wooden staircase, wearing the insignia of the Iltari house: a gold bar and an ivy leaf. Wealth and good fortune.

Not tonight.

Kullen inclined his head upward at the skybox. The covered

balcony built into the side of the Iltari tower offered the aristocrat and his esteemed guests a peerless view of the Court of Justice's fatal festivities. From there, high up on their perch, they offered the common people below them—always below them—an unobstructed glimpse of their "betters." The peasants, garbed in rough-spun tunics and work clothing, could gaze up at those holding positions they could never even hope to attain and bask in the opulence.

Magister Iltari was the wealthiest of the elevated nobility. Just the sale of one ring from one finger could rebuild the Embers, Dimvein's poor district. Where most noblemen were round, rotund, fat, slothful, lazy—repulsive even—Magister Iltari wore the shape of a trained guard, if one slightly out of service. His clean-shaven face was one for which ladies had swooned over for decades. Yet now, he'd become out of date. Near expiration. Ready to be tossed out with the trash.

He looked utterly foolish in his gold smallcoat, black tassels fluttering as he gesticulated, telling what was sure to be an exaggerated tale of his younger days. His face was already red, flushed from drink, and he leaned over to shout something at the aristocrat at his side.

The other man, Magister Estéfar, was a beast of a fellow, with a face like a boar and a vast belly bulging out of his garishly yellow shirt. He was so occupied with a goblet in his left hand and a little ball of molten metal dancing like a coin between his knuckles on his right, that he paid no attention to his companion's words. Until Magister Iltari flicked a handful of snow —*magically* summoned snow, plucked right out of thin air—at him. Estéfar's entire hand turned to ice and the lump of red-hot metal hissed like an angry snarler.

Magister Estéfar bristled, but Magister Iltari just laughed and clapped the smaller man on his plump shoulder.

It was all a show, play-acting for the little people below. They all hated one another, that was not to be mistaken. It was all white mustaches and fancy suits from the men, and resplendent dresses, sparkling jewelry, and big hair from the women, faces painted like whores. As if name and blood would somehow separate them from the poor souls littering the Embers' many brothels.

Sadly, it often did.

Kullen tensed as a patrol of Imperial Scales marched past in a clatter of clanking breastplates, rattling sabers, and tromping hobnailed boots. Not surprisingly, the Dimvein city guards paid as much attention to him as they would a shadow. They were far from the Emperor's finest—the sort more than happy to look the other way for a modest bribe or a bottle of wine from the right person. And perhaps they'd just beat the wrong person half to death with no provocation at all.

Luckily for Kullen, the Orkenwatch wasn't present. Not yet, at least. The Orken guard, headed by Arbiters like Chuldok, would be called out within the hour, though. The murder of an aristo-crat tended to draw Emperor Wymarc's attention. Kullen, however, intended to be long gone by the time the tusked bastards flooded the Court of Justice. If discovered, his head would be the next to roll... no matter who he was.

No one could know he served at the Emperor's pleasure—that was part of what made his task so intriguing. Hunt in silence, lurk in shadows. Never get caught. And above all, never, ever allow his connection to the Emperor to be discovered by anyone not already privy to such damning information.

What would the people say if they'd known Emperor Wymarc himself had called for Iltari's death?

Kullen snickered to himself.

They'd probably love him all the same for it.

He skirted the edge of the town square, slipping in and out of covered stalls, all but invisible in the settling gloom.

A booming voice drew the attention of anyone whose eyes weren't already fixated on the gallows.

"Dimvein!" Arbiter Chuldok sounded like a bear being strangled, like wagon wheels grating upon loose stone. "Justice witness you today! Sentenced to die, he is, this man. He do bad against Emperor Wymarc and against all Dimvein. He in Crimson Fang. Accused of murder, conspiracy, and high treason!"

The crowd gave a collective gasp as if they hadn't known why they were there. It was all a game—a mummer's farce put on by people with too much time and not enough purpose.

Chuldok stood before his audience, drinking in their adoration, clearly satisfied with their response. His feet remained planted like strong oaks, his voice rising and falling with a brutal intensity that more than made up for his lack of oratory.

"Confessed his crimes, this scum has, and admitted guilt. Now, we see price of treason, cost of raising hands to Empire. His suffering serves as reminder of..."

Kullen tuned out Chuldok's bloviated ramblings. The prisoner's crime, his sentence to torture and death, they mattered nothing to him. He cared only for the command given him by his Emperor. He labored only so that Iltari would die.

Sliding deep into a patch of shadow, Kullen noted a lone raven pecking at scraps of trash. Other than that, he was utterly alone. From within the folds of his cloak, he drew a dagger in his left hand and, with his right, reached for the small vial that hung from a silver chain around his neck. His thumb pressed into the vial's gold-embossed cap. A familiar needle-prick pain followed. Closing his eyes, he drew a breath, frigid as it entered his lungs.

A wellspring of power erupted within himself. Time seemed to freeze between heartbeats, the world grinding to a halt around him. His gaze followed the raven's ascent. Each individual flap of its wings was crystalline to him. Dust motes danced in what little light bathed the alley. Energy flooded his veins, set his nerves prickling, burned in his muscles. Strength of that power called out, drawing him into its depths as if he plunged into the pools of the dark, icy underground.

The reservoir of magic resided in the core of his being because of who he was—what he was—accessible only through drag-onblood within the vial through a process known as bloodsurging.

"*Have you need of me?*" came a voice in his mind. "*Do you summon me, Kullen Bloodsworn?*"

No, Umbris, Kullen answered, not with his voice but within, an internal coupling he and his dragon shared. *But I have need of your powers.*

"*They are yours, as always,*" the voice echoed, deep and calm.

Suddenly, Kullen's body began to tingle, lightning coruscating through his veins. In an instant, the world around him changed. Everything became nothing but light and shadow, black and white with varying shades of gray. It was some ancient magic he didn't begin to understand—simply embraced it, learned to master it in service of his Emperor.

Walking forward, he felt the gentle pull of his form toward shadow, one to another like the temptation of sin. Somehow, he managed to control his path, navigating through the cobbled street, unseen by anyone. The guards stood at the base of the stairs, looking almost directly at Kullen but noticing nothing odd or out of place.

Then, Kullen looked upward, finding a nook below the skybox's upper deck. The shadows beckoned, and he surrendered to them. As if he caught upon the very wind itself, he slipped through the darkness above Dimvein. Despite the glow of scrubbed lunar light, he continued on a spiraling path toward the upper levels of Magister Iltari's tower and the open skybox.

His eyes—or perhaps simply his consciousness—locked onto the flicker of lantern light, the glint of gold thread, the sparkling gleam of crystal goblets. He ebbed ever closer, watching the pride etched upon Magister Iltari's face—or perhaps it wasn't pride as much as rabid avarice.

In the Court of Justice below, Arbiter Chuldok proceeded to ramble about "justice" and "punishment" and all the other shit that offered him the legal shield behind which to hide his depravities. The man was a true ass-licking whoreson if any ever lived. He boasted his title proudly every chance he got, using it to his advantage in every fashion. There was no coin he couldn't plunder in the name of the Emperor, nor woman he feared to violate. And both things, by all accounts, he did often and with great vigor.

A loud crack echoed through the heavens, and the sky abruptly opened up. Cold pellets of rain hissed, but Kullen didn't feel them.

Thick sheets of rain sluiced down upon the skybox's covering, hammering against the tower's stone walls. Noblemen shouted in irritation as their fine robes and coats were soaked. The ladies scrambled for further cover.

Magister Iltari and his guests sprang to their feet, and attendants rushed forward to drag their throne-like chairs back from the railing and out of the rain.

The shadows embraced Kullen at the rear of the skybox, where he would find momentary rest. An icy chill seeped into his soul—a warning he dared not ignore—and he relinquished the bloodsurge. Then, he propelled himself upward, out of the font of power. This transition was far more difficult. He focused on the light, fixed the whole of his thoughts upon it. It felt like clawing his way out of quicksand. The Shadow Realm clung to him, fighting to trap him within its endless void. He could only fight it with the force of his Umbris's wills combined. His mind quivered with the effort of returning to skin and bone while his body struggled to once more find its place in this plane.

Color began to form around him, swirling and strobing light. He recalled the first time he'd experienced the return from the Shadow Realm. He'd retched countless times until his belly was empty but for the bitter bile within. But in the end, even that had come up upon his bedroom floor.

Now, from within the shadows came limbs, a torso, his cloak, and drawn dagger—things that had been touching his bare flesh before entering the Shadow Realm. This time, his lunch stayed where it was. The feeling was no less uncomfortable, but Kullen had mastered it.

Not twenty feet from him, Magister Iltari and company, had once again resumed their seats beneath the portico, protected from the downpour. Magister Iltari himself sat in the center of the twelve-by-twelve pace skybox.

Kullen assessed the ground between him and his target. The attendants had resumed their places behind the noblemen's chairs, faces dutifully turned toward their masters. No House Iltari guards stood on watch this high up, wrongfully believing they protected the only entrance at the stairs below.

It would be an easy kill. One knife was all he needed to end the threat against Emperor Wymarc. Kullen would make the throw ninety-nine times out of a hundred, and at this close distance, he had no chance of missing.

Kullen stepped out of the shadows. His arm went up and back, dagger gripped loosely between his fingertips. Even outside of the Shadow Realm, no one saw him; no one would. He was a ghost, invisible within the depths of his charcoal-gray cloak.

A wet thunk suddenly spread through the skybox. The chair beside Magister Iltari toppled backward, and the rotund honored guest, Magister Estéfar, collapsed on the balcony. His yellow tunic became a muddled brown as his own blood spewed outward in a geyser, a crossbow bolt protruding from his throat.

2

NATISSE

O ne bolt, two targets. Natisse had never faced such an impossible choice.

Her very soul cried out, anguished at the sight of her friend, Ammon—brave, handsome, charming Ammon who'd taught her to swing a sword and string a bow. He thrashed on the torturer's rack in the Court of Justice. Face bloodied and bruised, tongue now strained beneath his torturer's fingers, his one remaining eye wide in horror, he fought. Ammon always fought. But now, even his substantial strength proved useless against the steel manacles binding him to the table.

Natisse tasted bile at the sound of blood pooling in Ammon's throat. Each cry was gurgled and muted. She ached to end his suffering. The bodkin-tipped bolt loaded into her crossbow could serve a dual purpose, both ushering him into Shekoth, the realm of the dead, and stealing away Arbiter Chuldok's pleasure in an instant.

Tusks cracked and crooked, the smile on that oaf's pock-marked face would vanish. Or she could send the bolt straight through the Arbiter's tough hide and end his miserable life instead.

Yet, she could do neither. Uncle Ronan's instructions had been clear, and she dared not disobey. For all the torment roiling within her, she knew her task—the one for which she'd been trained and specifically chosen.

Her eyes settled on the lavishly dressed aristocrat sitting as the guest of honor in Magister Iltari's skybox. Pudgier than a suckling pig and with a pink complexion to match, Magister Estéfar was the reason Ammon would die slowly and in great pain.

Ammon, her brother in purpose if not in blood, Uncle Ronan's strong right hand, had been reduced to a screaming, struggling mass of flesh and bone.

And that bastard wore a smile, conversing gleefully with his lady companion as if what went on below were no more than a chariot race.

As much as Natisse desired to insert her hand, to sway the outcome of the Court of Justice, Magister Estéfar's death mattered more to the Crimson Fang than anything else—even Ammon's life.

Tears welled in her ice-blue eyes, but she swallowed them back. There would be time for such emotions, but not now.

Pulling her eyes from the Court of Justice, just for a moment, she gazed toward the Emperor's looming palace, high above Dimvein. There, atop its battlements, sat curled the scaled, white figure of Thanagar. Thanagar the Protector, the Emperor called him, though to her and the Crimson Fang, he was Thanagar the Cruel, Thanagar the Oppressor, Thanagar the Captor. The sight of the enormous dragon filled her with ice-cold fury that froze the white-hot anger burning within her.

Natisse turned back to her target, squinting to focus her rage-tinted vision on the skybox. As Ammon had taught her, she sighted in the range. From her perch atop the roof of Magister Corvus's tower, she had a clear view and clean shot straight to Estéfar's fat heart.

Sprinkling rain became a veritable downpour, but that only

reflected Natisse's mood. She embraced it, allowed the cold water to cleanse her of emotion.

Until...

Arbiter Chuldok must have relinquished his hold on Ammon's tongue. At least long enough for a fresh scream to echo from the cobbled courtyard below. What could make such a strong man sound so frail? An intangible dagger twisted in Natisse's belly. With some effort, she refused to remove her gaze from her target, fearing even her iron resolve might be tested at the sight of Ammon's suffering. She'd been waiting there for hours, long before the crowds had filled in the square. She'd positioned herself for this moment, and she couldn't blow it. She may not be able to shut her ears, but she could harden her heart.

The fire that had scarred her skin and destroyed her family had also burned away another part of her, the tether linking mind and spirit. As she had so many times before—and far too easily she worried—she pushed the emotions down deep, locked them away, until only the unbending metal of intention remained.

Ammon's agonized cries came again, registering in her ears, but this time, they failed to pierce the cold veil of ice encircling her heart. She steadied her breathing, tasted the coppery tang of blood that hung thick over the Court of Justice, and settled her cheek against the crossbow's solid blackwood stock. The instant skin touched wood, all thoughts faded from her mind. Nothing existed beyond the feel of the weapon in her hands and against her face. Moonlight glinted off the bolt's razor-sharp tip.

Magister Estéfar had to die today.

Blood for blood, she thought and squeezed the trigger.

The crossbow bucked, the bolt hissed, splitting the sky on a straight path toward her target. She couldn't hear the thud over the rain and Ammon's cries, but crimson bloomed just beneath the collar of Magister Estéfar's bright yellow tunic, and the aristocrat's posture went suddenly rigid. His head slumped, and his high-backed wooden chair toppled backward.

Natisse fled before the screams began. It was about time the nobles were the ones to suffer loss at the Court of Justice.

Seizing the bundled rope she'd used to ascend Magister Corvus' tower the previous night and dropped it over the roof's edge. Even before its weighted end struck the street far below, Natisse had donned her cloak and cast darkness over her face with its hood. Crossbow slung over her shoulder, she slid down. Leather gloves and leggings protected her flesh as she descended five full stories in the span of ten thundering heartbeats.

The instant her boots splashed on the muddy street, she broke into a sprint westward, not stopping until the shadows of a nearby alley embraced her. With the Imperial Scales—the Emperor's city guard—now focused on the mayhem within Magister Iltari's skybox, none were present in these meager backstreets. By the time they discovered her abandoned rope, Natisse would be long gone.

Dimvein was dark tonight—dark as once the whole city had been before the Emperor and his Lumenators cast their light upon the wealthier districts. She wouldn't complain. Darkness shrouded true intentions, and her actions today demanded secrecy.

She carried herself at an unhurried pace, careful to draw no undue attention. She would be just another pauper on the streets, a shadow amongst shadows. A new kind of shout grew louder behind her, one of alarm, but all she heard were Ammon's screams of pain. Whether they were real or just an imprint forever etched into her mind, she didn't know.

Magister Estéfar's death would stir the Imperial Scales into a frenzy. That coward, Emperor Wymarc, would doubtless let his Orkenwatch loose upon the city. But it was already too late to save the fat, pompous aristocrat. Magister Estéfar would go into death with his guilt and shame burned into his soul.

Natisse's lip curled into a sneer. After what he'd done, Shekoth was too kind a place. She sensed it before she heard it, a figuring gliding down from the shadows beside her. In one swift motion, her dagger slipped from its sheath, and she had it raised. A hand gripped her forearm, prepared for the defense.

Tall, rangy Garron glared at her, the lines on his face deeper than ever, his eyes dark with shadow.

"One of these days," Natisse said through pressed teeth. He said not a word, just shook his head dourly. Natisse stowed her weapon, and they walked together.

Around the next corner, a second figure joined them. Hulking Jad, uncharacteristically quiet, tears glistening on his craggy cheeks—as tender-hearted as he was enormous, with a deep well-spring of emotion Natisse often envied.

For her, however, this was still not yet the time nor place to allow the day's emotion to get the better of her. She would remain strong—for all their sakes.

Small, sweet Sparrow was the last to rejoin their procession through the cold, dark alleyways of Heroes Row. There was nary a lantern lit to guide the way—never mind one of the Emperor's Lumenators—their feet shuffled through the dust as they had a thousand times before. The polished facade of the district was lost off the main avenue. This was their world—here, with the people, in the muck and filth. Not in some posh palace, surrounded by luxury purchased with the blood of innocents.

Sparrow, barely fifteen years of age, could barely walk for the noiseless sobs that rattled her slender shoulders. Of all the Fang, she'd been closer to Ammon—save, perhaps, Baruch, the only one to claim true kinship with the man. Ammon's death would be a blow that Natisse was uncertain the girl would survive.

Silence, but for the occasional sniffle, hung like a thick pall, so heavy not even the mounting tumult in the Court of Justice could puncture it.

Natisse led them ever-westward toward through the maze of filthy, detritus-clogged alleys that marked their path to the One Hand District. She had no need for street signs—not that there were any in these narrow, muddy lanes—but followed the internal compass that always guided her aright. None questioned her; they'd long ago accepted Uncle Ronan's unspoken bestowal of command. They merely trudged along behind her, each lost in their own churning thoughts and sentiments.

Jad, big as he was, practically carried Sparrow the rest of the way, lending her strength when hers had failed. Which was often.

Who could blame her?

When they reached the One Hand District, Natisse led them away from the bustling markets—which doubtless would be thick with Imperial Scales and Lumenators. Instead, she headed deeper into the shadows and settling gloom.

A few hundred yards ahead, Baruch stood outside the crumbling warehouse that was their destination. Here, the winds whipped, and with them, the scent of fresh water from the nearby Talos River. The chill filling the air stung Natisse's eyes, making it even more difficult to hold back the emotion welling there.

Still, she remained the only one steadfast. Baruch, too, stood with puffy eyes, bright with fury and reddened cheeks, though he'd tried to scrub any trace of tears. His fists were white, clenched at his side.

Natisse frowned.

"What are you doing here?" she hissed at him. "Uncle Ronan said—"

"I know what he said!" Baruch snarled in a thick brogue. "And I don't give a thimbleful of dragon piss."

His vehemence surprised Natisse. She'd never heard him raise his voice before. At least not to her. Yet, she could understand. It was, after all, his brother condemned to die today.

"Garron. Key," she called over her shoulder.

Loquacious as ever, Garron answered her with a grunt that held a note of affirmation. Then, he slid past her to open the padlock that secured rusted chains barring the warehouse's faded, dilapidated door.

Natisse seized Baruch by his broad shoulders. "Get inside."

Though he stood a full head taller, Baruch allowed her to propel him past Garron, through the open door, and into the decrepit warehouse. He might've defied Ronan to stand in the Court of Justice to watch his brother's execution, but he was no fool. He knew as well as she what would've happened if either the Orkenwatch or Imperial Scales had spotted him. He was a wanted man—they all were—and they could afford no attention drawn so close to home.

Hidden in plain sight, they were. Just a stone's throw and then some from Dimvein's largest open-air market square, well off the beaten path leading westward the One Hand District toward the Embers. Plain sight, perhaps. But a place whose streets no fancy lord or lady would be caught dead traversing.

"Uncle Ronan's going to be pissed," she said, her voice sharp. "And he'll be right in it."

Garron grunted, once again signaling his agreement.

"Don't mean I'm gonna let it stop me," Baruch said. His voice was strained, tight with emotion. "He was my brother, Nat."

"I know." Natisse took his rough hand in hers, gripped it tight. "And I'm sorry, Baruch."

Baruch quickly averted his gaze, but Natisse had caught a glimpse of moisture brimming once more in his eyes. She let him have his private moment of sorrow and led him gently by the hand deeper into the building.

"Jad, a quick sweep," Natisse said. "Make sure we're alone."

"On it," the big man said, his voice deep as thunder and fraught with emotion.

Natisse stood with Baruch while Jad searched the warehouse's two small adjoining rooms—in truth, simply sagging wooden walls without doors or windows. Despite the padlock—which in its current state was little more than a visual warding. One good pull from a man Jad's size and the chains would crumble. Drunks often used the building to sleep off a bender, or the occasional beggar would find an opening in the structure's decaying façade and squat within.

Not that the warehouse offered much in the way of shelter. The roof had long ago caved in, leaving only wooden rafters and open skies beyond. The building flooded with every rain and provided scant relief from the strong bay winds that gusted through. Not the most hospitable place, even for the truly destitute of the Karmian Empire's capital city.

"We're alone," Jad said, lumbering out of the rooms a minute later.

"Good." Natisse turned to Baruch—who should've been keeping watch on the building rather than joining the rabble in the Court of Justice—and nodded. "Open it."

Baruch pulled his hand reluctantly from hers and strode toward the largest of the debris piles littering the warehouse's cracked and weather-beaten floor. Kneeling, he reached into what looked like a nondescript metal canister surrounded by trash. A moment later, a loud click echoed, and the entire pile of debris shifted to the side on hidden casters, revealing an opening and stairs that descended into darkness.

"Here." Baruch pulled out a torch he'd also concealed among the rubbish, and Garron used one of his firestrikers to light the oil-soaked rag wrapped around one end. Once the flame caught, Baruch handed it to Garron. "Lead the way."

Garron accepted it with a nod and hurried down the stairs. Sparrow followed, Jad still at her side, with one huge arm wrapped around her shaking shoulders. At least she'd managed to do the walking on her own by now.

"Wouldn't mind a Lumenator among us," Jad said, not for the first time as he disappeared below.

That left Natisse and Baruch. She motioned for him to go first. "You're going to face Uncle Ronan's tongue-lashing like a man, you hear me?"

Baruch just shrugged. "I just thought—"

"No, you didn't," Natisse snapped. "Brother or not, he wouldn't have wanted you to see him like that." He looked down at her. "It would've killed Ammon, knowing you were there, hearing him suffer. And Uncle Ronan knew that, which is precisely why he told you to stay put, to guard the Burrow."

Baruch's jaw muscles clenched. His words came out like they pained him, like each one dragged knives across his throat. "I had to see him. I needed him to know he wasn't alone. I knew he was gonna be in pain, but if it was me on that table…"

His voice cracked, and this time, he did nothing to conceal the tears.

Natisse pulled him in close. He was so strong, like a weathered oak, yet he trembled like a storm-blown leaf in her arms.

"He knew you loved him," she whispered into the man's ear. "And that's what he's taking with him to Shekoth. That knowledge. That assurance."

"Aye, I know," Baruch sobbed into the crook of her neck. "'Least deep down, I do. But why him? It should—"

"Don't you dare say it should've been you!" Natisse pushed Baruch up until she could look him dead in the eyes. "You know that what happened wasn't anyone's fault. Just sheer rotten luck, that's all." She gripped his strong chin in one hand. "We all know the dangers we face doing what we do. Ammon…"

She let out a long breath.

"He just got unlucky. Running into Magister Estéfar's guards like that and breaking his leg while trying to flee. There's nothing you could've done. Nothing any of us could've done. But what we can do is continue the mission Ammon gave his life for."

"The mission," Baruch repeated, his voice a raspy whisper. "The mission above all."

"Mission above all," Natisse echoed. Ammon had always said that; always lived it. He would've done what she'd done, too. He'd have put the bolt into Magister Estéfar, even if it had been Baruch on Arbiter Chuldok's bloody table.

"And that mission's not done," she continued. "We've hit another target, but there are many more left to eliminate."

The memory of that rose blooming on Magister Estéfar's sun-bright shirt remained affixed in her mind—as vivid as the memories of the yellow-and-crimson flames that had destroyed her childhood.

Baruch brushed the tears from his cheek, gave himself a light slap, and nodded. "Aye, you're right."

"So c'mon, then," she said, playfully shoving him toward the staircase that led to the Burrow. "Time for you to face Uncle Ronan. Once you're done getting chewed out, we'll pick up what's left of you, and together, we can find out which damned aristocrat he wants us to kill next."

3

KULLEN

*S*hekoth's icy pits!

The sudden violence froze Kullen in place for a single heartbeat. He stood, staring at Magister Estéfar's body nailed to his toppled chair by a crossbow bolt buried in his throat. Blood fountained from the aristocrat's wound, and open mouth, pooling around his head. It stained the wooden planks and seeped through the slats. Kullen could imagine it watering the flowers below, splashing the commoners, baptizing them in unholy glory.

Though here, above, the overfed lord managed one weak gurgle and a twitching convulsion or two before falling deadly quiet.

A high-pitched, panicked scream shattered the stillness in the skybox. Most still watched in stunned silence, but one woman dressed in a yellow satin dress that matched Estéfar's own tunic dropped to her knees beside the dead Magister. There could be no mistaken, this was Lady Estéfar sobbing wetly over her fallen husband.

Magister Iltari leaped to his feet and scrambled backward toward the railing, eyes like great shields in horror.

Instinctively, Kullen's arm flashed forward, his fingers loosing the throwing dagger he'd readied. The blackened blade spun end over deadly end and found its place embedded into Magister Iltari's right eye. The man's head snapped back with the force of it, the impact sending him reeling into the railing. Without a sound, he went over, dead before his body hit the ground.

Where there had just been chaos, there was now pandemonium. Panicked screams and howls of alarm rang out. Those nearest Magister Estéfar's corpse scrambled, no doubt sure their lives were next to be forfeit. But Kullen had no other targets. One such coward staggered to escape the widening scarlet puddle, and lost his footing at the stairs. Each crack of the man's head resounded until he collided into the ascending guards and all three lay at the bottom.

The guards rose, but the man did not, his neck bent at an unnatural angle.

While those who'd seen Magister Iltari go over the edge voiced their confusion, Kullen went unnoticed. His hand flashed to the vial around his neck and, pricking his finger to activate the blood magic, summoned Umbris's power to him.

The world flashed to light and darkness around him and his body plummeted deep into the Shadow Realm. Within the space of a single breath, he was gone from the skybox and cavorting from shadow to shadow above and throughout the Court of Justice.

Kullen maintained little control over the course of his flight, just the force of will and his goal in mind: escape the Court of Justice and the soon-to-be-there Orkenwatch. He barely managed to preserve cohesion until he drew within level of the rooftops overlooking the Court of Justice. Releasing his bloodsurging, he returned to his human form and collapsed into a sodden heap on the slanting tiled roof of a three-story building.

For long seconds, he lay there, mind and body torn between

realms, his thoughts racing. Only one question prevailed: where in Shekoth's embrace did that bolt come from?

He raised his head—which still felt light—and analyzed Magister Iltari's skybox and the possible perches from which the assassin had loosed the missile that had taken Magister Estéfar's worthless life. He summoned to mind the image of the bolt protruding from the aristocrat's thick throat, looking for any hint at its owner's purpose or identity. None came, but he used what he could recall. The shaft had been angled upward, which meant it could only have come from above the skybox.

The only structure within crossbow range offering such a vantage point would've been the roof of one of the other Magister's towers surrounding the Court of Justice. He hadn't seen the shooter, not even a glimpse. By now, they'd have vanished into Dimvein's latticework streets, a phantom in the night. Just like him.

No, there were none others like him.

But this one... who was this killer?

Kullen slid down the rooftop and dropped onto a second-story balcony, then scaled down the building's façade to reach the street below. No one was looking his way—all eyes were fixed on the spectacle in and overlooking the Court of Justice. The Imperial Scales would be spanning outward to search by now, but the Orkenwatch wouldn't be there for at least half an hour.

Plenty of time for Kullen to pull his own vanishing act.

A grimace tugged at his lips as he slipped into the darkness behind the butcher's shop, the smell of blood heavy on the air. Fitting for such a day. Then, he steeled his heart and girded his mind for the conversation he was about to have.

Kullen loathed a great many things. Noblemen chief among them. Pompous lordlings who thought a great deal of themselves, but who were little more than worthless twats contributing nothing to Imperial society. He also hated Arbiter Chuldok and his cruel torments—everything about the Arbiter, really. The Orkenwatch, though that was a matter of principle. After all, they were tasked with enforcing Emperor Wymarc's laws throughout Dimvein, and Kullen had spent his entire life on the wrong said of said laws. At least publicly—not even Turoc, Tuskigo of the Orkenwatch, their highest rank, knew of Kullen's secret service to the Karmian Empire.

Onyx sharks ranked fairly high on Kullen's list, but what sort of idiot wouldn't dislike such voracious creatures?

A dull edge, a poorly balanced sword, and a broken crossbow string deserved their rightful places as well amongst his most detested things.

But, as always, Kullen found himself utterly despising the secret tunnels which led into the Imperial Palace almost as much as loathed men like Magister Iltari and Arbiter Chuldok.

The place stank like what it was—the drainage system for the Emperor's piss and shit. The walls were covered in a thick film that Kullen dared not hypothesize its origin. None of the Emperor's Lumenators cast their light upon these tunnels, nor were there torches to light the passage since the passage's contents were highly flammable. Instead, the ceiling was open to the city in intervals of thirty or so kilometers, allowing thin strips of moonlight in—and tonight, rain.

It was no matter. Kullen didn't need a torch or magical light—thanks to Umbris's magic. This particular ability required no transformation, no entering into the realm of shadows. The bond formed between them allowed Kullen to see through Umbris's eyes. Or, in this case, to transform his eyes into those of his dragon companion.

In the darkness of the tunnels, he didn't fear them being seen, but he knew from time spent gazing upon them in the reflections of mirrors and water that the dragon eyes were a sight to behold. Gleaming yellow orbs with vertical-slitted pupils, capable of seeing in all but the deepest darkness. Much like when he traversed the Shadow Realm, everything lacked the vivid hues seen by human eyes, but appeared washed out, a mess of grays and blacks and whites with only hints of color. It'd taken him years to grow accustomed to seeing the world through such limited vision but now, it was all but natural to him.

By now, news of the events at the Court of Justice would've reached Emperor Wymarc's ears. Better for Kullen to get out in front of the mess than to wait until he was summoned to the royal palace. He owed his Emperor an explanation, after all.

Kullen neared a stone wall. It was no different from any other wall except for the distinct lack of sludge covering it. Kullen spotted a crack that looked like nothing more than that, but when he slid his stiletto blade into it, he was rewarded with a soft click followed by a long groan. The wall shifted, gliding to one side and then out toward him.

Kullen stepped back.

When he emerged into the lower dungeons, a new flavor of stink accosted him. The stench of shit was joined by sweat and sorrow. Down here, the worst of Dimvein's criminals sat awaiting a trial that would never come. In this, Kullen was reminded that there was a worse thing than losing one's head in the Court of Justice.

He stalked forward through the opening. This was the kind of place the guards only entered when forced to do so. Even what little food the prisoners were given came three meals at a time and was delivered by young porters desperate to earn the favor of the Imperial Scales.

And none but Kullen, the Emperor, and a select number of the

Emperor's confidants knew of the secret passage in the rear-most cell. The barred door was broken and the room was in a right state of disrepair, ignored by all for that very reason.

Kullen slipped out into the corridor, not bothering to enter the shadows. Soon, he found himself stalking past occupied cells.

"Get away, demon!" one man shouted.

"The dark one has returned!" another joined. "Take me this time! Take me!" he begged.

By design, Kullen led these poor creatures to view him as an otherworldly entity, taunting and threatening them so that any words they spoke to guards about his presence would be met with suspicion at best and the blunt end of a club at worst.

"You'll rest soon enough," he told the man, glaring at him with yellow dragon eyes.

Kullen reached the staircase at the end which led to the upper dungeons. Instead, he slipped beneath its rounded edge and engaged yet another lever hidden within the stone wall's depths. Out of sight of any prisoners, he slid in and climbed a hidden ladder.

Kullen's dragon eyes illuminated the lines of the walls and rungs of the ladder. Kullen moved upward, inching closer to the top where he would emerge through a hatch behind a wall in the Emperor's private study.

Kullen's heart sank as he snuck out and caught sight of the well-dressed, youthful figure seated in a plush reading chair, legs crossed. However, he wasn't reading. Instead, he sipped from a golden goblet, apparently waiting for Kullen's arrival.

Prince Jaylen, the Emperor's grandson, was like a particularly sharp pebble in Kullen's boot.

"Assassin," Prince Jaylen spat, rising to his feet. He placed his drink down on the table beside him and moved to smooth down his already perfectly flat tailored coat and straightening his ruffled shirt cuffs. "What in Shekoth dead depths happened out there?"

Kullen found himself momentarily stunned. Never before had the prince acknowledged him as such. How long had he known?

Prince Jaylen fixed Kullen with what he doubtless thought was a piercing gaze, but looked more like the bug-eyed stare of a drunken blind man. He was scrawny and pointy, a nose like the sharp end of an axe and a brow that appeared to be hit by the flat side.

"Yes," Jaylen said with a little smile. "That's right."

Kullen regarded the Prince through narrowed eyes. "Say what now?"

"What I say is that news of Magister Estéfar's… passing has reached Our ears."

Kullen groaned inwardly at the Prince's use of the royal "Our"—something he'd never have done if Emperor Wymarc were present. He was too young, inexperienced, and far from taking the Imperial crown to start speaking as if he were the Emperor.

Prince Jaylen seemed not to notice.

"So," he said, drawing out the word before retaking his seat. He took a small sip from the goblet. "I'm interested to hear your report."

He leaned forward, pursing his lips—another of those facial expressions he apparently thought made him appear lordly. Instead, he looked like a puckered asshole. Kullen supposed that was precisely what the boy was. On his slim face, it just served to drive home how young he was at twenty-two summers. Barely out of swaddling clothes, in Kullen's mind.

He motioned with a flat hand for Kullen to sit but found himself ignored. A sneer disappeared from his face as quickly as it arrived, and he lowered his hand to the arm of the chair as if that was what he'd meant to do all along.

Clearing his throat, he said, "What happened out—"

"None of your pissing business," Kullen snapped.

Prince Jaylen recoiled as if Kullen had struck him.

"My grandfather—" he began, standing once again and taking a step toward Kullen.

"May have told you who I am and what I do," Kullen said, "but that doesn't mean I answer to you." He stepped closer to the Prince and jabbed a finger into Jaylen's chest. Jaylen stumbled back and into the chair. "If the Emperor wants to fill you in on my report, then he'll do so himself. Otherwise, you and I have no business."

"Well—You—I—You'd do well to remember to whom you're speaking so rudely," Prince Jaylen said, bristling. He glared up into Kullen's face like a toddler in a highchair. "I will be the Emperor one day, and it behooves you to treat me with the respect I am due as the future heir to the Imperial crown and your eventual ruler."

"What behooves me," Kullen snarled back, "is to not waste my time dealing with a snot-nosed kid who barely knows which end of the sword points where." He loomed over the young man. "As to whether you'll be my eventual ruler, time will tell, won't it?"

Prince Jaylen blanched. "Are you... threatening the crown prince?"

"Crown prince," Kullen scoffed. "Be it threat or promise." He bared his teeth in a snarl. "What are you going to do about it, princeling?"

To his credit, Prince Jaylen found it in him to rise again. Kullen could see the tremor in his legs but the prince didn't recoil from his fury. He had heart, Kullen had to admit. Not an over-abundance of brains or caution or good sense, but courage in spades. Unfortunately, in the Karmian Empire, that trait would both get him killed at a young age and, should he manage to stay alive, make him a far less effective ruler than his grandfather, Emperor Wymarc.

Prince Jaylen's lips parted, a defiant snarl forming, but the opening of the study door cut off his words.

"Well, now we've got ourselves a damned party," Kullen said, eying the only man he'd wanted to see even less than the prince.

Assidius, Imperial Seneschal, glided into the room. He too was lean, like Jayden. However, where the prince lacked in matters of intimidation, Assidius abounded. Though it had little to do with his appearance.

The dark-haired man wore his goatee trimmed to a far-too-precise point, his mustache, perfectly manicured. Two sharp eyebrows cast shadows upon deep brown eyes, making them appear like pitch. He looked almost comical standing beside the lavishly dressed Jaylen. The Seneschal's simple clothes—a long, flat-collared frock of frumpy brown over an equally drab cream-colored shirt and black trousers—gave the appearance of one who had worked for his position, yet they only served to accentuate his whip-thin frame. Even Prince Jaylen was well-proportioned juxtaposed with the Seneschal.

"Assidius," Prince Jaylen said in a tone that barely stopped short of whiny, "tell Kullen that he is to accede to my authority as the crown prince of the Karmian Empire, and to answer me as he would my grandfather."

Assidius glared at the prince—a boy by all definitions.

"I'm afraid I cannot do that, my prince," Assidius said.

The seneschal's voice always made Kullen think of mating snakes—even his name carried the hiss. The man had just the slightest lisp on his sibilant sounds, despite years spent attempting to conceal the impediment.

"Not in this matter, at least," he continued. His lean face contorted into a displeased frown. "Despite my earnest objections, Kullen serves at the pleasure of the Emperor alone."

Kullen grinned, knowing those words hurt Assidius to say aloud. There was no love lost between the two, and neither attempted to conceal it much. Kullen shot the seneschal a smug grin. He had no doubt that Assidius would love nothing more than to be rid of him—after using him to dispatch of those he considered enemies to the Empire, of course. Emperor Wymarc had been right to make clear that Kullen answered to him alone. Otherwise, there'd be far more blood in Dimvein's streets.

"However," Assidius continued, his voice growing harsh, "it is the duty of all loyal citizens of the Empire to show deference to its Imperial rulers." He returned Kullen's look with a dagger-sharp glare. "Including, of course, your prince."

"Crown prince," Jaylen interjected.

"Quite," Assidius said, not turning his gaze.

Kullen met the man's icy expression with calm disdain. The Emperor might rely heavily on the seneschal for the day-to-day running of the Karmian Empire, but Kullen had no need of the man. Just as he had no need of the prince.

Sliding around Jaylen, Kullen bumped the prince's shoulder roughly as he passed.

"I'll be seeing the Emperor now," he told both men. "Where's he—"

"Hold!" Prince Jaylen's voice echoed behind Kullen, accompanied by the rasp of steel on leather. "First, you insult me, then you assault my royal person. I don't care who you are—you will answer for your impudence, peasant!"

Kullen turned to find Prince Jaylen standing in a fencer's position, the sword that had been sitting on his belt moments earlier now leveled at Kullen's chest.

"Ah, so you do know which way to point it," Kullen said. "Bravo." He crossed his arms, making it clear to the prince that he would not make efforts toward his own blade. "Now, let me tell you where you can stick it."

"How dare you!"

"Prince Jaylen—" Assidius began in a tone rich with exasperation.

"This does not concern you, Seneschal!" Jaylen snapped. His eyes blazed, locked on Kullen. "Draw your weapon, knave."

"Is that really what you want me to do?" Kullen snorted in derision.

"Draw, foul beast," Jayden said.

"All these names," Kullen said, shaking his head. He let his hand slide to the pommel of his sword, then sighed. "You've made it clear that you know what I do for your grandfather."

"You're an ass-ass-in," the Prince said, succinctly splitting the word into thirds. His tone was cold, as if disgusted by Kullen's mere presence. "You lurk in the shadows, drive your knives into the backs of better men. But have you ever—"

Kullen moved so fast the Prince had no time to react before he was disarmed, his wrist twisted to the side, and Kullen's blade resting against his throat.

"Respect is earned, Prince," Kullen growled into the young man's face.

"Unh-hand me—"

"Your grandfather earned it the day he plucked me off the streets. Your father earned it by kicking the snot out of me in the training ground. Your mother..." He swallowed. That was one memory he had no desire to dredge up. "Your mother was good and kind and decent." He leaned closer, until his nose was nearly touching the prince's. "But what have you done to earn my respect, eh?"

Prince Jaylen swallowed, but to Kullen's surprise, he didn't cower. His eyes filled with something akin to fear, or anger, or both. His expression hovered between defiance, determination, and rage. Kullen's estimation of the prince rose a single notch— not that it had been particularly high to begin with.

Lowering his dagger from Jaylen's throat, spinning it on a finger, he sheathed it in one motion. Then, he released his grip on the young man's wrist.

"Your birth to the Emperor's son does not give you the right to demand respect from those who serve you," Kullen said, his voice hard. "You want that, you do something worthy of it. Understood?"

Prince Jaylen rubbed his wrist, grimacing, but he actually nodded his ascent.

"Good." Kullen turned sharply on his heel, spinning away from the flustered prince only to find himself staring into Assidius's grinning face and the bared swords of two white-armored Elite Scales aimed at his throat.

4
NATISSE

Natisse triggered the mechanism that shut the mechanical trapdoor. It rumbled slowly closed, plunging the underground tunnel into near-total darkness. Garron and his torch were fifty paces ahead, Jad and the weeping Sparrow mere shadows in the taller man's wake. Only Baruch hung back, waiting for Natisse.

The two hurried to catch up to their three companions. He walked close by Natisse's side, as if seeking reassurance that he could reach out and touch her. No surprise, given what he'd just lost.

Despite their familiarity with the place—or perhaps because of it—they knew it was never truly safe to be alone in the pitch blackness of the ancient tunnels that honeycombed beneath Dimvein. Creatures, ever-hungry for tender human flesh, deprived of the sun's warmth, dwelled within the stone and earth. Though the torch's light kept the worst of them at bay, there was still a good reason behind Uncle Ronan's insistence that they never travel the tunnels without a torch or lantern, weapons, and at least two companions.

"And never neglect to look up," he'd always say.

The journey through the underground passages took the better part of half an hour. Garron led them unerringly as always —he alone knew the twisting, turning maze of tunnels better than Natisse. Above ground, no one rivaled her internal compass, but here? She'd never known the rangy man to get lost. Just one of the things that made him so valuable to the cause.

The silence and gloom enveloping them, suffocating them, only compounded the party's somber mood. Sparrow's laments had finally subsided, though the occasional snuffle and sniff emanated from within the depths of her ragged hood. Jad followed her closely but allowed the young girl the space she needed.

Finally, a flickering glimmer shone in the tunnel ahead. Emerging into a high-ceilinged stone cavern ringed with glowing oil lanterns, they were careful to stay true to the path. To the right and left, the stony ground dropped off into sharp cliffs, beyond which flowed an underground tributary of the deep, icy-cold Talos River and a smaller offshoot that flowed westward beneath the eternally barren Embers.

On a normal day, Garron would have stopped to drain himself off the ledge, silently decreeing to all that his piss would run through the gullets of the rich and lazy. Though today, he did no such thing, just led them down the single path, barely two paces wide.

When, at last, they reached a heavy steel door set into the stone wall, he drew from within his pouch a heavy brass key. This he inserted into the door's lock, giving it a slight twist until the mechanisms within issued a quiet click. However, he didn't open the door immediately. To do so would've spelled death—the traps framing the door would open a spiked pit beneath his feet and send a volley of needle-thin poison darts soaring across the stony passage. Instead, he quickly twisted the key in the opposite direction until the lock click-clicked twice more. Only then, with the traps disarmed, did he dare push the heavy door open.

It was impossible to tell which groaned louder, the door or the man, but finally, it stood wide for them to enter. He waved them in with an exaggerated bow.

Jad gently led Sparrow through, the big man stooping nearly double to avoid the low ceiling of the tunnel beyond—another safeguard against intruders. Even Natisse was forced to duck as she and Baruch passed the threshold and entered the rough-hewn stone-walled corridor that led to the common room of the Crimson Fang's secret underground headquarters.

Uncle Ronan sat within the Burrow, scowling at the large wooden table that dominated the space. One strong, scarred hand toyed with an empty glass bottle that Natisse knew had once held a fine Karmian red—the only thing he drank besides the occasional glass of water. The other rubbed at his neck where there was a wide burn mark. His square jaw muscles clenched and relaxed, chewing on the inside of his lip as usual. His gaze slid past Jad, Sparrow, and Natisse to lance Baruch with the force of a crossbow bolt.

"Uncle—" Baruch began.

Uncle Ronan held up a single finger and shook his head. "Not here."

Baruch's mouth snapped shut. He'd disobeyed a direct order once already today, and in doing so, earned their leader's ire. Not even he was stupid enough to go for round two.

Uncle Ronan's eyes returned to Natisse. "It is done?"

"Yes, Uncle," Natisse said. "Not even the Emperor's personal healers could save Magister Estéfar from a bolt to the throat." She was surprised by the calmness of her voice. It sounded more like a cobbler explaining how he'd managed to fix a boot sole than someone who had just skewered a man to death from a hundred yards.

A job was a job, she supposed.

Uncle Ronan nodded. "Good." He rose from the comfort of his upholstered seat, the old coat he always wore whispering around his knees as he approached. He never spoke of it or its many adornments, never mentioned time spent in any army. Likewise, Natisse had never asked about where it came from. Rumors around the Burrow were that it was a trophy of sorts, spoils earned through the slaughter of its previous owner.

Natisse thought it more likely part of a disguise that he'd adopted for its comfort and versatility. He'd even modified it, concealing metal plates around the torso. Very effective against blades and bolts.

His gaze strayed to Sparrow, and for a moment, his grizzled face took on a kind affectation. He stopped where the forlorn young girl stood in Jad's shadow.

"I know this has dealt you a grievous blow, little bird," he said, his voice quiet and filled with compassion. "We will all feel the weight of Ammon's absence in the hours, days, and weeks to come."

He then lifted his gray eyes to regard the rest of them. "Come sunrise, we will commemorate his life and celebrate his passage to the Realm of the Dead. But for now, affix this thought firmly in your minds: Magister Estéfar's crimes have been punished. No more will he harm the innocents of the Empire who cannot defend themselves from his cruelty, greed, and unbridled lust for power. No more will his dragon rain molten metal upon farmers, villagers, and townspeople unable to fight back."

Natisse looked around. No one seemed bolstered by the words.

Uncle Ronan then raised a clenched fist. "Ammon dedicated his life to protect all in the Empire from men like Magister Estéfar. We have succeeded because of Ammon's very life."

He unclenched his fist and brought his hand gently down on Sparrow's hooded head. "Weep for him, little bird," he said gently, "and let that sorrow harden your determination to further the cause for which he sacrificed himself."

"Y-Yes, Uncle Ronan," Sparrow said. Her voice was unnaturally high-pitched for a girl of fifteen summers, which, combined with her slim figure and youthful face, allowed her to pass unseen as both boy and girl amongst Dimvein's plethora of street urchins. She kept the cause well-funded, taking from the rich that which they could afford to give. Uncle Ronan referred to it as philanthropy.

He gave Sparrow a kind smile that clashed with his hard features. "Go now. Eat, rest." He looked to Jad and gave the big man a meaningful look.

Jad nodded back.

He'd take care of Sparrow, just as he'd cared for Natisse when she'd broken her leg two years earlier or when Garron had taken ill with the flu three months back. Among their little group of foundlings-turned-crusaders, the hulking Jad was the closest thing they had to den mother, and everyone loved the big man for it.

While Jad led Sparrow away, Uncle Ronan turned his attention to Garron. "Any undue attention from the Imperial Scales?"

Garron shook his head.

"The Orkenwatch?"

Garron shook his head again.

"Good." Uncle Ronan's eyes narrowed. "After dark, take Tobin to the Court of Justice and listen to what's being said."

Garron raised an eyebrow.

"They made a spectacle of torturing Ammon as a member of the Crimson Fang," Uncle Ronan said. "I want to know how Arbiter Chuldok knew he was one of us. And, if they suspect us, what Emperor Wymarc might be doing about it."

Garron, never one to say more than absolutely necessary, nodded and strode after Jad and Sparrow, deeper into the warren of tunnels that served as their base.

Uncle Ronan turned back to Baruch, but before he could speak, Natisse stepped between them.

"He knows what he did," she said. "And you know why he did it. Does he really need the lecture, today of all days?"

Ronan frowned down at Natisse, silent for long seconds. Then he nodded. "Fair enough." He looked to Baruch. "You have my sympathies, lad. Just don't let this"—he tapped Baruch on the chest—"get you killed because it stopped you from using this." He moved his tapping finger to Baruch's temple.

"I know, Uncle Ronan," Baruch said, his tone far meeker, more humble than it had been just moments ago. "I just..." He cleared his throat. "I had to. I... I just had to see him once more. Even though he couldn't have known for sure I was there, I needed to be. Perhaps he felt it—felt me there. I don't know. I just... I couldn't stand for him to be alone at the end. Not after failing him al—"

"That's enough of that," Natisse said, stepping in. "I already told you once, no one could have helped it."

Baruch's eyes blazed, his fists clenching. "I could have!" He folded at the waist, leaning heavily on his knees, his breath coming in spurts. "I should have," he said, his voice strangled by guilt. "I should have. His own brother should have!"

"All right. All right," Uncle Ronan said, inclining his head. "Natisse is right. But so are you."

Baruch looked up.

"We all should have," Uncle Ronan continued. "Each of us here and those not. Every Crimson Fang has a responsibility to one another. Any of you sees another doing something stupid or careless, it's on you to stop them. And ultimately, every pound of guilt weighs heavily upon my shoulders."

Natisse's brow furrowed. This line of thinking could drag them all down a dark path from which it would be very difficult to return.

"Uncle Ronan," she said, "that's unfair."

"No, Nat. It's the truth. And it's why I'm not feeding shit to Baruch. Perhaps no one is responsible for Ammon's capture.

Perhaps, we all are. Either way, we have jobs to do. We must press on. Blood for blood."

Baruch did his best to repeat those words through clenched teeth.

"Blood for blood," Natisse agreed. "The mission above all."

"Yes, and for this reason, I'm not sitting you out the next mission," Uncle Ronan told Baruch.

A twinge of a smile—relief if nothing else—painted Baruch's lips.

"Ah-ah," Uncle Roman said. "Don't get too excited. My instincts suggest otherwise. We simply can't afford to be another man down. Don't let me catch you disobeying another direct command. Is that understood?"

Baruch stiffened behind Natisse and nodded once. Natisse held her peace—Uncle Ronan would be right to keep Baruch down here, as Baruch's grief could prove a costly distraction.

"Go," Uncle Ronan said, dismissing Baruch with a wave and a heavy sigh. "Mourn your loss. Then, recover your wits and prepare for what is to come."

"Yes, Uncle." Baruch gave a perfunctory little nod and, turning sharply on his heel, strode out of the common room.

Natisse made no effort to follow. Uncle Ronan had purposely left her for last, which meant he had something important for her ears alone. Indeed, his whiskered face grew pensive and solemn, his gray eyes following Baruch's exit.

Natisse moved to one of the wooden cabinets set against the common room's stone wall and drew out another glass bottle identical to the one sitting empty on the table. Uncorking it, she poured a measure of wine into a pewter cup and drained it in a single long draught. She served herself more—only now having realized just how parched she'd grown after a night and half a day spent lying on the rooftop of Magister Corvus' tower.

"How bad was it?" Uncle Ronan asked quietly.

"Bad," Natisse answered, her voice equally low. She turned to find Uncle Ronan seated heavily in a chair opposite her. His weathered face instantly looked a decade older.

She took a seat across from him and extended the bottle by the neck. He stared at it as if battling internally before accepting it with a nod.

"Arbiter Chuldok was administering 'justice.'" She sneered the word. What had been done to Ammon was a far cry from anything resembling true justice—merely cruelty for entertainment's sake. "He brought out all his worst tools."

"Damn it all to Shekoth." Uncle Ronan ran a scarred hand over his face.

He hadn't shaven in weeks, and his stubble had thickened to a proper beard. More than anything, he just looked tired. He still only held the wine bottle, twisting it between fingers crooked from being broken so many times before.

"I'm going to see what I can figure out on my end," he said, finally taking a long swig before passing the bottle back to Natisse. "Figure out how the Arbiter learned Ammon's true identity; how he knew he was Crimson Fang."

"Torture reveals a great deal," Natisse said. "They no doubt worked on him long before he was strapped to that table." Again, she was struck by how cold her voice sounded to her own ears.

"How do you know this?"

Natisse recalled the moment Ammon was dragged out onto those gallows. He was covered in his own blood, bruised, one eye already missing.

"I just know," was all she said.

Uncle Ronan grimaced. "Poor boy shouldn't have been tortured. When Magister Estéfar's guards snatched up him, they couldn't have suspected him of being anything more than just one more thief. They'd take his hand, not deliver him over to the Arbiters."

Natisse frowned. Uncle Ronan was right, of course. Ammon's luck had soured during one of his and Baruch's reconnaissance trips into Magister Estéfar's mansion estate in the Upper Crest. According to Baruch, his brother had pushed his luck, tried to follow a servant in through one of the many passageways used by the help to stay unseen. Baruch tried to call him off, but it was too late. Moments later, Baruch watched as his brother was dragged away by the guards, favoring a newly broken leg.

There had been nothing marking him as a member of the Crimson Fang. Tattoos and brands were for the foolish, children playing games or acting a part. No, Uncle Ronan's crew wore no insignia of any sort. So how had Ammon been identified? Had he? It seemed so. The proper punishment for his crime of breaking and entering, attempted theft or burglary of a minor aristocrat's house should've ended at the severing of his right hand in the Court of Justice.

"So, how did he end up in Chuldok's hands?" Uncle Ronan voiced the question that had already begun to form in her mind as well. "Something happened in there, something I need to know about."

"You've heard Baruch's tale, same as us," Natisse said. "He ran. Must've broken a leg and got caught."

"Yes." He leaned forward. "But now it's time to learn the truth."

"You think him lying?"

"Baruch? No. But something doesn't add up. I just had to make sure you all got back safe and sound before I went out."

"We're good," Natisse said. "Sparrow's going to take it hardest, but she'll have Jad to look out for her."

"Baruch will need you," Uncle Ronan said.

"I'll look in on him," Natisse promised. "Once he's done grieving alone, he'll talk to me. I'll get his head on straight for the next mission."

"Good." Uncle Ronan nodded. "Dalash says the pieces are all in place; the time set." He reached out a leathery hand and rested it on hers. "You'll be okay?"

"I will," she said, giving him a smile she knew he expected. She also knew it looked more genuine than it felt. At the moment, she felt very little at all.

"Unfortunately, this one hinges on you again." Uncle Ronan's tone grew solemn, his voice deepening. "I know it puts a great burden on you, but—"

"No," Natisse said, shaking her head. "This is what you trained me to do. This is who I am." Who she needed to be to ensure that no one else suffered as she had, lost as much as she'd lost. "I'll be ready."

Uncle Ronan stared at her silently for a long moment, then nodded.

"Good." Patting her hand, he pushed back his chair and stood. "I'll see you at sunrise."

"Sunrise," Natisse echoed.

She watched him leave, taking one last pull from the bottle. Then, with a sigh, she stood and left the common room.

Her steps led deeper into the Burrow and toward her underground quarters. Just beyond the common room, the passage split off into three additional corridors. Natisse chose the right-hand path, passing the many doorways behind which her companions dwelled. Her own door stood at the end of the hallway and bore no lock. None was needed. Here, amongst her brothers and sisters serving the cause of righteousness, she had nothing to fear.

Yet, it was only after she closed the door behind her that she felt truly safe. Safe enough to relax, to let down the guard she always maintained even around Baruch and Uncle Ronan.

She plopped down on her bed, drawing in long, deep breaths. Closing her eyes, she reached within herself. There, beyond a gap that felt like a yawning chasm, lay her true emotions. The swirling, seething maelstrom she shoved deep within, only allowing them to manifest in moments of quiet isolation. Only then, when she was finally alone, safe, did she permit herself to truly feel.

It started slowly, quietly. First, a slight trembling in her right hand—the hand that had squeezed the trigger and loosed the bolt that killed Magister Estéfar. Then, a welling within her chest, like water bubbling up from a hidden wellspring beneath stone. Once it began, however, she could no more control it than she could convince her heart to stop beating.

Sorrow assailed her like a tidal wave, slamming into her chest with the force of a battering ram. A tear fell. Just one at first. Then.. it felt like a dam breaking, giving way to hot, fast, wracking sobs.

She did her best to remain silent as the memories of Ammon flashed through her mind. Her shoulders bobbed while her mind replayed visions of them together on the practice grounds—that mocking grin, the embarrassed-yet-proud flush of his cheeks when she finally bested him in hand-to-hand combat and sword-play. His strident laughter as he and Baruch traded jests. His quiet, calm voice and comforting presence during the dark nights when the dreams of fire had overtaken her. His confident aura and self-assurance when detailing their plan of attack or recounting the findings of his reconnaissance.

Natisse wept for her brother. A true brother, one who had loved her and shielded her in a way only he ever could. Not the screaming, weeping, bloodied man strapped to Arbiter Chuldok's table—she refused to remember him that way. She clung to the bright memories of Ammon, the moments of happiness they'd shared over the fifteen years they'd lived together.

But as much as she wished it to be false, Ammon was gone. His absence ripped a hole in Natisse's heart. And for just a few brief minutes, she could allow herself to truly feel that pain.

5

KULLEN

The threat of two drawn swords pointed at Kullen, sharp as they were and skilled as their bearers might've been, failed to impress. He simply raised an eyebrow.

"Really, Assidius?"

"I'd be well within my rights," Assidius shot back, his grin turning malicious. "Laying hands on a member of the Imperial family... Not even the Emperor would fault me."

"I hardly think an accidental bump to the prince's shoulder could be considered 'laying hands on' anyone."

"I beg to differ," Assidius said, his dark eyes sparkling with menace. "I believe all those present would attest to assault—an offense punishable by death."

"And you would so like to see me tried for such an act, wouldn't you?"

"Nay." Assidius affected a look of mock sympathy. Then he grinned. "I would give the order and have you cut down where you stand—"

"I tire of your games, Assidius," Kullen said. "Either make true your words or step aside."

"Very well," Assidius said. "Guards—"

49

"That won't be necessary." Prince Jaylen hurried to plant himself between Kullen and his would-be killers. "It was I who challenged him." He glanced over his shoulder at Kullen, his face flushed like a ripe plum. "He, too, was within his right to respond to my challenge."

Kullen's estimation of the young man rose yet another notch.

Assidius's face pinched as if he'd just sucked on a particularly pestilence-ridden pair of bollocks. He had no chance to speak, to protest the prince's words, or give the order to take off Kullen's head.

"My grandson is right, Assidius," said a strong, commanding voice coming from behind the two Elite Scales. "There is no need for such nonsense."

All in the room whirled toward Emperor Wymarc. If ever there was a man whose appearance screamed "regality," it was he. White hair, stark as fresh-fallen snow topped a face etched with deep lines. However, age had not slowed his precise militaristic march nor bowed his shoulders. Though it was true, he'd lost much of the musculature he'd gained during his years of service in the Scales, he radiated an assertive, decisive air that marked him unquestionably as ruler of all he surveyed.

"Imperial Majesty," the two guards said in unison, lowering their swords and bowing. Prince Jaylen followed suit, albeit with far more familiarity.

Assidius swept a deep bow—so low, in fact, that the tip of his goatee nearly touched the floor. Even Kullen found himself genuflecting before his Emperor—he owed the man a great deal more than just his respect.

"Rise," commanded Emperor Wymarc. He turned to the man at his side, a shorter, stockier aristocrat at least a decade his junior. "I will speak to you later on this matter, Carritus. Once I am done sorting out this mess."

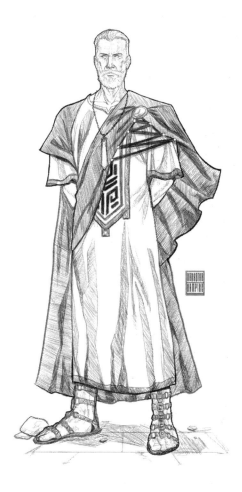

He flicked his hand, gesturing toward the argument in such a way to make Kullen feel like a child being scolded on the playing field.

"I don't know why you allow him to stick around," Branthe said. "Friend to your late son or not."

"That's enough, Carritus," the Emperor said.

"Of course, Imperial Majesty." Magister Carritus Branthe's

long locks bore only hints of gray within his thick dark brown mop. Numbering among the highest-ranked noblemen in all the Karmian Empire, he served as confidante to the Emperor. Yet, even he bowed in veneration before marching away—though he cast a inquisitive glance at Assidius, the guards, Prince Jaylen, and finally, Kullen himself.

The two Elite Scales parted to make way for Emperor Wymarc, who swept into the room with a scowl for Kullen. "Still having trouble playing nice, Kullen?"

Before Kullen could respond, Prince Jaylen spoke up. "A misunderstanding, grandfather, nothing more." He shot Kullen a sidelong glance. Evidently, the dagger pressed to his throat had driven home Kullen's words about respect. If he was trying to earn Kullen's by defusing the situation, this would prove to be a good first step. "Kullen was merely awaiting your presence to report on the night's... questionable events."

Emperor Wymarc's piercing stare remained fixed on Kullen as if his grandson hadn't spoken at all.

"Questionable, indeed," he said, arching an eyebrow imperiously.

"My Magister," Kullen began but stopped when Emperor Wymarc's hand rose.

To his Scales, the Emperor said, "Leave us."

The men snapped their feet together, eliciting a loud clank before turning and departing the room. Only when they were gone did the Emperor lower his hand.

Still, Kullen remained quiet, showing deference to the Emperor.

"I believe my instructions were to eliminate Magister Iltari, but I said nothing about Magister Estéfar. Much as I loathed the man, personally, he was, by all accounts, a loyal servant of the Imperial crown. Am I not right, Assidius?"

"He was, Divine Majesty," the Seneschal said, barely sparing the sneer when his eyes flittered toward Kullen. "A true son of the Empire, basking in your radiance as we—"

"For the love of Ezrasil, Assidius," Emperor Wymarc said, sighing, "save such saccharine adulation for when we are in public. On long days like today, my ears grow truly weary of flattery."

"Yes. Yes. Of course, Majesty. Apologies, Your Excellence," Assidius said, with an expression that reminded Kullen of a rebuked puppy.

"So, tell me," Emperor Wymarc said, turning back to Kullen. "What exactly happened?"

Kullen had spent much of the journey in the underground tunnels pondering precisely that question. However, nothing he had come up with felt sufficient. There was no point in perjury.

"I killed Iltari as requested," Kullen said simply. "Someone else loosed the bolt that pierced Magister Estéfar's heart."

"Ah, someone else," Assidius said, frowning and nodding along.

"I suspect," Kullen continued, "they were lying in wait atop one of the nearby towers—"

"Magister Corvus' tower," Assidius interrupted.

"Would you like to tell this story?" Kullen asked.

"Assidius?" the Emperor said.

The Seneschal struggled to conceal his gloating smile. "The Orkenwatch found a rope evidently left behind by the killer as he fled."

"Any sign of where he went?" Prince Jaylen asked, taking a step closer, hoping to join in the grown-ups' discussion, no doubt.

"None."

For all his earlier castigating of Kullen's disrespect for the prince, Assidius appeared no less eager to give answer to the Emperor's grandson. He didn't even glance Jaylen's way, but addressed Emperor Wymarc directly. "The Orkenwatch has put its best sniffers to the task, but Tuskigo Turoc is less than optimistic. As he explained, the Embers tend to be far too… aromatic for his people to find any clear trail."

Kullen snorted. "Tuskigo Turoc couldn't find his own ass with both hands and the entire Orkenwatch pointing at it."

That wasn't quite fair. The Orkenwatch were, in fact, surprisingly effective enforcers of the Emperor's law—significantly more so than the Imperial Scales, as they'd proven on many an occasion. But Kullen disliked the Orken Tuskigo on a personal level. Turoc took the Orken "vows of loyalty and service" far too seriously, carrying himself as if he had the world's thickest, thorniest spear up his mud-hued rear end.

He made that Arbiter Chuldok seem like a pleasant dinner guest.

Turoc embodied "unyielding" in every sense of the word. The Orken Tuskigo was doubtless, even now, attempting to track Kullen down for the deaths of Magister Iltari and the many other noblemen assassinated on the Emperor's orders, and that made it easy for Kullen to stir up a little disdain for him.

"And you suppose you could do better?" Emperor Wymarc asked Kullen, an amused smile tugging at his lips. "Have you suddenly developed the senses of a bloodhound or the eye of a dragon?"

That last was said as a private joke shared only between the two of them. After all, it had been the Emperor who'd first introduced Kullen to his dragon, Umbris. He was, in fact, the very reason Kullen and Umbris had bonded so quickly all those years ago. Emperor Wymarc had even helped train Kullen in some of the more… unusual traits bestowed upon him by the bloodsurging.

"Forgive my forthrightness, Imperial Majesty," Assidius put in. "However, I must strongly protest against Kullen's involvement in this inquiry. His methods are…" He gave a little sniff of disdain that made his angular face appear even sharper. "… far too clumsy in the situation."

"Clumsy?" Kullen said, fighting the urge to ring the bastard's neck.

"I'm sorry, did I say clumsy? I meant calamitous. Nevertheless, it requires a more delicate touch and keener mind to uncover the identity of Magister Estéfar's killer. A killer who, I suspect, also had a hand in Magister Oyodan's death as well."

That caught Kullen's interest enough to forget the many insults. At least for the moment. "Two noblemen killed by the same man?"

"Perhaps even more," Assidius said, radiating smugness at knowing something Kullen did not. A petty man winning a petty victory. "Do you worry your reputation as Dimvein's most deadly assassin is at risk?"

"Assidius," the Emperor warned.

Assidius bowed quickly and continued. "It's just... there have been a number of unusual deaths over the last few months. Deaths that cannot be attributed to your Imperial assignments, Divine Majesty. Arbiter Chuldok and his inquisitors suspect they are connected to the Crimson Fang."

Kullen frowned. "Conspiracy theories."

"I think not," Assidius retorted.

"Haven't you, yourself, disproven the Crimson Fang as nothing more than a hoax?" Kullen allowed the contempt he harbored within to echo in his voice. In all his work digging into the nobles he'd been assigned to kill, Kullen had heard rumors and whispers about the Crimson Fang, though nothing concrete. "A group of rabble-rousers at worst. And at best, a watchword spread about by those seeking to foment discord in Dimvein."

"There is evidence the Crimson Fang is more than we previously believed," Emperor Wymarc said, his expression growing somber. "That man who was executed this evening—" He glanced to Assidius.

"Baronet Ammonidas Sallas," the Seneschal supplied.

"Yes. Yes. Baronet Sallas was believed dead years ago, and his recent return has led to some concerns."

"Concerns?" Prince Jaylen prodded.

Assidius took over. "Concerns that, when explored under Arbiter Chuldok's direction, revealed deep psychological conditioning in Baronet Sallas's mind."

"Brainwashing?" Jaylen asked, fear crossing his features.

"Indeed. I'm told for hours, he would say nothing more than 'blood for blood,' and 'the mission above all'."

"Is that so?" Kullen asked.

"The Crimson Fang's rallying cry, it seems."

Kullen's jaw muscles clenched. He'd seen those words, "blood for blood," painted on far too many walls of homes and buildings in the Embers. Though he'd dismissed them at the time, to hear them here, now, proved just how concerning the rumors could be.

"If the Crimson Fang is behind this," Kullen said, "then all the more reason to put me on this matter. Who better to kill the killer?"

"Literally anyone else," Assidius muttered, though loud enough that everyone in the small room heard.

As was becoming practice, Kullen ignored the Seneschal.

"All due respect," Kullen said, approaching the Emperor slowly. Assidius moved to block him as if he posed some kind of a threat. "Imperial Majesty, but you know how Turoc is going to approach this matter. This requires a scalpel, not a sword. For all of Assidius's accusations toward me, the Orken will muster all the delicacy of a giant's mallet."

"In his own way, it's an approach that gets the job done," Assidius cut in. "Especially with my assistance in... directing his focus."

Kullen shot a scowl at the lean Seneschal, but Emperor Wymarc spoke before he could follow it up with another insult.

"Do it," said the Emperor. "Set Turoc and his Orkenwatch on it."

Kullen sighed audibly. Perhaps a little too loudly.

"Of course, Imperial Majesty." Assidius bowed, not quickly enough to hide his self-satisfied grin. He turned to take his leave.

"But Assidius," Emperor Wymarc called, halting the Seneschal in his tracks, "do tread with caution. The situation is already fragile enough. Our attempts at alleviating the misery of those in the Imperial Commons—or should I say, the Embers?—are far from sufficient, and the nobility are furious at the latest tariffs imposed upon goods flowing up and down the Talos River. And, as if that wasn't bad enough, I'm now hearing murmurs that cases of Aching Fever have begun to crop up throughout the city." He let out a heavy breath and shook his head. "Do nothing that will cause further unrest unless absolutely necessary. Is that understood?"

"Of course, Divine Majesty." Assidius swept another exaggeratedly low bow and left, vanishing from the room in a flutter of his frumpy coattails.

"If he keeps bowing like that, he'll get stuck that way," Kullen said. "At least it would place his lips closer to your royal ass."

"How dare you?" Jaylen said, aghast.

"Oh, cut it out, Grandson." The Emperor then moved to get a good look at the two of them. "And this thing between you two stops now. Am I clear?"

Kullen gritted his teeth but nodded.

"Of course, Grandfather. Now, I do understand your hesitance to assign Kullen the task, but surely I could be involved in the investigation, aid Tuskigo Turoc and the Seneschal in—"

"No." Emperor Wymarc said, terse. "Your place is here in the palace, Jaylen."

"But, Grandfather," Jaylen protested, "I have spent my entire life cooped up in the palace!"

"Where it is safe," the Emperor said, nodding.

"And boring!" Jaylen rolled his eyes, his face shriveling into a childish frown. "There is nothing here for me but lessons, tutors, and affairs of state."

Emperor Wymarc's face hardened. "Which is precisely what should occupy the time of the Imperial Crown Prince."

"But how am I supposed to be a good Emperor if I don't know anything about the Empire I'm ruling?" Prince Jaylen's voice grew plaintive. "Not just the numbers and statistics, but the actual people! I need to get out, to—"

"Enough!" Emperor Wymarc's voice thundered. Kullen thought it might've rattled the wine goblet on the table, though that might have been his imagination. "You will obey me, Jaylen."

Jaylen's protests immediately died. "Of course, Grandfather," he said, bowing. Kullen didn't miss the hurt look on the young man's face, the shadows darkening his eyes. "If you'll excuse me, I have a fencing lesson to be about." He hurried quickly from the room. Kullen would've bet marks the boy's tears were flowing freely already.

"Ezrasil's bloody hand!" Emperor Wymarc swore, slumping into the plush chair where Jaylen had been upon Kullen's arrival. Though the man never looked a true elder, in this moment, he looked as old as he ever had. He ran a ring-adorned hand down his face. "I swear, his father was never half as difficult. And that's taking into account the fact that he fell in love with a common woman and married her against my Imperial orders."

Kullen smiled. "Prince Jarius was a bit headstrong. Especially once he met Hadassa." His smile cracked. He hadn't said her name aloud—even after all these years. It still brought him pain. "But Jarius's father was far less protective than Jaylen's grandfather."

Emperor Wymarc shot Kullen an irritated glare. "Do not presume to lecture me, Kullen."

"Never, Emperor," Kullen said, though he couldn't help a faint smile.

"Jaylen is..." Emperor Wymarc let out a long breath. "He is

Jaylen. Twice as enthusiastic as Jarius but without half his father's brains."

"Or a quarter of his mother's," Kullen interjected.

"Right you are." The Emperor grunted and shook his head. "He is right about one thing, though. He does need to get out of the palace, see the Empire for himself, if he is to be a good ruler. But after what happened to Jarius..." His eyes darkened and his gaze grew unfocused, lost in painful memories.

Despite Kullen's words, the Emperor was right to be protective over his grandson. Jaylen was all Wymarc had left of the son he'd adored and the daughter-in-law he'd grown to love and regard as his own. Their deaths had been unexpected and tragic.

In the wake of devastation unleashed by a fire dragon gone rogue, the Prince and Princess had traveled into the Imperial Commons, the city's westernmost district, to minister to those affected.

Yet their good intentions had been repaid by evil when Jarius and Hadassa had found themselves at the mercy of a violent crowd—the very people they had come to help. Those who suffered the worst of Golgoth's fiery fury believed the Imperial crown responsible for their fate and filleted the both of them right there in the streets.

The Emperor had yet to overcome his own feelings of responsibility. It was then that he'd employed the power of his own dragon, Thanagar the Protector, setting it permanently atop the centermost spire of the palace. Its charm extended like a dome over the entire city, serving as not only a warning of potential threats, but defense against them as well.

However, it went unnoticed by most of Dimvein that Thanagar's protection ended a mile west of the Mustona Bridge spanning the Talos River, leaving the vast majority of the Imperial Commons—which all in Dimvein had taken to calling 'the Embers' since its destruction—outside of its barrier.

A moment of silence stretched on, then Emperor Wymarc

seemed to come out his reverie. "But the prince is not your problem, Kullen. What *is* your problem, however, are the assassination plots Assidius has continued to uncover."

Kullen's lips pulled into a tight line. "More threats against your life?"

"Perhaps it would be better said as 'more of the same.'" Emperor Wymarc sighed and pushed himself to his feet with visible effort. His knee joints popped and crackled loudly as he stood, again reminding Kullen of just how much the Emperor had aged. By Shekoth, Kullen had been just ten years old the first day they'd met!

"I've got another name for you," the Emperor said. "Magister Athos Taradan."

Kullen frowned. "I know the little piss. Don't much like him."

"Our feelings toward Our nobility matter little," Emperor Wymarc said, his tone just short of reproach. "But if, as Assidius believes, he is involved in a plot on my life, then you have Our permission to eliminate him. Permanently."

Kullen bowed. "It shall be as you say, Divine Majesty."

"Shekoth's pits, not you too!" Emperor Wymarc rolled his eyes and marched from his study.

6

NATISSE

She dreamed of fire.

Brilliant scarlet-and-gold flames consumed her world, tongues of blinding heat licking at her clothing, her flesh, ravaging the air in her lungs.

She screamed—or tried to, but she could not draw breath. Thick smoke choked her voice and blinded her. She clawed at the flames, desperate to escape, frantic in her efforts to find them. Their names rose to her lips, but her throat was parched and scratchy like she'd swallowed cotton laced with razor blades. All she could do was watch, helpless, horrified, as the pillar of dazzling dragonfire closed in on her, engulfing her whole world in agony and death.

Natisse bolted upright, gasping, her fingers raking empty air. Cool, dark air. No fiery currents snarled at her flesh or devoured her clothing. She was blinded not by brilliant flames but by pitch blackness. The heat washing over her skin came from within, from the sweat drenching her and soaking her bedding.

Her breath came fast, as if her mind still labored beneath the force of that recollection, drawing what air she could before the fire burned it away. For long moments, Natisse had only strength enough to sit there, bound to her bed by that fear of her past. After time, her brain reconciled the fact that it was just a dream. One she'd experienced so many times before. Every muscle in her body trembled.

It took all her willpower to move her legs, pulling them from beneath sodden blankets, lowering them to the floor. Her feet touched cool stone, and she focused on that sensation. Focused on the cold, the chill in the air. Anything to drive back the memories of the flames.

Her left hand stole toward the burned, wrinkled flesh that marred the right side of her neck, shoulder, and the back of her right arm down to the elbow. The skin felt thick and rough under her fingertips, yet registered no sensation.

It was dead. Dead, just as everyone else she'd lost that day.

In her dreams, she always remembered their names. Yet when she awoke, they vanished from her mind, scoured away by that blinding, agonizing blaze.

She could not recall who exactly she'd lost, nor anything else from her past beyond that day. Her mother, father, brothers, sisters, the life she might've once lived... all gone. Lost to the holocaust of that day.

Only Uncle Ronan truly knew her plight. He'd told her of repressed memories, things that hide deep within, only to revive themselves as night terrors. And revive themselves they did, like biting, nagging, scraping beasts within her heart and mind. They hated her, and the feeling was mutual.

Finally, Natisse stood, forcing her unsteady legs to hold her upright. It was always the same. She should've been used to it by now, but how could she be? Dressing quickly, throwing on a simple, lightweight cloth tunic and belting on her breeches, she found her boots. Immediately, she missed the sensation of cold against her feet. It grounded her.

From the chest at the foot of her bed, she drew a pair of cloth-wrapped swords. They'd been a gift from Ammon on her last birthday—a day they'd chosen since she could no longer remember such things. She hadn't yet had the opportunity to bring them on a mission, but she would put them to use now. In his memory.

She hurried from her room and down the silent hallway bordered by closed doors. At the intersection, she continued straight into the corridor that led toward the training room.

As she'd expected, the massive room stood empty, lit only by a single lantern near the door. Natisse moved the lantern from its hook to a post beside the row of straw-filled training dummies standing in neat ranks along the training room's western wall.

She unwound the cloth from around the two swords. They were fine weapons, made of quality Dimvein watered steel, perfectly balanced with heft sufficient for deflecting a heavier long sword while still being slim and light enough for Natisse's more graceful style of combat. One was a hand's breadth longer than the other, the main-gauche that served as defensive and offensive weapon both.

She spun one, then the other, smiling at the feel of the blades in her hands. Ammon had taught her this manner of fighting—a far cry from Uncle Ronan's more brutal, workmanlike technique, which was better suited to a soldier or street brawler than a fencer. It was one of the few remnants of the years before his and Baruch's lives, too, had been burned to ash in the Embers five years earlier.

Natisse moved through the first cycle of sword forms, each move precise and purposeful, just as Ammon had taught her. The long, thin blade in her right hand carved deadly circles in the air while her off-hand weapon wove a defensive net of steel to deflect the swords of her imaginary foes. Completing the exercise, she moved on to a more complex series of movements. Sweat soon streamed down her forehead and across her brow. Her arms burned from exertion, yet she would not slow. Could not. The fire coursing through her heightened the intensity of her concentration and force of her actions. She trained harder to forget—both the flames that haunted her dreams and the pain of losing Ammon.

Faster and faster, her swords sliced until they were a blur in the lantern light, sharp edges reflecting the faint glow. Natisse's body moved in perfect unison, every motion of her hands and feet utterly controlled and deadly. She cut and thrust and parried as if each blow she struck would be her last. As if she could somehow cut down every one of the bastards who had played a role in Ammon's death.

Blood rushed in her ears. Her vision darkened, shadows creeping closer until nothing remained but her tormented thoughts and the swords spinning in her hands. She refused to feel... anything at all. She simply was—a whirlwind of imagined death and destruction. It was who she had to be for the sake of everyone in the Crimson Fang.

Uncle Ronan was their leader, but oftentimes, Natisse felt like the glue that held them all together. Many of them had only joined because of devotion to her—even Ammon. She couldn't help fight the feeling it was her fault he was no longer with them. What if she hadn't convinced him and Baruch to join their cause?

A new rage rose within her, and she struck harder than intended. Her sword form cycle ended with a whirling, sweeping arc intended to decapitate the final enemy. She screamed, stopping in a low crouch. Rising, she found she was no longer alone.

Baruch stood by the training room door, arms folded across his broad chest, his eyes riveted on her. Natisse felt suddenly self-conscious. How long had he been standing there, watching her? Had he spoken to her, his voice lost beneath the tumult in her mind? His expression revealed nothing.

Heat rose to her cheeks, and she turned away from Baruch quickly, sheathing the swords. When she turned back, the man had moved from the door and now strode toward her.

"I tried to get your attention," he said, almost apologetically, "but you looked... focused."

Lost, more like, Natisse thought but didn't say. For she had indeed been lost in her mind, swept up by the single-minded focus on her training. It was one of the things that made her the warrior she was. She'd defeated all but Uncle Ronan, a feat not even Ammon had claimed before...

"Did you need something?" she asked, then winced inwardly at the sharpness of her tone.

"Uncle Ronan's back," the man said, his voice mild, as if she hadn't just snapped at him. "Said to gather everyone for the ceremony."

Natisse nodded. Like she needed another reminder of Ammon's death. Like any of them did. However, no one could deny him the sendoff he deserved, especially after the death he hadn't.

"Lead the way." She once again had control of herself, her breathing steady and her mind returning from the empty, dark void where it often traveled during her training. She hurried to belt on the swords and, catching up to Baruch, took his hand in a silent apology.

Baruch just shot her a tired, sad smile and said nothing.

Then, she decided silence wouldn't do.

"Baruch," she said, forcing him to stop. He stared at her, a pleading look in his eyes. "I'm sorry."

It looked like he'd just been struck.

"You're sorry?" he said. "I... you're sorry?"

"That day," she said, looking down. "If I'd just left you alone..."

Baruch pulled her closer. "Nat, stop it."

"Ammon—"

"Made a choice, just as I did," he said. "My brother chose the Fang and I..." A moment of silence passed while Baruch waited for Natisse to look up from the ground. Once their eyes met again, he continued. "I chose you."

"Don't," Natisse said, shaking her head. "Even if..."

Her words trailed off. She considered how their training together might've been better, but Ammon taught her everything she knew with a sword. It was not blade-work, or the lack of it, that had gotten Ammon caught.

"If what happened to Ammon was anyone's fault but his own, it was mine."

"Don't say that. Please."

"You weren't there," Baruch said, a harsh edge creeping into his tone. He immediately adjusted it, and his voice grew softer. "I should've stopped him."

Natisse laughed. A sound that felt out of place even to her own ears. "No one stopped Ammon from doing anything once his mind was set."

Baruch's eyes closed. His mouth pulled up at the sides. "That stupid bastard."

"C'mon," Natisse said, grabbing his arm. "Uncle Ronan calls."

Together, they strode from the training room, past the common room, and out the heavy steel door that barred the entrance to the Burrow. Beyond it, she knew, snarlers stalked and crept, but their way was oft traversed, and those beasts preferred solitude when they weren't hungry.

Natisse was surprised to see nearly all the Crimson Fang gathered on the narrow cliff-edged pathway outside. Jad stood with one colossal arm wrapped around Sparrow, whose eyes were still red-rimmed from crying. She'd run out of tears someday, but not now.

Garron had returned from his mission, the sandy-haired, freckled Tobin in tow. Stern-faced Nalkin and her opposite, the eternally smiling L'yo, stood talking with Athelas. Natisse hadn't seen the three of them in the better part of a week, not since they'd departed on a scouting mission downriver to the village of Argencourt, the most recent victims of a dragon attack. She wanted to talk to them, to find what secretive task Uncle Ronan had set them to, but at that moment, someone else caught her eye.

Grabbing Baruch's arm, Natisse pulled him toward the tall, willowy man who stood apart from the rest of the Crimson Fang.

"Dalash," Baruch said, his voice heavy.

Dalash turned and bowed slightly to Baruch. He was only a decade or so older than them, with a kind face and the prim look of a scribe or manservant.

"You managed to get away?" Natisse said by way of greeting.

"Just for a short while," he said, smiling. His delight at seeing her faded into a somber frown. "After what happened with Ammon, I knew I had no choice but to return, if only for a spell." He looked to Baruch. "Haston and Leroshavé send their condolences. They wished to be here—"

"—but the mission comes above all," Baruch said, gripping Dalash's shoulder in solidarity as he echoed Ammon's favorite words. "We cannot all get what we desire in all regards."

"Too, true."

"He'd be glad to know you're here for this."

"As am I, brother." Dalash folded his long, slim fingers in front of his slender waist and turned to stare wistfully down into the fast-flowing Talos River. "He was a good man, Ammon. Perhaps the best among us. He will be missed."

"Aye, so he will." Baruch, too, turned toward the river.

Natisse rested her hand lightly on Baruch's arm. She glanced around and read the pain written upon every face in the cavern. Though only Baruch had shared his blood, Ammon had been like an elder brother to all of them, even those like Dalash and Garron, who were, in fact, older by more than a handful of years.

Though she saw their pain, she no longer allowed herself to feel it. She couldn't. Not now. Uncle Ronan's return meant he'd either found the information he hunted, or there was nothing to be found. Either way, he'd want to discuss with her both it and the mission to come. She needed to be clear-headed, not wrapped up in her emotions like the others. She would be strong for her brothers and sisters who could not be.

Uncle Ronan joined them now, emerging from within their underground stronghold. His gray eyes reminded her of a cold winter's day, even the way they shimmered as if he, too, held back tears. He strode to stand in their midst, at the cliff's edge, facing the frothing waters. His scarred hands pulled something long and sharp from the pocket of his duster.

"Children of the Fang," he started, holding up their most sacred possession—one of Thanagar the Protector's own fangs. "Nieces, nephews, brothers, sisters, friends, and family. All of these things, we are one to another. These days have been filled with unease and heartache."

He let a second pass, the roar of the river behind him filling the silence.

"But we all knew the risks when we entered into this fight. Ammon included, perhaps more than any other. His service, dedication, devotion to this cause should be a beacon of light to which we look when we find ourselves so buried in the shroud of darkness around us that we cannot fight our way out."

Everyone cried now. Some, like Sparrow, held back very little, if at all. Others, Natisse could tell, were trying and failing. But not her. She would not allow the others to see any form of weakness in her. She would have time to mourn the loss of her friend when she was dead and by his side in Shekoth, and then, there'd be no need to mourn.

Uncle Ronan turned toward the water.

"Does any know where the current takes us? Does any begin to understand the depth to which the oceans delve? So, too, is Shekoth a mystery to us all. One thing is true, Baronet Ammonidas Sallas is watching us. He is cheering on as we bring the nobility and their cursed dragons to their knees."

"Blood for blood," they all muttered.

"Our loss in his brutal murder—for that's truly what it was—will only spark us to burn hotter. It will be like a whetstone upon which we sharpen our own fangs as we sink them deep into the hearts of our enemies."

Sparrow's weeping had become a deep groan by now, and Jad concealed her within his strong embrace, muffling the sounds.

Somewhere above, bells tolled, signaling the change in the Orkenwatch. It might as well have been for them as they all stepped closer to the edge and stared down into the swift-moving waters of the powerful Talos River.

"May his spirit soar high above the dragons," Uncle Ronan said.

"May it be so," they all agreed.

Silence prevailed for a long while. Natisse didn't know what the others were thinking, but she considered the day she'd encountered Baruch and his brother Ammon for the first time. Dressed pitifully, look half-starved, they'd been tossing dice in the street when one of the Imperial Scales had passed by. The soldier slid from his horse, approached the two of them. She couldn't hear their words, but there'd been quite an exchange that led to the soldier taking their betting money and returning to his steed.

As he trod away, Baruch held his brother back.

Natisse had found her opening. It was the job of every Crimson Fang to find those who were ready to stand up to injustice, and fruit ripe for picking these were.

"Ammon will not likely be the last of us to fall," Uncle Ronan said, breaking her from her thoughts. "But like him, each drop of blood spilled will cry out from the dirt. Each life stolen for this cause will bolster the resolve of the rest. Each moment spent mourning will be fuel to set us blazing against injustice, and ultimately, we will see this Empire crumble."

"Hear, hear," a few said.

"I said we will see this Empire crumble!"

"Hear, hear!" they all cried, voices weak but as strong as could be in the moment.

"Blood for blood," Uncle Ronan said, holding up Thanagar's

fang.

They all repeated those words with vim and vigor.

She once again considered how things would've ended up if only she'd let them go upon their way that day.

"Natisse, Baruch, with me," Uncle Ronan said softly as he passed behind them.

She stared into the churning waters, taking note as Garron strode at Uncle Ronan's heels, glancing over his shoulder when Natisse didn't immediately move to follow.

The grizzled leader nodded to Dalash, too, and the slender man silently fell in step behind them. The five marched into the stronghold, past the common room, and up the passageway leading straight through the intersection and into the chamber Uncle Ronan had dubbed the "War Room."

The War Room was dominated by a massive wooden table into which had been carved an impressively accurate replica of Dimvein. Dalash had spent a few months apprenticed to a cartographer, and Tobin's skill with woodworking had breathed life into the spectacular map. Countless minute details were etched into tabletop, from the hangman's nooses in the Court of Justice to the maze-like back streets of the Embers to the enormous bulk of the white dragon that wrapped its sinewy frame around the upper battlements of Emperor Wymarc's palace.

As always, the sight of that monstrous creature—even in effigy form—set anger burning in Natisse's gut. Though she'd never drawn within a league of the beast, she hated everything it and its fellows represented. Power unchecked, wealth, and greed that corrupted everything it touched, and the boot that trod the poorest Imperial citizens into the mud. That foul dragon was a reminder to all in Dimvein and the entire Karmian Empire that they were little better than slaves beneath the iron-fisted rule of an Emperor that permitted men like Magister Estéfar to commit atrocities without recompense.

Seeing it there every time she entered the War Room

reminded her why they fought.

Not that she needed the reminder. Not truly. It came every time she closed her eyes, and the dreams of fire returned. Or when she heard the tale of some new village or township like Argencourt destroyed by a dragon unleashed by its noble master.

"Oh, you failed to pay taxes?" she could hear the foul lords say as they beckoned forth destruction.

Magister Estéfar was just one among scores of men who would soon feel the Crimson Fang's bite. Natisse's anger turned to grim anticipation, eager to find out who would be their next target.

When they were all gathered around the table, Uncle Ronan turned to Dalash.

"All is ready?" he asked.

"Almost, Sir," Dalash said. "Haston has located what we need, and Leroshavé is securing our means of escape. By the time we make our move tomorrow eve, we will have a clear path out."

"And our way in?" Ronan asked.

"Of course." From within his simple, dull-colored jacket, Dalash produced an envelope. It bore a wax seal stamped with the crest of a noble Imperial house, and a delicate perfume wafted up from the parchment.

"This will suffice," he said, handing the envelope to Natisse. "You and your entourage will be granted entry without question, as befits our lord's honored guests."

"Entourage?" Natisse cocked an eyebrow. She peeled open the envelope. Written in an elaborate script on the paper within, she saw the name and groaned. "Lady Dellacourt? Really?"

Uncle Ronan seemed to be struggling to keep a straight face. The bastard! He knew how much Natisse would hate this particular disguise.

Garron said nothing, but his eyes twinkled with a glint of humor. Baruch, however, failed entirely to hide his mirth.

"You'll make a fine lady, indeed, Natisse." He chuckled evilly.

"Just think, all the lace and velvet you could ever ask for, and your hair done up in—"

She cut him off by digging the sharp point of her elbow into his ribs.

"This was the best way in," Dalash said, almost apologetic. He, too, knew her feelings on the matter. "If we had any other option..." He shrugged. "If it's any comfort, it will be just for one night."

"One night too many," Natisse snarled. With effort, she tamped down her irritation and turned to Uncle Ronan. "Do you have any idea what we'll be facing?"

Uncle Ronan nodded. "Aye. Dalash has learned the nature of our target's powers." His expression tightened. "I cannot overstate the importance of an instantaneous kill, Natisse. Should he be allowed to bloodsurge—"

"Things will go to shit, I know," Natisse said.

It was ever the way with the noblemen who had become the Crimson Fang's targets. They not only commanded the loyalty of their winged beasts but somehow, their mastery of the dragons imbued them with strange and varied magical abilities.

Magister Estéfar had been able to withstand immense heat as if his skin was made of the same bronze scales of his dragon. Magister Oyodan—their last target—had possessed such uncanny luck that their assassination had only succeeded due to Uncle Ronan's thorough planning, Baruch's dogged persistence, Natisse's skill with blade and crossbow, and the multiple contingency plans Garron and Ammon had put into place. Even still, they'd barely escaped with their lives.

Perhaps that explains how Arbiter Chuldok had known Ammon's identity. The Imperial Scales had come dangerously close to capturing half their ranks that night. Uncle Ronan's contacts had informed him that the Orkenwatch had learned more about the Crimson Fang during that one mission than had been known for five years prior.

Whatever the case, they'd just have to be doubly cautious on this one. They could afford no more losses, not even in the name of eliminating another of the dragon-controlling pricks who hid behind titles and wealth.

Dalash filled them in on the remainder of the plan, and Uncle Ronan added details as needed. Garron remained silent as ever, seemingly content with the proposed plan of attack. Natisse followed his lead and held her tongue. At the end, she concluded that, despite the distasteful nature of the role she was to play, the strategy was solid.

"Any questions?" Uncle Ronan asked, glancing around the table. "Good," he said when no one responded. "Then get into place."

Dalash and Garron nodded in response.

Then, Uncle Ronan's gaze settled upon Baruch and Natisse. "You think Sparrow's up to this?"

Natisse exchanged a glance with Baruch.

"I'll have to check with Jad," Baruch said. "If not, we can always use Tobin."

"Sparrow's the better choice," Uncle Ronan said.

"No doubt about that," Natisse agreed. "But if she can't keep it together, then we've got no option but to go with Tobin."

Uncle Ronan grunted, a sour look on his face.

"So be it." He stared down at the map of Dimvein. "What we do here..." he said quietly. "It matters. Not just to us, but to all of the Karmian Empire."

He lifted his gaze to regard the four of them.

"The Emperor refuses to hold his nobility to account, to punish them for their crimes. So it falls to us." He raised a clenched fist—a fist scarred not only by wounds sustained in combat but by old burns he'd earned in the dragon attack that slaughtered his wife and three children nearly two decades earlier. "For his crimes against the people of the Empire, Magister Perech dies tomorrow!"

7

KULLEN

The sun had not yet risen fully over the eastern horizon when Kullen slipped into the Wild Grove Forest to the north, just outside Dimvein's city walls. He avoided the broad, heavily traveled trade route that cut through the woods, instead choosing a narrow game path that led him toward the forest's western edge.

Trekking in silence for the better part of half an hour, eternally wary of his surroundings, his hand never strayed far from his sword. Whitespine wolves, predatory owl raptors, and wildeboars all made their homes in the Wild Grove, their footprints evident in the deep mud bordering the murky swamplands ahead of Kullen. Even the snarlers who normally made their home deep within the warrens beneath Dimvein weren't complete strangers to these woods.

And that was just the fauna. Half of the Wild Grove's flora was carnivorous, some large enough to ensnare and devour small animals or wayward children. Poison plynar, a vine that grew rampant throughout the groves, could sear the flesh quicker than any dragon's fire.

Of lesser concern for Kullen, bandits, too, were known to lurk in the trees. The merchant wagons and lightly guarded caravans which oft traveled these parts made for easy targets—a source of great consternation among the Dimvein nobles, who petitioned the Emperor to send the Imperial Scales to patrol the broad highway.

But this far to the west, Kullen had only the biting, stinging insects and the occasional venomous croakers to worry about. The latter tended to hop out of his way, but the former seemingly took great delight in plaguing him, engulfing him in a swarming cloud that made breathing a task of great difficulty.

A familiar trail led through the swamplands. Few knew of its existence, and fewer still could pick out the sparse patches of solid ground betwixt the bogs and marshy lowlands. Kullen trod carefully through the tall, wet grass, planting his feet with care so as not to slide into the scummy green water. Within the pools and swamps were far too many species of serpents that would love nothing more than to take a bite out of fresh meat. The corpses of hares, deer, even beasts of prey scattered along the water's edge served as a stark reminder that he had to be constantly vigilant.

Soon, however, the ground grew firm and sloped upward once more. Finally, it gave way to a crest, a small grassy rise. Dense underbrush nearly barred his passage, but he pushed through, careful to leave no trace of his presence.

Beyond the thick hedge, Kullen found himself in a glade that contrasted sharply with the gloomy, murk-laden swamplands he'd just traversed. Early morning sunlight streamed through a gap in the canopy, casting warmth over the clearing and warming the air. A deep chasm tore through the earth like a jagged scar. Dewdrops glistened on a thick carpet of emerald grass.

It was peaceful and serene in a land that rarely was.

Sunlight disappeared as he crossed into a thick copse of elms on the western-most edge. Hidden in darkness stood a small shrine made of oval-shaped river rocks stacked waist-high.

Kullen moved to stand before it, scraping away the moss that had formed there with his gloved hand. Three letters had been carved into the stone's smooth surface: K for Kullen, the newest of the set, J for Jarius, and H for Hadassa. This shrine stood not as a testament to the ancient Mosleon peoples who once ruled this part of the world when darkness reigned like death. No, these letters represented the friendship shared between three youngsters in a time that felt like an eternity long gone.

Jarius had been the one to find this glade, but it was Hadassa's idea to build the little stone monument. At the time, they'd been just ten summers old—eleven, Hadassa would always correct, as if the fact that she was a year older than them somehow made her their superior—and Prince Jarius had been given free roam of Dimvein, provided he brought the redoubtable Sir Reffri along.

Kullen had been in the Emperor's care for less than a year, but he hadn't forgotten any of the children with whom he'd shared the stone walls of Mammy Tess's Refuge for the Wayward—or, simply, "the Refuge" as it was known by its orphaned inhabitants. Hadassa had been one of the few friends he'd made during his years in the Refuge. She'd been equal parts sad to see him leave and elated at his newfound fortune. Kullen had sought any opportunity to welcome her into the games and schemes he concocted with the then-young Prince Jarius.

Kullen's smile faded, and he quickly turned away from the small shrine. Too many painful memories that he'd rather forget.

He gently stroked the stone one last time before continuing his journey through the glade toward a dense stand of towering walnut trees, which cast deep shadows over a patch where the grass had withered, and only bare earth remained. He slowed as he approached—how many hours had he spent lying in the shade, talking with his old friends? How many secrets had passed between them in this very spot over the years?

A lump rose in Kullen's throat. Even after all this time, the pain proved hard to shake. His grief paled in comparison to Emperor Wymarc's, though. The man had lost the son he'd adored, his only heir, and the woman who'd captured Jarius's eye and heart. Yet, Kullen had possessed so little that even a small loss could crush his soul. And the death of Prince Jarius and Princess Hadassa had been far from "small" for him, though only Emperor Wymarc ever knew just how much it had pained him.

With effort, Kullen pushed the grim reverie aside and reached for the vial hanging about his neck. He pressed his thumb into the gold-embossed cap and felt the needle prick his skin. The pain helped to clear his mind. Closing his eyes, he drew in a breath of the cool forest air and reached for the wellspring of power deep within the core of his being.

Come to me, Umbris, Kullen said, speaking through the bond he and his dragon shared.

The reaction was instantaneous and, as always, disorientating. Though, this time, instead of a surge of power welling up within Kullen, he felt it draining away inside himself.

When Umbris rested in the Shadow Realm, his power became Kullen's, allowing him many of the attributes natural to his dragon. But the moment Umbris was called to this plane, that power was ripped from Kullen like a lodged arrow—and felt nearly as painful.

Disorientation overcame Kullen briefly, as if the breath had been sucked from his lungs. His arms and legs grew weak and numb, his head light, stricken with a sudden headache.

Then, as fast as the symptoms onset, they were gone. There remained a strange absence of sensation as if he'd gone blind or lost his ability to feel. The forest around him was colorful and bright, save for the shadows in which he stood. Yet, without the dragon's power coiling within him, it appeared somehow duller, the scents of fresh, damp earth less distinct.

Kullen's eyes scanned the shadows beneath the dense walnut trees. It seemed he blinked, and where there had just been empty air and cool shade, now, a mighty dragon suddenly stood before him. He'd traveled in shadow himself and seen Umbris appear enough times to not be startled... almost. No matter how familiar they'd become, there was no preparing oneself for the sight.

Umbris stood, a ten-ton mountain of black scales, leathery wings, and gleaming yellow eyes. His maw was open in a restful position, fangs the length of mankind's longest blade rose and fell like stalagmites and stalactites within.

Then Umbris threw back its head, neck whipping, horns thrashing. Though under certain circumstances, this could be perceived as a threat, Kullen recognized the greeting.

"Greetings, friend," Kullen said.

Umbris rumbled low in his throat.

Kullen, he said through their mental bond. *Have you brought it?*

"Of course," Kullen said aloud.

Umbris couldn't speak, but the dragon—like any other—was highly intelligent and more than capable of comprehending the human tongue.

Kullen pulled the bag he'd carried out of Dimvein from his shoulder and let it *thud* on the grass.

"You really think I'd forget your favorite treat?" Grinning, Kullen bent and drew out what he'd promised: an entire honey-and-applewood-smoked pork shoulder, plum-glazed and delicious.

Umbris's golden eyes gleamed bright, and he dropped into a crouch, head between his enormous taloned fore-claws. Though the dragon stood twice again as tall as any man, in that moment, he reminded Kullen of a hound eagerly awaiting a long-awaited reward.

With a chuckle, Kullen threw the fifteen-pound chunk of meat to Umbris. The dragon's jaws cracked open, further revealing those razor-sharp teeth, then quickly snapped shut on the pork shoulder before it hit the ground.

Delightful! Umbris rumbled in Kullen's mind. *It has been far too long since last I tasted Master Bainquo's fine cuisine.*

"Yes, I know." Kullen tied the now-empty sack into a tight

bundle. "That's my fault. I should be bringing you treats like that more often. I just—"

Get too busy? Umbris looked up from his feast and eyed Kullen with a look of very dragon-like amusement. *Remember that I see through your eyes even when you cannot see through mine. I know what occupies your days and nights. The hunt for your Emperor's enemies is a time-consuming endeavor, indeed.*

"It really bloody is." Kullen ran a hand through tangled hair in great need of a trim. "Every time I put one down, seems two more pop up as his replacement. I can't kill the ass lickers fast enough."

Certainly not for lack of trying, Umbris said.

Reaching out, Kullen patted Umbris's snout. The dragon snorted, sending steam rising from his nostrils and, along with it, the scene of burned pig flesh. He waited until the snack was fully devoured before speaking.

"Are you doing well, friend? Truly?"

A long serpentined tongue whipped out and lashed across Umbris's black lips.

Better now, he answered, rising. *And better still should this become regular.*

Umbris lumbered forward and lowered his head toward Kullen. With a smile, Kullen reached under the dragon's neck and scratched the spot where he knew Umbris liked it. A low rumbling growl reverberated in Umbris's throat, and the dragon's enormous body shivered all over. The movement set his scales rippling like a thousand shields upon the battlefield. The sunlight glinted off each one. Hints of luminous violet that dappled the obsidian intermingled in the darkness, revealing the truth of Umbris's nature. He wasn't a true black, but something akin to amethyst.

Umbris existed in what Kullen had named the "Shadow Realm," the layer of reality occupying the space between light and darkness—a Twilight Dragon. The only of his kind.

Decades earlier, when Emperor Wymarc had first explained to

Kullen the bloodsurge, he'd spoken of where the dragons had originated. They existed on two planes of reality, tethered to both the physical, tangible world and a world of pure elemental forces. The bond between human and dragon enabled those who possessed the vials to summon their dragons into the physical world. For a time, at least. The dragons needed to feed on the elements they embodied. Red dragons that could breathe fire also required the presence of fire to sustain their forms in the physical realm. Blue dragons could not live long outside of water.

For Umbris, too much time out of shadows caused physical pain and weakened him.

At the same time, the dragons needed to be summoned once a day in order to maintain the bond. Kullen didn't understand the reasoning behind it, but he lumped that in with everything else he didn't truly understand about bloodsurging. For more than twenty years, he'd done this. For more than twenty years, his questions went unanswered.

Kullen regularly made the journey this far out into the Wild Grove for Umbris's sake far more than his own. Though he owned a handful of hidey-holes and empty warehouses throughout Dimvein, all large enough to contain Umbris's bulk, out here, he had no fear of the dragon being seen. He was no aristocrat with a long lineage to trace back millennia to the first humans who bound themselves in mutual service to the dragon. He was just a child plucked from the streets and trained to become the Emperor's assassin. The "Black Talon," Emperor Wymarc called him, a title passed down to those who served the Empire from the shadows. No one outside the Emperor, Assidius —and now Prince Jaylen, it seemed—knew who he really was.

But it was more than just operational security. Umbris had always loved this isolated glade—just as Kullen had when in the company of Jarius and Hadassa—with its deep shadows. The dragon could warm himself in the bright sunlight but retreat into the shade when the brightness grew too taxing. In years long past, he'd loved playing with Jarius and Tempest, the prince's silver wind dragon.

"Jarius's son now knows of my duty," Kullen said.

Though he knew Umbris had seen the very exchange shared in the Emperor's study, the dragon never spoiled a good conversation.

Is that so?

"The little shit now thinks I answer to him."

And, surely, you showed him his place?

Kullen laughed. "I believe I smelled the piss staining his breeches when we were through."

Umbris joined in the mirth, shaking the ground like an earthquake. Then, the smile vanished from his face.

Kullen. Umbris's tone grew heavy.

"What is it, friend?"

I long to fly. To be amongst my brethren in the clouds.

Pain wracked Kullen's heart. While all the other dragons were free to roam during their beckonings, Kullen needed Umbris to remain hidden. Not for the dragon's sake... but for his.

The guilt felt like a millstone tied around his neck.

"I'm sorry, Umbris. You did not choose this."

Umbris sighed. *Will you bring me more pork soon?*

"Twice what I brought you today," Kullen swore. "And Umbris... I promise, soon you will soar."

Umbris whipped his head again, and Kullen closed his eyes. Two steady breaths and the bloodsurge ended, Umbris's essence flooding back into Kullen's very being. It was like he'd down a keg of ale. His head swam for moments while his body adjusted to the power.

When his eyes opened, the glade spun. Umbris was gone, back to his lonely Shadow Realm where no other dragons dwelt.

Kullen gathered up the empty sack and strode across the clearing, pausing only to glance at the childish shrine of stone before pushing through the hedge and back into the swamp.

Emperor Wymarc had given him his instructions, pointed the blade where he needed it to go. Now, it was up to Kullen to determine whether or not Magister Taradan truly was guilty of his plot against the Emperor. And if he was, Kullen knew precisely where to find and execute him.

8
NATISSE

Natisse loathed everything about Lady Dellacourt. The endless simpering, fan-fluttering, giggling, and eyelash-batting nonsense was enough to drive her to absolute fury. The dress—a monstrosity of flowing, puffy fabric in a sunny shade of yellow—only compounded her utter hatred of this disguise that Uncle Ronan and Dalash had cooked up for her. She'd never seen so much lace, frill, chiffon, and ribbon in her life. And the corset... It felt as if she were being crushed by Orken arms, her ribs already aching as she struggled just to draw half a breath. If there was one thing worse than walking in high-heeled shoes, it was doing so on a ship that rocked to and fro.

It wasn't her first time playing this role, but each time, she hoped it would be her last.

Truly, the only saving grace to be found in the getup were the multiple hiding places it offered to conceal her weapons. Secreted about her person were three throwing knives, two push-daggers, a pair of spiked iron knuckledusters, a leather blackjack, and, of course, her lashblade. The hairpins holding up her fiery red hair in an excessively ornate and high-stacked coiffure were also sharpened to razor points and doubled as wickedly effective stilettos.

Natisse was both the least comfortable woman at Magister Perech's soiree and, without a doubt, the absolute deadliest.

Yet even she couldn't help a little flutter of worry as she stared over the edge of the pleasure boat. Hundreds of black fins sliced through the water—at Magister Perech's orders, servants had spent hours dumping chum overboard, ensuring the presence of hundreds of vicious onyx sharks. A show of his power, Natisse knew, just like everything else the preening aristocrat did.

"He likes to muster the sharks, then dive overboard," Dalash had explained during their mission briefing. "With his magic, he can outpace them even in the deepest, coldest water. He whips them into a frenzy, then swims back to his barge and summons his dragon to finish them off."

Natisse had heard tales of the nobility hunting gryphons with their dragons in the savage Grivaine Range or chimera in the Hostalleth Desert, but shark-baiting was new to her. Those in attendance tonight who had witnessed the spectacle at past gatherings refused to shut up about how "breathtaking" and "dazzling" and "utterly bewitching" such blood sport was.

Magister Perech would close the evening's festivities with a display of his magic and the power of his dragon.

"I can't wait," Natisse said under her breath with a plump dollop of sarcasm.

Looking at the man now, however, Natisse found it impossible to believe that Magister Perech could out-swim even his own prodigious belly. The man weighed nearly twice as much as Jad, stood only a little taller than Sparrow, and had roughly the same muscle tone as the ribbons sealing Natisse into this horrid dress—just further proof that the foul magic these noblemen wielded was truly evil. That much power did not belong in the hands of people who would misuse it.

She struggled to keep the sneer from her face. For once, her brilliant yellow fan came in handy, serving as a wall of silk behind which to hide her disgust.

"I know what you're thinking, my lady," came a familiar voice at her elbow. "And, no, you're absolutely wrong."

Natisse took in a deep breath before turning away from the barge's railing and toward the man. It was time to play the game.

Batting her eyelashes at the speaker, she said, "Wrong, my lord?" She arched an eyebrow delicately. "I am never wrong."

The man's face was pale as fresh fallen snow. He wore a pair of triangularly framed spectacles—the sort that raged within the Upper Crest—and a handsome doublet paired with a festive necktie-handkerchief combination.

Baruch smiled, though beneath that heavy layer of cosmetics. Natisse couldn't be certain it wasn't a grimace.

"Lady Dellacort," he said, "if I do not miss my guess, you were contemplating the state of your dress." His eyes twinkled with wicked glee. Much as he may've hated his own costume, he'd always enjoyed seeing her suffer through hers all the more. Yet, there was a spark of genuine admiration coupling his amusement. "You look utterly ravishing in marigold. Complements your hair and eyes."

"Such flattery!" Natisse made a show for those around them— a horrible high-pitched tittering that was somehow considered be "ladylike" among the women of the Emperor's noble court—and struck Baruch's right arm gently with her colorful fan. "Precisely the sort of thing that makes you the perfect companion, Baronet."

Baruch extended his arm, a gesture that pulled the perfectly tailored coat tight across his broad shoulders and well-muscled arms. "Would my lady care to be escorted to the refreshment table?"

"Of course, my lord." Natisse slid her arm through his. "Lead the way, Charlati."

Baronet Charlati of Delvehome was as much a work of fiction as Lady Dellacourt of Elliatrope, and equally necessary for the purposes of tonight's festivities. An unaccompanied lady could find herself the target of unwanted advances or excessive and unflattering attention from the unmarried noblemen of Dimvein —and more than a few of the married ones.

"Particularly when they look as stunning as you," Baruch had told her just before dismounting from their carriage upon arrival at the docks.

She looked out over the railing again, back toward where the jetty from which the pleasure barge had been launched hours earlier. It was not the stinky, decrepit docks west of the Embers. No, these were private docks positioned within eyesight of Thanagar.

"Could you imagine having ships for nothing more than entertainment?" she said in a whisper.

"I need not imagine, my dear," Baruch—Baronet Charlati— replied with no lack of sternness in his tone.

It wasn't like someone would overhear them. It was difficult to hear much of anything, even so close. Perech had spared no expense in the way of entertainment. A band of six musicians with the look of those from the southern province of Hudar graced a stage in the middle of the barge.

However, she understood his discretion.

With Baruch at her side, Natisse was considered beneath the scrutiny of the Dimvein capital nobility, who saw her as a country bumpkin unworthy of rubbing shoulders with them. Doubtless, more than a few had questioned her presence tonight—after all, Magister Perech's soiree numbered among the most exclusive events of the city's social calendar.

If Natisse had been given a choice, she would've chosen virtually anywhere else. Arbiter Chuldok's torture chambers and the Orkenwatch cells held a certain appeal when contrasted with the overly perfumed, lace-festooned, garishly dressed men and women swirling around Magister Perech's pleasure barge.

Unfortunately, she'd been given no such choice.

Magister Perech rarely left the safety of his island fortress, with its high stone walls, raised drawbridge, and shark-infested waters. Indeed, tonight was one of the few nights of the year when the aristocrat opened his doors and invited guests onto the islet upon which stood his lofty keep.

She looked back again at the stronghold's four towers rising nearly a hundred paces above the ocean's surface. Solid walls encircled not only the fort, but the vast gardens and manicured lawns that surrounded it. Patrols of heavily armed guards sporting the colors of House Perech—rusty orange and mauve—marched around the estate.

Up there, within Perech's fortress, Garron stood waiting with the rented carriage that had conveyed them to the island by way of the single heavily guarded bridge that connected the island to Dimvein's Upper Crest. Natisse doubted he'd be close enough at hand to help should the situation grow dire, but he'd be watching.

"This is where it happened, you know?" Baruch said. "Where General Andros defeated the Hudar Horde—the Battle of Blackwater bay. And now the Hudarians are serenading us with song. Incredible."

Baruch loved to tell stories about the Great General Andros. He, unlike everyone else in Dimvein, found it easy to forget that the General had been accused of treason. Though, perhaps Natisse couldn't blame him for rising up against the Emperor.

"He was acquitted," Baruch said, as if reading Natisse's thoughts.

Something brushed against Natisse's arm, drawing her attention and sparing her the need to respond.

A short, fresh-faced lad wearing the livery of House Dellacourt fell into step behind and to her right. Uncle Ronan had deemed Sparrow up to the task of tonight's mission. Though the girl's eyes were still dark and shadowed by grief, she played the role of Natisse's unobtrusive, always-hovering page to perfection.

Natisse allowed Baruch to lead her through the crowd filling

Magister Perech's pleasure barge. Their destination—the refreshment table—lay on the far end of the flatboat, which was a lot larger than Natisse had anticipated upon first hearing of their mission plan. Stretching easily three hundred paces long and a hundred wide, more than five hundred people mingled on the barge.

Amid them, no less than a dozen of the Emperor's Lumenators. These men and women had always rubbed Natisse wrong. No one truly understood where their powers came from, but she had to assume that, like all magic she was familiar with, it had something to do with Thanagar or one of the other nobles' dragons.

They each stood holding their shining globes, casting warm blue light over the entire barge. Their faces were entirely emotionless, barely even blinking. One stood up in the crow's nest, washing the surrounding waters with a faint magical glow.

Everyone ignored them, so used to their presence as they were in the Upper Crest. For Natisse, being accustomed to traveling the Embers, it was a wonder to see her own hand in front of her face this late at night.

"They couldn't spare a couple of these for the peasants, I guess," Natisse said to Baruch quietly, nonchalantly motioning to one nearby. She made sure a phony smile plastered her face in case anyone was snooping. "All the same. We already have to see the filthy place all day."

"My lady," Baruch said, changing the subject with intention. "Would you care for a candied quatberry?" He reached for a tray passing by.

"No, thank you," she said.

That didn't stop Baruch from popping a couple into his mouth.

"Perhaps my page would like—"

Baruch playfully raised one to her lips.

"I insist."

The dark berry touched her mouth and she pretended to indulge him as Lady Dellacourt would do, letting him feed her. He'd pay for it later.

Much as she was loathe to admit it, the taste was divine. Juicy, sweet, it was so unlike the things the Crimson Fang regularly ate. Finding fresh fruit in the Embers was damn-near impossible—at least any without rot or mold.

"Do try to enjoy yourself," Baruch said, leading her beyond a troupe of dancers, also having the olive-skinned appearance of Hudarians. They waved long poles, each streaming cloth ribbons dyed rusty orange and mauve.

Soon, they reached the refreshments table. Natisse gratefully accepted the crystal flute Baruch offered her.

"Boat's not in place yet," she said. Others gathered around the table in close proximity. She took a sip of champagne to conceal her moving lips. "No sign of Leroshavé, either."

Baruch grunted. "He'll be here."

He scanned the crowd, perhaps in search of Dalash, who was mixed in somewhere among the guests, albeit in far less ostentatious clothing. Dalash's role as Magister Perech's household scribe—a position he'd only recently filled after the previous scribe took suddenly ill from a particularly nasty concoction brewed up by one of Uncle Ronan's alchemists—ensured his presence here tonight. Magister Perech had a habit of making grand speeches that he wanted recorded 'for posterity's sake,' whatever in Shekhoth's pits that meant.

Natisse caught sight of the wisp of a man. "There, by the musicians."

Baruch nodded.

"Blayton," he said to Sparrow, using her alias, "find out what's the delay."

Without a word, Sparrow vanished into the crowd. None of the Crimson Fang could navigate a throng quite as adroitly as the young girl, a holdover from the years she'd spent living on the streets and earning a living as a pickpocket before Ammon and Uncle Ronan talked her into joining their brotherhood... to do the same for them.

Sparrow didn't talk much about her younger years, not to Natisse, at least. She'd spent most of her time training with Ammon, learning her letters from Baruch, or running missions with the rest of them.

Natisse felt a stab of worry. Sparrow might've been clear-headed enough to play her role here tonight, but she was still hurting badly over their collective loss.

Back in the Burrow, Jad would care for her, but what if she was suddenly overtaken with grief here amid Dimvein's elite? And caring as Jad was, he hadn't the slightest idea what it was like to be in Sparrow's shoes. In that moment, Natisse resolved to look in on the younger girl herself as soon as this eve was behind them. Ezrasil and the drunken gods knew she would've killed to have a womanly presence in her life when she was Sparrow's age.

"You absolutely must try the crab bites," one man said to Baruch.

Baruch gave the speaker a gallant grin, but the man was already turning away.

The enormous buffet table ran nearly half the barge's width, covered in anything and everything imaginable and then some. Natisse reached for one of the little balls of shellfish and pressed it playfully into Baruch's face, repaying him the favor.

He barely parted his lips in time.

"You just *must* try it," she said.

Baruch's eyes went wide. "He's not wrong. It's bloody good."

Natisse shoved one into her mouth as well, then noticed the other women picking sparingly at their food, little fingers pointing upward. She groaned almost silently. Much as she wanted to enjoy a proper meal, ladies of the Imperial court had to be dainty, delicate little fussbudgets who minced and flounced and giggled like brainless dolts.

Gods, I really do hate this whole disguise!

She'd have a stern conversation with Uncle Ronan about choosing a far less infuriating façade for the next job.

Sparrow materialized from the crowd directly in front of them.

"My lady," she said. "He's here." She was good at the game, making sure to keep details to a minimum. Though it was unlikely anyone at the party suspected them of foul play, keeping Leroshavé's name out of it was the smart move.

Natisse drained the last of her champagne—it was a truly delicious vintage with hints of lemon and green apple—and nodded.

"About time. Let's move."

"Five minutes for you to refresh, and then we dance, Lady Dellacourt," Baruch said, putting on airs.

Natisse graced him with a ladylike smile.

"Plenty of time."

She swept a little bow to him, as he'd taught her to, then wafted away from the refreshments table with Sparrow in her wake. It was a chore to get through all the big dresses and twirling couples on the dance floor, but soon, they emerged and had their target in sight.

Magister Perech stood near the barge's port-side railing, surrounded by a gaggle of sycophants and clingers-on—all of whom were interested in him for his power and wealth, no doubt. The man was an utter bore, totally self-interested, yet spoke as if he were Emperor Wymarc holding court in the Imperial Palace rather than just some half-a-century-old, too-rich aristocrat celebrating his birthday. The men and women clustered around him laughed too loudly at his terrible jests, cheered and stamped their heels at every fifth word out of his pudgy mouth, and played the role of suck-ups to perfection.

Natisse had no desire to play that particular tune. Instead, she went straight in for the kill.

"My lord!" she gushed, affecting a breathless, sultry tone. "I must insist that you offer me the courtesy of at least one dance. Even in faraway Elliatrope, it is said that Calaydris Perech's skill in the ballroom is unmatched." She slid close to him and whispered into his ear. "Except, perhaps, by his skill in the bedchambers."

Magister Perech was easily twice her age and three times her weight, but he was still a red-blooded man who'd once held the reputation for being quite the lothario, and refused to believe his heyday had truly passed. His confident smile turned into an enormous beaming grin.

"Quite right, quite right."

"Come, come," Natisse said, taking the aristocrat by the hand, making certain to brush up against his trousers with the thick of her thigh as she did so. "Before one of these other gracious ladies swoops in and steals you away."

Judging by the looks the ladies surrounding Magister Perech shot her, they had intended precisely that, but had simply been taking their time as befitted a lady of the Empire's capital. Natisse's status as "backwater nobility" gave her a great deal of leeway—along with plenty of anonymity when this mission was done.

Magister Perech allowed himself to be drawn away from his crowd and onto the dance floor. Natisse grimaced inwardly as his hands roamed the back of her dress, but she forced herself to ignore the discomfort at his pawing. She had to endure just a few minutes more, and it would all be worth it in the end.

In the middle of the dance floor, she turned to face the portly aristocrat. Up close, she was struck by the strange azure sheen of his skin. Even the sweat trickling down his brow had a distinctly... salty scent to it. Both were effects of whatever strange magic he wielded.

He was one with the sea, it was said. The scar behind his right ear, which disappeared beneath his upturned collar, brought back the stories she'd heard.

"That scar is legendary," she said.

"Ah, yes." His hand left her ass—much to Natisse's relief—to absent-mindedly stroke the calloused skin. "You know the tale, I'm sure?"

"Oh, I've heard much, but surely you could tell it much better than any traveling minstrel."

"Songs, about me? You don't say."

"So many." Natisse fought back bile as his hand traced the seam along her ribcage. She cleared her throat. "Each one more incredible than the last. Please, tell me about it?"

"If you insist."

"I do." She grabbed his hand more to keep it from exploring any further, and laced her fingers with his.

"Well, in the season when kings went to war, I found myself at Emperor Wymarc's side. He'd always chosen me as a kind of... personal bodyguard, you might say."

He paused, waiting for her to respond with the typical oooo or ahhh.

She obliged. Then he went on to tell of the naval battle with the Hudarians.

"It was the day they surrendered, believe it or not. I like to think that was my doing."

"That's what the songs say," Natisse lied.

He'd been injured by a man he described as twice his size and thrice the strength, which likely meant a lady. The attacker's sword dug deeply into the flesh of his neck and sent him toppling overboard—precisely why Natisse needed him away from any railings. That was when he'd called upon his dragon and the bloodsurge took hold. The sea water healed him instantly, leaving only that scar as evidence of the day's events.

"Amazing," Natisse said.

Magister Perech grinned. "Truly."

Natisse leaned in close, letting her hot breath tickle his ear. Then she purred, Tell my, my lord, is it also true that you and

Magister Estéfar were responsible for the destruction of Halfvale?"

The words registered slowly in Magister Perech's mind. When they did, he jerked back. "What?"

Natisse didn't give him a chance to retreat. She yanked him in close. "Is it true," she hissed, "that Magister Estéfar sent his dragon to burn the forests around Argencourt to clear a path for you to cut a new waterway for your cargo vessels to navigate the river to Delvehome without being forced to pay the Emperor's taxes?"

He stuttered, and she slid a hand beneath his arm. Clasping his back, she pulled the portly man even closer.

"And that," she continued, "started a forest fire that killed two-thirds of Halfvale's population and destroyed the entire village? A fire that you could have put out with a simple bloodsurge... my lord?"

Magister Perech bristled. "I don't know what—"

A high-pitched scream from behind Natisse drowned out Magister Perech's protestations.

"Help!" Sparrow cried. "Oh blessed Yildemé, someone help! The Baronet... he's dying!"

Natisse didn't bother to glance back—she didn't need to see the show Baruch was putting on, holding his breath until he grew red in the face, flailing wildly, hands at his neck, staggering around like a drunken sailor. But all those around turned toward the commotion, hundreds of pairs of eyes locked onto the ornately dressed "Baronet" and the terrified pageboy.

Only Magister Perech's eyes were fixed on Natisse. Outrage flashed across his face, turning his blue-tinged skin a furious purple.

"You little bitch!" he snarled, spittle flying. "I don't know who you think you are, but I will not be addressed with such disrespect at my own celebration. I'll have you flogged and..."

But Natisse paid no heed to his tirade. Reaching up, she drew one of the stilettos from her hairdo.

Suddenly, not two paces away from her, a tall, handsome aristocrat wearing a finely tailored long coat of crushed velvet staggered backward as if struck by an invisible fist. Natisse's eyes widened at the sight of the dagger's hilt protruding from his neck, and the sudden gush of dark red blood that sprayed down the front of his white shirt.

Confused, but unwilling to let her opportunity escape, Natisse quickly returned her attention to Perech.

"Blood for blood," she whispered into his face, and prepared to drive the razor-sharp metal needle into his fat body.

9

KULLEN

Kullen had spent the day tracking Magister Taradan down. And now, as he watched as the soft-fleshed ninny toppled to the deck of Magister Perech's pleasure barge, a grim satisfaction welled within him. The traitorous bastard deserved far worse than the quick, near-painless death of dagger to the brain.

The ship at sea was a bit of fortune to Kullen's mind. Magister Perech's island fortress, with its many guards would've proven a more difficult killing ground. However, he'd been prepared to do what needed doing.

He'd used its high stone walls and perfectly maintained gardens as cover. Shaded corners had shrouded him, providing ingress into the mansion proper. From there, he'd slipped from shadow to shadow until finally spotting Magister Taradan seated with one leg crossed over the other in Magister Perech's office, his little loafered foot bouncing with some unheard rhythm.

Though he'd arrived on the tail-end of the hushed conversation between the two noblemen, Kullen had heard enough to convince himself that Magister Taradan was, indeed, moving against the Emperor.

What else would Magister Taradan have meant when he'd said, "I want in"?

Kullen hadn't missed the hand-off of an envelope bearing Magister Taradan's seal, which Magister Perech had stored in a locked desk drawer. And then that sleazy smile from Perech. It took all Kullen had not to kill them both right then and there. But he'd been forced to flee the office when Magister Perech's manservant brought the afternoon meal and prepared to throw open the curtains—thus dispelling Kullen's shadowy concealment.

The day passed and the sin cruise began, giving Kullen precisely the distractions needed to do the task. He couldn't afford another kerfuffle, even if the last one wasn't his fault. With Assidius undermining him at every turn, tonight's assassination would need to be perfect.

As providence would have it, some idiot by the refreshments table had begun choking, and the panicked shouts of the fool's page provided the perfect distraction for Kullen to make his move. He hadn't even needed to disappear within shadow. Dressed in finery to match the rest of the nobles, he was just one face among a sea of pompous, overweening men and women.

Presently, Kullen sheathed the second throwing dagger he'd drawn as a backup in case the first missed or failed to kill Magister Taradan. Though it took effort not to drive it through Perech's arrogant face as well.

Magister Taradan gasped and gurgled. His hands clawed at the dagger embedded in his throat, each failed attempt to remove it resulting in lacerations on his palms. One finger had been severed entirely and now fountained blood along with his neck.

Kullen's blade had sliced his windpipe, severed a large artery, and fractured the silver chain upon which Taradan's dragonblood vial had hung. Now, it lay a half-dozen paces away, well out of the dying aristocrat's reach. Even if it had been closer, Magister Taradan was too weak to reach for it, much less bloodsurge and summon his dragon. Not that it would've saved him either. As varied as each aristocrat's bloodsurging abilities may have been, none of them would remove the weapon and repair the damage Kullen had done.

The man's flaxen hair, aureate eyes, and bronzed complexion were all indicative of his bond with his gold dragon. All the gold in the world—including the vast fortune rumored to have been created by the dragon's own breath—couldn't stop him from bleeding out.

He watched Magister Taradan's frantic struggles growing weaker, his body gripped by jerking spasms. And still, no one took notice—all eyes were turned toward the commotion near the buffet, the shouting pageboy, and the choking aristocrat. Slowly, the light faded from Magister Taradan's golden eyes until they were as inert and still as the precious metal they resembled.

The Black Talon's job was done.

Kullen was preparing to turn away and vanish into the crowd when something caught his eye: a flash of fiery red hair and brilliant yellow dress just a few paces from where he stood. A woman, locked in an embrace with Magister Perech, the aristocrat's face buried in her luxurious locks, body smashed up against hers. Only they paid no heed to their surroundings. Indeed, they were far too intent on each other to even notice the dead Magister Taradan not five feet from where they danced.

Magister Perech seemed to sag in the woman's arms, leaning heavily on her. Doubtless, the lush had drunk too much. Kullen pitied the poor woman who'd have to endure Magister Perech's sweaty, clumsy pass. She was in for a rough night.

Then, to Kullen's wonder, Magister Perech slumped, his knees buckling and his legs giving out. The woman could no longer hold the overly inebriated aristocrat upright and he thumped to the deck of the barge, sprawling onto his face, a mere yard from where Magister Taradan twitched.

Instead of calling for help or stooping over the fallen Magister

Perech, the woman simply strode away. No hurry, no concern, but her pace was slow, steady. She didn't bother to glance back.

Something was terribly off about the woman, Kullen knew. He slid closer to Magister Perech, and his eyes widened as he caught sight of the trickle of blood seeping out from beneath the aristocrat's ornate clothing. He didn't need to turn the man over to understand what had happened. Magister Perech's chest no longer rose and fell with life's rhythm.

Kullen's head snapped up. His eyes darted in the direction of the woman, but she'd vanished into the horde of gawking noblemen and women, leaving her victim dead on the floor behind her.

Shekoth's icy pits! For a moment, surprise rooted Kullen in place. *Can she be…?*

A cry from behind him shattered his train of thought. A corpulent, white-haired woman with a heavily powdered and painted face stood over Magister Taradan's body, loosing a blood-curdling cry that threatened to shatter all the glass aboard the pleasure barge.

"He's dead!" she wailed.

Kullen slid away from Magister Perech's body and sought the refuge of the barge's railing. It would only be a matter of seconds before the second corpse was discovered, and he couldn't let anyone suspect him as the killer.

Sure enough, a moment later, another cry of alarm rang out.

"Magister Perech is dead, too!"

"There's a killer aboard!" cried another.

A stampede ensued—absolute madness—as noblemen and women alternately crowded around the bodies and fought their way clear of the ever-widening pool of blood. Others panicked and ran for their lives as if there were an exit other than the cold, dark, shark-infested waters.

Kullen had gotten clear just in time. No one was paying him

any heed. His eyes, however, darted up and down the barge in search of the red-haired woman in the brilliant yellow dress. He spotted a single flash of fiery locks near the aft end of the boat, gone in an instant.

Without hesitation, he pushed through the throng of partygoers, heading in pursuit of the fleeing woman—the fleeing assassin.

His mind flashed back to the night he'd killed Magister Iltari. Someone had put a crossbow bolt into Magister Estéfar's chest just mere moments before Kullen had thrown his own knife. Now, Kullen had been the first to eliminate his target, only to have Magister Perech die a moment later. It couldn't be a coincidence!

But who was the woman, and why had she killed Magister Perech?

He burst through the panicking multitude and raced along the barge's starboard side. He barely managed to evade the pile of brilliant yellow lace, chiffon, and ribbon that lay discarded beside the railing. The woman had ditched her clothing—he recognized the quick-loosening ties utilized by stage actors needing to make a quick costume change between scenes.

Kullen shook his head, left the dress where it lay, and raced onward.

Despite the chaos, the Emperor's Lumenators stood fast to their spots, lending their magical light to illuminate an otherwise pitch blackness. Kullen approached one, grabbing him squarely by the shoulders.

"Did you see her?" he said. "Did you see a woman? Red hair. Dispatched of that dress." He pointed. However, as the were trained to do, the Lumenator stayed perfectly silent. Perfectly still.

Kullen groaned, frustrated.

He grasped the railing, and peered out over the inky blackness. A small, sleek rowboat bobbed in the larger vessel's wake, secured by a mooring rope. And there, Kullen saw the red-haired woman leaping agilely from the barge's lower deck onto the smaller ship. She landed lightly on the craft without so much as causing it to sway. From twenty yards away, Kullen could hear her barking orders to the two men sitting at the oars.

"Cast off, now!" she shouted.

"What about—" The man said a name, but Kullen didn't quite understand it. Barak? Baroa? Their voices were being drowned out by now beneath the waves, the wind, and the tizzied nobles.

"He'll find his own... back," the red-haired woman shouted. "But... got... oh!"

A dark-skinned man—a Brendoni possibly?—who hadn't yet spoken scrambled toward the front of the smaller vessel and reached for the rope securing it to the pleasure barge. Kullen poured on the speed and reached the boat before the man could loosen the knot. He leaped over the Brendoni to the lower deck, then bounded across the narrow gap and landed on the smaller craft. Just as the mysterious woman had done, his balance was perfect. He drew a long hunting knife, pointing it with purpose.

"I don't know who in Ezrasil's name you are," he growled to the red-haired woman, "but—"

Kullen stopped, sensing the attack behind him. He ducked beneath the inevitable swing by the man who'd attempted to loose the moorings. Kullen drove his elbow backward, and it caught the man beneath the chin. The impact reverberated all the way up his arm but he never let his eyes stray from the red-haired woman.

A groan. The thump of the body collapsing. Another thud as it came to rest.

"—I bloody well intend to find out why you're killing noblemen," he finished, sweeping his knife up to point at the woman's throat.

The woman was positively radiant. She was possibly the most intriguingly beautiful thing Kullen had ever laid his eyes upon.

The spray of the ocean as it beat against the boat's side soaked her undergarments—all she wore after ditching her dress.

Before he could find himself further distracted by her lithe frame, he raised his attention to her eyes. Ice blue, no trace of fear or trepidation. On the contrary, they narrowed warily upon him.

"I don't know what you're talking about," she snapped. Her hand dropped to her lower back. "But unless you want to swim with the onyx sharks tonight, get the hell off my boat."

Kullen didn't miss the way her eyes darted cautiously past him. If she'd killed Magister Perech, she'd be worried about the aristocrat's guards. She was no accidental murderer; that much became immediately clear. She was cool, calm, and fully in control of herself. The other oarsman had risen and drawn a weapon of his own—a long, iron-spiked wooden club—yet seemed to be looking to her for direction.

This grew Kullen's interest exponentially. Who was she?

As he was about to ask that very question, she whipped her arm around and something darted toward his face. Instincts alone saved Kullen's life. Just as he had with the first attacker, he sensed it before he saw it coming. One knee cracked against the bottom of the boat as he dropped into a low crouch. Sharp steel snapped the air where his right eye had been a second earlier. The woman's yanked back and a length of steel uncoiled to form a long, straight blade.

He remained ducked, feet spread wide, leg muscles ready should he have to spring into action. His off hand slipped toward a throwing dagger hidden in his boot. She struck out with that strange whip-like sword, but he deftly deflected it with his right hand weapon and hurled the knife at her before she could pull back. Much as he'd hate to put an end to this mesmerizing, beautiful assassin without a chance to question her, survival trumped everything else.

Boots thumped behind him, and Kullen half-expected to hear a cry of alarm or a shout of "There are the killers!"

Instead, the boat rocked as something heavy boarded.

Torn between his need to keep a watchful eye on the whip-wielding woman and a desire to scrutinize the new threat, Kullen had no chance to dodge the blow that crashed into the back of his head.

IO

NATISSE

N atisse's eyes widened at the sight of the finely dressed aristocrat leaping onto her boat. The bastard had cleared Leroshavé with ease and now stood near the bow of the skiff, his dull, gray eyes locked on her.

"I don't know who in Ezrasil's name you are," he growled, "but—"

His elbow drove into Leroshavé's chin, knocking the smaller man down with a single blow.

His face scrunched into a snarl, his long hair wet from sweat and matted to his face, tangling in a freshly trimmed beard. On second glance, he may've worn the clothing of an aristocrat, but this was no highborn man of means.

"—I bloody well intend to find out why you're killing noblemen."

She noted that he didn't say "us"—why you're killing *us*. He said noblemen. That meant something.

A knife flashed upward toward her and Natisse's muscles tensed at the sight of it. Like the man, this was no fancy, bejeweled poniard or eating dagger used at a lavish feast. Instead, the blade was plain, unadorned, with an edge that gleamed in the moonlight. It matched the knife she'd seen protruding from Magister Taradan's throat. His grip on the dagger was loose—almost casual in its familiarity–yet his posture, poise, and expression screamed predator.

This man was a killer. The question was, who did he call master? Was he working on his own?

"I don't know what you're talking about," she snapped. She slid a hand behind her back, reaching for her lashblade. "But unless you want to swim with the onyx sharks tonight, get the hell off my boat."

She didn't give him a chance to respond, but tore the weapon free of its concealment and struck out at him. The segmented blade snapped forward, elongating to its full ten-foot length, and darted straight for his head.

Impossibly, the man ducked, far faster than Natisse had expected. She whipped her right arm back to retract the lashblade. The segments clacked together in her hand, re-forming into its sword shape.

Natisse caught a glimpse of the man's own hand grasping at his boot—readying another hidden weapon—and braced herself for the attack. He had both skill and speed, but Natisse was far from helpless. The ribs of her corset had been reinforced with whalebone for added protection against bladed weapons, and she'd fortified her under-dress sleeves with bracers of thin brass strong enough to turn aside a blade. Haston stood at her back, and Leroshavé was shaking off the blow that had knocked him down. The moment the stranger sprang at her, she'd be ready.

Movement from upward, aboard the pleasure barge, caught her eye. A broad-shouldered figure in ornate clothing broke free of the swirling knots of people screaming about the dead noblemen. Baruch charged toward the barge's edge and leaped across the narrow gap, landing onto the skiff immediately behind the armed man threatening her. From the folds of his robes, he pulled a leather blackjack and brought it crashing down onto the back of the man's skull.

Again, impossibly, the dagger-wielding man seemed to sense the danger and moved with otherworldly speed. He couldn't evade Baruch's blow, but he rolled forward to soften the impact. It was for this reason alone that Baruch's attack hadn't taken the man's head clear off his shoulders. Instead, his legs sagged and he dropped to one knee, but he was back on his feet in an instant and spinning to slash out at Baruch. Baruch barely managed to evade the knife blade, though it tore a long, ragged gash in his coat and silken shirt.

Cursing, Natisse whipped her lashblade forward. It found its mark, striking at the back of the man's head. A single blow to the base of his skull ought to put the bastard down, once and for all.

But it was like the man had eyes in the back of his head. He twisted out of the way, giving her a sly smile. Before Natisse could retract her lashblade, he half-spun and hurled a throwing knife at her. Only the whalebone ribs of her corset saved her life, turning aside the blade. The impact, however, staggered her backward a step. Her heel struck the seat behind her and she toppled into Haston's arms. For a few brief moments, they fought to regain their balance.

Leaving Baruch to face the stranger alone.

The man's attacks were well planned and executed, like he was trained. Baruch parried, dodged, and did his best to keep the blade at bay. As they fought, the man's coat and Baruch's robes fluttered, concealing much of the fight but it was clear, the armed man hacked and stabbed at Baruch with terrifying speed.

In the seconds it took Natisse to find her feet, the man had knocked the blackjack from Baruch's hand, cut a deep gash into his left arm, and driven a short push dagger into his leg. Baruch staggered backward, off-balance and bleeding. He tried to recover, to draw his brass knuckles and launch a counterattack, but his blows struck only empty air.

The man was just too fast.

Natisse saw the end coming before it happened—but too late to stop it. Baruch threw a vicious right hook that flew wide and high, and he stumbled forward, overcommitted to the blow. The armed man simply stepped inside his guard and buried his knife into Baruch's gut.

That was it. Just like that. No fancy slice or thrust. No dance... just a step and a stab and Baruch's lifeblood was pouring out onto the skiff.

A scream bubbled up from Natisse's throat, but she stifled it and snapped her lashblade forward at the man's chest. This time, he couldn't evade, even when he twisted his body lithely to the side. The razor-sharp edge of the segmented lashblade tore a long, jagged line along his ribs, and Natisse was rewarded with a grunt of pain.

She recoiled the lashblade and struck out again with all the speed and strength she could muster. The steel tip flashed toward the stranger's throat, but he twisted aside. Barely. The lashblade scored a thin line on his cheek. Blood welled from the gash and dripped from his beard.

Despite the wound, he anticipated her third strike in time to bring up a throwing knife to block. At the same time, his other hand whipped up to trap the segmented lashblade using the crossbar of his smaller dagger. They stood there, joined by steel, gazes locked. Hate burned within Natisse's icy eyes. In his, she saw the cold, calculating look of a killer. No hate. No fire. No storm cloud brewing. If he cared one bit that he'd just taken the life of another, he showed none of it on his face.

Frost slithered down her spine. She hauled on the lashblade, but the man held it firm, his grip like iron.

"You vile piece of horse shit."

"Who are you?" He spoke, softly. "And why in the Emperor's name—"

His words cut off in a half-grunt, half-gasp of pain, and he staggered forward, off-balance. His grip on Natisse's lashblade weakened and she tore the weapon free, pulled it back to reform a sword blade. She didn't know what happened, but as she begin to press her attack, she noticed Baruch.

He'd torn the dagger free of his stomach and driven it deep into the stranger's leg. Now, the two of them were locked in a grapple, grunting and straining to gain the upper hand. Baruch was stronger and larger by far, but his opponent was wiry and had muscles like corded rope.

Though Natisse had never seen anyone defeat Baruch in a wrestling match in the Burrow's training room, the man in his arms seemed to slither free with terrifying ease, breaking Baruch's hold on him with a vicious wrist lock.

Yet he could not break away, not fully. Baruch drove a punch into the man's stomach, doubling him over. Lurching to his feet, Baruch hurled himself at the stranger once more, his arms snaking around the man's throat and beneath his arms. With a roar, Baruch lifted his enemy off his feet and swung him toward the skiff's edge as if to throw him over. But with those injuries, Baruch couldn't last.

Again, the stranger did the impossible, swinging his legs to increase the momentum of Baruch's spin. His free arm snaked around Baruch's neck and grabbed him beneath the chin—a hold that would snap Baruch's spine if he tried to execute his intended throw. Barely, Baruch somehow broke free, but his attempt to throw the man overboard had failed. Worse, he was in a position where the man had the upper hand. A single vicious wrench of his chin and it would be over.

The stranger knew that as well. His lean, corded muscles tightened and yanked hard on Baruch's chin. Baruch's broad shoulders tensed, his neck straining. For a gut-wrenching moment, the two of them looked like statues. With Baruch's back to Natisse, she couldn't see the look on his face. She swore, his body squarely between her lashblade and the armed stranger trying to kill him.

Suddenly, Leroshavé appeared behind the two wrestling men, Baruch's blackjack in hand. His eyes still wobbled and he appeared half-dazed, but he had presence of mind enough to strike at the stranger's spine. The impact knocked the breath from the man's lungs and his grip on Baruch loosened. Just for a moment, but it was enough for Baruch to free himself.

The stranger managed to land on his feet. He tore the dagger from his thigh with a snarl and lashed out. Leroshavé brought up his club to block, only for the stranger to bring his knife spinning downward, shredding the front of Leroshavé's shirt and the dark flesh beneath.

Baruch loosed a wordless roar and hurled himself onto the stranger. His huge arms encircled the man's lean abdomen and swept him up in a bear hug.

Then, the tip of a dagger punched out through Baruch's back. Rich blood darkened Baruch's coat, staining the yellow fabric a deep crimson.

Natisse couldn't stifle the scream now.

"No!"

Her arm, poised to drive the lashblade forward, froze, her muscles turning to rigid ice. He could've survived the knife to the gut—Uncle Ronan knew some of the finest chirurgeons in Dimvein—but not this. Worse, with Baruch in the way, she couldn't strike out at the man who'd killed him.

Baruch gave a weak, wet cough. The man struggled in his arms, yet somehow Baruch refused to let go, stubborn even as he died. His strong legs sagged but he half-turned his body so he could take one final look at Natisse. A strange expression shone in his eyes—a mixture of fear, sorrow, and relief.

"Go," Baruch whispered, his lips stained crimson. "The mission..."

Before he could complete his brother's famous words, the big man hurled himself off the side of the skiff. Baruch and the assassin plunged into the dark water and vanished beneath the surface in an instant.

Natisse flung herself toward the edge of the boat. Even as she scanned the water, she was pulling at her underclothes, trying to strip them off to dive in unhindered.

"No!" A man's voice echoed at her elbow. Something grabbed at her left arm. She brushed off the grip and continued her frantic efforts to disrobe.

"Don't you do it!" Leroshavé snarled, and this time he wrapped both arms around her, dragging her physically away from the skiff's edge.

"Let me go!" Natisse raged. "I can still get him. I can still—"

"Natisse, no." Leroshavé's voice barely filtered through the war raging within her. "It's too late. That blood will draw every onyx for a hundred miles. Look."

The arms encircling Natisse loosened, and she surged up to her feet once more. Horror twisted in her gut as she caught sight of the white-churned water where Baruch and the stranger had disappeared. Dozens of black fins already swarmed around the spot, and the splashing of onyx sharks echoed even through the blood pounding in Natisse's ears.

She slumped backward, collapsing into the boat's deck.

"No!" She thought she'd screamed. Bile roiled bitter and hot in her throat. Her stomach heaved.

No, no, no! It can't be!

Dimly, she heard Leroshavé calling, "Get us out of here, now!"

"What about Sparrow?" Haston answered, his voice distant faint.

"She's with Dalash. They'll find a way out. But we need to go or we're dead!"

The words sank home in Natisse's mind. They weren't out of danger—far from it, in fact. It fell to her to ensure they reached safety.

Though it tore at her soul, Natisse pushed the raging emotions down, down, down, until she could no longer feel them. She'd already done it with Ammon, what was it to add more? They were there, she knew, threatening to overwhelm her the moment she released them from within their prison. But for a time, they couldn't touch her, couldn't deter her from doing what needed to be done.

She picked herself up off the floor of the skiff and slid onto the nearest bench.

"Leroshavé's right," she said, her voice eerily calm. "We need to get out of here before Magister Perech's guards see what's happening and send up the distress signal."

"That won't be a problem," Haston said, gesturing toward the bow of the boat.

Natisse turned. The barge was off in the distance now, churning up water and leaving them in its wake. Leroshavé had loosened the ropes that tied them to the pleasure craft, and in their struggles with the armed stranger, the skiff had drifted away. The Lumenator's presence upon Magister Perech's boat were growing distant too. The light was faint and growing fainter. Cloud-hazed moonlight dappled the sea's surface around them—including the spot where the onyx sharks still circled, hungry to feed on the two men who had gone overboard.

"You got what we came for?" she asked hurriedly.

"Right here," Haston said, hefting an oilcloth bag. "Raided the pecker's office and cleaned him out good."

"Good," Natisse nodded. "Get us out of here. The mission's done. Dalash and Sparrow know what to do. They'll return when they return."

"Aye, aye," Leroshavé said.

Sorrow still darkened his face—he'd been friends with Baruch, as had all the Crimson Fang—but he no longer appeared worried for her. They'd cleared enough missions that he and Haston both recognized her recaptured serenity.

"You know what to do," she told Haston, taking up an oar. "With just the three of us, we'll have to row hard to reach the Ember-side docks before sunrise. Best we vanish before the Imperial Scales think to start searching for us on open water."

With a nod, Leroshavé and Haston both settled onto the benches and took up oars as well.

They'd rowed a few minutes in silence before she heard the sniffle behind her. She didn't know who that man was, but one thing was certain... he deserved worse than the sharks.

II

KULLEN

The shock of the cold sea water drove the air from Kullen's lungs. He struggled to break free of the dying man's grip, but the arms encircling him refused to release their hold on him. If Kullen's situation hadn't been so dire, he might've admired his enemy's tenacity, the sacrifice the man had made for the red-haired woman and the others aboard the boat.

But Kullen's situation was dire, indeed. The man's weight was dragging him steadily downward, farther from the surface, and though the pitch-black water hid the sleek black forms, he had no doubt the onyx sharks were even now closing in on them. It would only be a matter of seconds before their razor-sharp teeth ripped his flesh to shreds. He'd be as dead as the man bleeding out behind him.

He did the only thing he could: he tore his right arm free, fumbled in his shirt until he felt the dragonblood vial hanging from the chain around his neck, and jammed his thumb into the gold-embossed tip. He couldn't feel the needle-prick pain—the cold had already begun numbing his limbs, but it was as nothing compared to the icy surge of magic that burst to life within him.

His thoughts melted inward, a swirling cloud of vague images of the Shadow Realm.

Umbris! Kullen cast out, speaking through the connection he and his dragon shared. *I need you!*

In that moment, the first shark appeared in the darkness around him. At the sight of the twenty-foot long beast, his focus was wrenched back to the corporeal realm. It's lithe body undulated, shimmering the purest black, almost invisible at this depth. White eyes locked on him as it sliced the water on a deadly path toward him. It smelled blood in the water and had come to feed. It wouldn't care whose blood it was.

Kullen's heart leaped into his throat as the gaping mouth opened and the six rows of serrated death came for him. He managed to interpose his right arm, and the teeth closed around the decorative leather vambrace worn as part of his aristocrat's costume. The pressure alone as the jaws clamped shut should have crushed bone but the reinforced steel bracers within the leather held. However, the crushing bite tore through fabric and leather, scoring Kullen's flesh. The shark thrashed at the water, tearing its teeth free, and circled around for another pass.

Kullen watched in horror as his own blood mingled with the already red waters. By now, his lungs were screaming for air. To his relief, it seemed the man behind him had finally entered Shekoth. His arms had grown weak, the muscles slackening. Yet they were so far from the surface, he could barely see the faintest glimmer of starlight piercing the water's inky darkness. In desperation, Kullen reached around and grabbed hold of the dead man, then thrust his fresh corpse toward the circling onyx shark.

The creature wasted no time, thrashing and shredding, tearing flesh by the chunks. It was bloody and tragic, but it gave Kullen a chance to break free and kick out toward the surface.

It would do him no good, he knew. The onyx shark would finish that small meal quickly. Not to mention the dozens more Kullen knew were on their way. He cut through the waters as fast as his arms and legs would allow, blood trailing from the wound on his arm.

The silence was the worst part. The beast made no sound as it sliced toward him at terrible speed. Kullen peered over his shoulder just in time to pull his legs inward and avoid becoming a beggar on the steps of Our Grand Maiden's Cathedral. He managed one powerful kick of his legs, even as he drew a dagger. The little blade would be like a butter knife against a beast of that onyx shark's size. But he'd fight to his last breath, or until—

An enormous black shape suddenly flashed through the darkness and collided with the approaching onyx shark. Huge, gleaming teeth snapped shut onto the shark's frame, ripping it in half. Milky white eyes turned toward Kullen, and a moment later, a scaly body barreled into him.

Hold on tight, Umbris said within Kullen's mind.

The cold-numbed fingers of Kullen's right hand instinctively closed around one of Umbris's wing spines. A painful jolt rippled up his arm and tugged at his shoulder, nearly jerking the joint from its socket, but he held on.

The ocean became a force all its own as Umbris dragged him through the water. It was like shards of ice against his flesh, he closed his eyes but he wasn't sure his lungs would last much longer.

Finally, just as Kullen felt he couldn't wait any longer to draw breath, Umbris burst free of the ocean's surface. Kullen dragged in a great, ragged gasp. He was dizzied and disoriented as he went from the depths of the ocean to the cloud-filled sky.

Do not relinquish your hold, Kullen.

Umbris must've sensed Kullen's subconscious intention. The dragon's words spurred him to action, reaffirming his grip on Umbris's wing. The wind whipped at him, biting cold on his wet hair and clothing, but he welcomed it. Better to be miserable than dead.

Air filled his lungs and he began to gain his bearings.

I don't believe it's necessary for me to advise against swimming with the sharks, yes? Umbris said in Kullen's mind. Su*ch things ought to be common sense.*

"Gee, you don't say!" Kullen scowled, fighting to keep his teeth from chattering. "Next, you tell me that sticking sharp things into my eyes is a bad idea, too."

Umbris's huge body rumbled and a sound Kullen recognized as laughter rolled like thunder from the dragon's lips.

"Thank you, my friend."

It wasn't as if I had better things to do.

The words were spoken in levity, but Kullen knew better. He knew that even something such as this was preferable to him being stuck, alone in his realm. It pained Kullen to know that Umbris was there without any of his kind. While the other dragons shared their realms with others like them, Umbris had no other Twilight Dragons to keep company with.

His were a kind thought too dangerous to remain. While the others would be seen coming from miles off, the Twilights were one with the shadow and could appear instantly in nearly any situation, delivering death as quickly and silently as an assassin. It made Kullen and Umbris perfect for each other but did nothing to ease either of their loneliness.

Kullen went to respond when Umbris dipped into a steep dive. He leveled out just above the waves, the sea spray whipping up against them. Then, as quickly as he'd descended, Umbris whipped back upward.

Kullen peered over the edge of Umbris's wing. They were high above the ocean, Magister Perech's pleasure barge far below and south of them, but there was no sign of the small skiff or the redhead. He doubted they'd be spotted. Umbris's purplish-black scales were all but invisible in the darkness. He had no intention of returning to the party anyway. He'd handled one of the two tasks he'd set for himself this night. Magister Taradan was dead, which left just the envelope the aristocrat had handed off to

Magister Perech. An envelope which should, even now, be locked away in Magister Perech's office on the fourth floor of his island fortress. With all the commotion aboard the barge, it should prove a simple matter to slip through the shadows and gain entrance.

But first, Kullen thought as a fresh gust of wind sent icy knives cutting through his soaked clothing and flesh, *I need to get bloody warm*!

Midnight found a now-dry Kullen hunkering down in the shadows, tucked within the crisscrossing beams below the bridge that led from the mainland to Magister Perech's island fortress. Umbris had flown him to his nearest safe house—a small apartment a mile inland from the Upper Crest—for a change of clothing and to bandage his wounds. He'd lost his hunting knife, but had replaced it with a long stiletto, perfect for tonight's infiltration. Armed, with Umbris's power once more replenished within his inner reservoir, he'd made his way on foot to the estate of the now-deceased aristocrat.

Just in time to see the Orkenwatch arrive. The death of not one, but two of Dimvein's wealthy and powerful, had inevitably drawn the attention of the elite guards. Turoc himself marched at the head of the six Orken platoon. In the moonglow, their tusks gleamed like lit candles, the light reflecting off saliva. They all wore dark fur-lined cloaks, crafted from the hardened skin of dryland lizards. They were proud people made prouder by their roles given by the Emperor. It was as if they didn't realize they were being used for their strength and brawn.

It had been centuries since Emperor Wymarc's line had called upon them to take up arms. Long ago, men entered the

Korpocane Caverns, deep within the Kingdom of Trill. For years, they were considered lost to this world until, finally, something emerged. Human they were no longer... but the offspring of man and whatever dwelt within those caves. It was that day, the Orken became known. They were savages, uneducated, and violent, but the Emperor saw use for them; decided they, too, had a right to life—true life.

He had them taught, trained, and tamed. And now, they served the Empire.

At the moment, they did their job well, their presence keeping Kullen from re-entering Magister Perech's mansion. He had no desire to draw any closer to the Orken than necessary—and not just because of his personal dislike of their Tuskigo At Turoc's side marched Bareg, his Ketsneer—the Orken word for second-in-command—and the finest Sniffer in the Orkenwatch. Better to keep his distance until Ketsneer Bareg and his far-too-keen nose departed.

The arrival of the Orkenwatch had been proceeded by a veritable stampede of carriages conveying frilly, lace-festooned men and women away from the fortress-like mansion. The drawbridge remained down, but the gate had been sealed behind the departing nobility.

Kullen settled in to wait for the Orkenwatch's withdrawal. There was no need to hurry—no one was getting in or out of that fortress, at least for the time being. Furthermore, with the Magister dead, the contents of Perech's office would remain undisturbed for at least a few more hours. He was just glad to be dry, warm, and outside the bellies of those damned onyx sharks.

In his mind, he replayed the evening's curious events. He'd noticed the red-haired woman in the brilliant yellow dress earlier in the night—how could he not?—but had dismissed her as just one more vacuous noblewoman as vapid as the others flitting and flouncing around the barge. Yet Magister Perech's death, her attempted escape, and the fight aboard the skiff had irrevocably burned her into his mind.

Who was she? He couldn't help wondering. And why did she kill Magister Perech?

There were all manner of reasons for wanting the aristocrat dead. Gambling debts, a spurned lover, a jealous business rival, enemies more vicious than the man himself—the list was long, indeed. She hadn't acted alone, either. Her plan had been damned clever, he had to admit. She'd been bloody skilled with that strange whip-sword, whatever in Shekoth's frozen pits it was.

Her accomplices had been mostly beneath his notice—the usual rough-and-tough sort, low men skilled in the typical arts of duplicity and death—though the one he'd killed had seemed somehow... familiar. Kullen couldn't place the man's face, but he had the nagging suspicion that he'd seen the man somewhere before.

Not that it mattered much now. The man was a corpse—if that —doubtless ripped apart by onyx sharks. His act of sacrifice—for the woman's sake, of that Kullen was certain—was certainly nobler than might be expected of a street thug or hired killer.

Then again, men do ignorant things for women when their little brains do the thinking. Fool.

Regardless of the man's intentions, something about the whole situation tugged at Kullen's curiosity. And not just because of the woman's beauty and ferocity with that strange weapon of hers. There was something amiss. He just couldn't put his finger on it.

He had no more time to contemplate the matter. Half an hour after the midnight bell, the gate rumbled open and the Orken-watch marched out onto the drawbridge. Kullen pressed himself deeper into the shadows and waited in tense expectation for the six Orken to pass his hiding place. Turoc and Bareg spoke in voices too quiet for Kullen to hear, though their expressions were grave—graver even than their ugly mugs normally were.

The Orken vanished into the night, and Kullen let five

minutes pass before emerging. Only then did he make his move, drawing his dagger with his left hand, reverse grip on the hilt and blade pressed against his forearm. With his right thumb, he gripped the dragonblood vial hanging around his neck.

The familiar pinprick, a trickle of his own blood mixing with that of Umbris and the already calm, quiet night became still as death itself. It seemed even the ocean breeze stilled, the starlight itself freezing in place. Energy bathed him, drowning out the pain of his wounds, the fatigue of a long night, the cold permeating his skin. Thousands of red-hot stingers flickered through every nerve in his body. Inexorably, he was drawn into the depths of the inner reservoir of magic.

"Trouble with sharks again, Kullen Bloodsworn?" came Umbris's voice in his mind.

"No," Kullen retorted mentally, pouring a generous helping of scorn through the bond he and the dragon shared. *"But I do have need of your powers."*

"They are yours," Umbris said. *"But know that while you wield them, I cannot save you from whatever trouble you get yourself in."*

The tingling, crackling power rippled through Kullen's veins, and the colors of the world around him faded to blacks, whites, and grays. The shadows of night tugged on his body, as if seeking to tear him apart into a million fragments. It took all of Kullen's concentration to keep his shadow form cohesive—too much effort for him to muster a retort for Umbris at the words he'd heard so many times before.

His consciousness locked onto a patch of shadow atop the walls surrounding Magister Perech's mansion. There, no lanterns shone, no fires burned in braziers, and even the light of the moon and stars were now shrouded behind thick clouds. Kullen willed himself toward it, and it felt as if an invisible grapple yanked him across the vast, intervening distance in heartbeat's span.

Once atop the wall, he sought out more darkness in the mansion below. Thick gloom beneath a stand of dense trees called to him, and he heeded their call, again dragged across the expanse in a breathless instant. Time bore no meaning to him in this form. He knew only light and dark and what lay between.

Flitting through the night, weightless as a leaf on the breeze yet moving in the blink of an eye, each shift sapped his strength, drained the wellspring of power within him. Umbris had warned him of his capabilities. He could only manage seven transitions—eight, at full strength—before the shadow magic would consume him, turn him into a creature that knew only shadow, as intangible and lifeless as darkness. Damned forever in the Shadow Realm like the Twilight Dragon himself. But unlike Umbris, there would be no one to beckon him from that realm. No respite from the loneliness and isolation. Cold. Alone. Formless.

Once in the garden, he had a clear line of sight to the third-floor window of Magister Perech's office. To his relief, the chamber, too, was dark, not so much as a candle burning on the aristocrat's desk. A final shift through the shadows sent him hurtling toward the unlit room, passing through the glass window as if it didn't exist. Glass could not deter shadows, nor could it deter him.

Returning to his tangible form proved difficult as always. With every shift, the icy chill of nothingness seeped deeper into his soul, and his body forgot its original state, magic transforming it more into the shadow. More into a creature akin to those he never truly glimpsed but *felt* every time he entered the Shadow Realm. He clawed his way back to permanence with effort, dragging his consciousness through the quicksand of the power that battled him as if the darkness itself wanted him. A dangerous power, one he used all his substantial might to oppose.

He was once again Kullen, no taint of shadow. Gasping, he bent and wretched but nothing came up. His stomach turned, but it was empty. It was only then he realized his hunger that would have to wait. Numbness spread across his limbs. He had to rest. Try as he may, his legs wouldn't carry him forward.

It took him nearly ten minutes to regain his strength and for sensation to return to his extremities. Even once he could move, his muscles dragged as if beneath an immense weight. His mind felt slow, his head thick with wool.

Blinking to push back the fatigue, Kullen stood and slipped around Magister Perech's desk and knelt in front of the drawer where Kullen had watched him store Magister Taradan's envelope. No surprise, the drawer was locked. Kullen slid the tip of the stiletto blade into the mechanism and gave a sharp twist. Metal snapped, surprisingly loud in the silence of the dark office. Kullen ignored it—no one was around to hear anyway—and pulled the now unlocked drawer open.

He blinked in shocked surprise at the empty drawer.

Confused, he reached in and fumbled with the wooden base. No hidden panels or secret caches he could find. The contents of the drawer—and importantly above all, the envelope—were simply… gone.

Thinking he must've been mistaken, Kullen pulled open the other drawers. Empty, empty, empty. All of them, empty. Someone had taken every scrap of parchment, every envelope, even the silver stamp and wax stick Magister Perech used to mark and seal his documents.

Kullen's mind raced. How was this possible? He'd been in this very room just a few hours earlier, had seen Magister Perech's drawers filled to bursting with all manner of papers and scrolls.

Scanning the office, his gaze traveled over the books on shelves, the plush armchairs where Magisters Perech and Taradan had shared a drink earlier, the serving cart that had born their refreshments. A wooden cabinet sat against the room's southern wall, a few steps away from Magister Perech's desk. But, as Kullen feared, it too had been ransacked.

All this for nothing.

Kullen slammed the desk. "Shit!"

The connection the Emperor had mentioned that would lead

Kullen to uncover the conspiracy to assassinate him was in that envelope. Of that he was certain. And it was gone. In the last three hours, someone had taken them. But who?

The trail had just gone frigid.

Damn, the Emperor's not gonna be happy…

12

NATISSE

Natisse fled to her quarters the moment she, Leroshavé, and Haston entered the Crimson Fang's underground lair. Uncle Ronan was nowhere in sight—for which Natisse was greatly relieved—and for a few brief moments, no one needed her. No one had questions for her or expected a report on what had happened—not that she would have known how to answer that question. For now, she could allow the emotions to well up within her and mourn Baruch.

Even as she closed the door to her chambers and surrendered to the embrace of the cool darkness, Natisse felt the veil of ice she'd thrown over her emotions shatter into a billion pieces. The sorrow, anguish, and grief welled up within her like a geyser of lava, burning through the restraints holding her feelings in check. Her legs gave out and she collapsed to her knees, forehead pressed against the door, tears burning hot tracks down her cheeks.

First Ammon, now Baruch. Her two best friends in the world. The two with whom she'd spent most of the last five years of her life, who'd trained her, watched over her, and loved her in a way only they could. Ammon had been as much an older brother to her as he'd been to Baruch. And Baruch…

Just thinking about him ripped Natisse's heart into pitiful shreds. She struggled to draw breath but couldn't fill her lungs for the fist of iron crushing her ribs. A low, animalistic moan bubbled from her lips, a keening cry so deep and furious she couldn't control it, couldn't bottle it up.

Why? The question hammered at her mind again and again. Why did it have to be him? Why them?

Her fingers clenched and she beat at the solid stone walls of her chamber until her fists bled. Exhausted, she slumped to the ground and lay with her face pressed against the cold stone floor. Eyes open or closed, she couldn't escape the image of Baruch's pale, pain-twisted face, his final words to her.

The mission above all, he was going to say before both he and their attacker plunged into the onyx shark-infested waters.

He was on death's doorstep—they'd both known it—yet he'd chosen to hurl himself and the stranger overboard. With his final act, he'd purchased her freedom. Her escape from the stranger who'd killed Magister Taradan and tried to do likewise to them. Had the bastard not gone to the sharks, Natisse would have dedicated her life to hunting him down and tearing his still-beating heart from his chest. The knowledge that Baruch's killer had died should've given her a shred of satisfaction. In truth, it only compounded her anger. There was no one to pay for what had happened. No one upon whom Natisse could unleash her hatred and rage and grief.

Her last true conversation with Baruch played through her mind—not the flirtatious show they'd put on as Baronet Charlati and Lady Dellacourt, but the few quiet words they'd shared in the training room before Ammon's funeral.

"If I'd have just left you alone that day," she'd said. It was déjà vu. The same thoughts she'd just had for Ammon.

And meant it, then as much as now.

They'd cut such pathetic figures, the two young brothers in bedraggled finery crawling through the rubbish of the Embers in a desperate search for food. Half-starved and going feral after weeks of living on the streets, the pair had drawn Natisse's pity... and curiosity. At the time, she'd wondered if they had stolen the noblemen's clothing or simply found it abandoned in the refuse in which they hunted scraps.

When those soldiers accosted them, stole what little they had, Ammon had tried to stand up to them.

When he'd fallen to a vicious backhand, Natisse simply couldn't help but insert herself. Had she been quicker, she might've killed those bastard Scales.

The fire in Ammon's eyes as he'd spoken to them, how he'd shielded his brother with his own body had intrigued Natisse. That evening, she'd returned to them with a single meat pie—all she could afford with the meager coins Uncle Ronan had given her. Despite being ravenous, Ammon had restrained his appetite long enough to ensure Baruch ate his fill.

The sight of such sibling loyalty had tugged at something within Natisse. Every day for the following fortnight, she'd visited the rundown shanty they'd called home. The more she interacted with the brothers, the more curious she grew. Until, finally, Baruch had told her the truth: the pair of them were the sons of the once-prosperous Sallas family, the only survivors of a red dragon attack that had slain the rest of their household and destroyed their mansion. All because some aristocrat had felt slighted by Baronet Sallas in some deal gone rotten.

She had to wonder if it was the same one she'd dreamed of so many times.

Her mind returned to those days, practically courting Ammon and Baruch in an attempt to draw them into the fold of the Crimson Fang.

It is all your fault. The words echoed in Natisse's head, a pounding rhythm louder than the beat of a dragon's wings.

My fault.

Because of Natisse, Baruch was now dead too.

Baruch's voice cut through her mourning. "My brother chose the Fang and I chose you."

He'd chosen her—the day he'd accompanied her underground to become a member of the Crimson Fang, the day he'd returned here to her rather than taking up his sword and fighting to free Ammon from Magister Estéfar's guards, and now tonight, hurling himself to the sharks for her sake.

"Baruch, you damned fool," she said under her breath. It wasn't true though. He'd been brave and kind and intelligent, and his last act had been far from foolish. Yet anger came more easily than sorrow. It was easy to hate, and so much harder to live through the pain twisting in her chest.

A gentle knock sounded at the door. Natisse had no need to ask who was there—only one person would come to her quarters at a time like this.

"Natisse?" Uncle Ronan's voice echoed through the heavy door. "Let me in."

Natisse couldn't bring herself to speak; she hadn't the strength. The best she could do was shift her weight, clearing the path for the door to swing open.

When no answer proved forthcoming, Uncle Ronan tried the door handle. The door swung open, and faint light brightened the darkness within her room. Natisse didn't bother bringing her hand up to shield her eyes. She just sat there, overwhelmed by her misery, externally numb but blazing with an inner fire not even her typical chilly detachment could quench.

Uncle Ronan entered the room. His gaze fell across Natisse's empty bed, the desk and chair in the corner, until, finally, it made its way to her, pathetic and broken on the floor. He closed the door gently behind him, set the lantern down on the desk chair, and lowered himself to the ground beside her. His hand fell beside hers, but said nothing, simply sat there at her side in silence.

"I..." Natisse tried to speak, but her voice cracked. Words deserted her. What could she say? *I got him killed?* How foolish that sounded, like a child weeping over a dropped toy. Yet that was exactly how she felt. Logic and reason meant nothing in the face of the emotions she couldn't quite yet master.

"Leroshavé and Haston told me what he did," Uncle Ronan said. His voice was so soft, so gentle, a far cry from his usual stern manner. He turned toward her, kindness in his eyes. "Ammon would've been proud."

Those words shattered Natisse all over again. Fresh tears streamed down her face and she wept, great silent sobs wracking her shoulders. Uncle Ronan turned away—not to ignore her sorrow, she knew, but to let her grieve in private—but his presence, his strength consoled her. She reached for his scarred, callused hand and clung to it with all her strength.

Uncle Ronan squeezed her fingers with surprising gentleness.

"I know it's not much comfort," he said, "but at least now he's reunited with Ammon. Ezrasil knows the two of them hated being apart for long, Little Bird."

Little bird. He hadn't called her that in years. As a teenager, she'd hated the name. She wanted nothing to do with "little," no matter the context. After years of her insisting, he'd relented and called her by her name, though she knew it pained him. That is, until Sparrow came around and Uncle Ronan found his new "little bird."

Somehow, hearing it now both amplified her grief and soothed her. The words reminded her of the early days spent with Ammon and Baruch, the countless hours the three had spent training together. The hardships they'd endured for the Crimson Fang's cause and the joys of their intertwined lives. The memories, though painful, helped alleviate the burden weighing on her. Her tears slowed and soon dried up.

"I'm sorry," she said, wiping the moisture from her cheeks.

"Don't be," Uncle Ronan said. "It wasn't your fault. Leroshavé and Haston told me everything."

"Did they tell you that the bastard killed Magister Taradan just before I put a knife in Magister Perech?"

Uncle Ronan's face pulled into a frown. "No, they didn't."

"I had Magister Perech right where I wanted him. Then, suddenly, Magister Taradan toppled to the deck, a dagger in his throat. I didn't see who killed him, but I knew I had to act quick and make a run for it before someone found out."

She continued recounting the story until Uncle Ronan scrubbed at his scruff-cover cheeks and interrupted.

"Did you get a good look at the little shit?"

"Oh, yes." Natisse nodded. "He wore his hair long, but had it pulled back into a tail. His beard was like yours, short and full. He wore aristocrat's clothing, but no insignia, nothing to identify him as belonging to any house."

Though the memory of the night's events still brought her immeasurable pain, the retelling helped her to manage the grief—and recall more details she'd missed or forgotten since Baruch's death.

"And the way he fought, there's no way he was one of Magister Perech's guards. He..." She frowned, replaying the battle in her mind. "He moved far too fast, and he was good, Uncle Ronan, better than anyone I've ever seen."

"Hmmm." The musing sound rumbled in Uncle Ronan's throat. "Anything else you can think of to identify him?"

Natisse called to mind the man's face. She'd never forget it until the day she died. It was burned there, alongside Baruch's last words to her and his final act of courage. She scrutinized every detail of the man she could remember.

"No. Nothing." She shook her head, feeling ashamed though she knew she needn't. "He looked utterly ordinary. Aside from the way he fought—like a demon out of Shekoth—there was nothing to mark him as special."

Uncle Ronan pondered. "I will see what I can find out about this extraordinary ordinary man." He tugged at the tuft of beard beneath his lower lip. "If someone else is offing nobles, we need to know. I won't risk any more of you without a full understanding of what's going on."

Natisse squeezed Uncle Ronan's hand. He was strong, but she knew him well enough to see that he, too, felt Ammon and Baruch's loss.

"Haston and Leroshavé," Natisse said, "their part of the mission was successful?"

"Damned right," Uncle Ronan said, nodding once. A look of grim satisfaction skewed his features. "Jewelry enough to feed a sizable swath of the Embers for a month, with more to distribute among the extra needy."

Natisse couldn't help a small smile. At least one shred of light had come from the dark night.

The Crimson Fang's purpose was two-fold: first, to visit righteous justice and retribution upon the nobles who abused the power their riches, position, and their so-called bloodsurge magic they wielded. Second but no less noble, they distributed the wealth of those who had far too much amongst those with far too little.

Natisse, Baruch, Ammon, and Garron had spearheaded the former along with Nalkin and L'yo. Their training under Uncle Ronan—and, eventually Ammon—had tended to the martial, the art of combat and dealing death. None of them knew precisely where Uncle Ronan had learned to fight, but he'd trained them well, turned them into sharp daggers to plunge into the hearts of the corrupt nobility.

The remainder of the Crimson Fang, however, carried out the latter. They adopted disguises, infiltrated noble houses, picked gold-lined pockets, broke into heavily-guarded mansions, and did whatever else needed doing to ensure the wealth was properly distributed among the destitute—particularly those in the Embers. Dalash, Sparrow, Leroshavé, Haston, Jad, Tobin, and Athelas were the unseen fingers that dwindled the coffers of those who wouldn't miss it.

"Not only that," Uncle Ronan continued, "but they found some particularly intriguing—and actionable—information."

Among the skills Uncle Ronan had taught them was the gathering of intelligence. Leroshavé and Haston, in particular, had a knack for breaking into hidden safes, locked cabinets, and secret hiding places. But another skill was *listening*. It was shocking what kind of information noblemen would discuss when they'd thought they were alone. It was, perhaps, even more shocking how their eyes never seemed to notice those who looked like they belonged on the streets.

Any information found was handed off to Jad and Dalash, who sifted through numbers, letters, and boring legal documents to uncover intelligence of use to the Crimson Fang.

"So, what was it?" Natisse asked. "What did they find?"

She couldn't help the curiosity burning within her.

"They found *it*!" Uncle Ronan's eyes burned with a bright light.

Natisse's eyebrows shot up. "Truly?"

"Well, not exactly." Uncle Ronan's lips twisted into a frown. "But they've found the first new piece of actionable information we've had in months—since Magister Ariadas."

"That's wonderful!" Natisse tried to sound excited, but in truth, she couldn't summon the emotion. She felt mostly numb, hollow, as if a part of her had been wrenched away and left only a void behind.

Uncle Ronan must've heard it in her voice. "Little B—Natisse, I know this hurts. I can only imagine what you feel inside. But the mission is bigger than the individual, bigger than the sum of us. It is all that matters."

Natisse nodded solemnly.

"It was Ammon who'd said it first," he continued. "The mission above all."

"Those were—" her throat felt like she'd swallowed cotton. "Those were Baruch's last words."

"You see! We must continue on. We must shove down the hurt

and revive it when the opportunity comes to strike at their hearts. Blood for blood."

"Blood for blood," Natisse repeated.

"Yes, exactly. I don't know who this attacker is. I don't know what he's up to. But perhaps our purposes align."

Natisse's lips pulled up into a snarl. "He killed Baruch."

Uncle Ronan nodded. "The mission…"

Natisse shook her head.

"The mission…?"

"The mission above all," she said through clenched teeth.

"The mission above all," Uncle Ronan agreed. He was quiet for seconds that felt like hours. "I know it's going to be hard to go on. But you have to. We all do. And as much as it pains me to say it, I need you now."

Natisse's head shot up. "Now?"

"Indeed. We've made a monumental breakthrough." Uncle Ronan rose, retrieved the lantern, and turned to her. "I know it's asking a great deal, but I need you." He held out a hand. "With Baruch and Ammon gone, I'm leaning on you more than ever."

Natisse reached up and, taking his hand, pulled herself to her feet.

"I'm here, Uncle Ronan. Whatever you need from me."

She swallowed the last of the emotion roiling in her stomach and once more, cast the icy veil over it, disconnected herself from the grief and loss and misery. She had to be strong, to focus on the mission. She had to make certain Baruch and Ammon's deaths weren't in vain.

"Then come, Natisse," Uncle Ronan opened the door for her. "Let's find how Magister Perech was connected to those slave fighting pits we've been hunting for the past three years."

13
KULLEN

K ullen needed to report to the Emperor his findings from Magister Perech's office—or, more accurately, his lack of any findings. But it could wait until morning.

Bloodsurging to escape Magister Perech's little party on the sea had sapped his strength, left him exhausted. The shadow walking to his mansion had nearly done him in. There was simply nothing left in his reserves to allow for him to do so back to the mainland. Indeed, even the climb down into Perech's outer court-yard and the four-mile trek back to Kullen's nearest safe house felt like the longest journey he'd ever undergone. So much so, he'd had to fight the temptation to summon Umbris to fly him the last half-mile to the One Hand District.

It was with great relief that he came within sight of his safe house. It looked far from safe—indeed, the Apple Cart Mead Hall was anything but the quiet, secluded stronghold where one would expect to find the Emperor's Black Talon. A steady stream of boisterous men and women in various states of inebriation flowed in and out of the establishment. Laughter, shouts, jeers, and sounds of a fistfight reached Kullen even from two streets away.

Yet the activity of the bustling tavern was precisely what made it the perfect place to hide in plain sight. Kullen could easily blend into the crowd who frequented the establishment for food and drink. It wasn't only the commoners and locals of Dimvein either. Men of the nobility deigned to descend from the Upper Crest—and even visited from nearby cities—to sample Tavernkeeper Dyntas's renowned gold-apple honeymead, the drink that Emperor Wymarc himself was said to drink every morning with his breakfast.

Kullen knew better; Emperor Wymarc favored beer to break his fast, wine with his lunch, and dragonfire rum after dinner. But the Emperor did make certain the Imperial Palace always had a supply of the honeymead on hand to serve visiting dignitaries.

No matter what disguise he wore, Kullen would be just one more face among the crowd, a man no more remarkable than the thousands of others who flowed through the mead hall every day. Plus, his investment in Dyntas's mead distillery ensured that he always had a steady stream of income—and a guaranteed first sampling of the latest batch.

Kullen slipped through the swinging doors and entered the noisy mead hall. Sweet-scented applewood smoke rose from a half-dozen braziers that burned along the taproom's walls, accompanied by the slightly acidic tang of the apple cider vinegar with which Dyntas religiously cleaned his establishment. Colorfully painted murals and decorations of intertwined metal branches and leaves bearing round fruit completed the mead hall's "apple" motif. At the center of every wooden table, bench, and even the long bar had been carved with the likeness of the fruit that had brought Dyntas such prosperity.

The smell of roasting sausages, spiced potatoes, and fried onions set Kullen's stomach rumbling.

"Madam," Kullen said, flagging down a passing serving girl.

Dyntas's daughter, Sumaia, bore a similar likeness to her father. Her cocoa brown eyes bore the weight of someone twice her thirteen years, but she carried it like someone twice her age as well.

"Hello, Ku—"

A swift glare reminded her that names were not to be spoken during business hours.

"Well met, sir," she said instead. "Can I offer you some gold apple mead? Perhaps an apple pie topped with cheddar?"

"Honeyed mead and sausage."

Sumaia looked at Kullen as if she were hurt he hadn't taken her recommendation.

"And a slice of pie would be fine after," Kullen added.

Sumaia smiled, curtseyed, and went to fetch his order.

Kullen took the moment to find an empty spot in the far corner of the room, back to the wall so he could keep an eye on the entrance. From there, he could see nearly everyone in the tavern save those upstairs in private rooms.

A hearth burned beside him and a couple sat before it, smiling and whispering sweet nothings to one another.

Kullen had never been in love. Not truly—at least not with someone who returned his feelings. The floodgate of memories past threatened to surge his mind until Sumaia returned, beaming with pride as she brought his food and drink a few minutes later.

"Thought you'd left, I had such a time finding you," she said.

Kullen reached for the dish and quickly set to work on the meal. The steaming sausage was served with spiced potatoes and onions with a side of green beans. He hadn't realized just how starved he was until that first bite touched his tongue. His stomach responded in kind, begging for more.

"Fresh from the kitchen. And this—" She placed the tankard next to him on the chair's arm, only splashing a little over the wooden rim. "—is the first of a freshly tapped barrel."

"My compliments to your father, lass." Kullen said through a mouthful of potatoes. He placed a pair of coins on her tray—

enough to cover his meal and a gratuity that fell just shy of noticeably generous.

"Thanks, Ku—sir!" Sumaia said, pocketing the coins and bustling away.

Kullen hid a smile behind his tankard. Since her tenth birthday, the young girl had tried to convince her father to let her help with the serving. Looks like she'd swayed the stubborn old goat in the end, eh?

He made quick work of his meal—the potatoes and onions were hearty, the sausage only containing a modicum of gristle. And the buttery green beans—which gave off just the right *snap*—complimented both to perfection. Before he knew it, the plate contained nothing but crumbs and he drained his tankard in a long pull. A soothing warmth descended over him as the honeymead's alcohol took effect. His hunger satiated, Kullen rose and navigated the crowd that stood between him and the staircase that ascended to the establishment's upper floors.

The second floor was home to two dozen narrow, cramped rooms that Dyntas rented out to anyone with the coin to pay. The third floor, however, was reserved for those who wished for—or needed—a room for the night. Occasionally, however, an aristocrat would have too much to drink but no way to return home. Dyntas's hired bouncers would haul the unconscious men upstairs, then, when they awoke in the morning, stand guard to ensure the freshly awakened and often hungover aristocrat paid the high rate for the comfortable rooms. All the wealthy in Dimvein and beyond knew there was a high price for over-drinking and passing out in the Apple Cart Mead Hall.

Kullen glanced around to ensure the second-floor hallway was empty, then quickly slid up the stairs to the third floor. Dressed as he was in simple black clothing, he appeared innocuous enough for the taproom, but his appearance might draw questions on the exclusive top floor.

Like the previous, the third-floor hallway was empty, and

Kullen hurried toward the door at the far end of the corridor. Though it appeared identical to the rest, it was far from ordinary. The iron-cored wooden door had a built-in locking mechanism that not even the most skilled safecrackers of Dimvein could bypass. He alone carried the key, and Dyntas was the only one who shared his secret. Even the old Tavernkeeper didn't truly know Kullen was the Black Talon, just that he was a wealthy investor with a few... peculiarities. Kullen's gold kept Dyntas from caring overmuch about such trivialities as identity.

From his pocket, Kullen pulled a key, inserted it into the lock, and entered quickly, shutting the door behind him. Even though the hall appeared empty, one could never be so certain. It was being over-cautious that had allowed Kullen to remain a ghost for so long.

There was one small window, and a small circular shaft that ran from the ceiling to the roof about the size of a man's head. Moonlight poured in through the glass-covered sun hole. Just enough between the two to illuminate his small quarters enough for him to locate the lantern hanging from a hook on the wall. He gave it a light before placing it on his bedside table.

He collapsed into bed with a groan for his tired, aching body. Closing his eyes, he took long, slow breaths, letting the weariness and tension drain away from his muscles. The pain of his arm, his back where the big man's cosh had struck him, and the tear along his ribs remained. In fact, they throbbed deeper now that the adrenaline of the night's exertions had all but worn off.

"No sleep for the wicked," he said aloud with a sigh.

Grunting, he rose from the bed and moved toward a small cupboard on the east wall. Opening the doors, he rummaged among its contents—simple foodstuffs, spare bits of parchment and swatches of fabric and leather for quick repairs to his clothing and armor—until he found the item he sought: a vial filled with a gold-colored liquid that seemed to glow even in the meager light of the lantern. Gryphic Elixir, a wondrously potent remedy that could cure all but the most severe of wounds.

Funny how something so miraculous could be found in a place so dangerous.

That tiny vial cost as much as a man would pay to stay on the second floor for a month, but Kullen had stockpiled a large enough supply over the years that he felt its use at present was justified.

Popping the cork, he downed the glistening golden liquid in a single draught. He hated the taste—it was bitter, metallic, and had a nasty edge that reminded him far too much of that taste one gets when they retch stomach bile—but the effects were worth the barely palatable flavor.

Instantly, his many wounds began to mend and a sense of calm came over him.

He strode to his bed and buried himself in it. His eyelids, heavy as boulders, shut and he let the sensations of the elixir wash over him. In Kullen's younger years, he and Jarius had been no stranger to the malek leaf. If that dulled Kullen's senses and gave his mind rest, the elixir was ecstasy in a bottle.

He was dragged inexorably toward sleep, and made no attempt to fight it. As he drifted off, his mind was filled with two faces. One belonged to the red-haired woman who'd tried to kill him mere hours past. The other was one he hadn't dreamed of in a long time. Thoughts of Jarius and their youthful indiscretions must've triggered another memory. Or perhaps it was his journey to the glade that had brought back thoughts of Hadassa—and all the torment that accompanied such recollections.

Sleep might have come easily, but rest would be an elusive friend.

Sunrise streamed through the open window, shining directly into Kullen's eyes and coaxing him out of slumber. Despite his dreams, the Gryphic Elixir had combatted his expected restlessness, and he'd slept longer and better than he had in weeks.

Rising, he changed into a simple pair of pants, tunic, vest—the caliber and style of clothing most citizens of Dimvein wore. He slipped a long coat atop the outfit, and checked to ensure the usual assortment of weaponry remained firmly in place within its many hidden pockets. A sword would be unnecessary today, but Kullen could do just as much damage with a pair of long hunting knives as his primary armaments. If push came to shove, he'd trained long and hard to hone the skill, enabling him to disarm his enemies and turn their own weapons against them.

Instead of returning down the stairs toward the taproom, Kullen slid out the window. He stood on the sill, overlooking the Apple Cart Mead Hall's back alley. Below, not a soul traveled except perhaps Dimvein's most unsavory when the moon was high. A plain, windowless wall looked back at him, the rear end of the Coal Miner's Guild. That didn't stop him from a quick glance about to ensure he would not be seen as he clambered up the hanging rope ladder onto the rooftop. One more little secret Dyntas didn't know about. From there, it was an easy journey across the flat roof to a wooden beam that spanned the gap to the rooftop of the adjoining building—the distillery where the renowned gold apple honeymead was brewed.

Kullen continued westward across the rooftops for a quarter-mile, until he finally reached another hidden rope granting him access to the streets below. He could've covered half of Dimvein without touching boot to stone, but he had one stop to make before heading to the Palace. Thoughts of Hadassa the previous night had reminded him of the duty he considered second only to his service to the Emperor.

Dimvein during daylight was almost a different city. It was the kind of place where one could lose or find themselves. The capital of the Karmian Empire. The light within the darkness.

Kullen hadn't been alive when Dimvein got its name, but he'd heard all about the unholy gloom that once hung over these lands. All until the Wymarc line entered the fray and built this glorious city. Above, the thin veil of Thanagar's dome shimmered like crystals reflecting the brilliant sunlight.

Kullen joined the traffic flowing across the Mustona Bridge, crossing the deep, fast-flowing Talos River on his journey west. The crowds thinned quickly once he descended the high-arching stone bridge and approached the boundary marking the end of the One Hand District.

Entering the Embers felt like stepping into an altogether foreign world. The One Hand District was among the busiest of Dimvein's sectors, filled with color and life, bustling with endless activity as the city's vendors and merchants eked out a meager living. Yet compared to the Embers, it might as well have been the Upper Crest.

Kullen felt the moment he passed through Thanagar's protection—like a little shiver running through the core of his being, a touch on his mind, faint yet unmistakeable. He smelled it, too. The stink of decay, rot, and abandonment.

Thanagar's dome ended where the Embers began, and outside the dragon's magical reach, only the faintest hints of nature flourished. The fire dragon's attack had burned the district to the ground, but in the years since, it seemed as if plants had refused to spring forth from the barren ground. No amount of rainfall could bring back the life destroyed so long ago, nor wash away the charnel pall that seemed to hang permanently over the Embers.

Stone streets turned to dirt, and wattle and daub homes transitioned into what would best be described as mud huts. Where, men and women gleefully shopped for trinkets and fineries a few hundred yards to the east, here, children begged for food and coin.

"Spare a mark?" said a young boy whose face was so covered in dirt and grime it looked as if he'd never had a proper bath. "Even just a little bit?"

"Where's your family?" Kullen asked, squatting beside the boy.

A sullen look washed over the child. "Mum's dead. Dad's in the dungeon. I've got a little brother. Don't know how old he is."

"You live here?" Kullen asked, meaning the streets.

"All my life."

Kullen dug in his pockets and he could tell the boy was fighting an internal battle to keep the excitement from his face.

"Spend it on food," Kullen told him, tossing a gold mark, "for you and your brother."

"Wow." The boy stared at the treasure in his hand, eyes sparkling. "Thanks, mister!"

Kullen rose without a word. He rounded a corner onto muddy Pawn May Avenue and his stomach knotted as he came in sight of Mammy Tess' Refuge for the Wayward. Children played in the streets as if they hadn't a care. Had Kullen once been so small, so carefree? Perhaps the former, but the latter... never,

The squat brick building had been his home for seven years and it was beginning to show its age. Another survey of the place changed his mind; it was decrepit and rundown, near death. The roof was crumbling like week-old bread. The wall closest to him had a hole large enough to fit a carriage. Someone—likely Groundskeeper Voyles—had shoddily repaired it. Wooden planks crisscrossed haphazardly, barely managing to cover the gaping maw.

Kullen shook his head and climbed the stairs leading to the front door which looked as if it would fall over any instant.

There was a groan and the door opened.

Mammy Tess, too, had grown more worn and weary since Kullen had last seen her. The woman stepped through the sagging doorway onto the front porch. Each step creaked and protested under her weight but she ignored it.

Instead, she clapped and barked numbers to a pair of children skipping rope in the quiet street. Her clothing was faded, fraying at the seams, the color long ago leeched away by frequent washing, leaving it a drab, pale hue.

Yet her eyes still shone as bright as ever as she spotted him. Though more wrinkles appeared at the corners of her mouth, her smile still warmed his heart. His life in the Refuge had been far from easy—he'd been among the smallest and weakest of the children his own age—but Mammy Tess had made it all more tolerable.

Her arms were wide as she waddled toward him. Like she'd always done, she enveloped him in a fierce hug. When she broke off, she held him at arm's length and studied him up and down.

"You're not eating enough." It wasn't a question.

Kullen couldn't help laughing. "Nowhere I can find cooking half as good as yours, Mammy."

"Oh, hush, you!" But her eyes said something different. "We both know that my best dish is that boiled porridge that everyone chokes down because there's naught better to eat. Why else d'you think I handed off my wooden spoon to Quelly as soon as she was old enough to cook without burning herself half to death?"

Kullen grinned. "Well, I suppose if we're being honest—"

Mammy Tess drove a sharp finger into his chest. "Not too honest, mind you. I raised you to mind your manners; to be kind to little old ladies."

"Old?" Kullen raised an eyebrow. "You haven't aged a day."

"That's what they taught you up in that fancy place, eh? Flattery and lies to get what you want?" Her eyes darted toward the Imperial Palace and Kullen followed them. There, Thanagar was, wrapped around the tallest spire, casting off his magic to protect the city. Well, most of the city. His power barely reached the

Embers and Golgoth's attack on the district had been proof enough of that.

"They took good care of me," he said.

Mammy Tess was among the very few who knew what had become of the orphaned child Kullen, though she wasn't privy to all the details. To her knowledge, he'd been chosen by the Emperor to be companion to Prince Jarius. Because he was a nobody, he would ostensibly be loyal, and thus protect the Prince from all threats.

Small as Kullen might've been at the time, that frailty had taught him to be scrappy. And as he grew, hitting more than a few growth spurts before his teenage years, he was not only formidable but cut quite an intimidating figure as well.

A companion to Jarius... That had indeed, been the case initially. Only after his fifteenth birthday had Kullen learned the true purpose for why he'd been chosen, the reason for which he'd spent every spare hour training alongside Prince Jarius. It was true that Emperor Wymarc had desired someone to watch the Prince's back, but he'd also conscripted Kullen into his personal service. To be the Black Talon, the Imperial dagger in the dark.

The Emperor had maintained, and Kullen had agreed, that shielding Mammy Tess from the truth of his activities as the Black Talon was best for all involved. He'd fed her a half-truth about being in the Emperor's service but played loose on the details.

"No lies," Kullen said. "Just the truth." He squeezed her shoulder gently. "Spirit like yours never grows old, Mammy."

"Spirit, maybe, but the body?" Mammy Tess gave a theatrical groan and pressed a hand to her lower back. "Can't keep up with the kids as well anymore."

At that, Mammy Tess went into one of her cough fits. She'd had them as long as Kullen could remember, but now, it seemed different. Where she'd once had a dry sound to her throat, it was now wet and sounded... At that moment, Kullen resolved to bring her one of his Gryphic elixirs the next chance he got. She was worth every mark and more.

"Maybe it's time to hire additional help, then?" Kullen asked. He saw the retort forming on Mammy Tess' lips—they'd had this conversation a dozen times in the last few years—but before she could speak, he pressed a heavy purse into her hand. "Think about how much it will benefit the children to have additional caretakers. Maybe even a tutor to learn their letters and sums."

Mammy Tess' eyes widened. "Kullen," she whispered, "this is too much!" She tried to push the money back at him.

"No, Mammy." Kullen closed her aged fingers around the purse. "It's more than usual, but you can't tell me that you, the children, and the Refuge don't need it."

Mammy Tess' lips pressed together, fine frown lines appearing at the corners of her mouth.

"I'm not going to take no for an answer, Mammy." He fixed her with a mock stern gaze. "And trust me, I learned stubbornness from the absolute best."

For long moments, Mammy Tess remained silent, her 9 locked with his, indecision etched into her wrinkled face. Then, slowly, the lines smoothed out and she gave a reluctant nod.

"If you insist, dear," she said. She stopped trying to push the purse back toward him, and allowed him to close her other hand around it. "I suppose this would serve us well. Some better food for the young'uns, a tutor or two—"

"And a new dress for you?" Kullen glanced down at her frumpy, dull outfit.

"Oh, don't be silly!" Mammy Tess snorted. "What possible use could I have for a new dress? Since Sylla passed…" Her expression grew sad.

"I know." Kullen squeezed her hands gently. Sylla—or Mammy Sylla, to all the orphans—and Mammy Tess had been the great loves of each other's lives. Even though consumption had taken Sylla a decade earlier, Mammy Tess hadn't once thought to move on. All her love and attention was lavished on the children in her care.

Mammy Tess quickly recovered, a little smile on her lips.

"Thank you, Kullen." She slid the purse into one large pocket on the front of her dress. "This'll also come in handy next time Magister Deckard comes to visit."

"Magister Deckard?" Kullen frowned. "What's that bag of shit want with the Refuge?"

"Kullen, language."

"Sorry, Mammy." He let his anger at the mention of the man's name quell, then added, "But I've heard you say worse when you lost at cards." They both shared a smile. "Now, what does he want with you?"

"He's trying to buy the building," Mammy Tess said, giving a dismissive wave. "But he's been trying for the better part of a year now, and every time, I tell him we're not for sale." She gestured to the building. From this vantage, it looked even more rundown, like no one had been there in a decade. "The Embers just wouldn't be the same without the Refuge."

"The Embers wouldn't be the Embers without Deckard either," Kullen said quietly.

"What's that, dear?"

"The Princess wouldn't have wanted you to sell, either." Kullen's said, raising his voice slightly.

Mammy Tess gave him a soft smile. "Oh, beautiful girl. No. She wouldn't have."

Together, they turned toward the orphanage. A large bronze plaque hung on the wall next to the door. It was the only thing on the building not touched by age or wear. Someone had polished the metal to a brilliant shine. Kullen's heart twisted. Even from ten feet away, he could read the words burnished into the gleaming metal.

Beloved Of The Empire

It was a gift from Hadassa—Imperial Princess Hadassa—given to Mammy Tess on her last visit to the Refuge before her death.

The sight of that plaque always raked at Kullen's heart. Hadassa had been the only other good thing in his life all those years ago. He'd lost her more times than he wanted to remember. To Jarius. To Shekoth. He hoped not to lose her to memory as well.

He swallowed the lump rising in his throat and turned to face Mammy Tess.

"Magister Deckard gives you trouble, you let me know," he said, squeezing her hands again. "This place isn't going anywhere. It saved me and countless others like me. Still does. It's going nowhere."

"You're a good one, Kullen." Mammy Tess lifted up on her tiptoes and kissed his cheek. "Now, off with you. I'm sure you've got better things to be about than chatting with an old lady."

Kullen laughed. "I can't think of a thing."

He turned slowly toward the steps and his eyes fell on the little boy he'd given charity to, peering around the corner at him. His little brother was beside him. Couldn't have been more than half a decade old.

"Mammy," Kullen said, turning back.

"Yes, dear."

"Do you have room for two more?"

14

NATISSE

J ad sat alone in the War Room. Didn't even look up when Natisse and Uncle Ronan entered. A pile of papers were spread out across the carved wooden table in front of him. The big man hunched over a solitary sheet of parchment bearing columns and rows of numbers, letters, and symbols that made absolutely no sense to Natisse. However, the gleam in Jad's eyes made it clear he'd found something to pique his interest.

"Uncle Ronan, look!" No hello. No startled expression as he looked up. He just thrust the paper toward the Crimson Fang leader. "This one has it, too!"

Uncle Ronan took the parchment and frowned down at it. He possessed neither Dalash's training or Jad's innate skill with numbers, but as with nearly everything else, he had at least a rudimentary understanding of balancing books, even those as complex as Magister Perech seemed to have kept.

"You're right," he said a few seconds later. "The exact same sum for an entirely different cargo."

"But delivered to the same person on the same day of the month," Jad finished.

Uncle Ronan offered the paper to Natisse but she shook her head.

"I'm no bookkeeper," she said. The details on those pages would make her head spin. She vastly preferred the intricacies of combat and subterfuge to accountancy. "Just tell me what you've found." She fixed Jad with a baleful glare. "In simple terms, if you please."

Jad grinned.

"Of course."

He and Dalash could spend hours talking complicated mathematical theorems and racing each other to calculate enormous sums. Thankfully, both men were also smart enough to boil the mind-boggling reckonings down to something that they could all understand.

"I've gone back through Magister Perech's books for the past four years, searching for anything that could lead us to the slave pits."

The Crimson Fang had long suspected Perech's involved in the vile underground fights but as of yet, they hadn't been able to pin anything on him.

Until now, so it seemed.

Jad from his seat and Natisse had to look up to keep eye contact. Men his size were often thought to be simpletons, but Jad was anything but. He took the paper from Uncle Ronan.

"Every month for the last two-and-a-half years," Jad continued, "Perech has paid out fifteen hundred gold marks for the delivery of cargo shipped down the Talos River. The exact same price, yet a different cargo every time."

Natisse raised an eyebrow. "And that's interesting because...?"

"Because of the cargo." Jad rifled through the stacks of parchment on the War Room table and plucked one up. "Look!" He thrust it out toward her, his huge finger tapping a specific row of numbers and symbols. "One thousand five-hundred gold marks."

"And?" Natisse said again, growing impatient of games.

"What's it for?"

His finger followed the row to the end.

"Cotton," Natisse read.

Then he snatched up another.

Natisse looked to Uncle Ronan who wore a rare smile.

"I still don't under—"

"And this one?"

"Fifteen hundred gold marks." Natisse followed the row with her eyes. "For raw iron ore from Lanercost."

"Precisely," Jad said. "And yet another. Same amount for pickled herring all the way from Blencalgo on the eastern coast."

Natisse grimaced. "Who in Ezrasil's name wants that much pickled herring?" She'd seen a few of the riverboat sailors eating the foul-smelling stuff at local riverside inns, but the gentry of Dimvein never touched it. "There's no reason for him to import such quantities."

"Exactly!" Jad's eyes sparkled—he loved a good riddle or puzzle to solve, particularly if it involved numbers. "And all that raw iron ore from Lanercost? He spent twice what he'd have paid had he bought it from any of the mines within a hundred miles of Dimvein. Only an utter fool would purchase such poor quality material from a low-yield mine on the far side of the Empire."

Natisse began to understand what he was getting at. "So you think it's fraudulent purchases?"

"I do!" Jad's big head nodded. "And look where the cotton is supposed to come from." He thrust the first paper into her face. "Argencourt!"

Natisse's gut clenched. There was no way Magister Perech could have purchased anything from Argencourt—three weeks earlier, a forest fire had razed the village, its people, and its crops to the ground. Both Magister Estéfar and Magister Perech had paid the price for their rapacity, sent to an afterlife of eternal torment and misery by her hand. Yet the Crimson Fang's vengeance would not bring back the eight hundred and nineteen people murdered that day.

"All of these cargo shipments are fraudulent," Jad continued, his face growing animated as his voice rose in excitement. "But what's really important is who they're being delivered to. Magister Onathus!"

Natisse frowned. "I'm not familiar with him."

"Another minor noble," Uncle Ronan said.

He seemed to know everything about the Imperial nobility, especially those residing or owning serious holdings in Dimvein.

"Made his fortune running cargo up and down the rivers," he continued. "The bastard's been dodging tariffs and taxes since the day he took over the house and business from his father, but he's damned good at covering his tracks—good enough that the Empire's never been able to bring him up on formal charges."

"He'll pay in blood," Natisse said.

Uncle Ronan nodded and gestured to the parchment in Jad's hand. "I'd wager Onathus is the one who concocted this scheme. No one would look amiss at cargo being delivered to his shipyards by the river, no matter whose ships did the hauling. And it would be simple enough to explain his connection to Magister Perech as a secret merger or alliance for mutual profit."

"With Magister Estéfar getting a cut of the revenue," Jad added. He held up another stack of parchments. "Half of the contracts Magister Perech signed had Estéfar's name on it, too. I'd wager he put up at least a quarter of the funds to get this venture off the ground."

"Indeed." Uncle Ronan's face hardened. "This sort of thing happens all the time amongst nobles."

Natisse followed the complex thread of thought to its final conclusion. "So those fraudulent shipments delivered to Magister Onathus's shipyards are, in fact, the slaves that we've suspected are being smuggled into Dimvein?"

Jad gave a glance over to Uncle Ronan and said, "I believe so.

Onathus's cargo ships are among the most heavily guarded in Dimvein—a measure taken against recent river piracy, he's claimed publicly." A frown twisted his blocky face downward. "But transporting slaves would also require a lot of armed men. And his shipyards are also walled, gated, and patrolled day and night by his own private guards."

"A great deal of protection for a shipyard," Natisse remarked.

"Both to keep the slaves in and prying eyes out," Uncle Ronan said.

"I know it's little more than conjecture at this point," Jad said, shrugging, "but it's the first solid bit of information we've had to go on in a while."

"It's good work, Jad." Uncle Ronan cuffed the man amiably on his massive shoulder. "Anything else of interest in what we took from Magister Perech's office?"

Jad swiped up an envelope. "I don't know if it's of interest, but there's this." He pulled out a paper from within. It's a title deed for an abandoned factory building somewhere in north Dimvein. Magister Taradan's the seller, and Magister Perech and Magister Estéfar are both listed among the buyers. I can't find anything connecting them to Onathus though."

"Damn," Uncle Ronan swore.

"But there is someone named Baronet Ochrin." He looked up from the paper to Uncle Ronan, then to Natisse. "That name mean anything to either of you?"

Natisse shook her head.

"Nothing," Uncle Ronan agreed. "But dig into him. And that building. See if you turn up anything of interest."

"Yes, sir." Jad returned to his seat and back to the pile of documents. "Perhaps there's something of interest at Magister Perech's caravan yard?" He rummaged among the parchments until he found the one he sought. "Right here, there are a few more of these fraudulent payments for cargo delivered over land. Different goods—copper ingots, Brendoni jade, and silk from

Taishi—but the same pattern. Identical sums and the same delivery dates every month."

Uncle Ronan ran a hand over his hoary beard. "Where's the caravan yard?"

Jad shoved aside a handful of papers covering the section of the table's carved map that displayed the Talos River wending through Dimvein.

"Here in the Western Docks," he said, pointing to an area at the northern edge of the city. "And Magister Onathus's shipyards are here." His finger traveled an inch farther to the south.

"That's less than a quarter-mile apart," Natisse said.

"Perfect." Uncle Ronan's gray eyes settled on her. "I'll take Leroshavé and pay our recently deceased Magister Perech's caravan yards a visit. Take Haston and get to the shipyards. See if you can find a way to break in, and, barring that, find somewhere high enough that we can watch the comings and goings unnoticed."

Then, turning to Jad, he asked, "When's the next fraudulent shipment due?"

"If it follows the same pattern that has repeated every month for the last two-and-a-half years," Jad said without hesitation, "it was delivered two days ago."

Uncle Ronan grunted acknowledgment. "We're likely too late to witness the slaves being offloaded, but it's still worth getting an eye on the place; watching it until the next shipment."

"Understood." Natisse inclined her head.

"Jad, when Garron gets back, tell him where we've gone and what we're doing."

"Of course, Uncle Ronan." The big man nodded.

With that, the Crimson Fang's leader strode from the War Room. Natisse turned to follow—she had a few things to prepare before grabbing Haston and departing on her mission.

"Natisse," Jad's quiet voice stopped her. She glanced back and found the big man moving toward her. He rested a hand on her shoulder. "I'm sorry. About Baruch." Sorrow darkened his big, round eyes. "I know what he meant to you."

Natisse felt her emotions welling up, a stone rising in her throat. As always, Jad was so sincere, so compassionate, his looming presence, comforting. He squeezed her shoulder gently, his touch soft and kind.

Yet Natisse refused to let the feelings bubble to the surface. She swallowed hard, and mentally envisioned herself securing a lock and chain upon her heart, stowing away the sorrow, grief, and loss down deep. She'd already mourned Baruch as much as she could allow herself to for the time being. Now was the time to focus on getting the job done. There would be plenty of time to mourn once all those rich, selfish, worthless, above-the-law bastards were dead.

"Thank you," she said, hoping the hate she felt for the nobles didn't reach her voice. She reached up and placed her hand atop his.

A smile lit up his face, almost turned his craggy face hand-some. "You need anything—"

"I know who to come to," she said, patting his hand.

Jad squeezed her shoulder again, then let her go.

She smiled, though she didn't feel like it, and left the room.

"Good luck on the hunt, Natisse!" he called after her, before the door to the War Room closed, and Natisse stood alone in the cold stone tunnels.

"Any luck?" Natisse asked as Haston settled into place at her side.

"Nothing." The man shook his head. "After dark, I'll head down to the riverbank and see if I can find a way through, under, or around the wall. But Magister Onathus's shipyards live up to their reputation. Not even a bloody mouse could find a way in."

Natisse muttered a curse. She'd hoped Haston would have luck where she'd failed. The man had an uncanny knack for breaking into even the most heavily guarded strongholds.

Shifting her weight from one knee to the other, ignoring the protest in her back and legs, she peered over the crest of the rooftop toward the shipyards spread out below. The stockade wall rose nearly two stories high. Thick logs with tips sharpened like spears stuck up from like ancient palisades to prevent anyone from attempting to climb over. Six armed men in heavy chain mail guarded each of the three gates granting entrance from the north, east, and south—but not to them.

Over the last hour, she'd counted an additional twenty-four men patrolling the interior. The four-guard units moved at five-minute intervals, and there were always at least three patrols out.

Simply put, even if they found a way inside Magister Onathus's shipyards, it would take damned near a miracle for them to evade the guards.

At least luck hadn't fully deserted them. The rooftop they now stood upon was two stories tall, and was strategically located just a couple of streets east of the shipyards' perimeter.

It had been a simple matter to scale the adjacent building using grappling hooks and climbing spikes—items never left behind during such an occasion. The flat warehouse roof provided an excellent vantage point from which to surveil Magister Onathus's property.

Thus far, they'd seen nothing of particular interest beyond the already stated. There were two river boats docked along the pier, and a handful of dockhands working to load a seemingly innocuous assortment of barrels, sacks, and crates onto both. No sign of slaves... yet.

Natisse shifted to a more comfortable position and prepared for a long day of watching and waiting. Magister Onathus might be clever enough to forge his accounting records, and with the backing of Magisters Perech and Estéfar, have the gall to try and cheat the Imperial taxmen. But even he wasn't brave enough to openly defy the Emperor's strict laws against slavery.

That was possibly the only good thing Natisse could lay at Emperor Wymarc's feet. He'd outlawed slavery nearly two decades earlier, and—mostly—made good on his promise to liberate all those in thrall to the nobility. He'd even been the one to grant the Orken an opportunity for work where most cities would've cast them out as vile beasts.

Granted, his "work" was as brutal enforcers and murderers— like that prick who'd killed Ammon in cold blood.

Natisse shook the thought away. She had to.

Yes, the decree against slavery had enjoyed a less-than-gracious response from the nobility, but Emperor Wymarc had followed through on his word.

Officially, slavery did not exist in Dimvein or the entire Karmian Empire. Unofficially, however, it was still alive and well. Some trafficked slaves from outside the Imperial borders. People went missing in the capital city regularly, never to be seen or heard from again. Men, women, and even children from small towns along the Empire's fringes could vanish without a trace.

The official Imperial word on those matters were that many were unable to see the glorious light of the Empire. They failed to recognize the need for Thanagar's protection and simply ran away.

Including, Uncle Ronan believed, some who had once called Argencourt home. He'd dispatched Nalkin, Tobin, and L'yo to the razed village in the hopes of finding evidence to back up that belief. The trio, however, had returned empty-handed. There'd been no one left alive to identify the charred corpses of those slain in what was being spun as a forest fire—a fire, which in reality, had been started by Magister Estéfar's pet dragon. Heavy rains immediately following the conflagration had erased any wagon, animal, or human tracks to indicate the presence of slavers.

Yet with this new connection to Magister Onathus's shipyards and Magister Perech's cargo vessels, Natisse had begun to suspect that survivors—if there had been any—might have been hauled away from the destroyed village via the river that passed just five miles from Argencourt.

Knowing that slavery existed in Dimvein and the Karmian Empire was just the first step. The Crimson Fang needed to find proof so incontrovertible that even Emperor Wymarc would be forced to descend from the lofty heights of his grand palace to deal with it.

That was why Natisse and Haston crouched on that warehouse's rooftop, surveilling the shipyards. Nearly three years earlier, Uncle Ronan had heard rumors of a fighting pit where the strongest, toughest slaves were pitted against each other in blood sport to the death. The Crimson Fang had tried its damnedest to uncover its whereabouts and been unsuccessful... until now. This was the first big discovery they'd made. They were on the right track—Natisse could feel it all the way to her bones.

Scanning the guards patrolling the shipyards, she marked their routes and patterns as she'd been trained to do. Something nagged at the back of her mind. She couldn't quite place it, but there was something... off about their movements. The patrols along the northern edge of the shipyards took twice as long as the eastern and southern patrols. It couldn't be that the men were resting—the guardhouse was located just inside the eastern gate—but, try as she might, Natisse had not yet figured out the reason for the delay.

Worse, from her perch, she didn't have a line on the patrols once they reached the northern section of the shipyards. The piles of sacks, stacked crates, and storage structures obscured an entire quarter of the walled-off area from her view. And there were no buildings that offered a better vantage point.

That was why she'd set Haston to find a way into the shipyards. She needed to see what lay to the north, why the guards—

The scuff of heavy boots on the rooftop made Natisse start. Whirling toward the sound, her hand darted to a throwing knife at her belt. The blade was out of its sheath and halfway out of her hand before she recognized the lean, rangy man in the nondescript gray cloak.

"Garron?" she hissed. "What are you doing here?"

The lines of Garron's face were even graver than the previous night—he must've heard about Baruch.

"Uncle Ronan sent me," he said quietly. His shoulders hunched as he slipped toward her perch.

"How did you know—"

"Where to find you?" Garron gave her a blank look. "We were both taught by the same man, Natisse. Minute I saw this building, I knew you'd be here. No better vantage point."

Natisse grimaced. She hated the idea that anyone could so easily predict her actions or thoughts—even someone like Garron, someone on her side.

"Found anything?" he asked, crouching.

"Nothing." Natisse shook her head. "No way in yet. Haston'll take another look after dark."

"If it comes down to it," Haston put in, "we might be able to use the river to slip in. Just have to get in upstream and swim down, if the rocks aren't too treacherous."

Garron grunted and nodded. "Good. Keep an eye on things. Athelas will be here in a quarter-hour to join you." He turned to Natisse. "As for you, you're with me. Uncle Ronan wants you at his side, quick as you can. You're going to want to see what he found at the caravan yard."

15

KULLEN

Noon.

It was the only time of day Kullen needn't question where to find the Emperor. For all Wymarc's countless duties and the ceaseless parade of Imperial functions, the man never let a day go by without a midday visit to his garden.

And what a garden it was. In a place that once knew only darkness, where vegetation and greenery scant survived, the Emperor had cultivated a veritable paradise. And it had been him who'd done it, by hand. No gardeners or those tasked to tend the place.

But what Emperor Wymarc loved best about the garden was its location atop the roof of the Imperial Palace. Up there, high above Dimvein, Kullen knew it allowed the Emperor to disconnect from the city, its people, and the troubles that consumed his life. While there, on the rooftop, he could sit in the quiet and, for a few brief moments each day, set aside the burdens of rule.

Kullen, too, had loved the rooftop garden from the moment Prince Jarius had shown it to him. But, perhaps, Hadassa had loved it even more. The three of them had spent their free hours playing among the karodine bushes, sitting beneath their broad, nearly black leaves, and, inevitably, wrestling on the grass. It was in that garden that sixteen year-old Kullen had intended to share his feelings with Hadassa—only to find Prince Jarius had beaten him to it.

There was something truly magical about the garden, with its variety of plants that were said to exist nowhere else in the entire Empire—blooming red opeuses, dellias that seemed to glow. Like so much else in Dimvein, the garden only flourished because of Thanagar.

Kullen quietly pushed through the very same karodine bushes he'd spent so long under. It was no accident that was where he'd chosen for his warren of passages through the palace to dump out. He moved like a whisper, spotting Emperor Wymarc in his usual spot, perched on a padded stone bench by his favorite tree. Beside him lay an enormous white dragon that glistened blindingly bright in the midday sun. His scales seemed to take in every color in sight, reflecting them back in a glorious prism.

Thanagar, called the Protector by all in the Empire, mightiest of all dragons, was close to a hundred and fifty feet long with a wingspan that stretched two hundred feet across. He more than filled up the lawn that spread before the Emperor's seat. His huge eyes were closed, and the rumble of his great chest set the grass trembling beneath Kullen's feet.

Emperor Wymarc sat with a book open on his lap, his eyes fixed on the page, one hand stroking Thanagar's tail. Kullen knew he was reading to the dragon through the bond they shared—a favorite pastime of the Emperor, one that Thanagar, too, seemed to enjoy.

At Kullen's stealthy approach, Thanagar cracked an eyelid, revealing a gleaming orb, ruby red, nearly as wide as Kullen was tall. It was all for show—the dragon had sensed Kullen the moment he stepped out of the hidden passage, but coming face-to-face with such power was intended to drive home just how serious the dragon took any threats to the man with whom he was bonded.

"Ah, Kullen," Emperor Wymarc said, looking up. He gently closed the book and folded his hands atop it. "I was wondering when you'd appear to deliver your report on last night's… occurrences."

"Took a quick detour by the Refuge," Kullen said. "Made sure Mammy Tess was in good health." He made no mention of Magister Deckard's attempts to purchase the orphanage. He'd stay quiet about that unless it became a problem requiring the Emperor's permission to deal with.

"Oh, dear Tessaphania. How is she?" Emperor Wymarc smiled, an expression that made his aged, stern face appear much more like a kindly grandfather than the ruler of an entire empire. He always used the woman's full name—one Kullen only found out after leaving the Refuge. It's no wonder. What child would be capable of saying such a mouthful? "It has been too long since I last paid her and Sylla a visit."

Long, indeed, if the Emperor didn't know of Mammy Sylla's passing. "She is well. Sylla…"

As Kullen's words trailed off, the Emperor put his book down on the bench beside him and sadness fell upon his features.

"I'm so sorry," he said.

"As am I," Kullen agreed. "However, like Mammy Tess, the Refuge is showing its age, but I left coin enough to see to the repairs."

"I will have Assidius send more," Emperor Wymarc said. "Such beneficence is rare, indeed, Now more than ever. That place is a beacon almost as bright as Thanagar himself."

The dragon stirred at his name and perhaps a bit more at the mention of anything coming near his splendor.

The Emperor smiled. "The Refuge cannot be allowed to flounder."

Kullen stepped forward. He stopped in front of the Emperor and stood at the pose soldiers referred to as "parade rest."

Thanagar's eyelid slid closed once more, the dragon evidently deciding he was no threat. Again, that was all for show. Thanagar possessed a power unusual even among his kind. He could sense the unique energies emanating from every living thing—man, beast, even the plants and trees of the garden—and, to a certain extent, manipulate those energies. The actual "how" far exceeded Kullen's understanding, but the garden in which he stood was the merest shred of proof of what the dragon could accomplish.

In the years that Thanagar had stood vigil over Dimvein from his perch atop the Palace roof, the dragon had caused the city to flourish. Apart from driving out the unnatural darkness and granting the Lumenators their power, crops grew faster, larger, and produced a higher yield. Fish flourished in the oceans surrounding the city, and the fauna dwelling in the Wild Grove multiplied exponentially. The rate of births had skyrocketed, while the number of stillborn children plummeted.

Thanagar's control over the energies of humans was limited, but he could sense them as clearly as he could see the sunlight that even now warmed his shimmering white scales. He'd no doubt recognized Kullen while he'd still been sneaking through the passages, and had known him since the day he was brought into the Palace.

To most others, Thanagar's magical abilities were mysterious… and, of course, terrifying, given his sheer size. Yet the true nature of the dragon's power was known to few outside the Emperor's inner circle—of which Kullen was a part—albeit in secret to all save the Emperor himself, Assidius and, apparently, Prince Jaylen. Kullen had spent enough time under Thanagar's baleful stare to no longer quake in fear. At least not outwardly. The dragon was still a powerhouse, twice the size of Umbris, and capable of destroying life as easily as he could cause it to thrive.

Thanagar kept Dimvein safe and protected.

"So," Emperor Wymarc said, drawing Kullen's attention away from the dragon, "tell me about last night."

Kullen raised an eyebrow. "You mean why Magister Perech ended up dead alongside Magister Taradan?"

"Indeed." Emperor Wymarc leaned forward, his expression stern. "That is twice now that two of Our nobility die on the same night, side by side. Had I not personally overseen your training, I might believe you were getting sloppy."

"Your confidence in me is overwhelming," Kullen said with a snort.

Thanagar's eyelid cracked again, and the fiery red eye fixed on Kullen. Evidently, he wasn't thrilled with Kullen's sarcastic tone.

Emperor Wymarc, however, was accustomed to it. In truth, Kullen suspected the man actually relished his occasional irreverence, having spent most of his waking hours surrounded by fawning lickspittles and toadies like Assidius. The court had to be suffocating, and though he bore the burden with the dignity that characterized everything he did, even he doubtless enjoyed feeling less the "Divine Majesty" and more the man beneath the honorific.

Before he'd inherited the mantle of Emperor, Wymarc had been a career military man. Despite being the son of the Emperor, he marched alongside salt-and-vinegar soldiers. Jarius had been much the same way. Yet, Jaylen… Kullen didn't quite know what had gone wrong with that boy.

"Let me guess," the Emperor said, raising a steel-gray eyebrow, "it was not your hand wielding the dagger that ended Magister Perech's life."

"Not my hand, foot, nor any other part of me," Kullen said. The Emperor went to speak, but stopped as Kullen raised a hand, though his silence was accompanied by a severe glare. "But I did catch a glimpse of the woman who killed him."

"Woman?" Emperor Wymarc's other eyebrow shot up and his sternness turned to wonder. "Truly?"

"And what a woman she was!" Kullen described the stunning redhead and the way she'd used the distraction to put a dagger in Magister Perech. "Either she had impeccable timing, or—and I find this most likely—her accomplices created the diversion." Now that he'd taken the time to think over last night's events, it seemed all the more likely that the choking man and his page had been plants.

"Accomplices? How many?"

Kullen frowned. "Three that I saw—two rowing the boat, and a third who came to her aid when I attacked—but it's possible there were more. Were it my plan, I wouldn't have counted on fortune to aid me. I'd have created my own."

"And have you any clue as to her identity?" the Emperor asked, a lour tugging on his lips. "What manner of woman she is to so brashly murder Magister Perech on his own pleasure barge, in open water?"

"I caught just one name. One of the men asked, 'What about Baruch?'"

Emperor Wymarc's expression grew pensive. "That name... why is it so familiar?"

"I don't know, Majesty," Kullen shrugged. "Not one I have heard before—"

Emperor Wymarc sat up abruptly. "Sallas!"

Kullen frowned. "Related to the Ammonidas Sallas executed in the Court of Justice?"

"On the same day our first double assassination occurred," the Emperor said.

"Ezrasil's bastard son," Kullen swore.

The Emperor glared at him for a moment.

"What? I'm not one of your frilly men," Kullen said. "Who is—was—he, this Baruch?"

"Annonidas's brother." Emperor Wymarc narrowed his eyes in thought. "Younger, I believe. Truth be told, I did not know Baronet Sallas, the father, before their abrupt and mysterious disappearance, only that he had two sons—Ammonidas and Baruchel."

Kullen chewed on that. "If he is the brother of the man executed days ago, could he, too, belong to the Crimson Fang?" He raised a hand again. "If it indeed exists."

"That possibility cannot be discounted," Emperor Wymarc said, ignoring the gesture this time. He inclined his head, then rose to his feet. "If it is true, and it was, in fact, the Crimson Fang who eliminated Magister Perech, then they are a greater threat than even Assidius believed."

"Blood for blood," Kullen mused. "From what I gather, the only blood they've spilled has been that of the nobility."

"Which is, in itself, the greatest problem." Emperor Wymarc began to pace, though he never left the shade beneath the leafy oak tree. "There is a reason they are targeting the nobility, but until we know what that reason is, we cannot be certain of their true intentions, or the full extent of the damage they have the potential to cause."

"Nor how many they number," Kullen added. "There could be hundreds in the city, waiting to strike."

"Or there could be only a few." The Emperor spoke without looking at Kullen, his eyes on the ground before his feet as he paced. "Either way, the question remains the same: Are they seeking to exterminate all nobility and thereby destabilize the Empire at large, or is there a reason that Magisters Perech, Estéfar, and Oyodan were eliminated?"

"Oyodan?" Kullen cocked an eyebrow. "I had not heard of his passing." Not that he would have mourned the bastard. Oyodan had been insufferable and arrogant on his best day. Kullen was almost sorry his hand hadn't been the one to end the piece of shit's life.

"For good reason." Emperor Wymarc's scowl deepened. "It would not do for word to spread that the nobility of Dimvein are dying off at an alarming rate." He lifted only his eyes to look at

Kullen and lowered his voice. "Counting Magisters Taradan and Perech, that is eight noblemen who have gone to Shekoth in the last month alone."

The Emperor took a deep, steadying breath, removed his crown, and ran a hand through his snow-white hair.

Kullen shielded his surprise at the Emperor's words. He understood the need for concern. It had been Wymarc who'd ordered the deaths of Magisters Iltari, Alladace, Ladrian, and Nybus—all men who he believed had been conspiring against the royal crown. Magister Taradan's death, too, could be laid at the Emperor's feet. But the other three—Estéfar, Oyodan, and Perech—had not been by his command.

He had no more time to ponder the mystery, for Emperor Wymarc was once again speaking, his gaze boring into Kullen's.

"And Magister Taradan... You're certain that his killing was justified?"

"Absolutely." Kullen said. "I listened in while Magister Taradan sat in Magister Perech's office, plotting."

"Plotting what?" the Emperor asked.

Kullen shook his head. "I don't know." He continued before the Emperor could raise question. "But Magister Taradan passed off an envelope to Magister Perech to safeguard."

"And what was in the envelope?" Emperor Wymarc asked.

"I don't know."

Kullen was fixed with a hard stare.

"Surely you returned after Magister Perech's death to investigate."

"I did," Kullen said, nodding, "but it, along with every other document and scrap of parchment within Magister Perech's office had been taken."

Emperor Wymarc's expression hardened even more. "By whom?"

"I don't know." Kullen shook his head.

"What *do* you know?" the Emperor demanded.

Kullen ground his teeth. There was no doubt in what he saw in that office. Two men plotted something nefarious, of that he was sure. It wasn't like him to strive for answers like this. He felt... foolish.

"I know that something was amiss between the two."

"Amiss?" Emperor Wymarc arched a white eyebrow. "What you are telling me, my Black Talon, is that blood covers the streets of our fair city and we don't know why. It is your job to know why.

"What about Assidius?" Kullen offered. "Or perhaps you can ask Turoc. His Orkenwatch were—"

"Ask Turoc what?"

A growling, angry voice echoed through the garden, followed a moment later by the Orken to whom it belonged.

Turoc was a giant even among the Orken, standing seven-and-a-half feet tall, three feet wide in the shoulders, with arms thicker than Kullen's legs. Every inch of him—his close-set black eyes, two lower canine fangs, coarse, bristling beard, heavily armored frame—radiated menace. And how easily he moved despite the heavy two-handed sword sheathed on his back and the full suit of banded mail armor that covered him from his bull neck to his oversized boots.

He, like all Orken, wore rings etched with the crude symbols of his people's brutish and limited written language in their braided beards. The members of the Orken command wore gold rings while those below him wore silver. Any Orken male who couldn't grow a beard were unwelcome in the ranks as it was seen as a sign of weakness.

At the thought, Kullen pressed a hand through the scruff lining his cheeks.

"And what about Assidius?" another, slimy voice said.

Assidius was nearly invisible in the giant Orken Tuskigo's shadow, appearing all the more frail for the comparison to Turoc's powerful build. His lean face appeared pinched and strained, thin lips pressed so tightly together they disappeared against his pale skin.

Kullen felt a rumbling underfoot, and a breath of hot air snorted from Thanagar's enormous nostrils. The dragon lifted its huge head from its restful pose and fixed its ruby eyes on the approaching pair. Though Thanagar could not speak, Kullen needed no mental bond to sense the dragon's disdain. No doubt aimed at Assidius—the Seneschal experienced a similar reaction everywhere he went and from everyone he met.

Turoc's long, corded legs carried him across the garden at twice Assidius's speed, and he reached Kullen and the Emperor a full thirty yards ahead of the Seneschal. The Orken Tuskigo planted his feet solidly, folded his arms across his barrel-sized armored chest, and glared down at Kullen.

"Of what you accuse me, little man?" he growled.

Kullen wasn't the sort to intimidate easy, but even he felt the tiniest quailing in his stomach at the sight of the Orken towering over him. Malice glittered in Turoc's beady black eyes, his snoutish nostrils flared wide, and his outthrust jaw emphasized the length and sharpness of lower canines. Up close, he appeared a mountain of steel armor, framed by the fur that lined the ever-present Orkenwatch cloak with its shining twin-tusked gilded brooch bearing the insignia of the Emperor's personal elite policing force. Even those golden bands braided into his chest-length black beard somehow managed to appear threatening.

Though he'd never admit it aloud, Kullen would think carefully before picking a fight with Turoc. He'd seen the Orken Tuskigo swing his blade—as long as Kullen was tall—with deadly grace.

But he couldn't back down, either. So he squared up in front of Turoc and met the Orken's glare with a cold smile.

"Of taking far too few baths and eating far too many garlic bulbs." Kullen pinched his nose. "Or do your Orken women find the stench of your unwashed armpits and fetid breath somehow appealing?"

Turoc bristled, his back going ramrod straight—the "thorn-bush-up-his-arse" pose that characterized him so well. He bared his fangs and opened his mouth to snarl something down at Kullen, but at that moment, a huffing, puffing Assidius reached them.

"Forgive... the disturbance... Divine Majesty," the Seneschal said, his faint lisp growing more pronounced as he struggled to control his breathing. "I know… this is… your cherished time… but I thought… this was important."

"What is important, Assidius?" Emperor Wymarc said.

Assidius took the moment he needed to catch his breath, leaning heavily on his knees. He dashed sweat from his angular forehead and used his damp hand to smooth down his perfectly trimmed moustache and goatee.

"The dragonblood vials," he said, still slightly winded but willing himself to speak. "Magister Perech's and Magister Taradan's. They're both gone!"

16

NATISSE

Natisse followed Garron to the building that Uncle Ronan had chosen as his perch to watch the caravan yards. Unlike the shipyards, this spot was rife with opportune and strategic views. Even at a cursory glance, Natisse spotted several vantage points she would've or could've chosen. However, she saw with clarity why her leader had picked this one.

Once a grand theater, the four-story building stood empty, abandoned. Broken windows, trash in heaps around the outer walls, rats and other rodents chasing each other through the front porch balustrades.

Inside was no better. The wooden walls sagged and the catwalks that once ringed the upper levels had long ago crashed to the paved stone floor. Now, bits of rotting planks and shards of waterlogged wood were all that remained of what, by all accounts, had numbered among the finest playhouses in Dimvein.

It was the kind of place anyone who frequented this district would barely pay mind to. It would be all but invisible to anyone within the yards.

A knotted rope hung from the ceiling, swaying in the slight cross breeze. Given that the stairs and ladders had crumbled away

JAIME CASTLE & ANDY PELOQUIN

years earlier, it served as the only access to the roof. Natisse scaled quickly upward and pulled herself onto the creaking ceiling beam to which it had been secured. "Secured" was a generous word. Under her meager weight, the beam bent and sunk, threatening to shatter. She'd never been afraid of heights, but even she knew to respect the danger of unsteady footing this high up.

It was with great relief that she reached the section of solid, tiled roof where Uncle Ronan and the dark-skinned, compact but muscular Leroshavé sat watching Magister Perech's caravan. One of them had thought to bring along a small bottle of wine and a bundle of food—Natisse suspected Leroshavé's hand in the matter. He was the sort of man who always seemed to be hungry, even minutes after a hearty meal.

Natisse moved in a low crouch toward the two men.

"You called for me?" she asked quietly.

Uncle Ronan didn't so much as glance over his shoulder.

"Come," he said, gesturing for Natisse to take a place at his left side.

She obeyed, kneeling on the roof. Together, they studied the sprawling caravan yard on the other side of the broad avenue. It was a hive of activity. Hundreds of workers, carters, drivers, and strongbacks were visible within the three-acre lot, flowing in and around the sturdy two-story inn at the center of the yard. Hundreds of covered wagons and wooden carts, the stables where the draft animals were fed and cared for, and the enormous warehouse where goods moving in and out of Dimvein were housed were all bustling with activity. House Perech's guards, dressed in orange and mauve, kept a close eye on the commotion and their hands on the hilts of their swords.

Upon first glance, it appeared precisely as Natisse expected: a flourishing caravan yard belonging to one of the wealthiest Imperial nobles. A dead noble...

It was as if their boss hadn't just been stabbed to death the night before. Each just continued their duty like the drudges they were. After all, they had to earn their wages and doubtful cared who supplied the marks.

"Look," Uncle Ronan said, pointing toward the caravan yard. "South end, just along the river's edge."

Natisse followed Uncle Ronan's finger. Behind the huge warehouse, she could see what looked like a cargo ramp leading down into the ground—as if to a subterranean structure or passageway beneath the earth.

"So far, we've only seen a few head down there," Uncle Ronan said. "Only the guards, though, and never carrying anything to be stored."

Natisse frowned. "No boxes or barrels or carts?"

"Not a one." A furrow carved Uncle Ronan's forehead. "My gut's telling me there's something more to that. But until we get a closer look, we won't know what."

"I'll—" Natisse started.

"Not until after dark," Uncle Ronan cut her off. The look on his face made it clear he'd known exactly what she was going to say. "For now, we wait."

Natisse ground her teeth, but she couldn't argue. He was right. She could easily disguise herself as a worker and blend into the busy caravan yard. Even if the place was rife with Lumenators, it would still be easier with the cover of night. No need to risk questioning by Magister Perech's guards; she could simply evade them and get close enough to see what had drawn Uncle Ronan's interest. Age and experience had given the Crimson Fang leader far better instincts than the rest of them. If his gut told him there was something there, there was.

And so, Natisse settled into a comfortable position and prepared for a long wait. Night wouldn't fall for another five or six hours, which meant a hot day beneath the bright Dimvein sun, with scorching roof tiles beneath her.

For the rest of the day, she, Garron, Uncle Ronan, and

Leroshavé traded off keeping an eye on the caravan yard. Those not on watch rested or slept, as Uncle Ronan had taught them.

Natisse was resting, on the verge of drifting off into slumber, when a hiss from Garron snapped her awake. Scrambling to her knees, she moved to the edge of the roof beside him.

"What is it?" she asked.

In response, Garron just pointed in the same direction Uncle Ronan had previously called her attention.

Six men stood next to the ramp on the southern end of the caravan yard, lounging in the shade of the warehouse. These also wore orange and mauve—Perech's colors—but the other four donned blue and green—the mark of House Onathus.

Natisse's eyes widened. "Did they…?"

Garron nodded. "Right up that ramp."

Natisse's mind raced.

"Back at the shipyard," she said. "The guards patrolling the north end of Magister Onathus's shipyards always took longer to march their route than those on the south and eastern patrols."

"I thought you found nothing?" Garron castigated.

"How was I to know—"

"She's right," Uncle Ronan said.

Natisse had thought him sleeping.

"This could be something," he said.

"Or nothin'," Leroshavé cut in.

"I guess we are all awake now, huh?" Uncle Ronan said.

"No matter what," Natisse said, "this isn't nothing. This proves a connection between Perech and Onathus."

"Nobles intermingle all the time," Garron said.

Natisse shook her head. "Not like this. Their guards carousing within each other's property?"

"We'll need more than that to bring this to the Palace," Uncle Ronan said.

"We should just kill them all and let Ezrasil decide their fates."

"I believe you mean Yildemé," Leroshavé said with a smirk.

He was the one Brendoni amongst the crew; the one who believed Yildemé to be the maker and Ezrasil to be a mere fabrication within the Karmian people's imaginations.

"Let's leave the intricacies of religion for the scholars, shall we?" Uncle Ronan said.

"It's all bullshit anyway," Garron added under his breath.

Uncle Ronan shot him a glare and Garron raised both hands in surrender.

"If there's some sort of underground tunnel or passage connecting the yards, we need to find out," Natisse said.

She glanced at the sun. It hung low over the western horizon, splashing the sky with brilliant hues of orange, crimson, gold, and purple. Sunset was half an hour off, and it would be full dark in less than an hour.

When the time came to move, she'd be ready.

Natisse crept through the caravan yards, shrouded in the gloom of night and the folds of her gray cloak. Outside the inn, stable, and warehouse failed to fully illuminate the darkness.

For the briefest of moments, she wondered why they used lamplight when the nobles would have full access to the Emperor's Lumenators. Then, it dawned on her, giving her more reason to believe they'd located the source of the fighting pits. Perech and Onathus simply couldn't afford for the Emperor to find out what they were up to.

She slipped from shadow to shadow, silent as a wraith and twice as deadly. If anyone crossed her path, the throwing knives she concealed in the palms of both hands would silence them before a question could be raised.

Ahead of her, Leroshavé charted the safest, quietest path to their destination. He wasn't quite as adept at sneaking as Haston, but he had quieter feet and quicker fingers. Not that Natisse expected to crack any vaults tonight. She just needed to get close enough to see where that ramp lead.

Uncle Ronan's gut had been right.

They gave the inn a wide berth—the din of drinking, laughing, and shouting covered any noise of their movement, but the crowd of strongbacks and caravan drivers wagering on a wrestling match drew all eyes inward. Even the handful of Magister Perech's guards who should've been on patrol now gathered amidst the throng to offer wagers on which of the two heavily muscled brutes would be the first to thrash the other senseless.

Knots tightened in Natisse's shoulders as they drew closer to the warehouse. She forced herself to match Leroshavé's pace, to move slowly, quietly, despite the urge to quicken her steps. Some instinct or intuition screamed within her—this was the place. She knew it.

Drawing in a deep breath, she disconnected her mind from the eager excitement burning within her body. She couldn't afford to make a mistake now. She needed to be cold, calm, fully in control of herself. The nervous energy crackling within her stilled. Her pulse slowed, settled, her breathing once more relaxed.

Around the warehouse they crept, clinging to the shadows and using the enormous building to shield them from the eyes of Magister Perech's guards. They'd timed the patrols—a few were disciplined enough to remain vigilant in light of the spectacle taking place outside the inn, and the next company of guards wouldn't be passing for another quarter-hour.

Reaching the southwestern corner of the warehouse, Leroshavé raised a hand to halt their advance. Natisse waited, counting out the seconds by the steady beat of her heart. Her ears pricked up for any sound of movement on their back-trail. She heard nothing, saw nothing unexpected.

A quiet hiss from Leroshavé signaled their advance. The smaller man moved first, sliding out from the shadows and darting across a darkened stretch of ground toward the ramp. Natisse followed a moment later, her soft-soled boots near-silent on the grassy earth behind the warehouse. She raced toward the stack of crates where Leroshavé had taken cover just five yards west of the descending ramp.

No surprise, no Lumenators marked the entrance. Not even torches or lanterns. Perech and Onathus would want no undue attention drawn to the tunnels.

Natisse and Leroshavé remained motionless for half a minute, but no warning shouts rang out; no cries of "Thieves!" broke the silence. Natisse moved first, slipping out from behind cover to the ramp at the nearest edge.

Disappointment flooded her as she glanced down the descending ramp. She didn't know what she'd expected to see, but there was only darkness and silence.

She frowned. Had Uncle Ronan been mistaken? Was this nothing more than—

A low whistle came from Leroshavé's hiding place—their pre-arranged warning signal. Without hesitation, Natisse sprinted back toward the crates and threw herself into the shadows next to her companion.

Not a moment too soon. Behind her, lantern lights brightened the darkness, and the sound of heavy booted feet grew louder. Natisse crawled on her belly to peer around the edge of the crate. Just as the first of Magister Perech's guards came marching into view along the eastern side of the caravan yard.

Natisse's eyes widened. Shekoth's pits!

The guard led a small procession of shabby, rag-clad figures chained together by shackles at their necks, wrists, and ankles. Twenty men, women, even children, herded like cattle. Two more guards carrying lanterns flanked the line of captives, with two more bringing up the rear. Each crack of the guardsmen's whips drove a stake into Natisse's belly.

Anger boiled within her, threatening to burn the ice from her veins. She dug her fingers into the soft grass beneath her and forced herself to remain motionless, calm. To simply watch when instincts screamed at her to leap to her feet, slice down Magister Perech's guards, and liberate the enslaved...

Yet she could not. Not yet. She had to find out where these poor souls had come from, where they were being taken. The day would come, and soon, when everyone involved in Magister Perech's slave-trafficking operation received due justice—if not Emperor Wymarc's, then the Crimson Fang's. But for now, they needed more information.

Her eyes marked the five guardsmen herding the captives, assigning each a name that would ensure she'd remember them: Rat Face, Droopy Eyes, Pocked Cheeks, Flat Nose, and Four Teeth. She'd personally make certain they were punished for their part in this.

The guards marched their prisoners down the ramp, and Natisse heard a heavy clanging *thump-thump* of a fist banging on solid metal.

"Open up!" called a man's voice.

A moment later, there came the rattling of chains being loosened, the *clank* of a deadbolt being shot. Of course—there was a door at the bottom of the ramp! The line began to move forward again, whips cracking, the cries of terrified men and women rising into the night sky once more. Natisse waited until the last of the whip-wielding guards disappeared from view, then sprang to her feet and dashed toward the ramp. The last of the prisoners were just marching through a heavy steel door which stood open to reveal a rough-hewn stone corridor lined with chains, ropes, and wooden yokes.

Within, a brazier burned brightly. Even as she watched, a giant of a man with a face like a crushed potato lifted a red-hot branding iron from the glowing red coals. The man swung toward the next prisoner in line and pressed the scorching metal to his arm. The woman's shriek at the touch ripped a hole in Natisse's heart... and tore something free in her mind.

Brilliant scarlet-and-gold flames consumed her world, tongues of blinding heat licking at her clothing, her flesh, ravaging the air in her lungs.

A man's face loomed in her vision. Brutish features, a sneering smile, and enormous arms stained with blood. His laughter echoed in time with a terrified scream. A woman's scream. A voice she knew so well.

She tried to cry out, but couldn't. Thick smoke choked and blinded her. She clawed at the flames, frantic in her efforts to escape, to get to the woman.

Then, a silhouette above. Massive. And a pillar of dazzling dragonfire closed in on her, and she was swallowed in agony and death.

Natisse came out of the memory with a gasp. Her legs gave out and she dropped to one knee, heart racing.

Her mind reeled. What was that? She had relived that moment a thousand times in her dreams, but she'd never before seen the man's face. Never heard his laugh or the woman's scream.

She had no time to contemplate what she'd just relived. Light suddenly spilled across her kneeling figure, and from behind her, came a man's cry of, "Hey, what are you doing there?"

17

KULLEN

K ullen's eyes narrowed. "What do you mean, gone?"

"Precisely that," Assidius snapped in his lisping voice. His lips puckered up into a dissatisfied scowl aimed at Kullen, as if annoyed at a peasant who had the gall to speak in his presence. "Magister Taradan's vial was found nowhere on his person by the time Turoc's Orkenwatch arrived to inspect the crime scene. Neither was Magister Perech's. Of course, he came to me straightaway."

"Of course," Kullen mocked.

Emperor Wymarc frowned, a worried look in his eyes. Thanagar began to rise but Kullen could tell by the Emperor's expression he was speaking to the dragon through their bond. The Great White lowered its head but did not close his eyes.

"And no one you questioned at the scene had any idea where they'd gone?" the Emperor asked Turoc.

"No, sir," Turoc growled, his voice a booming rumble. "Strange, I thought it was at time. So ask I did. Thoroughly." His huge hands flexed, making his steel gauntlets creak. "No one knew nothing. Or said nothing of knowing nothing."

Emperor Wymarc looked to Assidius. "Have there been any

reports of the vials' appearance around Dimvein? Of any dragons appearing in unusual places?"

Kullen couldn't help but think the whole world would know of dragons appearing in unusual places but kept his mouth shut.

"No, Divine Majesty." The Seneschal fussed at his frumpy brown frock, smoothing out the wrinkles accrued during his hasty trip through the palace. He regained his composure and his expression once more went flat. "Though it has only been a few hours since their owners' deaths. It is possible that whoever looted them from the noblemen's corpses has no idea how to use them."

"Indeed." Emperor Wymarc nodded to himself. The secret of the dragonblood vials and the silent bond formed with dragons was carefully guarded. Just as carefully, Emperor Wymarc—and all the Emperors before him—had spread false rumors about how the magic worked. There were tales aplenty roaming Dimvein, but the truth was... unexpected. Indeed, Kullen had been surprised to learn it for himself nearly two decades earlier when he'd inherited Umbris.

"But that not all, sir," Turoc rumbled.

Kullen had never once heard Turoc refer to the Emperor as Majesty, merely "sir." The same for the other Orken. Judging by Assidius's ghastly expression, it was a point of contention for the uptight Seneschal. But if Emperor Wymarc allowed it, Assidius could not force the matter.

"Suspicious, became I when noticed the missing vials. Wanted to confirm that more gone missing. So checked, did I. Recent deaths, Magister Iltari and Estéfar, execution day at Court of Justice. Magister Oyodan, too, days before. All vials missing, too."

Emperor Wymarc's eyebrows shot up. "You're certain?" His gaze darted between Assidius and Turoc.

"I'm afraid so, Divine Majesty." Assidius's face puckered even more. "We just came from interviewing both the Imperial Scales nearest Magister Iltari's skybox and the Orkenwatch company that were summoned to the scene. Both men were, indeed, missing their vials, too."

Kullen could tell the Emperor was biting back more foul language, but he daren't speak that way in front of most.

"A grave discovery," he said through clenched teeth. Then he looked briefly at Kullen. "One that merits further and immediate investigation."

Kullen racked his brain. He had no idea where to begin the search for whoever had taken the vials—there had been hundreds of guests aboard Magister Perech's barge the night he and Magister Taradan had died. Any one of them could've taken the vial.

Ezrasil's bastard son, it could even have been her!

Kullen chewed on that. The red-haired woman who'd killed Magister Perech might've absconded with the aristocrat's dragonblood vial, and her companion—the big one who'd gone overboard with Kullen—could very well have stolen Magister Taradan's as he passed the corpse. If that was the case, Magister Taradan's vial was now at the bottom of the Karmian Channel or, more likely, in the belly of an onyx shark.

"Turoc," Emperor Wymarc said, head snapping away from Kullen to the Orken, "I want you on this personally, working with Assidius. We need to find those vials soon, before they wind up in the wrong hands."

Kullen's stomach sank. It felt as if a stone had been shoved down his throat.

"Of course, sir." The huge Orken gave a stiff-backed bow—the greatest sign of respect he could summon for the Emperor he ostensibly served.

Assidius gave Kullen a sly grin, then bowed even more deeply, nearly folding in half at the waist.

"It will be done, Divine Majesty. I will neither rest or sleep nor take food until—"

"Please," the Emperor said, a weary tone in his voice. "There's no need for such extremities." He then looked to Turoc. "And do not harm any Imperial citizens unless it proves absolutely necessary." His jaw muscles clenched. "Baronet Ammonidas Sallas was an aristocrat, and he deserved an execution befitting his rank, not torture and a public spectacle."

"Of course, sir." Turoc bowed again, but Kullen didn't miss the way the Orken's close-set black eyes flitted toward Assidius.

Interesting, thought Kullen. So that was the Seneschal's idea, eh? He wouldn't put it past Assidius to use the harshest, cruelest methods to root out traitors to the Empire, or anyone who threatened the Emperor's person. Doubtless, Assidius would love nothing more than to strap Kullen himself to that table and let Arbiter Chuldok ply his bloody trade—not for answers, merely to see Kullen humiliated, in anguish, and destroyed. The feelings between them were mutual, but only their service to the Emperor stayed both their hands.

When Turoc straightened, his gaze darted to Kullen.

"Beware your back, little man. Palace has many dangerous places where fools wind up dead." Spinning on his heel, he lumbered away across the garden, leaving Assidius to hurriedly bow to the Emperor, glare at Kullen, and scurry after him.

Kullen stared at the Orken's enormous retreating back.

"Exhausting, the two of them," the Emperor said when they were gone.

"What was that?" Kullen demanded.

"I'm sorry?"

"You should be."

"Watch your tone," the Emperor warned.

Kullen threw his hands in the air and turned his back to the Emperor, pacing across the garden grounds.

"Kullen, what is it?"

Kullen spun back. "Like you don't know? Why them? Have you so easily lost your trust in me?"

Emperor Wymarc laughed.

"Right," Kullen nodded. "Hilarious."

"Kullen, my boy, why would I waste your talents on something so menial as tracking down these vials when yet more of my people are being slain in cold blood?"

Kullen stopped. The incredulous look on his face turning quickly to something akin to embarrassment.

"A job like that belongs to a beast as dull as that one," the Emperor said. "And to have Turoc by his side…"

At that, Kullen laughed this time. "I apologize, *sir*."

"Don't push it."

"I think he's coming around, you know? Turoc." Kullen shot a sarcastic grin at the Emperor. "One of these days, I swear he's going to ask me to be his best friend and help him braid his beard."

Emperor Wymarc gave a little snort of derision. "Or bite off your head." He clucked his tongue. "And I mean literally. I've seen Orken do it. Snapped right off at the neck."

Kullen grimaced. "What a treat. I can only imagine what he'd do if he knew I was the Black Talon."

"Probably the same." Emperor Wymarc grinned and held up a pair of fingers. "Just in two bites to make sure you felt the first."

Despite the graphic imagery, Kullen couldn't help chuckling. Turoc's perspective of him was wholly incorrect, shaped by the Emperor's will. To the Orken Tuskigo's knowledge, Kullen was nothing more than Prince Jarius' companion, kept around by the Emperor like a pet intended to remind him of his son. Kullen offered the Emperor nothing of value Turoc could see, but, like a persistent cock-boil, always around and annoyingly impossible to get rid of. Or, to put it in kinder terms—which Turoc never would—a waste of breath and the Emperor's time.

Should Turoc ever learn the truth, however, Kullen's troubles would grow exponentially. The entire might of the Orkenwatch would be turned loose against him and he'd be hunted down across not only Dimvein, but the entire Karmian Empire.

Worse, Emperor Wymarc would not—could not—prevent it from happening. The Emperor required the services of an assassin, but only so long as those services remained a secret. The outcry from among the nobility, and likely the populace at large, would weaken the Emperor's already tenuous standing. Should Kullen ever find himself on the wrong side of the Orkenwatch, the Emperor would have no choice but to disavow him and leave him to suffer the consequences of his action.

Kullen had no doubt Assidius fantasized daily about such an outcome—was shocked the Seneschal hadn't secretly begun rumors already. And so, Kullen went to great lengths to ensure that nothing would ever tie him directly to the assassinations he carried out for his Emperor.

"These vials going missing," Emperor Wymarc said, settling back onto his stone bench, "they are worrisome." He stroked his smooth-shaven, age-lined chin, chasms deepening his brow. "Were it just one instance, I could write it off as nothing more than an enterprising thief lifting a treasured object from an aristocrat's corpse. I could even convince myself that one of Our nobility was ignorant enough to misplace the device. But twice? And two stolen each time?"

"I suspect the woman's hand in this," Kullen said without hesitation. The Emperor inclined his head. "She could've easily lifted it from Magister Perech's corpse, one of her companions done likewise for Magister Taradan's vial."

"Perhaps. But from what you and Assidius have told me about Magisters Iltari and Estéfar, there is no way she could have gotten close enough to abscond with theirs."

Now it was Kullen's turn to frown. "True."

The crossbow bolt that killed Magister Estéfar had come from the top of Magister Corvus' tower. He might've been able to slip close enough in the confusion to steal the vials, but unless she had magical abilities that rivaled those he possessed through his bond with Umbris, it would be impossible for her.

He thought back to the previous night, their clash on the skiff. She hadn't once reached for a vial around her neck or stashed in a hidden pocket. She'd drawn a throwing knife and that strange whip-like sword of hers. If she'd have possessed magic of any sort, surely, she would've used it against him—or to save the man he'd killed.

No, the more he considered it, the more convinced Kullen became that she fought without magic. Simply a surprising amount of skill—a fact for which he found himself admiring her all the more.

"So if it's not her," he said, "then who? There may be a number of Magister Perech's guests who knew the secret of the dragonblood vials, but surely they wouldn't risk the binding so soon after his death."

"That is my thought, too." Emperor Wymarc retook his seat and slumped forward. "And that might explain why we have not yet seen the dragons appear. Their new owners are simply waiting until the next dragon cycle begins to take command of the magic. That's not to mention the days after."

Kullen's thoughts drifted in time, back to when the Emperor had first taught him about the cycles. To the day he'd become Kullen Bloodsworn.

FIFTEEN YEARS EARLIER...

Kullen screamed. Agonized, blood-curdling cries that came from a place deep within that he was unaware of until this moment. It was like liquid fire ran through his veins.

"*No!*" the dragon roared.

The voice wasn't quite full, as if it somehow echoed within Kullen's mind. Though it fought with pain for dominance in that space.

Kullen had seen dragons—any who lived in Dimvein had. But not only had Kullen seen Thanagar the Protector, perched high above the city, he'd also seen Tempest, Jarius's dragon. However, nothing had prepared him for this creature that stood before him.

It was all black, but somehow… shimmering purples and blues and greens and all colors in between. And its horns… the curled back like a ram but with a razor's edge along the tops of each.

"I cannot! I won't," the dragon said. *"He is not Inquist. Where is Inquist?"*

Kullen didn't believe he could suffer more than he already was, but the mention of that name brought a soft whimper from his depths. He groaned. It was despair. Young as Kullen might've been, he'd felt that feeling before late at night at Mammy Tess's Refuge.

He was feeling the dragon's pain.

"She's is not…" the dragon croaked. *"She can't be."*

Another voice spoke, this one strong and full, echoing in the valley like the that of a god.

"It is true, Umbris," the voice said. "Inquist is dead. I am sorry, dear creature. She was kind and gracious. We all miss her dearly."

Kullen opened his eyes. They burned like hot coals. Tears streamed down his face, though he knew not whether they were the shared sadness or pain. Through blurred vision, he took in the Emperor, standing with his shoulders slumped. This was the man who'd rescued him from poverty and lack, gave him a place within the palace as Jarius's companion. He'd been the closest thing to a father Kullen could remember.

Kullen heard the rumble of the great Twilight Dragon strike the ground but turned only in time to see the great billows of dust like a tidal wave. The force struck him and sent him soaring backward. He landed hard, back cracking against the earth. Struggling, he lay there, desperate for air but inhaling only dirt. It filled his him, choking him. He coughed, heaved, gagged. Rolling over to his hands and knees, Kullen battled for breath and after what seemed a lifetime, finally won.

He sucked in deeply, his lungs expanding with life. But just as he was about to rise, the dragon's bellows started anew. Kullen's ears felt as if they would bleed, he heart thudding within his ribcage with each of the dragon's sobbing cries.

"Why?" Kullen begged. "Why this?"

"This is not how it was supposed to be," the Emperor told Kullen. "He is resisting the bond. He is…"

"Heartbroken," Kullen said.

Then, its voice rose within Kullen's head.

"*Inquist!*"

Kullen fell back, broken and defeated. He stared up at the full moon. It was larger than Kullen had seen it in some time, and bright red like blood. Such a beautiful and horrifying sight befitting a day like today.

Though it had been many months since the Emperor's assassin, the dragon's master, Inquist, had been murdered, it became so fresh in Kullen's heart. Though they hadn't bound one to another yet, Kullen had extended himself to Umbris like a handshake. He merely waited for the dragon to return the gesture. From Kullen's perspective, he was wide open and vulnerable. Perhaps more so than he'd ever been.

Inquist's dragon must've wondered what happened to her master, her friend. Surely, he would've sensed something wrong, if not because the bond had been so weakened after months without the bloodsurge being enacted, but because the bond between man and dragon superseded the confines of the physical realm.

Umbris would've felt Inquist's death almost as strongly as the woman herself had.

"Why must we do this?" Kullen shouted.

"For your sake and his," the Emperor said, gesturing to Umbris.

A ululation rose from Umbris's deepest parts, breaking a chasm in the earth.

"He should go to another," Kullen argued weakly. "An aristocrat."

"Umbris requires a man of strength and integrity."

"I'm a boy!" Kullen protested. "Not a man! Surely, Inquist had an heir who fits such requirements."

"No!" the Emperor shouted. "Inquist wanted this. She'd always wanted this."

At that, Umbris's head perked slightly.

"Where is this written?" Umbris asked.

"Alas, it is not," the Emperor said, shaking his head. "But know this, great beast, Inquist instilled her full trust in me to do what I believed would bind you to a man or woman who was not just noble in name but in deed."

"No!"

"You must make the choice, Umbris, but I know that Inquist would have desired your bonding to Kullen. He is a man of valor and honor."

Moments slipped by without word but the dragon's warm breath could be heard like rushing winds, staggered and stuttering.

"I cannot," Umbris said, finally. *"Not now. I must..."* Another low groan shook the valley, causing more stone and dirt to cascade into the earth's open maw just feet from Kullen. *"Please, release me to mourn my bloodsworn."*

"We have not the time," the Emperor said, looking up to the full moon. "It is now or never."

Umbris turned his head and continued his lamentations.

Kullen turned to the Emperor. "What will happen if he—"

"The Twilight Dragon's power is directly tied to the lunar calendar," Emperor Wymarc said. "Tonight, when the moon is red, the start of the Dragon Cycle. Tonight, the bloodsurge will be strong enough to bond. If we don't do it now, tonight, we will wait months more and by then..."

He didn't need to say it. Kullen could grasp from the heaviness of his tone that Umbris would pass on, lost to his realm without a binding to this world.

Emperor Wymarc walked forward to stand beside the dragon's massive head. He placed a hand against the creature's face and stroked. Kullen expected Umbris to respond violently, but instead, he seemed to lean into the touch.

"Umbris," the Emperor said. "I know your pain, for I feel it too. Each day, the sadness threatens to overwhelm me at the loss of my servant and friend, but I press on for the good of the people. They knew not the mistake they made when they killed her."

Umbris's head snapped up. *"Killed her?"*

It wasn't clear who'd recognized the mistake first, Kullen or the Emperor himself.

"Now, now…" Emperor Wymarc said, hoping to placate the beast before—

"Killed her?" Umbris rose and the entirety of the valley became pure darkness despite the light of the moon. Silence followed but only for a moment. Umbris roared and the force of it sent Kullen to his knees.

"Who did it? I will avenge my master!"

"No!" Kullen shouted, rising to his feet. He hardly knew why, but he moved in the direction he'd believed the dragon and Emperor to be, though he couldn't be entirely sure in the shadow. He could only hope not to misstep and wind up in the belly of the earth. "You mustn't."

"Why? Give me one reason not to lay waste to this whole world in retribution for my loss!"

Kullen breathed deep. "Because she wouldn't have wanted that."

"Lies!"

"Inquist protected the people of this city as well as protecting the Emperor himself."

"Kullen is right," the Emperor agreed. "This is not the way. However, I assure you, the one responsible for such pain will pay."

Umbris didn't respond.

The Emperor grabbed Kullen by the arm and pulled him aside.

"Kullen, this must happen tonight. There's no other choice."

"Surely, if we tell him the consequen—"

"I fear it will make no difference. Umbris would not be the first to perish due to a broken heart."

"Is there another way?"

"But there is one other way," the Emperor said at the same time. "Though it will not be pleasant for either of you."

Kullen sighed. Nothing was ever easy.

"What is it?"

"He must be broken."

"Broken?"

"Like a wild stallion," the Emperor said. "His will must become forfeit to yours."

"I have to break the will of a dragon?" his tone incredulous.

"Yes."

"One that I can't even see?"

"I said it would not be easy."

"Killing the Hudar Horde singlehandedly would not be a more difficult task."

Kullen felt a hand on his shoulder. "You underestimate yourself, Kullen."

"You're right," Kullen said. "But you underestimate me as well."

"Is that so?" The Emperor smirked.

Kullen took a step toward the dragon, the beast's pain of loss evident.

"Umbris," Kullen said softly, "I know I can't replace Inquist. Nor can I stop your pain…"

The dragon puffed air hot enough to bake bread. Kullen didn't so much as flinch.

"I can't replace her," he said again, "but I can do my best to pick up where she left off."

Kullen looked back at the Emperor who nodded.

"Where you must go," the Emperor said, "I cannot go with you."

"I understand," Kullen responded.

The Emperor backed away, leaving Umbris and Kullen standing alone.

Kullen reached for the gold-capped vial with a hand that trembled more than he cared to admit. Gritting his teeth, he pressed his thumb against the needle, letting his blood bring the magic to life.

He felt a tug on his body—no, his *soul*—drawing him toward the dragon. Yet something rebuffed him. Pushed him away as if he'd slammed into a wall. His head rang, his breath coming faster.

"If he does not accept you," the Emperor said, "the magic will not work. You must make him choose you. Convince him to embrace the connection."

Kullen studied the Twilight Dragon. He felt Umbris's pain. Felt it as raw and deeply as though it was his own. And he had pain enough to last him a dozen lifetimes over. He knew what the dragon was feeling; he'd felt it countless times over the years, every night he lay awake in the darkness wishing, praying, hoping.

He wasn't sure if such a creature could shed tears, but believed he would drown in them if it could. For all its great size and immense strength, the dragon could hurt as badly as the scared, helpless child Kullen had once been. In the pain, he'd clung to Mammy Tess, Mammy Sylla, Hadassa. They had anchored him, kept him from drifting away into shadow. Now *he* would be that for Umbris.

Kullen reached a hand—now utterly steady—toward the dragon and rested his fingers lightly on the beast's great snout.

"Umbris, I am terribly sorry for your loss. I did not know Inquist well, but I knew of her greatness. She will be missed."

"Who would kill her?"

"We are not sure," Kullen said. "But together, we can find out. If I am to be the next Black Talon, I will make vengeance my first mission."

At that, Umbris's neck rose ever so slightly.

"I intend for us to be friends for a long time," Kullen told the dragon. Lifting the vial, he pressed the thumb of his free hand onto the needle. "And I am prepared to do what I must to ensure it."

Umbris lifted his head, sadness in his eyes. As if in response, a puff of darkness began to swirl around him, then it reached Kullen and an icy cold feeling enveloped him. The chill was otherworldly, and in an instant, he was transported into the Shadow Realm.

"I do not know this word, 'friend,'" rumbled a shape that was Umbris and yet not, so immense and powerful in the endless void enveloping Kullen. *"But I see in you a kindred soul. One who has known loss such as I now feel, who has felt as alone as I do in these shadows."*

"But you are not alone anymore," Kullen called into the emptiness, his voice stronger than he felt. "We are together, and for as long as I live, I will be your friend." He thought of the word Umbris had used. "I will be your *bloodsworn*."

Thunderous silence echoed through the Shadow Realm, the cold growing icier still, seeping into Kullen's bones. He stood firm, staring into the darkness around him. He would neither bow nor retreat. Not from this battle or any other. The Emperor had asked this of him, and so he would do it. He owed the monarch a debt far greater than he could ever repay.

"Your determination and tenacity does you credit, young Kullen," said the dragon, using his name for the first time. *"Perhaps you are indeed worthy of being my bloodsworn."*

The word hung in the void, and power rushed through every fiber of Kullen's being.

"Kullen," the Emperor's words tore Kullen from his memories.

It took many years for Kullen to earn Umbris's trust, but now, he could hardly remember a time without the great Twilight Dragon by his side and in his heart.

"Sorry," Kullen said. "I—We have four stolen vials and no leads."

"Leave that to Assidius and Turoc."

"Yes, but it's all the same task in the end," Kullen said.

"How so?"

"Whoever is killing your nobles might just be after the vials. If true, the only factor they are taking into account—"

"Is that they are nobility."

"Precisely," Killen said. "And they want control... they want the dragons. Whoever has stolen them is awaiting the start of the next dragon cycle in just three days."

"Indeed." Emperor Wymarc nodded. "It is possible they do not know what they are attempting, but simply seek to use the vials to their own ends without understanding the bonds formed between human and dragon. Should they attempt the binding, they will find themselves—"

"Yes, I remember intimately the mental torment inflicted by Umbris's mourning."

"You were strong and have strong blood," the Emperor said. "If these thieves are not, they could die."

"You say that like it's a bad thing," Kullen said. "If someone's foolish enough to use a power they don't understand, they deserve to suffer the consequences of their own stupidity."

"Like you sought to do?" Emperor Wymarc asked, raising an eyebrow.

Kullen flushed. It hadn't been long after Umbris and Kullen had bonded that Kullen tested that bond, casting himself from the top of Ezrasil's temple, the tallest building second only to the palace itself. He did not understand how the bloodsurge worked —not fully. He'd expected Umbris to sense his danger, to swoop in and save him. Had it not been for Jarius and his Silver Wind Dragon, Tempest, he would have become a bright red stain on the streets of Dimvein.

"The consequences may not be limited to only the fool who attempts to bind themselves to the dragon," Emperor Wymarc continued. "Or have you forgotten why the Embers are called such? I know I have not."

"Of course I've not forgotten but—"

"Whatever the case, I have full faith that Assidius and Turoc will uncover whoever is behind this theft." Emperor Wymarc fixed Kullen with a piercing gaze. "But as I've said, for you, I have another task."

Kullen bowed low, exaggeratively so. Then, in his best impression of Assidius, said, "Of course, Your Most Highest, Royalest, Majesty."

The Emperor couldn't help but spare a small laugh.

"Who is it?" Kullen asked.

"Assidius has brought me proof that Magister Issemar is connected to the assassination plot against me.

"Proof?"

"Indeed. And it is... shall we say, undeniable."

"But?"

"But, convincing as it might be, it falls just short of incriminating."

Kullen sighed. "More proof of Assidius's incompetence."

"You can engage in a pissing contest with the Seneschal another time. Right now I—"

"Need me to find out if he's guilty," Kullen finished for the Emperor.

"Precisely." Emperor Wymarc sat and picked up the book he'd placed on the bench and re-opened it to his page. Looking up with just his eyes, he continued, "Should you learn that he is plotting treason, you have my Imperial permission to do what needs to be done."

"With pleasure," Kullen said.

Kullen pushed through the broad leaves blocking the hidden entrance to his tunnels. He took one final glance back at the Emperor, seated on his bench. A beam of sunlight practically highlighted him there. A dark foreboding fell upon Kullen's heart at the thought of a plot to take the man's life.

As if Thanagar had heard Kullen's thoughts, his long neck rose and those ruby red eyes bore into Kullen's. Smoke rose from his nostrils before he returned to his rest.

Perhaps the Emperor had nothing to fear. At least not here under the White Dragon's protection.

18

NATISSE

Natisse, acting on instinct hammered into her by Uncle Ronan and Haston, sprang to her feet and dashed eastward, away from the guards. They'd spotted her, no doubt about that, but couldn't possibly know who she was. She hoped they'd suspect her of being a—

"Thief!" came the shout behind her. "Thief!"

Natisse bared her teeth in a snarling grin and ran for her life. Literally. If Magister Perech's guards captured her, the was no telling what they'd do. At best, they'd settle for taking her right hand—the accepted punishment for thieves in Dimvein. But the moment they found the weapons hidden around her person, they'd get far more violent and brutal. She might very well find herself the next one in chains, walking down that ramp to vanish underground forever. Or die in whatever hellhole the slaves were sent to.

Then the vision of Arbiter Chuldok and Ammon drove itself into her thoughts and she hastened her pace. So, too, her grip tightened on the throwing knives she still carried. She'd be damned if she'd let them take her. Certainly not without one hell of a fight.

She raced for the warehouse on the eastern edge of the compound. Its dark shadows would hide her from the pursuing guards, buy her a few moments of their confusion for her to make a break for the front gate. If her luck held, the din of the crowd surrounding the two wrestling brutes would drown out the guards' shouts long enough for her flee the caravan yards and disappear fully into the nearby back streets.

There was no time to worry about Leroshavé. He'd have to make his own escape. Hopefully, her flight would draw enough of the guards to grant him a chance to slip through the darkness before a passing patrol stumbled upon his hiding place. She could only pray he'd not try to continue their mission without her.

Glancing back, hope surged within her. Only two guards stood at the nearest gate, warming themselves over a brazier. Their attention wandered between the glowing coals and the fight they could hear but not see. Natisse slid the throwing knives into her palms, gripping the hilts tightly. She'd keep a hold on them until the moment she had to choose to kill or be captured.

Her dark gray cloak concealed her within the shadows just long enough for her to close to within twenty yards of the two guards before they saw her. Even once they did, they reacted slowly, caught by surprise. One reached for the sword at his belt while the other stepped toward her, barring her path with his arms outstretched.

Brutish men like this always underestimated Natisse.

She charged straight for the man impeding her escape, shouting a wordless curse at him. The intensity of her voice caused him to flinch back and his right hand dropped to the cudgel dangling at his side. That moment of hesitation gave Natisse the perfect opening to dart to the side, evading his grasping hand, and redirected herself toward the open gate.

Something whooshed past her left shoulder, barely missing the side of her neck. She was unsure whether it was the cudgel or sword, though she hardly cared. She raced through the open gate before either guard could swing at her again.

Behind her, the shouts of "Stop that thief!" started up once again, her pursuers catching up. But Natisse was beyond their reach now.

Then her boot struck a patch of mud invisible in the night, and her foot flew out from beneath her. She managed to turn her fall into a desperate roll that brought her up to her feet once more, but she was off-balance and when next her foot struck an uneven cobblestone, she fell again. The impact knocked the breath from her lungs and set the world spinning wildly about her.

Unable to give up her advantage, she staggered upright, dizzy, and blinked furiously to clear her vision. Lantern light bounced not twenty feet behind her—the two gate guards had given chase, with the patrol close on their heels.

She swore, spinning and breaking into a staggering run. Her knee ached. Sharp twinges ran down the right side of her neck, and she'd scraped away a thin layer of flesh from her left forearm. But she couldn't afford to let pain slow her down. Not with the guards so hot in pursuit.

Spotting an alley between two buildings, she dashed toward it. She knew from her time spent surveying the yards from above, the narrow street would take her into the maze of back lanes that dominated much of northern Dimvein. From there, she hoped she could lose Magister Perech's guards. If she was just fast enough to—

"Got you!" A hand closed around her cloak and Natisse was suddenly snapped to a halt, then hauled backward as if by a noose. Her legs no longer beneath her, she crashed to the floor, hard.

Light blinded her and heavy steps set the cobblestone street trembling. She rolled onto her stomach, tried to rise, but an armored boot kicked her hands out from beneath her and she collapsed to her face once more. Mud-covered and likely bloody, she raised her head. Before she knew it, she was surrounded by five hard-looking guards waving drawn swords in her face.

"Well, look'it here!" sneered one, a man with the face resembling a boar, down to the beady black eyes and long snout. "Our little thief's a thief-girl!"

"What you hoping to steal, girlie?" mocked a second, a fellow with buck teeth and a nose that begged to be punched. "Or you so desperate you'll do anything for a coin?" He tugged at his belt with his free hand.

Natisse decided he would die first. Her right arm flashed forward, and her throwing knife spun like a silver streak through the night. He stood for a moment, the black, leather hilt the only thing protruding from the man's neck. He staggered, gasped, and coughed blood. His sword clattered to the ground, and his lifeless corpse followed it a second later. Crimson gushed down the front of his orange and mauve jerkin and stained the cobblestones before him.

Natisse was moving even before the man fell. Her right hand darted beneath her cloak, seized the hilt of her lashblade, and whipped out the weapon in a blinding blur of cold steel. She swung the segmented, whip-like blade in a circle around her, pirouetting with the grace of a dancer rising from her crouch to a standing position. The razor-sharp steel bit into exposed flesh from knee to neck and the four remaining guards howled in pain. Two dropped their swords, hands slashed to the bone. Another fell without a sound, blood pumping from a gaping wound in his throat. The last dropped to one knee and clutched frantically at the deep laceration in his leg.

Snapping her arm back, Natisse re-formed the lashblade into its sword and struck out at one of the two disarmed guards. The tip of the thin sword drove right into his open mouth, punching out the back of his head in a spray of blood. Natisse gave a savage twist of her wrist as she pulled the sword free.

The man staggered forward and fell face-first atop his bleeding companion. Both went down in a tangle of wet scarlet and dying limbs.

With a flick of her wrist, Natisse wrapped the lashblade's many thongs around the last guard's neck and gave it a soft tug. "Move a muscle, and it rends your throat," she snarled.

The guard went instantly rigid, releasing the cudgel he'd half-drawn with his uninjured left hand. The *thud* as it hit the ground was the only sound save for his whimpers.

"Please," he begged. "I've got a family. Kids. A few wives."

"Then let's not make them orphans and widows. Fair?"

The guard nodded.

"Now, tell me," Natisse snarled, stepping closer to the guard, "where do the slaves come from?"

The guard's eyes went from saucers to dinner plates.

"I... don't kn-know!" He looked like he wanted to shake his head, but thought better of it given the whip-like blade encircling his throat. His voice faltered a bit. "They come from all over."

Natisse waited a moment, sure the guy wasn't done. When he didn't offer more information, she pulled just enough to draw a dozen small lines of blood around his throat and neck.

"I... I answered!"

"You know more than that."

"I'm just a g-guard," he stammered. "I have kids and—"

"Wives. Yes. You've said as much. What do you do with the slaves?"

"We just take delivery of them. I swear. We bring them down into the tunnels for branding. After—af-af-after th-that, they're A-Joakim's problem!"

"Joakim?" Natisse demanded. "Big guy, face like a smashed potato?"

"Yeah! Yeah! That's him!" The guard swallowed, gave the tiniest nod. "He's the one who takes them. Brings them wherever they're going."

She was no fool. This man was choosing his words wisely. The problem was, it wasn't very wise.

"And where *are* they going?" Natisse's hand remained perfectly steady despite the fiery rage burning within her. "Where does Magister Perech send these slaves? Who does he sell them to?"

The guard opened his mouth to answer, but he never got the chance to speak. The man with the wounded leg surged toward Natisse, grappled her in a bear hug, and lifted her off her feet. The world blurred as he dragged her backward. Even still, Natisse refused to relinquish her hold on the lashblade, and the steel thongs sawed through her prisoner's throat. His head spun away from his shoulders and his body crumpled.

Natisse didn't bother retracting the lashblade into sword-form —it would do her no good. Her captor managed to take three steps before his wounded leg collapsed and they both toppled to the floor. As she fell, Natisse struck out with her foot as Ammon had taught her, spinning them both in the air. She landed atop the wounded guard with the points of both knees driving into his chest. His ribs gave way with a terrible *crack* of snapping bone. Air erupted from his lungs and his hold on her slackened. Rolling free of his now-limp arms, Natisse surged to her feet, bringing the lashblade up in an overhead strike that whipped the guard's neck. He died gushing blood from an attack that hacked through flesh, cartilage, and only stopped at bone.

Suddenly, Natisse stood alone in the street, surrounded by the bodies of five dead guards. She hadn't planned to kill them, but they'd left her no choice.

Her gaze flicked to the one who'd spoken and would never speak again. His decapitated head lay half a dozen feet from his bloody torso. She growled a silent curse. The bastard was talking, and about to tell her where the slaves were taken after the guards handed them off to the giant Joakim.

Bootsteps echoed nearby and figures burst from the shadows to her right. Natisse spun, lashblade coiled, raised, and ready to strike. But it was just Uncle Ronan, with Garron two steps behind.

"Run!" Uncle Ronan shouted. "There's more coming."

Natisse's attention fell upon the open gates and beyond, into the caravan yard. Sure enough, eight more orange-and-mauve-clad guards ran toward them, the light from their many lanterns bouncing to and fro. Each had swords drawn and were ready for a fight. The moment they spotted the Natisse surrounded by their dead brethren, they wouldn't hesitate to cut her down. Or try to.

Eight against three weren't the worst odds, not with Uncle Ronan and Garron fighting at her side. But there would be more coming soon—Natisse had counted close to sixty guards patrolling Perech's yards, and close to a hundred strongbacks hauling cargo and unloading wagons. There were too many to fight right now.

Natisse hated that she had to run. Hated that she had to turn her back on the slaves below, just as she'd turned her back on Ammon as he lay on Arbiter Chuldok's table in the Court of Justice. But she had to. The Crimson Fang's mission would only be carried out if they survived to fight another day. On the battle-ground they chose, after they had all the facts and knew what they were fighting for. Not only had they'd found a source of slaves entering Dimvein, but they had proof Magister Onathus and the late Magister Perech were connected. Now, they had to put that information to good use and figure out their next steps.

After they got the bloody hell away from the guards pursuing them.

Natisse spun away from the caravan yard and raced after her escaping comrades. Garron took the lead, sprinting down the broad avenue and ducking into an alleyway that led farther south. He was damned fast, and Natisse had to push herself to full speed to keep up. Uncle Ronan, too, managed to maintain the pace, but they all knew neither he nor Natisse could match Garron's speed for long. Yet she refused to slow despite the exhaustion in her legs and the burning in her lungs and the many aches she'd earned from the guards—especially her ribs where she'd been crushed. Uncle Ronan proved equally stubborn. Neither of them would give into fatigue or slow their pace until they'd left Magister Perech's guards in the dust.

"This way!" Garron shouted.

A maze of alleys cut toward a broad avenue half a mile south of the caravan yard. In time, the sounds of pursuit faded, Magister Perech's guards losing sight of them in the twisting, turning warren of narrow, debris-clogged back streets.

Natisse wanted to breathe a sigh of relief, but she hadn't the air to spare. It took all her willpower to keep running in pursuit of Garron when she wanted nothing more than to stop and catch her breath.

"Just… a little… more!" Garron called back. "Almost—"

His words cut off in a grunt as he barreled out of the alleyway and collided with an enormous Orken. He flipped ass over teakettle, his head nearly being clocked right off his shoulders by a plate-mailed arm.

"Shit," Natisse swore.

Under ordinary circumstances, the Orkenwatch likely would've paid them no mind, but a trio running like the birds of Shekoth chased them, nary a lantern between them, drew some attention.

If that wasn't enough, Natisse held a bloodstained lashblade and Uncle Ronan and Garron both sported weapons on their belts.

Natisse's heart sank as the patrol of six Orken turned toward them, bared their long fangs, and reached for their enormous swords.

19

KULLEN

One look at Magister Issemar's estate was all Kullen needed to immediately dislike its owner. The sprawling gardens were in a state of disarray, weeds flourishing among the choking flowers and trees. All of the bronze statuary decorating the grounds bore a patina that not even the most vigorous scrubbing would remove. The six-foot-high stone wall encircling the property was cracked in a hundred different places, and the mansion's front gates were unmanned, open, and squealing like a dying pig with the gentle breeze.

The man clearly had wealth—five stories of excess and opulence was enough to prove that—but he seemed determined not to spend it on the upkeep of his property. What had once been among the finest properties in Dimvein now looked more like the Wild Grove Forest than the home of one of the Karmian Empire's most affluential.

Magister Issemar himself reflected the slipshod sloppiness of his property. His thin blond hair hung in messy, lank ropes around his shoulders, and he wore robes two sizes too large, which hung off his spindly frame like last year's drapes. Even from where Kullen crouched, scoping out the property from a rooftop fifty yards south of the walls, he could see the food and wine stains on Magister Issemar's robes as the aristocrat sat sunning himself in his garden.

Kullen found it difficult to believe such a slovenly man could be caught up in any clever schemes to assassinate the Emperor—or what manner of fool would welcome him as a co-conspirator. But the information Assidius had given him proved that appearances were utterly deceptive. At least in this instance.

After leaving the Emperor's side, Kullen had tracked down the Seneschal, finding the frumpy man in his obsessively tidy office.

According to Assidius's intel, the bulk of Magister Issemar's wealth was derived from two sources: fishing and the transport of cargo overseas. Both required an enormous fleet of seaworthy vessels, most of which Magister Issemar owned outright. Some, however, were owned and operated by independent captains employed in his fleet, leaving Kullen questioning just how many of those men were involved in this plot as well. Time would tell but for now, Kullen had his mark.

Despite Thanagar's magic encouraging crops to flourish, Dimvein had grown so rapidly that the farmlands, forests, and fishing grounds surrounding the city couldn't come close to sustaining her populace. Emperor Wymarc had to ship food in from across his vast Empire. According to Assidius, nearly forty percent of that was hauled in on Magister Issemar's ships.

"Which is why he poses a problem," the Seneschal had told Kullen. "As long as he controls the vessels bringing in the food, he controls the food." ·

"That makes no sense." Kullen frowned. "It's purchased by Imperial coin, simply transported on his ships."

"True." Assidius's pinched face took on a patronizing expression, as if preparing to lecture a particularly dull schoolboy. "But once the cargo is aboard his boats, Magister Issemar can simply order his less-scrupulous captains to 'lose' their portion. There are all manner of excuses: a storm forced them to lighten their load, attacks by Blood Clan pirates, ships being lost at sea, and countless more. All of which he has employed on a multitude of occasions."

"To what end?" Kullen asked. "Starving the people..." His words trailed into thought. It made both terrible and perfect sense even as he spoke. "...turns them against the Emperor who should be caring for them."

"Thereby weakening his power of rule." Assidius nodded. "And priming the people for possible revolt should the situation grow more dire. Or, should the plan to assassinate the Emperor succeed—"

"Pave the way for a new ruler to arise."

"Ah, so you're not as stupid as you look."

Kullen ignored the cut.

Things were already bad enough for much of Dimvein, and Kullen could only imagine how much the rest of the Empire had to be suffering, too. The sharp rise in population had led to over-crowded cities, where crime flourished and available resources proved scarcer with each passing day.

Despite best efforts, the Embers were far from being rebuilt, and it seemed as if the slums spread farther outward, invading the surrounding city. Imperial taxes couldn't begin to cover everything—food, infrastructure, maintaining law and order in the city, the list grew larger the more Kullen thought about it. Yet, Emperor Wymarc found his heart burdened at the thought of taxing the people further.

"And you're certain he's doing this?" Kullen had asked. "Fleecing the Emperor using his ships?"

"An asset of mine was serving aboard one of those who were reported 'lost at sea' not two months ago." Assidius's thin lips pressed into a tight line. "He returned to Dimvein just yesterday morning, beaten, starved, and half-dead, but he managed to tell me the truth before he succumbed."

Assidius suddenly stopped talking, shuffling parchments on his desk.

"Which is?" Kullen prompted when he realized the Seneschal was considering his story finished.

Assidius sighed, then looked up.

"Magister Issemar had given orders to the captain: sail to one of the southern islands and unload the cargo to the Blood Clan at a quarter of the cost. He pocketed double profit and, in the process, deprived the Emperor of valuable resources."

"If you know this," Kullen had asked, "why not move against him directly?"

"Because my asset's death deprives us of proof that will hold up in the Imperial courts." Assidius looked mightily displeased at that. "And until we obtain more evidence, we cannot bring Magister Issemar to justice publicly."

And that was why the Emperor had set Kullen to the task of infiltrating Magister Issemar's mansion. If there was documented evidence proving the man's guilt, the Emperor could use it to order Issemar's arrest. Arbiter Chuldok would delight himself prying answers from an aristocrat, pointing the Emperor to other conspirators attempting to overthrow or assassinate him.

In the absence of evidence—if Magister Issemar was clever enough to keep his fraudulent dealings unrecorded—Kullen had the Emperor's blessing to eliminate the problem. Emperor Wymarc expected to ask the same questions as Arbiter Chuldok, his methods no less cruel or fatal. The difference was in their legality. Either way, Magister Issemar's treachery would not go unpunished.

Still, as Kullen watched and waited, he couldn't help considering the source of the incriminating evidence. It was Assidius's network of spies that had uncovered Magister Issemar's deceit. The Seneschal alone knew the identities of the "assets" who brought him information of this nature—information that neither the Orkenwatch nor Imperial Scales could corroborate until after an arrest was made.

So who was to say that Assidius was actually telling the truth? Kullen had no idea why the Seneschal would want to frame Magister Issemar—some past grievance or slight—but he wouldn't put it past the man. Assidius was absolutely the sort to nurse a grudge for decades.

In all the years he'd known—and loathed—the man, Kullen hadn't once seen a hint of anything other than utter loyalty to the Emperor. Yet his position would make it all too easy to conceal any traitorous inclinations or actions. Just because he'd shown no sign of ambition, that didn't mean he possessed none.

Kullen pushed the thought aside... for now. He'd be paying Magister Issemar a late-night visit, and he'd get the particulars required to refute or corroborate Assidius's suspicion. Whether from documents found in Magister Issemar's mansion or directly from the man himself, one way or another, he would learn the truth of Issemar's guilt. Then, the man would face the Emperor's justice—or punishment at the end of Kullen's blade.

Overhanging gardens, brown with neglect, made frail awnings about the courtyard. A single path, well-trimmed and weeded, led from the open gates to the mansion's front doors. A small retainer wall lined each side, keeping the long, waist-high grass around the rest of the property at bay.

Upon the building's lower level, dead leaves crunched under the heavy boots of guards decked out in pale green and gold. They seemed oblivious to his presence and he was barely attempting to conceal himself. Kullen snorted in derision. Between the crumbling wall, the overgrown gardens, and the inattentive guards, he'd have no trouble getting at Magister Issemar. He wouldn't even need his magic.

Something wasn't right. Many things, really. But Kullen decided to wait a moment longer, to really take in the situation. The guards patrolled only around the mansion, paying no heed to the vast estate surrounding the property. Anyone could simply hop over the wall, walk through the long grass, and—

The grass!

Kullen studied it more closely. Growing up with Jarius in the palace had its benefits. Though he wasn't the Imperial scion, Kullen helped Jarius and Hadassa study more times than he cared to recall. He recognized this strain of sod. Pervectuca Torialus. Poisonous to the touch. Little spines lined each blade—invisible to the naked eye. They would cause nearly imperceptible lacerations to the flesh, allowing its toxin to be released throughout the body. It worked fast, and the cries of the victim would be more than enough to alarm the guards.

Magister Issemar had no cause to worry about anyone reaching his mansion because there was only one way to reach it: right up the paved stone driveway. Any thieves or assassins attempting to infiltrate through the estate would be rendered helpless within a minute.

Kullen's jaw muscles clenched. It looked like he'd have to consider his approach more carefully. He'd underestimated the slovenly appearance of the man and his estate, to his detriment. Beneath the disheveled façade was a cunning mind, a man cruel enough to cause widespread starvation among the populace of Dimvein in the name of destabilizing the Emperor. Kullen couldn't help wondering how many times the man had reveled in the agonized screams of would-be interlopers dying horrible deaths in the Pervectuca Torialus.

A rumble stole Kullen's attention and he spun to see a carriage in the distance, heading his direction. Tall trees lined the outer walls, and Kullen clamored up the nearest one, hiding himself in the lower branches behind a shroud of green leaves.

It wasn't long before the carriage approached the iron gates. Though they were unlocked, the weren't fully open. He watched as the side door opened and a familiar face stepped down, berating someone still inside.

Then, he waited while his driver unloaded himself and rushed to pull the gates wide.

"I'll walk from here," Magister Barridas Deckard said. "Take her home and ensure she doesn't leave the house."

"Yes, sir," the driver said with a low bow.

Magister Deckard, the man who wanted to buy out Mammy Tess. The man who Kullen held personally responsible for Prince Jarius and Princess Hadassa's deaths. The aristocrat above all others against whom Kullen wished the Emperor would wield his Black Talon.

20
Natisse

Natisse cursed. She should've stowed the lashblade but hadn't had the time while fleeing Magister Perech's guard. The sight of her bared, bloodstained weapon had fixed the Orkenwatch patrol's attention inexorably on her. Shekoth's pits, the Orken might not have even seen Garron or Uncle Ronan's weapons.

The biggest of them glared down at her, all tusks and bristling steel. She couldn't tell if he was smiling, but could imagine the joy he found in breaking up the monotony of their patrol with something as exciting as a slaughter.

And a slaughter it would be.

She held no illusions regarding their chances of surviving a battle with the Orkenwatch. The smallest of the Orken stood head and shoulders taller than even Garron. Only Jad—who was not here—could match their enormous bodies rippling with immense muscle. Their greatswords alone had to weigh as much as she, yet they wielded them with terrifying ease.

"When faced with an Orken out for your blood," Uncle Ronan had repeatedly reminded them, "you've got just one shot at survival: outrunning the bastard."

Presently, he barked, "Go!"

Natisse didn't hesitate. She burst out of the alley and sprinted down the broad avenue away from the Orkenwatch patrol. She caught a glimpse of Garron rolling on the ground, evading a huge, grasping hand and Uncle Ronan darting back the way they'd come. Splitting up bought them the best possible chance of evading pursuit—the Orken would waste precious seconds deciding which of the three to chase. Or, if she was really lucky, they'd decide it wasn't worth the effort at all.

Luck was not on her side this night.

"After him!" growled a guttural Orken voice, and heavy boot-steps thundered after her.

At least if she escaped, they'd have a hard time finding her if they thought she was a he. Her loose-fitting cloak had done its job.

She risked a single glance back and her mental curses doubled. All six were on her heels, roaring for her to "Stop, by command of the Emperor!"

Worse, in the split-second that Natisse looked at her pursuers, she recognized one of the Orken was unlike the others. This one had tusks so small they almost didn't protrude from his blackened lips, and eyes set farther apart in his head to make room for a thicker nose with wider nostrils.

Her heart sank. An Ezrasil-damned Sniffer!

All Orken had a keen sense of smell, but Sniffers had noses keener than any bloodhound. It was said they could find even the tiniest needle in the largest haystack just by identifying the scent of its metal. The moment the Sniffer got her scent, her chances of outrunning pursuit dropped to near-nonexistent. Even if she somehow managed to shake the Orken dogging her heels—not bloody likely, as the bastards were impossibly fast despite their bulk—the Sniffer would simply track her by scent.

"Come here, little lady!" he growled. Seems he could smell that too.

Natisse had only one hope of escape now. Unfortunately, she had half a mile left to go. Winded as she was, the Orken hot on her heels, she wasn't liking her odds.

Hopelessness threatened to overwhelm her. She thought once more of suffering the same fate as Ammon and Baruch. Just when they'd uncovered a bit of truth...

Damn the odds!

She gritted her teeth and fought to ignore the burning in her lungs and legs as she leaned into the run. She'd be damned if she let the Orkenwatch capture her.

She slid around a corner, using her free hand to push herself upright. She knew the alley belonged to a fruit-seller, which meant...

She shoved a stack of crates over as she ran, then another, littering the passageway. Rotten red and purple fruit spilled out everywhere, the week's leftovers tossed aside for scavengers. Behind her, she heard the Orken grunt with effort. It wouldn't hold them off long, but she only needed a bit more time.

Not bothering to slow, she used a perpendicular wall at the far opening to alter her momentum, planting one foot and then the other in a move that put her horizontal for just a few seconds. The wall run put her on course to her destination, tearing down a main thoroughfare. People shouted from open windows as she passed, likely awakened by the bedlam in the alley.

Her heart leaped.

At the far end, the houses had been built close together, and the lane narrowed to barely a foot across—just wide enough for a slim human to slip through, but not a heavily muscled Orken.

The Orken on her heels seemed to recognize her intentions, for their guttural shouts of "Stop!" and "By order of the Emperor!" redoubled. He also began to add, "Stop her!" while screaming at other citizens. The thundering of their booted feet grew louder behind her. Natisse poured on a last desperate burst of speed and threw herself through the gap between the two walls, turning at the last second. She careened through the opening, bounced off the sharp corner of a brick, tearing more skin from her left forearm.

But she was through!

Behind her, a furious roar split the night. Natisse reveled in the frustration and anger echoing in that sound. She was right; the Orken couldn't fit through that narrow gap, not weighed down as they were by—

Something flashed through the air high above Natisse, and she let out another curse. She'd gloated too soon. One of the Orken—no doubt the Sniffer—had taken to the rooftops. The other five would have no chance of catching up to her, but she was far from home-free.

She ran on, her desperation mounting with every exhausted step. She could no longer feel her legs, only the fire that consumed her muscles, and her breaths came in sharp, ragged gasps. Sweat dripped down her face and her heart hammered so furiously in her chest that it felt ready to rip free. She couldn't run much farther before her strength gave out.

Yet Natisse, stubborn as ever, refused to cede.

Just... a little... more!

Her mind fixed on her destination: she was so close. Just around the next corner, and she'd be—

"Graahh!" A bestial roar tore the thin air and an enormous figure dropped directly in front of her. Moonlight shone off heavy plate mail, a bared greatsword, and the sallow skin of the Orken barring her path.

"By order of Emperor Wymarc," the Orken growled, barely sounding winded at all, "you are under arr—"

Natisse struck out with her lashblade. It was a desperate ploy, one paramount to suicide. Attacking the Orkenwatch was a crime punishable by death. Yet it was a risk she was willing to take considering she already stood to wind up on Arbiter Chuldok's table in the Court of Justice. Either way, if she didn't escape, she was as good as dead. So she did the only thing she could: she fought.

The segmented steel whip snaked forward and slammed into the dead center of the Orken's breastplate. The sharpened tip had no chance of penetrating plate mail, but Natisse hadn't attacked to kill. Her blow struck with staggering force and sent the Orken reeling backward and to the left. Natisse leaped right, evading the Orken's grasp, and raced two quick steps along the wall before dropping back to the muddy alley floor, up and over her attacker. She was past the Orken and sprinting around the corner before the brute could give chase.

Hope once again surged within her. Ahead, she saw another narrow opening set into the street. Thick streams of foul-smelling muck flowed toward the aperture. Draining water and sewage flowed into the underground system of tunnels, pipes, and rivers that honeycombed the earth beneath Dimvein. In desperation, Natisse threw herself into a sliding, feet-first skid through the mud—and into the hole.

She dropped into darkness, landing with a splash and falling to her knees in calf-deep mire. She nearly gagged at the stench that enveloped her, and only managed to keep down the contents of her stomach with effort.

Surging to her feet, she slogged southward through the sewer tunnel, away from the street-level opening through which she'd dropped.

A furious growling echoed above. A shadow fell across the opening, and Natisse caught a glimpse of fathomless, black eyes peering down after her. It could not fit through the small hole, and the nearest access to the sewer system was a quarter-mile away. The horrific stench around her was also her salvation. The Sniffer would never be able to track her now.

She bared her teeth in a snarl and gave the Orken a one-fingered salute. Its night vision far exceeded hers, and it roared in its own guttural tongue something that had to be a curse. The

Orken's fury only lifted Natisse's spirits as she plowed through the thick, fetid darkness, leaving her pursuer far behind.

Shekoth's pits!

Her elation quickly faded, drowned beneath her exhaustion and nausea born of the all-encompassing stench. Her hands trembled and her legs wobbled beneath her. That was too bloody close.

The night had nearly ended in capture and death. Twice.

But it had been worth the risk. The discovery she'd made in the caravan yard served as proof that Jad's suspicion had been correct. The deceased Magister Perech had been working with Magister Onathus to usher slaves into Dimvein—and perhaps traffic them out of the city as well, to Ezrasil-knew where.

Thanks to tonight's efforts, she knew where to look for the poor souls. Beyond that heavy gate, somewhere at the end of the stone tunnel, she would find those men, women, and children who had been chained, herded, and branded like cattle. Perhaps even the fighting pit itself. If it was deep underground, it would explain why the Crimson Fang had yet been unable to find it.

And now, she had a name. She tested it on her tongue.

"Joakim."

21

KULLEN

Kullen did not hate easily. He loathed and despised a fair number of people—heading that list was Assidius, of course, along with half of the pompous windbags who lorded their titles of nobility over the rest of Dimvein—but he could only truly claim to *hate* a few.

Magister Deckard made the list—perhaps topped it. Given what he'd done to two of the only people Kullen had ever cared for—or who had cared for him—how could he not?

It had been Magister Deckard who burned down the Embers. What most in the Empire believed to be a "rogue dragon attack" had actually been the aristocrat's failure to bind the Ember Dragon, Golgoth, to him. Only a fair number of dragons existed and only the wealthiest of the nobility possessed them. Deckard was neither exceedingly wealthy nor abundantly popular amongst the court. Where he'd obtained the dragonblood vial, not even Assidius had been able to ascertain, but from the Seneschal's investigating, it appeared Magister Deckard had foolishly attempted the binding ritual without the knowledge to ensure its success. Golgoth had broken free of the aristocrat's control and, in her fury, set fire to the Embers. Only the timely arrival of

Thanagar, summoned by the Emperor himself, had managed to restrain the red dragon.

Formerly known as the Imperial Commons, it was Magister Deckard's fault that the Embers had been renamed—and because of him, the crowd that blamed Emperor Wymarc for the damage and death had killed Prince Jarius and Prince Hadassa in cold blood.

In the years since that fateful day, Kullen had pleaded with the Emperor to let him go after Magister Deckard a half-dozen times. On every occasion, the Emperor had forbidden it, albeit with great reluctance. The aristocrat had nearly been bankrupted by the fines levied upon him, but he'd committed no crime under Imperial law. There was no reason for the Emperor to send the Black Talon after him.

Until now, perhaps. A grim smile touched Kullen's lips. If Magister Deckard was connected to Magister Issemar's treachery, then he'd have good cause for taking the aristocrat's head from his shoulders. Or perhaps he'd just start with his eyes, tongue, fingers... No matter what, it would be poor recompense for the loss of the prince and princess, but it was the best Kullen could ask for.

Unfortunately, he had no way to know if Magister Deckard truly was an accomplice. At the moment, the aristocrat was just a visitor to Magister Issemar's estate. And, with the sun still high in the sky and shining bright, it was impossible for Kullen to get close enough to spy on the two men.

Magister Deckard strolled down the pathway, fiddling with something on his sleeve, picking at it as if he'd spilled food there. Where Issemar was a mess, Deckard was the picture of trim and orderly. He licked his thumb and went back to work worrying over the stain. His clothes—a striped tunic with matching doublet, both pale green and white in color—were gorgeous, and Kullen recognized them as designed by Madam Wellington of Wickshire.

The man might've lost a good portion of his wealth when fined over his failed bonding, but it seems he'd earned it back... somehow.

That made Kullen even more convinced he was involved in all of this.

His jaw muscles clenched as he watched Magister Issemar rise to greet and embrace Magister Deckard. The two men disappeared inside the mansion like old friends, heads together in hushed conversation.

The afternoon passed in a dull blur of heat, impatience, and anger. Kullen couldn't help dwelling on the mental image of Jarius and Hadassa's mangled bodies—he hadn't seen them, but had little trouble imagining how they'd looked after being torn open by the enraged mob.

His waiting was punctuated by Mammy Tess's words in his mind. Over and over, he replayed the conversation where she'd informed him that Magister Deckard had been attempting to pressure her into selling the Refuge. Anger grew into fury and impatience into tetchiness.

If Ezrasil existed at all, he'd cause the sun to fall early to bring judgment upon these two money-grubbing sacks of shit. But, of course, no such thing happened.

And so, Kullen waited it out.

The only activity was the return of Deckard's carriage at the gates. It seemed his opulent carriage was too large to fit upon Issemar's driveway. Not long after, the driver slumped over, asleep on the bench. Kullen considered many things in that moment—killing the man and stealing his clothing, waiting for the right time to slit Deckard's throat on their journey to his home.

All of these things were nothing but daydreams and fantasies.

Finally, Magisters Deckard and Issemar emerged from within the mansion. To Kullen's dismay, it was still two hours before sunset. Issemar accompanied Deckard to the front gates where the pair embraced, exchanging a few final words that Kullen couldn't hear. Then Magister Deckard brushed off his clothing and marched toward the carriage. His face twisted in rage at the sight of his slumbering driver. From within his pocket, he plucked something and chucked it at his sleeping driver's head. He then quickly wiped his hands on a handkerchief.

The driver startled awake, a thin line of blood pouring down the side of his face, but he didn't cry out. The sign of someone used to being abused.

The driver slid down and quickly opened the carriage door, allowing Deckard to climb in without touching a single thing.

Kullen's eyes narrowed in hatred as he watched the man's departing coach. He ached to pursue to the man, to put Magister Deckard to the cruelest questioning he could imagine. His blades could easily pry the secrets from that little piss-drinker's lips.

It took all his self-restraint to remain in place. Emperor Wymarc had given him a task and expected him to carry it out. Though the Emperor would never needle over Kullen's means of fulfilling the jobs, he would not take kindly to Kullen disobeying him and pursuing Magister Deckard. Not until he had at least a shred of proof that the man was, in fact, as traitorous as Magister Issemar was believed to be.

Which meant Kullen had to sit and wait until full dark when he could make his move; when the shadows of night hung thickest. Perhaps he would even take advantage of the opportunity to give Umbris a chance to spread his wings. It was nearing the time to summon him anyway.

But still he cast one last glance at the carriage just before it disappeared around the corner. Silently, he vowed that if Magister Issemar was even slightly guilty, Magister Deckard would be the next person he visited. And he would not come away with clean blades.

Kullen reveled in the sensation of the cool wind whipping past him, the heart-pounding rush of soaring high above Dimvein. Umbris, too, seemed to enjoy the feeling of flying free. The dragon beat his powerful wings and soared high into the night sky. Below, the city became a dark blotch with hundreds of small bright lights—the Lumenators. Umbris swooped and plummeted toward the pinpricks of light far below. There was a time when Kullen feared falling, where his stomach would do flips at such a move. But now, he trusted Umbris with anything, even his very life.

The Twilight Dragon banked right as if reading Kullen's thoughts. It was with great reluctance that Kullen directed him toward Magister Issemar's mansion. It had been far too long since he'd ridden on Umbris's back as the dragon took to the skies— their most recent flight had reminded him just how much he loved it despite being a desperate escape from the onyx sharks. But he had a mission for the Emperor. More than ever, Kullen wanted to fulfill this mission. The promise of Magister Deckard's punishment once it was uncovered that he was involved in the conspiracy spurred Kullen onward. The sooner he linked Magister Issemar to the perfidious dealings Assidius had claimed to unearth, the sooner he could hunt down Magister Deckard and string the bastard up by his bollocks.

Together, Kullen and Umbris dove, silent now, wings tucked in tight, toward Issemar's disheveled mansion grounds. Umbris came in close to the rooftop and rolled. With a tight grip on the dragon's reins, Kullen allowed himself to hang, letting go and tucking into a roll of us own as he landed. Kullen rose, offered a salute to his friend and the dragon vanished into the darkness, back to the Shadow Realm until the next time.

Kullen was inundated with a feeling of strength as Umbris left, the dragon's energy filling Kullen once more.

"*Thank you, my friend. We must do that again soon,*" Umbris rumbled in Kullen's mind. "*My wings ache to feel the wind, my eyes to behold the stars and sun once more.*"

"*Soon,*" Kullen promised. "*Just as soon as this mess is cleaned up, I'll bring you another treat to the glade and we can fly over the forest.*"

The dragon's pleasure emanated through their shared bond, bringing a smile unbidden to Kullen's lips. He could feel Umbris's emotions just as the dragon could feel his. It was one of the blessings—and, on occasion, curses—of their joining. Just as Kullen had felt Umbris's loss of his former master Inquist, Umbris had suffered deeply along with Kullen in the months following Hadassa and Jarius's deaths. Even now, Kullen felt Umbris's longing to fly free in the mortal world as if it were his own desire.

With effort, Kullen corralled his thoughts, bent his mind to the task at hand. The rooftop was a garden like the Emperor's yet nothing like the Emperor's. In fitting fashion to the rest of Issemar's grounds, it was barren and dead. Thanagar's blessed could only do so much if the garden's owner refused to do any work at all. A door stood at the east end on a four-walled structure no larger than a horse stall. As expected, a ladder waited within. Kullen crept down to the fifth floor landing, then began the search for Magister Issemar's office, study, or whatever room contained his business records.

Unlike shadow walking, Kullen's ability to see like his dragon in the dark was a passive thing. As soon as the light was gone, his eyesight became that of Umbris. For a man in his profession, it was nice to have no need for a lantern or torch. Kullen would only be spotted should he want to be.

The fifth and fourth floor were relatively clean but only because of their spartan and disused nature. The fourth floor hallway had only one small table bearing an unlit candle.

The third floor was much the same, with one room that

seemed to have been used recently but with sheets covering nearly everything inside but for a tall full-length mirror. Kullen checked each room just to be sure before venturing to the second story and found several of them to be filled with basic beds he assumed belonged to whatever kinds of help Issemar employed.

Kullen was relieved to find the aristocrat's study on the second floor. A picture window on the room's southern end offered a breathtaking view from the front of Magister Issemar's estate—once you looked past the brown and dying gardens—and beyond the walls, the sprawling mass of Dimvein. Moon-glow flooded into the room. There was something marvelous about seeing so many lights twinkling in the darkness. Kullen wasn't even sure most people knew where the Lumenators' magic came from but for Kullen, knowing that Thanagar's magic was the antithesis of Umbris's, there was a wonder about it. Those little globes shone across the city like a million stars reflecting the gleam of those filling the heavens. Kullen wasn't one for opulence or luxuries— a man of humble beginnings, he had no need of such things—but he couldn't help a momentary longing for a room with a view such as this.

The sound of determined footfalls outside the study snapped his attention away from the panorama. He slid toward a nearby armchair and dropped to one knee behind it. His dark cloak offered ample concealment, but he gripped the dragonblood vial just in case he had cause to make a hurried getaway.

The door creaked open and a glimmer of torchlight washed the room. Kullen risked a glance around the armchair. A guard in pale green and gold, Issemar's colors, stood at the doorway, a lantern held aloft. He wore a pin on his chest, a hand holding something. Kullen wasn't sure what Issemar's house crest was but it appeared to be a quill or bolt of lightning. Either way, the pin betrayed the guard's position as captain. After giving the room a cursory once-over, the Captain retreated, pulling the door shut behind him and plunging the study into moonlit darkness once more.

Kullen shook his head. He was fortunate Magister Issemar's guards were lax, but had he been lord of the house, he'd have insisted on far more thorough inspections of every nook, cranny, and crevice where an assassin or thief might lurk. One more reason to avoid luxuries, he supposed. The more one had to lose, the more one feared losing it, thus the more fiercely it had to be protected.

Rising from his hiding spot, Kullen slipped across the comfortable study toward a wooden cabinet. Each of its three drawers was adorned with bronze ornamental handles and bronze filigree at its corners. He tried the top drawer, finding it locked. Kullen, however, was not just some brutal assassin. His stiletto blade made quick work of the cheap tin mechanism. He'd never call himself a master thief, but wouldn't correct someone else for saying it either.

The drawer slid open easily. Within, he found a small fortune in gold, silver, gemstones, and scrimshaw—the currency most favored by the Blood Clan pirates.

Kullen pocketed a piece of the carved ivory. It wasn't damning in and of itself, but it lent a great deal of weight to Assidius's accusations of Magister Issemar's collusion with the Empire's enemies.

After a moment's thought, he pocketed one of Magister Issemar's purses, too. It was heavy with gold—enough to feed every child at the Refuge for five months, half a year if they were frugal with it. Mammy Tess would have good use for it.

The remaining two drawers were overflowing with parchments, documents, and scrolls bearing Magister Issemar's seal. Kullen held the papers up to the faint moonlight streaming through the picture window. A hand holding a quill, indeed. It seemed Issemar valued the pen over the ship.

Half were title deeds to the vessels Magister Issemar owned, and the remainder bills of lading, shipping manifests, and written reports from the ship captains in the aristocrat's employ.

It took Kullen half an hour to examine all of the documents. He suspected Assidius could likely find something incriminating among them, but nothing leaped out at him as overtly suspicious. Magister Issemar either had the Karmian Empire's most meticulous bookkeeper working for him, or the outwardly messy façade concealed a cunning business mind. By the time Kullen completed his examination, he found himself leaning toward the latter.

He'd dredged up nothing damning, but he was far from done with his search. Replacing all the documents exactly as he'd found them, he ran his fingertips along the sides and undersides of the drawers. A smile tugged at his lips as he felt the catch of a hidden push lever beneath the bottommost drawer. Magister Issemar may have paid for the finest craftsmanship, but Emperor Wymarc had insisted Kullen *train* with the finest craftsmen to learn their secrets in the name of protecting the Empire.

Pressing the lever unclasped a false bottom, and in the space, Kullen spotted a small, thin leather notebook. His smile grew as he thumbed through the pages. The aristocrat's meticulous record-keeping didn't just extend to his legal enterprises—within the notebook were written detailed notes of his illicit operations as well. Every sale to the Blood Clan was documented, including sums, dates, the correlating shipping manifest numbers, even the names of the captains and vessels involved.

Kullen's grin turned fierce.

"Got you, whoreson."

He was just slipping the notebook into a hidden pocket of his cloak when something outside the window caught his eye. A hooded figure was striding out of the mansion, heading toward a groom holding a saddled and bridled horse. The young boy bowed and handed the horse's reins off to the hooded figure.

Without even acknowledging the servant, the hooded figure swung up into the saddle and turned to ride away.

Yet in the second it had taken to mount, Kullen had recognized Magister Issemar's long, messy blond hair pouring out over his shoulders and the angular features of his face.

Frowning, Kullen watched the man spur his horse into motion and ride toward the front gate.

"Now, where in Ezrasil's hairy asshole are you going?"

22

NATISSE

I t was with great relief that Natisse emerged from the sewer tunnels into a small tributary stream that fed into the Talos River far south of Magister Perech's caravan yard. Her sense of smell had long since died, overwhelmed by the horrible stench of ordure and offal, but she had no doubt she reeked to the high heavens. She was all too glad for the icy water to wash away the stink.

Not even that worked. Now she was just wet and smelly.

Soaking wet, cold, and slightly cleaner, she set off for home. A short climb up the riverbank brought her to a particularly run-down section of the One Hand District, which was saying something. Though it was quiet and dark, not a soul in sight at the late midnight hour, Natisse started at every sound. A rustling here, a scrape there. Likely nothing more than stray cats and vagabonds, but after what she'd just been through, vigilance was the name of the game.

She moved cautiously through the streets, taking a circuitous route that led through twisting alleys and doubled back on her path half a dozen times. Though she doubted the Sniffer could pick up her trail, she wouldn't take any chances that someone could follow her.

Finally, satisfied she'd evaded pursuit, she headed deeper into the One Hand District's alleys the dilapidated building that housed an entrance to the Burrow. Half an hour later, she was finally unlocking the heavy door that led into their secret headquarters.

Natisse frowned at the sight of the empty common room table. Uncle Ronan and Garron should've returned by now. In the training room, she found Jad busy at training. His huge fists set the weighted punching bag swinging with every blow. He wore no shirt, giving Natisse a clear view of his impressive musculature, which rippled like steel serpents with every punch and kick. He truly could've given those Orken a run for their money.

"Jad!" she called out, hurrying toward the sweat-soaked man.

Jad spun at the sound of her voice.

"You're back?" His brow furrowed. "And the others?"

"I was going to ask you that," Natisse said, her stomach tightening. "Garron, Uncle Ronan, Leroshavé? You haven't seen any of them?"

Jad shook his head.

"Not since you left this morning." He frowned and lowered his cloth-wrapped fists. "Haven't heard from Haston or—" His eyes went wide and he staggered backward as if struck. "Shekoth's pits! Natisse, you reek!" He clapped a hand over his nose, his face twisting in disgust. "What happened?"

She recounted what they'd seen in the shipyard and caravan yard, of the slaves being herded down the ramp, and her flight from Magister Perech's guards and the Orkenwatch.

"You did good using the sewers," Jad said, nodding his approval, "but damn, Natisse, didn't you think of taking a bath before coming back?"

Natisse scowled. "Washed in the river."

"Wash again!" Jad waved her away. "Twice, if you have to.

Stink like that, the Orkenwatch will smell you from the other side of the Karmian Empire."

Natisse was about to retort, but caught a sudden whiff of her clothing.

Gagging and swearing, she squeezed her nostrils between two fingers.

"You're right; that's bad." She backed away from the big man. "I'll bathe, but you let me know the minute any of the others return, got it?"

Jad nodded. "Got it, Stinky."

Natisse shot a withering glare over her shoulder as she turned to leave the training room. Behind her, Jad muttered and waved at the air in a vain attempt to banish the foul odor.

Natisse didn't return to her quarters—no sense bringing the fetor in there—but headed straight for the bathing room. It was another of Jad's amazing ingenuities: the power of the fast-flowing Talos River fed water through copper pipes to create a convenient shower. Ice-cold, of course, but still amazingly convenient.

Stripping off her soiled clothing and cloak, Natisse stood beneath the steady stream of biting water and forced her tired muscles to relax. The fight had taken a toll on her. She bore a mess of bruises and a cut on her left leg from a blow she hadn't seen coming. Likewise, her left arm had lost a portion of skin from her elbow to her hand and stung like the water was wasps.

Her shoulders slumped and her chin touched her chest. The flight from the Orkenwatch had drained the last of her energy. Her whole body trembled with fatigue, and her stomach growled a reminder that she hadn't had more than a few bites to eat all day.

The icy chill sharpened her mind, brought clarity to her tired thoughts. She mulled over the events of the last day and night, replaying everything over and over, etching the details of Magister Onathus's shipyards and Magister Perech's caravan yard into her memory. She would spearhead a plan of attack and help Uncle Ronan devise the best strategy possible for breaching the gate that led to the underground passages.

Then the memory returned, and the shiver that ran through her body had nothing to do with the frigid water.

She was there once more, trapped in flames, surrounded by blistering heat. Yet she was not alone. The man was there—a face she couldn't remember, a cruel laugh echoing loud above the blaze. A woman's scream, too. She should've known who cried out, whose voice was familiar and yet so alien. But she didn't. She just couldn't remember.

Absentmindedly, her fingers traced the thick burn scars that marked her neck, shoulder, and upper arm. Rough, dead flesh felt like gravel beneath her fingertips. Why could she not remember that day, what she'd lost in the fire? And why had the memory returned last night of all nights? Why had the scream and the sight of the red-hot iron burning flesh brought it back?

Too many questions, and Natisse knew she would find no answers. Over the years, she'd looked—by Ezrasil, how she'd looked!—but her past remained a mystery to all. Not even Uncle Ronan knew a thing. He'd told her that he'd found her wandering along the road ten miles south of Dimvein, hollow-eyed, pale-faced, her body a mass of blistered flesh and charred clothing. He'd uncovered nothing else about her, who she'd been before... before the fire.

Natisse gritted her teeth and forced away the grim thoughts. There was no time to dwell on what lay behind her. If she looked back, if she fumbled through the darkness of her past, there was no telling what she'd find. The pain of losing Ammon and Baruch was bad enough—how much more would she suffer if she learned of parents, siblings, friends, loved ones gone in the flames? The rational part of her mind, a part as cold as the icy water trickling down her bare flesh, refused to open up old wounds. Another part of her, the quiet, scared child she had fought for so many years to leave behind, was not certain she could bear any more pain.

Finishing her shower, Natisse gathered up her weapons and padded naked and barefoot toward her quarters. Her foul-smelling clothing, she left behind—she'd dispose of them later. A job for another time.

The tunnels were empty. No sign of any of her companions yet.

She forced herself not to worry. Uncle Ronan and Garron could take care of themselves, and if anyone could sneak out of a caravan yard filled with guards, it was Leroshavé.

Still, anxiety churned in her empty stomach as she hurriedly dressed, strapped on her weapons, and headed toward the common room. Some kind soul had left a bottle of wine and two-thirds of a steak and kidney pie on a plate in the middle of the table—Natisse suspected Jad as the guilty party, but was too hungry to bother wondering. She cut the remaining meat pie in two slices and gobbled down the larger piece.

Just as she spooned the last bite into her mouth, a compact figure in dark gray clothing slid into view down the tunnel.

"Evenin'," Leroshavé said. "Better have saved some of that for me." He spoke in a casual, carefree tone, as if he'd gone for an evening stroll rather than evaded Magister Perech's guards and the Orkenwatch.

"Nah," Natisse said around a mouthful of food, trying to match his demeanor. "This bit's mine, too."

Leroshavé scowled. "Now that's just selfish, Nat. Sneakin' around all night's hungry work."

Natisse made a show of contemplating the matter, then sighed theatrically and slid the pie dish across the table to him. Leroshavé gave her a cheeky grin and tucked into the pie with only his filthy fingers.

"That's it?" Natisse asked after a moment. "Just walk back in here like nothing happened?"

"Nothin' happened," Leroshavé said, chewing loudly as he spoke. "Everyone was so busy lookin' your way, they didn't search the caravan yard. I got out of there easy as you please and paid Haston and Athelas a little visit. See what the fallout was from our visit to Magister Perech's caravan yard."

Natisse waited, but the man seemed unwilling to speak further.

"And was there fallout?" she finally pressed.

"Nothin' we saw." Leroshavé shook his head and took another too-large bite of the pie. "Quieter than a whorehouse on the Day of Celibacy."

"Good." Natisse's eyebrows knit together in contemplation. "Wait… Day of what?"

Leroshavé waved a dismissing hand. "It's a Brendoni thing. Don't worry too much on it." He wiped his mouth with the back of his hand. "You get the point though."

"Yeah, I suppose I do. Did you hear Magister Perech's guards say anything interesting? Like who they might suspect the 'thief' they chased was?"

"Like I said, I got out of there while things were still in a tizzy." Leroshavé licked cold grease from his filthy fingers, seeming not to notice or mind the dirt. "Lots of shoutin' and fury over a few dead guards, but not much more. Seems Magister Perech's death has left things a bit…" He frowned, as if unable to find the right word. "… tumultuous. Yeah, that's it. Tumultuous."

Natisse raised an eyebrow. "Heard that one from Baruch?"

"Ammon." Leroshavé grinned. "Smart man, our Ammon." His smile faded. "Shame about what happened to him. To them both."

Natisse pushed down the rising swell of emotion; she had no time for that now. "Didn't seem like anyone even cared that Perech was dead."

"Hey, time don't wait around, right? Thing is, when a Magister dies, it creates a sort of an empty place where folks can rise. Back in Brendoni, we didn't have houses like here, but I've seen wars start when Recchin's die. They're like your nobles, I guess. Close enough."

"Guess people are people everywhere, huh?"

"People are people."

"Any idea who's running the caravan yard in Magister Perech's name?"

"Not a clue, but I can find out." Leroshavé stared mournfully down at the now-empty pie dish, then glanced toward the bottle of wine. "Though pryin' for information tends to be thirsty work."

Natisse growled low in her throat, but shoved the bottle toward the man.

"Many thanks!" Leroshavé scooped up the drink with a grin and stood. "I'll catch a few hours of sleep, then get myself over to the caravan yard and see what I can scope out. A few marks in the right hands—or a few drinks down the right gullets—might loosen some tongues."

"Good." Natisse nodded and sat back in her chair. "If someone's running things for Magister Perech, it might be another connection to the slave operations in Dimvein."

"Aye, so it'll be." Leroshavé took a long swig from the bottle and strode away from the common room, heading toward his quarters.

Wine-less and still hungry, Natisse pondered her conversation. Magister Perech's death wouldn't necessarily put an end to his ventures. Most businesses would simply function as normal, even with their benefactor deceased. It was possible that the caravans would continue traveling to and from Dimvein uninterrupted. Someone at the yard—some foreman or head guard or boss—would be running the day-to-day for Magister Perech anyways. Perhaps even the Joakim the guardsman had mentioned.

But more likely, someone would take over the dead aristocrat's enterprises. Leroshavé was right about one thing, a war could start for less. Magister Perech had left no heir, no one to whom his fortune and estate would be passed. People would scramble for that position. Or all his holdings could wind up in the hands of Emperor Wymarc. Or, if Magister Perech was colluding with other noblemen as the Crimson Fang suspected, he might've left legal provision to pass it onto someone else. Someone he trusted, no doubt another member of the nobility. Magister Onathus, perhaps? Magister Estéfar was dead, and they had identified no other conspirators.

A thought struck her. Who had taken over Magister Estéfar's estates and holdings? The aristocrat had been dead a few days now, which meant the legal proceedings passing everything on to his heir—or back into the Emperor's hands—would be complete. She had no idea; it wasn't her area of expertise, but she knew someone who would be well-suited to find out.

Pushing away from the table, she stood, bones and muscles aching for a long sleep. Jad had doubtless finished his training by now, which meant he'd either be bathing, in the War Room, or with Sparrow. If the big man didn't have the answers to her questions, she could always send Sparrow to run a message to Dalash. The prim man would remain in his post at the deceased Magister Perech's household a few days more, just long enough to avoid suspicion. He'd be ideally positioned to obtain the information she needed.

Natisse couldn't help glancing toward the Burrow's front entrance. Where were Uncle Ronan and Garron? The Orkenwatch had been pursuing her, and she'd been forced to take the long way back via the sewers and the Embers. They ought to have been here by now.

Once again, she shoved down fear. They could take care of themselves. However, doubt continued to nag at the back of her mind. She couldn't put her finger on precisely what, yet she knew without a shadow of a doubt, something was wrong. Something was very wrong.

She'd taken two steps down the tunnel toward the bathing room when the sound of the gate's locks echoed behind her. She spun around, eyes darting toward the opening gate. Torchlight spilled into the passage, illuminating two figures.

The shorter of the two was Uncle Ronan, his face slick with sweat and dark with worry. He had an arm around Garron's waist, and the taller, rangy man leaned heavily on his companion.

Natisse's heart skipped a beat as she saw the dark, crimson blood spattering Uncle Ronan's chest and Garron's entire left side.

23

KULLEN

Kullen tore through the darkness of Magister Issemar's mansion, cloak flapping loosely behind him, boots near-silent on the plush carpeting. He retraced his steps to the stairs at a dead run and charged up to the fifth floor. Even as he took the ladder to the rooftop three rungs at a time, he reached beneath his cloak and jammed his thumb onto the tip of the dragonblood vial.

Umbris, I have need of you, he told the dragon through their mental bond. *Looks like you'll get to fly again sooner than either of us expected.*

Energy evacuated Kullen with such force it nearly caused him to stumble. Accustomed as he was to the sensation, there was no getting used to it. There was no conquering it. One moment, the rooftop was empty; the next, the shadows seemed to ripple and distort, reality twisting in a way that set Kullen's stomach lurching. Umbris's sleek, shimmering, purple-and-black-scaled form materialized in front of him, stepping out of thin air. The dragon's wings were already extended, its huge legs bunched beneath him. Umbris could sense his hurry through their connection, and he was ready to vault high into the night.

Kullen sprinted the twenty feet to where the dragon crouched and, with a single powerful push, leaped onto his friend where wing joined body. No sooner had he slid into his usual place on Umbris's back, than the dragon's mighty legs propelled them both upward with such force Kullen had to brace himself to avoid his head slamming into the beast's scaled neck.

"*Easy there!*" He told the dragon.

"*Your mind does not scream 'easy' anything, Kullen Bloodsworn,*" Umbris retorted. "*Within you is an urgency I have rarely sensed in you.*"

Kullen summoned to his mind the image of the hooded Magister Issemar riding through his manor's front gate.

"*We must not lose him.*"

"*We shall not,*" Umbris said, his mental tone somber as his huge wings beat at the air, gaining altitude. Soon, they were flying high over the estate, soaring through clouds in pursuit of the figure riding through the darkened streets below. "*What is so important about this man?*"

"*He is a threat to my Honorsworn,*" Kullen told the dragon.

Though not as strong as the bond between man and dragon, humans had their own kinds of bonds and dragons could understand them. *Bloodsworn*, Umbris called Kullen. It was a term of endearment or affection for his human master. It had been a simple step from there to *Honorsworn*, a term Kullen had created to describe his relationship to Emperor Wymarc in a way Umbris would easily understand.

"*Why do we not simply destroy him if he poses such a threat?*" the dragon asked. "*He would not taste as fine as smoked pork shoulder, but he will make an adequate morsel. Him, and the horse that bears him.*"

Kullen had to admit it was an appealing image. No need to get his hands dirty when he could just let Umbris devour the man in a single bite. There' be no trace of evidence to pin the crime on Kullen. It would be over in a heartbeat.

"*We will destroy him, soon,*" Kullen replied, mentally filing it away as an option for later, once he had what he needed from Magister Issemar. *"But, right now, it is possible that he could lead us toward others who would harm my Honorsworn. I must learn more about the enemies that lurk in the darkness."*

"Darkness is our domain," Umbris said. *"The shadow, our realm. No enemy shall hide long."*

Kullen considered explaining that his use of the word darkness was metaphorical, but instead, just said, *"Indeed."*

So high above the city, Kullen could cover great distances and no one would even hear Umbris's huge, flapping wings. Not even the Emperor's Lumenators could send light beyond the night's clouds. Even if they were to dive lower, the dragon's dark scales blended into the night, giving credence to the name Twilight Dragon.

Yet though they flew hundreds of yards above the city, Kullen was not flying blind. Through their bond, Umbris shared what his keen eyes beheld. The dragon had a clear view of the figure that, to Kullen, was little more than an ant-sized silhouette moving far below. Umbris could see in the dark as if it were day—but with him no longer in the Shadow Realm, Kullen could not. It felt as if Kullen had gone blind, but he trusted his dragon to guide them and knew he had a clear view of Issemar.

When Issemar turned, so too did Umbris. The man followed the Talos River, a ribbon of glistening silk far below and led them to a nondescript building that to any onlooker would appear as any other factory-type structure in the Western Docks. And like any other, it was in quite the state of disrepair. The only thing of note was a pergola in the side yard, choking vines crawling all over it.

"Lower us over there," Kullen told Umbris, setting his eyes upon another, more stable-looking building not far off.

"As you wish."

Kullen always wondered at how graceful Umbris could be. They landed, together, on a nearby rooftop.

"Thank you again, friend," he told the dragon.

Umbris lowered his head in a gesture Kullen had come to know well. He reached up and patted the dragon's head before dismissing the beast back to the Shadow Realm.

Kullen crouched and neared the far edge of the rooftop, hunkering down to watch.

"What are you doing here, you stain?" he whispered, watching as Magister Issemar dismounted in front of the building.

He didn't have to wait long. Within a few seconds, two men appear from the shadows, presumably from a door Kullen couldn't see from his vantage point. They approached a closed iron gate. So too did Magister Issemar. It was quiet and their voices carried on the air, but they were still too soft for Kullen to understand the words, just a series of hisses and pops.

Whatever Magister Issemar said, however, seemed to be please them. They pulled the gate open and ushered the hooded aristocrat inside. One, a flabby man with a tunic many sizes too small, took the horse and tied him off to await its owner's exit. The other, a dark-skinned man—perhaps a Brendoni—led Issemar into the darkness.

The building appeared to have two stories, though it might have just had a tall ceiling—a third if it had a basement like many of the properties in this district. Unlike the flat rooftop Kullen now spied from, this one had a slanted top, red tiles cascading down the sharp incline. A stovepipe or chimney stuck up from the western side and what appeared to be a sky light spread across the other.

Kullen unclasped his cloak and let it fall around his feet, leaving Issemar's stolen notebook and other valuable items he wouldn't desire to lose within the Shadow Realm.

Umbris had already granted him full rein of his powers so all that was left was the uncomfortable slide into the dark. With a deep breath, Kullen shifted into the in-between, finding shadows as if by instinct. His incorporeal form jumped through nothingness until he crouched on the rooftop. Releasing his hold of the bloodsurge, Kullen's body snapped back to the mortal realm and his insides curdled. Pain coursed through him but he held steady long enough for it to pass.

Now that he was there, it became evident that what he'd thought was a skylight was nothing more than a giant hole in the roof, barely being held together by crisscrossing beams. From here, he could see that it was one story, tall ceiling, mostly barren.

Planted on one of the crossbeams, he caught a quick glimpse of the aristocrat's hooded cloak vanishing into a short corridor as the exterior door closed. A guard wearing an unfamiliar insignia and colors stood there, weapons sheathed but a visible wariness painted his posture and expression.

What is this place? Kullen wondered. *And what is Magister Issemar—*

A series of sharp cracks sounded and Kullen suddenly found himself falling. The beam, unable to bear his weight, shattered beneath him.

24
NATISSE

"Uncle Ronan!" The shout burst from Natisse's lips unbidden. All other thoughts fled from her mind as she sprinted up the hall toward the two blood-soaked men.

"Help me here!" Uncle Ronan called back. "We need to get him to Jad, now!"

Natisse's breaths froze in her lungs as she spotted the source of all the blood. Garron's left arm had been severed just below the shoulder. Whatever had cut off the limb had continued on to carve a deep gash into his left side, doubtless crushing bone on its path. Garron's face was deathly white, his breathing shallow, and his eyelids fluttered like moth wings but there was no fire behind them. Natisse reached the rangy man just in time to catch him as he fell, his last reserves of energy depleted.

"Got him!" Natisse struggled beneath Garron's weight. Even with Uncle Ronan's help, the man was damned heavy, all corded muscle and lanky limbs. He hung limp in their arms, his head lolling against his chest. "What the hell happened?"

"The Orkenwatch," Uncle Ronan snarled, teeth clenched

against fatigue. "Or at least that's what he told me when I found him bleeding out half a mile from where we split up."

Natisse sucked in a breath. "How? They were chasing me!"

"I don't know," Uncle Ronan shook his head. "But he's passed out four times already. I barely managed to get him here on his feet. He needs Jad now, or he's going to bleed out."

Together, they hauled the unconscious Garron down the hall and into the common room.

"On the table," Uncle Ronan ordered.

Natisse helped Uncle Ronan lower Garron's limp form onto the table where only moments earlier she'd sat eating.

"Go, fetch Jad!" Uncle Ronan moved around to Garron's side, stripped off his blue tunic that was now dark and colorless with Garron's blood, and pressed it against the stump of Garron's left arm.

For a moment, Natisse stood transfixed, her eyes locked on Uncle Ronan's back. She'd never seen him shirtless before, never seen the litter of knotted, tangled scars that striped his back and sides. The sight sent a chill down her spine—what torments had he suffered, and at whose hands?

"Natisse, now!" Uncle Ronan's voice snapped her out of her thoughts.

She spun away, mad at herself for entertaining such distractions during such a dire time. She simply couldn't help it. All of this was... They'd been together so many years and had suffered more deaths and injuries in these past days and weeks than all of those combined. Who was next? Her? Uncle Ronan? Dear, sweet Sparrow?

She raced toward the intersection that led to the training room and private quarters where she hoped to find Jad.

She shouted his name. Then again. "Jad, where are you?"

Jad appeared from Sparrow's room. "What is—"

"Garron!" Natisse said, racing toward him. "He's hurt. Bad."

Jad's face darkened. "How bad?"

"He—" Natisse cut off as Sparrow emerged from the room behind Jad. The young girl's eyes were no longer rimmed red, but she appeared even more gaunt and haggard than after Ammon's death. Natisse swallowed hard. Sparrow had lost enough, seen death enough.

"It's not good," she said, her voice grim. "He's lost a lot of blood."

Nodding, Jad rushed past Natisse toward the common room. Sparrow made to follow, but Natisse stepped in the young girl's path.

"No, Sparrow," she said, her voice firm but kind, "you don't want to see it. It's…" She shook her head. "Trust me on this. You're better off—"

"No, I'm not!" Sparrow's unnaturally high-pitched voice cracked like a whip. "I'm not just some kid—not anymore." She drew herself up to her full height—still nearly a head shorter than Natisse. "I'm fifteen now. And I've seen the same things you all have. I was there…" her voice cracked and Natisse could see the girl's anger rise. "I was there in the Court of Justice to see what they did to Ammon."

Natisse's gut clenched. That was one spectacle she wished she'd missed.

"I know you were, Sparrow," she began, "and I know you're not just—"

"Good! Then, right now, if Garron's in bad shape, I have to go." Fire blazed in the young girl's eyes. "Jad's been teaching me all his healer tricks for weeks now. I can probably help him more than any of you." She evaded Natisse's outstretched hand. "I'm going to help him."

Natisse didn't try to stop the young girl again. Sparrow was right—she'd seen and endured more than most of the Crimson Fang ever knew. Her life on the streets had been hard on the best of days. But it was more than that. Until that moment, Natisse had thought of Sparrow as just a kid. She was barely fifteen, for

Ezrasil's sake! Natisse couldn't imagine anyone that young enduring everything the Fang had faced—anyone beside her, that was.

Yet Sparrow's response now proved there was steel at her core, the same strength of spirit that drove Natisse onward every day. Perhaps it was time she changed her perception of Sparrow. The girl might not have the ice that coursed through Natisse's veins, but a fire burned in her belly.

Natisse just hoped that would be enough to keep Sparrow alive.

Striding back to the common room, it felt like stepping into an abattoir. Blood covered the table beneath Garron, spilling over the edge like a waterfall and staining the chairs, the floor, Jad, Uncle Ronan, and Sparrow. The two men wrestled with cloths in a desperate effort to stanch the bleeding from the large artery in Garron's severed arm. Sparrow dug into one of the common room's cabinets for the healer's bag Jad always kept close at hand.

The sight of so much blood sickened Natisse. It was Garron's blood. It was her friend lying on the table where she'd just enjoyed a meal and drink minutes earlier. The pie and wine in her stomach roiled. She swallowed hard, forcing down the acid bubbling in her throat.

Ammon. Baruch. Garron... She was losing people far too fast.

No. Garron wasn't dead. Not yet.

She tried to disconnect her mind and heart, tried to draw upon her inner well of ice-cold dispassion. She'd turned off her emotions the day Ammon died, and again the night of Baruch's death. But here, now, she couldn't ignore the claws tearing away pieces of her heart. She wasn't strong enough to feel nothing.

"Go!" Uncle Ronan's shout snapped Natisse's attention back to the table. "And hurry!"

Sparrow took off at a sprint and passed Natisse in the blink of an eye. She vanished down the corridor that led to their quarters. Natisse frowned. Where was the girl going?

A moment later, Sparrow appeared again, heading back toward them. She no longer ran, but still moved at a fast clip. In her hands, she cradled a small glass vial filled with a golden liquid that gleamed in the lamplight.

Natisse's eyebrows shot up. Gryphic Elixir? Where in Shekoth's pits had that come from?

"Hurry," Jad called without looking up from Garron's still, bleeding form. "He's fading fast!"

Sparrow quickened, moving as fast as she dared. She treated the glass bottle as if she held a delicate, priceless relic. Priceless wasn't too far off. One bottle of the magical healing remedy cost more than someone in the Embers saw in a whole year. Maybe two.

And for good reason.

"Here," Sparrow said, holding out the bottle.

"You're sure about this?" Uncle Ronan asked. His jaw muscles were clamped tight, his face pale beneath the spattering of Garron's blood. "You know we're not going to get another one of those anytime soon. This could be the last hope for a serious—"

"This is damned serious!" Jad's usually soft voice thundered off the common room's stone walls. "He's lost half the blood in his body already. Any more, and he doesn't wake up. Ever." He snatched the vial from Sparrow's hands and ripped the cork free. "This is his only chance."

Uncle Ronan hesitated, but only for a moment.

"Okay. Fine. Do it," he said, giving a sharp nod and pulling away the cloths he'd been using to stanch the blood-flow..

Jad emptied half the contents of the vial over Garron's wounds, then poured the rest down the man's throat. Garron coughed weakly but managed to swallow the gleaming gold liquid.

Nothing happened for a moment. There was a palpable disap-pointment that overtook everyone but Jad, as if he knew something no one else did. And perhaps he had, for not a minute later, Sparrow gasped and took a wide step backward.

Natisse inched forward, realizing that until that moment, she hadn't allowed herself to be too close to the makeshift operating table. As she did, she heard a sound like the fizzle of a fresh-poured ale. Skin was beginning to form over Garron's wound, re-knitting, pink, raw-looking, but skin!

So too it was happening where what must've been a wide ax-head had torn into his side. The blood was no longer gushing but had slowed to a trickle. Even the color had begun to return to Garron's face.

"Incredible," Uncle Ronan said under his breath. "Miraculous even."

"What is it, though?" Sparrow asked.

Jad shook his head. "No one knows."

"Someone must," Sparrow argued.

Jad didn't respond, just hovered over Garron, two fingers pressed against the man's neck. Once satisfied with whatever test that was, he lifted Garron's eyelids. Two brown eyes darted back and forth at a dizzying pace. Jad pressed his ear to listening to Garron's heartbeat. Finally, the big man turned and gave them a nod. "He'll live."

Natisse let out the breath she hadn't realized she'd been hold-ing, and all the tension, fear, and worry drained away. Sparrow actually smiled, her eyes brightening. The girl laughed and cried simultaneously, a bubble of spit forming and popping on her lips. Jad turned and put an arm around her, pulling her in tight.

Uncle Ronan's face remained hard, but his shoulders relaxed a fraction.

"Good." He looked down, and for the first time, seemed to realize that he wore no shirt and his chest, arms, and face were splashed with blood. "You've got him?"

Jad nodded. "Go." He squeezed Sparrow's shoulder. "We've got him."

Sparrow's face glowed, and for a moment, Natisse caught a glimpse of who the young girl might've been had her life been kinder.

With a grunt, Uncle Ronan strode from the common room. Natisse hurried on his heels. She allowed herself only a moment to wonder again at the scars crisscrossing his back, but quickly pushed the thought aside.

"Where did you find him?" she asked. "And what made you go back?"

"Instinct," Uncle Ronan said without glancing her way. "After I was sure I got clear, I remembered I heard a man's cry mingled with the Orken shouts. I had to be sure, so I followed the route I figured he'd take to get here. Good thing I did."

"Good thing, indeed." A shiver ran down Natisse's spine. What if Uncle Ronan hadn't followed his instinct and gone back to search? Garron might've been found in the morning by some urchin boy, lying dead in some back alley.

Uncle Ronan stopped at the intersection and rounded on her.

"Look, I know it's a lot to ask, but I need to ask it anyway." The intensity in his voice and the harshness of his expression surprised Natisse almost as much as the abrupt halt. "Until I know Garron's really going to pull through, I need to stay here. That means I need you to get back to Athelas and Haston. Let them know what we found, and what happened."

Natisse opened her mouth to speak, but Uncle Ronan cut her off.

"You're exhausted, I know. You've had a rough few days, but right now you're the only able-bodied fighter still standing." He ran a hand through his steel-gray hair, and the lines on his face deepened, as if he'd aged a decade in the last hour. "I don't want to risk you, but the others—"

"Uncle Ronan." Natisse laid a hand on his solidly muscled arm. "I was only going to say of course I'll go. We've finally found our first solid lead on the location of the slaves. Whatever it takes to see this through, I'll do it." She straightened. "Blood for blood, right?."

Relief washed across Uncle Ronan's face, and he nodded.

"Blood for blood." His voice grew heavy, but he managed a tired smile. "Thank you, Natisse. Truly. I don't know where we'd be had I not found you all those years ago."

She smiled.

As Uncle Ronan turned to walk away, she stopped him.

"Uncle Ronan…"

He stopped and turned.

"That elixir," she said meekly. "Where did we get it?"

Something cold passed over the old man's face for just a brief second—so short, Natisse convinced herself she'd imagined it. He shook his head…

"Something Ammon found many years ago on one of his excursions."

The mention of Ammon's explained Uncle Ronan's discomfort, for she felt it, too.

"Oh."

"That all?" Uncle Ronan asked.

"Well…"

"What is it?"

"It's just… that stuff is worth an absolute fortune. We could have funded this whole operation for years to come. You could have sold it."

Uncle Ronan stepped toward her, looked beyond her at the now-closed door behind which Garron was recovering.

"Aren't you glad I didn't?"

At that, he strode off down the hall. Natisse got one last glimpse of his scarred back and bloodstained hands before he vanished into his quarters.

25

KULLEN

K ullen had just a split second to react as the beam crumbled beneath him. He had no hope of vaulting to another, sturdier beam—the nearest support was five yards away—and he doubted he'd reach his dragonblood vial in time to employ his magic to shadow-slide to safety. The only thing he could do was leap off the collapsing beam in a controlled descent toward the floor two stories below.

He hit the ground in a forward roll that diminished the impact of his fall—just enough that he didn't break any bones. A painful twinge ran up his legs, and his shoulder struck the floor with jarring force. Yet he rose smoothly to his feet a heartbeat after the collapsed roof beams crashed into the floor behind him.

The cacophony immediately arrested the attention of the guard standing by the door through which Magister Issemar had vanished.

"Oi! What's there!" the man barked. "You! Stop!"

It was an odd thing to say to a man barely standing in rubble, making no effort to move.

The man stomped toward Kullen, and his eyes fixed on the

figure in the dark clothing who'd seemingly dropped from the sky. His hand dropped toward the sword at his belt.

"What are you doing here? Where'd you come from?"

His sword was drawn now, but Kullen posed little threat as he was, hand pressed firmly against his side, doubled over.

"You're under arrest for breaking and—"

Kullen never gave him a chance to finish the sentence. He crossed the remaining short distance to the man in a single leap and drove the knife's edge of his flattened hand into the guard's throat. Cartilage collapsed beneath the blow, crushing the windpipe. The guard staggered back, hands flying up to his ruined throat. The sword clattered to the ground and with a single, smooth motion, Kullen brought his boot up and around to land a spinning hook kick into the man's temple. His heel struck in the exact location for which he'd been aiming, and the guard's neck gave a sickening snap. Instantly, the man sagged, limp as a fish and already dead.

Knowing the shouts might've aroused other guards, Kullen seized the body and hurled it back toward the roof beams that lay collapsed on the floor. It flopped into a boneless heap a few feet away from the nearest chunk of rotted wood.

Without hesitation, Kullen reached beneath his tunic and jammed his thumb onto the dragonblood vial. The world veritably froze around him. As he shifted into shadow and darkness, he spotted a door opening and two more guards spilling out.

With a thought, he darted from his place within the building back up to the rooftop and then across the street to the spot where Umbris had dropped him only minutes ago.

Then, returning to his physical form, he allowed himself to crumple, gasping, a new weight on his muscles. There were limits to bloodsurging. Though he hadn't dared test it, he knew. Having called upon the Shadow Realm and Umbris's power so many times in the space of only a few minutes, Kullen could feel himself unraveling. He'd told himself that he would suffer the same fate that Umbris would if he and Kullen hadn't bound one to another so many years ago. If he used too much magic too quickly without proper rest, he believed he would wind up trapped with Umbris in the Shadow Realm with no hope of return. He would become one of *them.* A creature of nothingness, as cold as the void itself.

He had no proof of this, but something within him, some instinct made it true in his mind. Even now, the multiple blood-surges took a toll on him. He lay on the rooftop, grateful it was solid, and remained there for long minutes, breathing heavily and struggling to regain control of his racing pulse.

Shouts from across the street drew his attention back to the building he'd just barely escaped. Rising, shifting his position to peer over the rooftop, he spotted the same two guards now running through the front door in answer to the outcry from within as if no time at all had past. The crumbling walls obstructed his view of the building's interior, and the distance was too great to make out what the guards were saying. But he suspected—in truth, he hoped—they were seeing what he'd wanted them to.

Killing the guard with bladed weapons would have been much easier, but no one would believe the guard had cut his own throat or stabbed himself in the chest. The beams that had nearly been Kullen's undoing were also a golden opportunity. Anyone who found a man with a broken neck next to the pile would be hard-pressed to suspect the presence of an assassin in a guarded building, not when there was such a convenient answer handy. The guards would, hopefully, write it off as sheer rotten luck and ill timing on their companion's part. He'd simply been walking or standing in the wrong place at the worst possible time.

Kullen let out a shaky breath and reached for his cloak, which remained where he'd left it moments earlier. From inside one of its many pockets, he produced a small packet of twine-wrapped wax paper. Untying it, he opened the packet to reveal five knuckle-sized capsules made of a gelatinous purple substance. He hadn't bothered to ask the alchemist for their exact contents—with alchemy, it was sometimes better not knowing what odd and exotic ingredients were mixed into remedies—but popped one into his mouth without hesitation.

Instantly, a torrent of energy surged through him. It was an artificial stimulus, he knew. The capsules did not provide him with external energy like food or drink, but simply diminished the fatigue sensations in his brain while increasing his body's natural adrenaline production. The rush was potent and instantaneous, but when he came down within an hour or two, the crash would leave him even more drained.

He rewrapped the packet and slid it back into its proper pocket, then donned the cloak once more. Every nerve in his body seemed to be vibrating, his muscles quivering with the fire that channeled through him. His heartbeat sped until it felt as if it was hammering in his throat and screaming in his ears.

The benefit and detriment of the stim-pops walked hand in hand. They made him feel invincible, which made him reckless. During the time the synthetic energy coursed through him, he could fight the entire Imperial army single-handed—or at least thought he could. That was the danger. Just one of the strange effects of whatever stimulants had been mixed into the alchemical remedy.

It often seemed waiting was chief amongst Kullen's duties as the Black Talon.

After some time, the doors reopened and out stepped Magister Issemar himself. He turned back as he walked, engaged in conversation with another figure who stood just inside the doorway. Kullen could faintly hear a man's voice, though, once again, not what was said between them. Shifting to a better vantage, he tried to gain a view of the man speaking to Magister Issemar, but—whether by intent or sheer luck—he was positioned too far inside the building for Kullen to get a clear look. He caught only the flare of a well-tailored cloak as what could only be another aristocrat turned away from Magister Issemar and vanished inside the building.

Kullen ground his teeth.

That man, whoever in Shekoth's depths he was, might well have been another co-conspirator in whatever nefarious enterprise had brought Magister Issemar to this seemingly abandoned building. Had Kullen been able to get a good look, he might have identified another aristocrat for elimination. Or, at the very least, someone else for Assidius to dig into for potential treachery. Ezrasil knew there had been far too many duplicitous cunts involved in the plot against the Emperor. Magisters Iltari, Taradan, and Issemar were just the latest in a long succession of traitors that Kullen had dispatched in the name of safeguarding the Empire.

The door clattered shut behind the mystery man, and Magister Issemar marched across the side yard toward his horse, temporarily disappearing beneath the pagoda before his head could be seen once again above the wall. It was only when he swung up into the saddle that Kullen had the presence of mind to think his next course of action.

Magister Issemar would be riding away from this place, almost certainly back toward his mansion. If Kullen could get ahead of him, set a trap, he could take the aristocrat by surprise, disarm him of weapons and, more importantly, his dragonblood vial. Issermar would lose whatever advantage his filthy grounds and their poisonous grasses granted, and Kullen would have the man at his mercy. A few minutes in a dark, deserted alley was all Kullen would need to extract answers from the man. And should Magister Issemar prove difficult, he wouldn't be the first corpse Kullen had disposed of within Umbris's chasm in the Wild Grove Forest.

Magister Issemar's horse trotted at a leisurely pace away from the meeting place. The man clicked his tongue and off he went down the street heading south. Kullen knew that street well. Pawn May Avenue ran straight for two hundred feet, then narrowed and curved to the west. He'd practically grown up here, the Refuge only a few blocks away. The moment Magister Issemar made that turn, he'd be out of sight—and earshot—of the guards. Likewise, there were no Lumenators for miles. Why would anyone wish for a place like this to be better seen, after all?

All of these things came together to make this the perfect time and place for Kullen to make his move.

He made certain the daggers in his arm bracers were still touching his skin—the only way they'd shadow-slide with him— and did the same with his boot knives and those concealed inside his belt. He had no need of a sword for this work.

Bare-handed, he grasped his cloak, ensuring it and all its possessions would likewise travel with him. He fixed his eyes on the shadows of the adjacent rooftop just north of the spot where the road curved west, and reached for his dragonblood vial and summoned the magic.

Weightless, he was launched forward as if upon a gust of heavy winds. In an instant, he was in place and in position to accost Magister Issemar. One more jump brought him to rest on street level under the dark cover of the goods store's front porch. Emerging from the Shadow Realm was a battle—he could feel the icy claws sinking into his soul, the whispering threads of nothingness tightening about him—but he managed. Crouching, he waited, glad for a moment to recover from the magical exertion.

He readied a throwing knife, fingering the sharp blade with anticipation. He envisioned the cold steel carving a gash through the man's shoulder, his horse rearing and tossing him into the muddy street.

On second thought, he sheathed the knife and drew a long-bladed dagger with a heavy metal pommel. A solid throw and the impact of that pommel to the side of Magister Issemar's head would knock the prick from his saddle. Then it could be said that he'd had a simple accident.

Besides, Kullen would have plenty of time to slice and dice the man should such things prove necessary.

Knots tightened in his shoulders, and the stim-pop in his veins set his nerves ablaze.

It was quiet but for Issemar's hooves *clap-clapping* and splashing small puddles, growing louder. Kullen's heartbeat fell into rhythm with the sound. These were the moments he lived for.

Suddenly, a cry of "Get him!" echoed around the corner, and Kullen heard booted feet, the rasp of weapons being drawn, and a panicked, terrified screech from Magister Issemar.

26

NATISSE

Exhaustion dragged heavy on Natisse's limbs with every step through Heroes Row. She'd long since stopped being impressed by the thirty-foot tall statues of men and women like Trent "The Titan" Timball, or Marien the Maiden. The main avenue was lined with many such effigies. One look at Dimvein in its present state was enough to know the age of heroes was gone.

The noonday sun shone down hot and so bright it stung her eyes, turned her eyelids heavy. She couldn't remember the last time she'd slept—before Magister Perech's party, perhaps? That was two days ago. She needed to rest, if only for a few hours.

But not yet. Not until after she carried out Uncle Ronan's orders. First, she'd hear what Athelas and Haston had to report after nearly a full day reconnoitering Magister Onathus's shipyards. Then she'd close her eyes.

"Hot, fiery Fenish Fish Whips!" cried one of a hundred hawkers stationed between statues.

Natisse hadn't just stopped being impressed by the place where people visited from all over the Karmian Empire; she'd truly grown to detest it.

"You'd look great in these," said a woman, drawing close to Natisse, stopping her dead in her tracks. The woman held a set of gold earrings up to Natisse's ears.

"My ears would be green by supper wearing those," Natisse snarked.

"My word!" the woman cried. "These are pure—"

Natisse didn't hear another word. She just shoved past the woman. She hadn't made it ten steps before she was nearly bowled over by a young boy cursing up a storm.

She hopped back, out of his way, only to be almost knocked down again by the boy's pursuer.

An Imperial Scale shouted behind the boy, cries of "thief!" and "halt!"

No thief had ever stopped because he was told to, Natisse knew. She watched the boy scale a short wall and couldn't help but think how much of an asset someone with his youth, drive, and tenacity could be to the Fang.

What—so you could get him killed too?

The voice was cold, full of hate, and it belonged to her.

Visions of Ammon, bloody and broken on Arbiter Chuldok's table flashed followed by Baruch being shredded to pieces by onyx sharks and then crimson flames.

Natisse stopped, bent, and nearly retched.

"Oi, lady, ye a'kay?" another boy about the same age as the runner said.

Natisse turned to appraise him. He was dirty and wiry like he hadn't showered or eaten in a week.

"I'm fine," she lied.

"Ye dun't look fine."

"Ya," another chimed in just out of view enough for her to turn bodily toward him. "Ye look like shite in a barrel, pissed in."

"I'm fine. Where are your par—"

"Ye got any money?" the first asked.

"We'd be fine wit bronzers even."

"I don't have..."

Natisse spun quickly and grasped hold of a skinny arm. She came face to face with a girl who couldn't have been a day older than her first dozen years. Her hair was cropped short like a boy's cut and she wore loose, dirty clothes.

"Oi! Let'er go!"

With her other hand, Natisse pulled a small blade and pressed it against the would-be thief's neck.

"Sommun, help!" shouted one of the boys. Natisse was too distracted to care which.

Natisse quickly sheathed her knife and pulled out a small sack filled with sand and in one motion, pelted the boy hard with it in the gut. His cries for help immediately stopped.

No one moved.

"Now, you listen up," Natisse said. "I don't care who you rob out here, but it won't be me. That understood?"

Still holding the little girl's arm, she turned to look her in the eye. The girl nodded. Then Natisse looked to each of the others in turn. The one she'd winded slowly straightened while the other stared in abject horror. After a moment, they also nodded their assent.

"That hurt," the boy said.

"It was supposed to," Natisse said, releasing her grip on the girl to retrieve her sand sack.

"Why you carry that?" the girl asked, pointing to the bag.

"Sometimes," Natisse answered, "you don't want to kill." She tossed the sack in the air and snatched it on the descent. Then, taking her knife out once more, she said, "Sometimes you do."

Just then, a particularly posh looking couple strode past, not even bothering to pay attention to the scrawny kids and knife-wielding redhead. Natisse quickly swiped her blade and quickly as she'd grabbed her sand sack, she swiped up the coin pouch she'd cut clean off the man's belt and tossed it to the little girl.

"Go, all of you, have a good meal and find a safe place to sleep tonight."

The girl stared down in wonder at the pouch. Without even seeing its contents, Natisse could imagine it was filled with more marks than any of them had seen all in one place. Then, the girl looked up at the two boys and, together, they ran off. After a few seconds, the girl turned and shouted, "Thank you!"

Natisse raised a hand in reply. Shaking her head, she continued on her way.

Heroes Row emptied out into the the One Hand District, which led west to the Embers, south to High Reach, north to the Western Docks. She headed north, and it wasn't long before she reached the rooftop perch overlooking the shipyards, where Haston was on watch with Athelas dozing at his side. Beneath the ever-present layer of grime that covered his clothing and matted his long blond hair, Athelas was actually a strikingly handsome young man. Four years her junior, he was among the newest and most inexperienced of the Crimson Fang recruits, yet he'd taken to Haston's training in stealth and thievery with impressive skill. And Uncle Ronan's lessons on grabbing sleep wherever and whenever he could. That was a talent Natisse hadn't quite mastered, but Athelas appeared supremely comfortable with a faded slouch cap pulled lower over his face.

She gave a quiet whistle to alert her comrades to her presence. Haston spun toward her, hand darting toward his belt knife. Athelas, light sleeper as he was, rolled to a low knife-fighter's crouch, his weapons—two long, curved blades attached like claws to brass knuckledusters—ready for battle.

"Anything of interest?" Natisse asked nonchalantly.

Tucking his knives away, Athelas glanced to Haston. "I miss something while I was out?"

Haston shook his head and released his dagger hilt. "Nothing noteworthy in the last hour. Just before dawn, though, there was a bit of a ruckus."

"Aye," Athelas said with a nod.

"What kind of a ruckus?" Natisse asked.

"Lots of running and shouting and fussing about Ezrasil-knows-what. Not sure what bee's gotten into Magister Onathus's bonnet, but that stockade's sealed up tighter than a nun's chastity belt."

Natisse slipped across the flat rooftop and knelt at Haston's side, peering over the lip of the roof. Sure enough, the number of guards visible below had doubled—perhaps even tripled—since the previous day. There had to be close to a hundred armed and armored men guarding the shipyards.

Natisse grimaced. "Looks like last night's fuss didn't go unnoticed."

The two men fixed her with curious, quizzical glances. She recounted what had happened—their discovery of Magister Onathus's guards appearing in the caravan yard as if out of thin air, the ramp that led down into the underground tunnel, the slaves being branded, the flight from Magister Perech's guards, and the consequences of their clash with the Orkenwatch.

"Garron?" Haston asked in a gasping whisper, his eyes going wide. "He's—"

Athelas's handsome face grew grim, pale.

"Alive," Natisse reassured them. "Uncle Ronan got him to Jad in time." She didn't mention the Gryphic Elixir. Uncle Ronan might've claimed it to be something Ammon had found, but as much as she hated to admit it, she had her doubts. Uncle Ronan was no liar, but she had trouble believing Ammon would keep something like that a secret from her, and why? That would've been the find of a lifetime.

It seemed they all knew but her.

Perhaps she was just being paranoid. Of course Jad would know. As their healer, he had to. She and the big man had been firm friends since he was first recruited away from the smithy where he'd been an indentured child servant. He probably just assumed everyone knew about it. It wasn't something to discuss in day-to-day affairs. Right?

But… Sparrow knew where to find it as well.

Of course, she did. Jad had been training her.

And now she was keeping the secret from Haston and Athelas. Why?

She pushed the thought aside, cleared her throat, and said, "But his arm's… gone."

"Gone?" Athelas said, his voice weak.

Natisse nodded.

She still had a hard time believing it. Garron was no fencer like Ammon had been or a brawler like Uncle Ronan, but he still numbered among the most skilled fighters in the Crimson Fang. He'd only ever suffered minor wounds in the past, but now… "He's going to be out of commission for a while."

Haston and Athelas exchanged dire looks.

"What do you need from us?" Haston asked.

"Athelas, I need you to stay here," Natisse said, indicating the younger man with a thrust of her chin. "Keep an eye on the ship-yards. See what Magister Onathus's men do."

"Yeah," Athelas said solemnly. "Okay. Yeah. I can do that."

"Haston, you're with me," Natisse said. "We're headed to the caravan yards to see if Magister Perech's men are doubling down on security, too."

Haston nodded. "Let's go."

Natisse led the way through the winding alleyways, heading back toward the old theater where she, Uncle Ronan, Garron, and Leroshavé had spent the previous day watching the caravan yards. Uncle Ronan and Garron, in their haste to reach her side and flee the pursuing guards, hadn't had the chance to gather the knotted rope that ascended to the roof. Natisse let Haston climb first—her muscles were fatiguing, her stamina reaching its limits and she didn't want the man to see her struggle.

She was sweating heavily and laboring for breath by the time she reached the rooftop. Haston seemed not to notice or was kind enough to not mention it. He barely spared her a glance when she knelt at his side—in the same spot where she'd knelt a few hours ago.

"Looks like a damned anthill in there," Haston muttered.

As Natisse had feared, the activity within the caravan yard had increased tenfold. Patrols had been beefed up, and the strongbacks hauling cargo now carried clubs, short swords, and knives visible on their belts. A few of the caravans had departed, but those remaining in the yard had been moved closer together to form a solid barrier that guarded the northern edge of the property.

A stony smile touched Natisse's lips. She'd been pondering how best to get near that underground tunnel again. Sneaking past the stockade encircling the shipyards had been challenge enough even before the guard had been doubled. Haston hadn't mentioned anything about finding a way to slip past the defenses protecting Magister Onathus's property, so she'd written it off as a lost cause.

She'd hoped her break-in the previous night had been dismissed as nothing more than attempted theft, but evidently the deaths of five guardsmen had made whoever was now running Magister Perech's caravan yard wary.

In this case, though, wary didn't necessarily mean smart. The order to circle the wagons and carts might've been intended to heighten security, but it made for one enormous flaw. All that wood, canvas, and rope would burn easily. Magister Perech's guards and strongbacks would have their hands full keeping the caravans from going up in flames—perhaps too full to notice anyone sneaking through the shadows.

She hoped.

"Keep watch," she told Haston. "I need to close my eyes for a few hours. Haven't slept in days."

"I'll wake you when the sun's set," Haston said.

Nodding approval, Natisse settled onto her back, pulled her cloak over her face, and closed her eyes. The combination of fatigue, the stress of the previous days, and the heat of the sun above and the roof tiles beneath her lulled her to sleep almost instantly. She slept like a stone, but was awoken all too soon by a hand shaking her shoulder.

Her eyelids popped open and her hand gripped her attacker in breath's span. It was only Haston crouching over her.

"What is it?" she said, relaxing slightly and sitting up. She yawned and wiped sleep from her eyes. "Something wrong?"

True to his word, he had waited until after sundown to disturb her rest. He shook his head. Night hadn't fully descended over the city, but an evening gloom hung over everything, dulling the colors and bringing a chill to the evening.

"Anything?" she asked.

"Just more of the same," Haston muttered. "More guards, too."

Natisse rose, ignoring the stiffness in her muscles, and knelt next to Haston to peer over the roof's edge at the caravan yard. Torches illuminated every nook and cranny, driving back the shadows completely. Thankfully, there were still no Lumenators.

"Didn't think the place could fit any more," she said.

Haston laughed mirthlessly.

Magister Perech's guards had set up braziers all around the perimeter and had guards stationed at each. The strongbacks, too, seemed to be on watch. The heavily muscled men moved around in small clusters far too relaxed to be a proper patrol, but they were warm bodies and watching eyes that effectively barred her path.

She cursed.

"No way we're getting in there now. Not tonight, at least," she said.

The expense of keeping that many guards and workers on duty had to be enormous—not a cost anyone, even an aristocrat as wealthy as Magister Perech had been, would sustain for long. It might take a few days, but eventually, the security at the caravan yard would relax and Natisse could make another attempt to investigate the tunnel beyond that heavy gate.

But did she want to wait that long?

Could she?

Her gaze traveled the south, roaming across the rooftops of Dimvein. In the distance, the Lumenators' light brightened the sky. The city looked like skeletal fingers grasping at the heavens, spires and towers poking up into the sky. Her eyes fell upon the Upper Crest where each filthy mansion was worth more than every mark in the Embers, and beyond to where Thanagar perched atop the palace.

Then her gaze passed over Magister Perech's island fortress.

There was another way to find the information she wanted. She'd seen proof that Magister Onathus and Magister Perech were in league. She wouldn't know who was running Magister Perech's estate until Leroshavé did some digging—he ought to be poking around even now—but she could find another way to cut straight to the heart of the matter.

"Stay here," she told Haston. "Keep an eye out for Leroshavé. He might be coming here with valuable information that needs to get to me—and to Uncle Ronan."

Haston raised an eyebrow as she rose to a crouch. "Where are you off to?"

"How many guards does Magister Onathus have at his command?" Natisse asked.

Haston frowned. "Four, maybe five score."

"And how many of them did he have guarding the shipyards?"

"Seventy or eighty." Haston's frown deepened. Then his eyebrows shot up. "You're not going to—"

"Damned right I am!" Natisse flashed him a hard smile. "If

Magister Onathus has all his guards protecting his shipyards, he'll have only a handful on his property." She drew a dagger and twirled it in her fingers. "I'm going to pay our aristocrat friend a little visit and get him to talk, even if I have to slice the answers out of him."

27

KULLEN

Surprise rooted Kullen in place for a heartbeat. What were the odds that someone else would attack Magister Issemar in that precise moment?

Before he could think any deeper, he was on his feet and rushing down the two steps from the general store's porch toward the broad street. As much as he despised Magister Issemar, he needed the aristocrat alive long enough to answer his questions, to implicate others wrapped up in his conspiracy against the Empire. That meant he had to save the bastard's life from whoever intended to kill or abduct him.

Kullen barreled around the corner just in time to see Magister Issemar being dragged from his saddle by four burly figures clad in tunics, leather jerkins, and hooded cloaks and face masks—all of black. Two more were struggling to stop the nervous horse from panicking.

Kullen's left hand reached for one of the throwing knives tucked into his belt, drew, and hurled it in a single fluid motion. The knife shot straight through the night like a crossbow bolt and buried deep into the lower left side of one of the men wrestling with Magister Issemar, just under the ribs. The attacker screamed and released his grip on the struggling aristocrat. His hand turned scarlet as he reached for the wound and dropped to his knees.

Kullen wasted no time, rising and hurling himself at two more worrying over the frantic horse. He shouldered one away and swept the leg of the other who fell face first into the mud. Then, snatching the reins, Kullen whispered for the horse to be calm but it refused, still bucking wildly.

A shuffling told Kullen the attackers were rising now.

"Stay down, shite-lick," he warned.

Of course, the black-clad men didn't listen. They never do.

Kullen's heavy dagger carved a deep gouge across the closest one's back, cutting to the bone. Blood spattered Kullen's face and dark clothing as the assailant once again screamed. His hands and knees gave way beneath him and he fell to the street in front of the horse. Still in a frenzy, the fearful beast finished the job, its front hooves coming down and crushing the man's skull with a sickening, wet crunch.

Kullen felt a sharp jab to his left side. He spun and before he could even lock eyes with his assailant, caught a fist to the jaw. He anticipated the strike and turned his head, letting the blow graze and roll off.

The man ducked low, then charged back in. Kullen caught a glimpse of a rusted, notched long sword flashing in the faint moonlight. The blade sang, but it was no wild swing. The timing was perfectly in synch with his charge—the blow was aimed at Kullen's head, powerful enough to hack through his neck.

Now it was Kullen's turn to duck and leap back, evading a second slashing blow, and interposing his long, heavy dagger to block a third. The man in black was more skilled than his rough appearance and inferior weapon suggested. Instead of letting Kullen get close with him, get inside knife-fighting range, the attacker darted once again backward, covering his retreat with another well-aimed blow that forced Kullen, too, to backpedal.

Even with no sword of his own, Kullen was far from at the man's mercy. His left hand sprang toward his belt and drew a second knife. His underhanded throw was too fast for his opponent to perceive, and the throwing dagger lodged itself deep into the man's leg.

To his credit, there was no agonized scream. The man just yanked the blade free and tossed it to the ground. It was a foolish move, Kullen knew. With the blade embedded, it would staunch the flow of blood. Now, however, the precious fluid would run freely until the man fell slack from blood loss.

"What do you want?" Kullen demanded.

Before a response could be made, Kullen charged forward, darting into the off-balance man's guard and deflecting a desperate swing of the long sword. A vicious twist of his wrist sliced his enemy's forearm, creating another fountain. This drew a sharp gasp, but still, the man fought. He made a weak attempt at a forward thrust—one that Kullen easily evaded. Then, stepping in, Kullen swept the dagger inward across the man's neck, opening his throat to the gristle.

Blood sprayed across Kullen's face and chest, staining his clothing, but he didn't back away. Instead, he drove a vicious kick into the dying man's torso, hard enough to propel the man backward to crash into the two men kneeling next to Magister Issemar. The three went down in a tangle of flying limbs.

"What are you doing?" cried Issemar. "Stop! Help!"

"Shut up," said one of the men, his voice deep and hateful.

The one who Kullen had initially attacked then crawled toward Issemar, knife still sticking from his side. Injured as he was, he attempted to drag the aristocrat by the robes. Issemar put up no fight but to scream.

What kind of a soft, worthless man couldn't fight back against someone with a blade embedded in their side?

"You're pathetic," Kullen said to Issemar, making his move to save the fool.

For all his efforts, the wounded man stumbled and fell atop the dirty Magister and his compatriot.

"Get the hell off me!" the uninjured man shouted.

Two more steps brought Kullen to them. He lifted his boot and stomped down hard on the protruding knife hilt. The blade drove deep, piercing the man's lungs and tearing a vicious path toward his heart. The act elicited such a primal scream that the horse took off at a gallop, slipping and sliding in the muddy puddles before finally vanishing around the corner in a clatter of steel horseshoes on cobblestone.

Blood leaked from the deep wound that had lacerated his kidneys, staining the ground in a grisly crimson halo around him. Kullen bent beside him. Blood bubbled to the man's lips in an attempt to seek mercy. Kullen had none. He sliced the brigand's throat without emotion.

The man managed a one last bloody gasp before he died.

Kullen tore his dagger free and wiped it off on the dead man's robes.

The other attacker was still alive but writhing beneath his friend.

The smell of blood, the unfamiliar men, and Magister Issemar's muffled screams coming from beneath the corpse were bound to bring guards or, worse, the Orkenwatch.

Wiping the blood and sweat from his face, Kullen stood and shoved the dead man to the side.

Before Kullen took two steps, however, the last man scrambled out from beneath his dead comrade and took off at a mad dash back the way they'd come. He shouldered his way through the general store's front door and vanished, disappearing into the darkness in a moment.

Kullen broke into a run, pursuing them through the unoccupied building. His eyes adjusted instantly to the darkness, but somewhere in the distance, a door creaked open. A glimmer of moonlight shone for the briefest of moments before the same door slammed shut. The rapid back and forth between his own sight and Umbris's left him stunned.

By the time Kullen exited the building, the man was long gone. The narrow alley running behind the shop led into a half-dozen adjoining back streets. This part of the city had many such maze-like avenues that made tracking his prey all but impossible. The men who'd attacked Magister Issemar doubtless knew their way around, and they'd chosen the ambush site for that precise reason.

Clearly this wasn't just any ordinary attack. The man with the sword had been far too skilled for a street thug—reflecting on his fighting style, Kullen recognized the military-like precision to the attacks. Either he was, or once had been, a member of the Imperial army.

Kullen hurried back through the general store, pondering the implications.

Soldiers sent to capture Magister Issemar? That seemed unlikely. The Emperor had only assigned him the task that morning. If this was an official military operation, Wymarc would've informed him.

Scratch that, he thought as he reached the aristocrat.

This was no abduction. Those men were sent to kill Magister Issemar.

The filthy Magister lay still, his protests now silent. Kullen didn't bother to check for a pulse—the gaping tear in Magister Issemar's throat still leaked. Kneeling by the body, Kullen frowned down at the wound. It was far too thick and jagged to have been made by a knife. A dull dagger would've torn as much as cut, but a sharp dagger would've left clean, precise edges. This looked like the man's throat had been ripped open by a clawed weapon of some sort.

Or an actual claw.

Kullen narrowed his eyes. He cast his mind back to the encounter, trying to recall details of the two assailants who'd escaped. They'd both looked like burly men beneath their dark clothing. Yet, their faces were shrouded—he hadn't made out any identifying features that could mark them as human. Not all Orken were towering muscle-bound behemoths like Turoc. There were more than a handful small enough to pass for a large human.

But why would the Orken want Magister Issemar dead? That was a question Kullen couldn't answer.

All Orken were sworn to the Emperor's service—repayment to their savior, Emperor Wymarc's great-great-great-grandfather, Emperor Lasavic, for giving them a place when they had none.

No, the more Kullen considered it, the more likely it was that Magister Issemar had been done in by a clawed weapon. He could think of at least three off-hand—sharpened climbing claws, claw-tipped knuckledusters, even a sharply curved knife—that could inflict such a wound. Easier to believe the assailant had carried an unusual weapon than to consider the Orken were involved in an assassination not sanctioned by Emperor Wymarc.

Just to be certain, however, Kullen examined the corpses scattered around the dead aristocrat. He pulled the mask off the one who'd fallen at Magister Issemar's side. He had the look of a sellsword, a bully boy, a common thug. But a further examination revealed something of interest. Inked into his bare forearm was a tattoo Kullen recognized as belonging to Imperial military—specifically, the Fourth Imperial Infantry Regiment, as made plain by the four vines wrapped around the sword and shield insignia.

The sword-wielding assailant bore a similar tattoo—this one belonging to the Third Infantry—though something about the man had suggested more than a mere foot soldier. A non-commissioned officer, perhaps? One look at the man's hoary features and the scowl etched on his face even in death suggested a sergeant.

The other, however, bore no military tattoos, no identifying marks at all. He appeared like the usual run-of-the-mill street tough, complete with the obligatory bronze-capped truncheon, brass knuckledusters in his pocket, and brutish features.

Kullen considered the corpses. Soldiers—or, more likely, former soldiers—working for hire to kill Magister Issemar. The ambush had been well-planned and executed with precision. It had taken them less than two seconds to drag Magister Issemar from his saddle, and the aristocrat was dead less than a minute later. This was no capture attempt gone wrong. These men had come for blood.

Why? Kullen might never know. The assailants had died or fled without offering any answers. And Magister Issemar's slit throat would make it damned hard for Kullen to find out what his connection with Magister Deckard was, what he'd been doing at that dilapidated old factory, or who his fellow traitors against the Empire were.

Kullen left the bodies where they lay and moved back toward Magister Issemar. He rummaged through the man's pockets, and to his surprise, found the man's purse remained securely tied to his belt. Odd. Also still present were the rings on Magister Issemar's fingers, a golden necklace that had been snapped in the scuffle, and twin diamond-studded earrings in his right ear. Jewelry worth a small fortune, yet the assailants hadn't bothered to take them?

That all but confirmed his theory. This was an assassination like the others. Magister Issemar had been targeted for death, and executed with impressive speed. His assailants had likely known of the magic he wielded, and opened his throat before he could reach for his dragonblood vial.

The vial!

Kullen's eyes widened, and he stared down at the golden necklace once again. It lay atop his bloodstained shirt, perhaps pulled out by one of the ambushers? The necklace hadn't broken in the scuffle—one of the men had torn the dragonblood vial free, snapping the gold in the process.

A quick search of Magister Issemar's person turned up empty. No dragonblood vial.

Kullen frowned. What in Ezrasil's hairy asshole was going on? That made nine vials taken off dead noblemen in the past few weeks.

"Ey! You! Don't move!"

Speaking of Orken.

Hands bloody and surrounded by dead men, including one of nobility, Kullen stood staring at three members of the Orkenwatch.

28

NATISSE

atisse had been right: the bulk of Magister Onathus's guards were occupied protecting the shipyards. Only a handful remained to watch the gates and the sprawling estate surrounding the aristocrat's mansion.

It stood proudly at the top of the hill in the Upper Crest—which meant that, besides the palace itself, Magister Onathus's home was the highest point in all of Dimvein.

Scaling the tall wall proved a simple matter—a grappling hook and climbing spikes made short work of the ascent—and once inside Magister Onathus's property, his vast gardens offered ample shadows for concealment. She drew within fifty yards of the mansion proper before encountering her first patrol. Hunkered down behind a thick oak tree, she waited for the two lantern-carrying guards to march past, then resumed her approach in the full darkness once more.

Once again, Onathus seemed to have no Lumenators in his employ—a clear sign that he wanted his business kept secret from the Emperor.

She might not match Haston's stealth, but right now, a herd of stampeding aurochs could slip through Magister Onathus's security unnoticed. Like all noblemen, Onathus was so assured in his safety that his confidence had turned to complacency. After all, what fool would dare raise a hand against one of the most wealthy and powerful men in Dimvein? Dispatching the bulk of his household guards to secure his business holdings had left him utterly vulnerable here.

With a grim smile, Natisse slid into the shadows of the towering three-story mansion. The staggered stone construction made for easy climbing to a third-floor balcony, which opened into a suite of rooms so opulently decorated that they could only belong to the lord of the house.

An antique armoire sat in one corner, topped with a gold and pearl vase with overhanging greenery. Natisse could only imagine how the servants kept it watered. Many taxidermied fish adorned his walls, including one the size of a small whale hanging over a tall couch made of polished leather. The carpet was plush like the pelts of a hundred wolves were strewn together and laid corner to corner.

A dresser against the far wall twinkled with jewelry. Onathus had always been a flashy man.

The place looked fit for a king.

She did her best to ignore the ornamentations. Her mission tonight demanded information first, and stealing to feed the Embers second. Besides, she would have a damned hard time moving in silence if she stuffed her pockets with coin, gold trinkets, or jewelry.

Her soft-soled boots made not a sound on the carpet as she approached the huge double doors leading into what she suspected to be a bedchamber. Sure enough, the sound of loud snoring echoed even through the solid wood. She pulled the door open just wide enough to slip through and into the room beyond, then shut it silently behind her.

Pale moonlight spilled through a floor-to-ceiling window at the far end of the room beyond which could be seen dozens of

Lumenators globes. The chamber was even more opulent and lavish than last. Magister Onathus slept on a massive four-poster canopy bed larger than Natisse's underground quarters. Silk hung from each corner, draping like dragon wings. A crystal chandelier hung at its center, light refracting in a prism all over the room.

Natisse let out a silent breath. Magister Onathus was unmarried—much to the delight of the ladies of the Karmian Empire, both eligible and... ineligible. The man had a reputation for being a lothario, a connoisseur of Dimvein's brothels, particularly those that catered to a clientele with exotic and bizarre tastes. Natisse had half-feared she would find the bed empty or, perhaps worse, occupied by one or more "companions" Magister Onathus had invited to his mansion.

But Ezrasil had smiled on her. Perhaps fear for his business had driven all thoughts of pleasure from Magister Onathus's mind, or he'd simply spent his energy and returned home to rest. Whatever the case, he was alone and vulnerable.

As vulnerable as a man of his power can be.

The Magister was a giant of a man, easily seven feet tall with a barrel chest, auroch-like shoulders, and beefy arms thicker than Natisse's waist. Natisse suspected he could outmatch even Jad in size and sheer brawn—and that was before accounting for his foul magic. It was said that his powers imbued him with the strength of ten men.

Natisse, however, had come prepared to deal with the man. She slipped lightly up to the bedside, drawing a stiletto as she moved. The blade was six inches long and half an inch thick, razor-sharp and perfect for slicing flesh. Clamping a hand down over Magister Onathus' mouth, she pressed the tip of the dagger into the skin just beneath his right eye.

"Make a sound or move a muscle, and you meet Ezrasil!" Natisse snarled quietly.

Magister Onathus's body jerked instinctively as his eyes burst open. As a result, Natisse's dagger sliced a shallow cut into his flesh, drawing blood. For a moment, she feared she would have to follow through on her threat and drive the dagger home, for Magister Onathus's enormous body tensed, his muscles coiling to strike. She twisted the stiletto's tip and pressed down harder on the aristocrat's face.

"Your strength won't save you here, *my lord*." She sneered the last two words. "I'll bury this blade in that tiny brain of yours faster than you can blink."

The threat sank in, driven home by the flash of steel in the moonlight and the pain of his sliced flesh. Slowly, Magister Onathus relaxed, his arms falling to his sides and his fists unclenching.

"Good." Natisse nodded. "Now, I'm going to take my hand away from your mouth. Don't even think about calling for help."

Magister Onathus fixed her with a baleful glare, but could not nod his head for fear of the dagger threatening his right eye.

Natisse removed her hand but made certain to keep the blade tip pressed against the flesh just beneath his eyeball. "One twitch I don't like, and this blade is the last thing you'll see. Understand?"

"Ezrasil can suck my giant cock," Magister Onathus said. His voice was impossibly deep, like thunder rolling over distant hills. "But you first."

He made to lunge for her but Natisse drew a broad dagger in her free hand and slid the tip into Onathus's open mouth before the giant realized it. His wagging tongue sliced itself along the edge of her blade, drawing blood and earning a rumble of pain from the aristocrat.

"Suck that, you piece of shit," she said, bearing her teeth in a snarl. "For once, Magister Onathus, you're not in charge. One more word out of your mouth that isn't a direct answer to my question, and you'll find yourself short a tongue." She leaned closer and dropped her voice to a harsh whisper. "And maybe a few other important parts, too."

Fury blazed in the Magister's eyes, a flush rising to his cheeks. Yet for all his anger, he managed to remain silent and motionless.

"Now," Natisse said, "I've got one question for you." She slid the dagger out of Magister Onathus' mouth. "Answer it, and everyone's night gets a whole lot better."

"Ask," Magister Onathus growled, his words slurred by pain and pooling blood.

"I know of your secret dealings," Natisse said. "That you, Magisters Perech and Estéfar have conspired to bring slaves into Dimvein—both through your shipyards and Magister Perech's caravans."

The slight widening of Magister Onathus's eyes told Natisse that Jad's deduction had been correct. Though they'd seen no sign of slaves moving through the shipyards, the connection was impossible to ignore. And Magister Onathus had just confirmed it.

Natisse hid a smile and kept her face a scowling mask of anger.

"What I want to know is who else is involved?" She pressed the dagger tip harder against the skin beneath his eyeball—it didn't hurt to remind him of what happened if he didn't cooperate. "It's not just the three of you in league, not for something of this magnitude. Give me the names of every aristocrat who is in on this, and I'm just a bad dream."

Magister Onathus's face remained expressionless for long seconds, then a slow smile spread across his face. He spit blood and it dribbled down his face and chest.

"Really?" A harsh chuckle rumbled from his enormous chest. "You really think I'll give in just like that? Just spill my guts and betray my fellow noblemen? You think you can frighten me so easily?"

Natisse's gaze was fixed on his face, but from the corners of her eyes, she saw his hand inching upward. He was going to make a move—either to wrest the dagger from her hand, or simply hurl her across the room. A clever, if desperate ploy—one that might've worked on an ordinary thief.

Natisse smiled.

"Yes."

With a flick of her wrist, she slashed the stiletto across Magister Onathus's right eye. The razor-sharp dagger tip cut deep into his eyeball, sliced away half his eyelid, and carved a deep gash into his nose. Natisse dropped her other dagger and clamped a hand down on the giant's mouth—just in time to stifle his screams of agony.

She didn't give the man a chance to struggle, to writhe free of her grip. Quick as a striking serpent, she leaped atop his barrel chest and pressed the bloody tip of her stiletto against the aristocrat's left eye.

"Be silent or be dead, *my lord*," Natisse snarled. "Choose wisely."

Magister Onathus froze, his breath coming fast as he fought to gain control over the searing pain in his right eye. He breathed deeply, the anger in his features slowly resolving to something akin to determination.

"You've made a huge mistake, coming here."

"Don't waste your breath on threats," Natisse warned. "Use it to give me the information I need—if you want me to leave this place without drenching your sheets in blood. Or, taking this from you." She twisted the stiletto tip, cutting into his left cheek. "You'll have a bloody hard time hunting me down and ripping me apart if you can't see."

Magister Onathus's remaining eye glared murder up at her. She'd known exactly what he was thinking. A strong man like him would want to inflict terrible tortures with his own hands. No doubt he was already picturing how he'd break her bones and tear her limb from limb. But she needed him focusing on the matter at hand.

"I offer you another chance, Onathus," Natisse said, purposely dropping the honorific. She removed her hand from his mouth and leaned forward until their faces were merely inches apart. "Give me what I want, or I start amputating."

"Threaten me all you want," Magister Onathus rumbled, "but I am not afraid of you." The way his eye darted to the threatening dagger belied his words.

"No?" Natisse asked sweetly. "Then I guess you don't need this other eye!" She pretended to tense, readying herself for another cut of the stiletto.

Magister Onathus bought the act.

"Wait, wait!" His huge chest rippled beneath her, his jaw muscles clenching.

Natisse raised an eyebrow. "Changed your mind?"

Magister Onathus scowled.

"I'm not afraid of you," he snarled, though it sounded as if he was trying to convince himself more than her, "but I'm not a damned fool, either. I'm not risking my neck to protect anyone."

Natisse hid a smile. The greed of the nobility was matched only by their self-serving desires.

"I'll give you the names," Magister Onathus rumbled. "Give me a quill and ink and I'll write—"

"I'm not a fool either," Natisse said with a sly smile, pressing the dagger deeper into his skin. "The names!"

"All right!" Magister Onathus arched his back, trying to shift his head away from the knife threatening his eye. "I'll tell you, I'll tell you!"

Natisse eased the pressure on the knife. "You have my full and undivided attention, my lord."

Magister Onathus scowled up at her.

"You were right that Magisters Perech and Estéfar were in on this. But you're still missing one more name. The one who came up with the grand scheme, the man who has been bringing slaves into Dimvein since the day Emperor Wymarc's decree of abolition."

293

Natisse leaned forward but dared not move the dagger.

"Tell me."

Magister Onathus's lips curled into a feral smile.

"Magister Branthe himself."

The name froze Natisse in place, set her mind racing.

Magister Branthe? She knew that name—all in Dimvein did. He was the most powerful aristocrat in the Karmian Empire, second only to the Emperor, believed to be Wymarc's trusted advisor. Could he—?

Magister Onathus had known what his words would do, and he was ready. He twisted his torso and bucked upward, his head snapping back in the same undulating motion. Suddenly, Natisse's dagger no longer threatened his eye and she was hurled off him, flying through the air. Landing face down atop the enormous bed, dagger burying into the cloth and goosedown stuffing, she was a sitting duck. Before she could rip the blade free, a massive hand clamped down her leg and dragged her.

"You dumb bitch," Onathus said.

Natisse scrambled to roll over, kicking out with her booted foot as she did. Her heel connected with something hard, but to no effect. Suddenly, she was on her back, and Magister Onathus's enormous frame loomed over her.

Both hands wrapped her throat.

"I won't even waste time threatening to have my way with you," he said. "You're not my type." His ruined right eye loomed close to her face, dripping blood into her open mouth. "You'll die tonight. But slowly, painfully. I'm going to take my time and savor every moment."

One arm was pinned beneath her. Natisse grasped with her free hand, pulling, tugging, clawing. His grip was tight. She beat against his chest with her fist. He just laughed and squeezed all the harder.

She pressed her palm against his face, pushing. Then, her thumb found his left eye and dug in deep.

He roared but didn't relent. She pressed in deeper and deeper. She saw black closing in around her vision. Finally, she was able to pull her another arm free. With every bit of effort she had, she stretched her arm upward and placed it against Onathus's other eye.

Shink.

A blade erupted from her wrist bracer and penetrated his eye and brain. The Magister was dead in an instant. The corpse collapsed onto her. She didn't even bother retracting the blade, just shoved the man off her, slicing him several times in the doing.

Somehow, she managed to roll him over. Breathing heavy, gagging from the taste of the man's blood in her mouth, she lay there.

She stared over at Magister Onathus's corpse. She'd come tonight knowing he would die, but Shekoth's pits, he'd nearly taken her with him.

Throat raw and sore, skin burned from the strain of the giant man's hands, she rose and staggered away from the blood-soaked bed and the dead aristocrat lying there. She had to leave, quickly, before a servant discovered her presence or the guards were alerted.

She rushed back through the adjoining room and out the window, nearly descending the stone wall in a freefall. She had to get back to Uncle Ronan and tell him who the real culprit was, the real power behind the slave trafficking in Dimvein.

Magister Branthe.

The Crimson Fang was about to go to war with the most powerful aristocrat in the Karmian Empire.

29

KULLEN

Kullen was about as screwed as a man in his line of work could be. Had it been the Imperial Scales, he might've gambled on their inattentiveness and average physical conditioning to buy himself a chance to escape. Beneath the shiny armor, many of the Imperial Scales were little more than men who believed it easier to walk a patrol than do a day's hard work. Oh, there were some who'd served in the Imperial army or truly believed in their calling as protectors of Dimvein, but those were often in short supply.

But the Orkenwatch was a different matter entirely. Most Orken stood between six and seven feet tall. The largest—those like Turoc—could reach eight feet in height. Their heavy musculature and the full suits of banded mail did little to slow their impressive speed once they came to a full run. Armed with just his daggers, Kullen had no chance of piercing their armor—and his odds of cutting through their thick hides were little better. He'd be chopped down the moment any one of the Orkenwatch drew the enormous two-handed greatswords they carried on their backs.

Worse, they had a Sniffer with them. The Orken at the front of the patrol was smaller than the rest—shorter than Kullen even—but with a canine snout and dark eyes set wide apart in his leathery head. One whiff of Kullen's scent, and that Orken would be able to track him to the ends of the Karmian Empire.

Kullen did his best to steer clear of the Orkenwatch, but whenever he found himself too close to a patrol, he had just one chance to avoid capture.

He fled like his life depended on it.

Before the Orkenwatch could cry out, Kullen sprang to his feet and darted into the building through which he'd pursued the ambushers mere minutes earlier. He banged into a wall, crashed off the doorjamb, but reached the rear door with ease and burst out into the darkness beyond. He didn't slow, but barreled down the nearest alley in a desperate attempt to escape what was sure to be certain death by Chuldok if caught.

One did not simply outrun a Sniffer. Fleeing an Orken patrol was nearly impossible, unless the one doing the fleeing was extremely lucky or extremely clever.

Or, in Kullen's case, extremely well-prepared.

Kullen charged through the darkened alleys, heading west toward the one part of North Dimvein he knew for certain he could lose his pursuers. Already he could hear the Orkenwatch's armor clanking and their heavy boots thundering along behind him. They were perhaps two, two hundred fifty feet behind him and gaining fast. In mere minutes, they'd be on him. The moment he was forced to slow and engage, to defend himself, he might as well lie down.

But he *did* have minutes. In Kullen's experience, that counted for a great deal.

His heart surged as he caught sight of an open window on the second level of the old stone mill. There was a third floor balcony that wrapped around and would grant him access to the rooftops where he would have a hope of losing them.

He poured on a burst of speed, then wall-ran up several feet before pushing off to the side and planting a foot against a perpendicular wall. The move launched him up the necessary remaining yards to grasp onto the sill and pull himself up.

Without hesitation, he climbed inside. The room lit up with Umbris's vision and Kullen scanned the building for any way to the roof.

Catwalks ran the length of the building, heavy chains and cables hanging down. He'd just chosen a route that would allow him to reach them when the door below burst open.

"Come back, killer!" one Orken growled.

Unwilling to waste time, Kullen mounted an iron railing, ignoring the twenty-foot drop, and leaped. He caught hold of his target, a catwalk a half a dozen or so feet away and a few feet up. It swung with his weight but Kullen held on.

"Up there!"

With effort, Kullen hefted himself up and tore off down the wooden skybridge.

He couldn't slow, not with the Orkenwatch hot on his heels. Their shouts of "Stop, in name of the Emperor!" echoed and their heavy bootsteps sent dust and dirt to floating throughout.

Kullen's heart galloped in his chest by the time he reached the balcony. He skidded to a halt as he nearly barreled into the stone bannister. Gasping for breath, he sheathed his dagger—it would do him no good against the Orkenwatch—and instead, ensured everything of import on him was securely touching flesh.

He did two things at once. First, he pulled a small, round, black sphere from his belt pouch. With the other hand, he closed his hand around his dragonblood vial, keeping it hidden from Orken eyes.

The instant his left hand closed around the dragonblood vial at his neck, the first of the Orkenwatch had found their way onto the catwalks. Six opal black eyes gleamed, fixated on Kullen. Their weapons reflected the pale light of the waning moon. Though it went against every instinct, Kullen turned away from the oncoming threat and faced the darkness of Northern Dimvein.

The city spread out before him, arched and bulbed rooftops, the faint light of Lumenators near the Upper Crest and finer sections of the city. Kullen eyed a rooftop two hundred yards away and drew on his mind to call upon his inner reservoir of magic.

He threw the sphere at the ground. It exploded, eliciting a dark gray smoke, filling the air and shielding him from view. Then, he pressed his thumb against the dragonblood vial's topper but nothing happened. At least, he thought nothing happened. Usually, the bond with Umbris was immediate, but this time, there was a hesitation that concerned Kullen. How many times had he called upon the beast without resting?

Too many, it seemed.

Finally, time slowed to a crawl. He was thankful for the concealment of smoke. His heart paused between beats, the hot blood freezing in his veins. Somehow, he could even sense the enormous Orken greatsword being drawn from its sheath as his pursuers burst out onto the balcony.

Something felt off. The Shadow Realm begged to take him completely, its all-consuming void and phantasmal inhabitants hungering for his life force with the endless, gnawing hunger. He knew he was entering dangerous grounds and both he and Umbris needed rest.

But first, he needed to live.

Giving in to the call of the shadows, Kullen willed himself to shift. Like a mighty gust of wind upon the sands, he was swept up and the focus of his mind took him to the next shadow, safely upon the distant rooftop.

He felt the Orkenwatch's hot breath as they gasped in shock at the sight of empty space where he'd just been. He heard their angry growls as he seemingly vanished into thin air. A part of him wanted to gloat at the escape, but years spent training and operating as the Black Talon had taught him the value of over-caution. He wasn't truly free and clear, not yet. The wind blew westward; within a few seconds, his scent would be carried to the Sniffer's sensitive nostrils, and the Orkenwatch would follow, baying for his blood.

Kullen focused again, willing the shadow to carry him a hundred and fifty yards to the south—a direction the Orkenwatch wouldn't expect him to be fleeing. There would be no logical reason for him to travel toward the One Hand District—the marketplace just south of Heroes Row—which would be crawling with Imperial Scales even at this late hour. Only a fool would flee toward that manner of danger.

But Kullen was no fool. His actions, as always, were careful and precise.

The shops would have all closed, but guards patrolled those streets vigilantly, watching over each stall and their locked up goods. Lumenators had regular positions at every intersection, their large magical globes shining light on every dark corner.

No thief would even dare. It would be easier to steal from there during broad daylight.

He landed and a vicious tugging occurred where his stomach would be in solid form. The shadow dragged at him. It felt as if his very skin were being raked from his flesh. Like a sandstorm, tiny pinpricks of pain all over his body.

He dropped to his hands and knees, the urge to retch strong.

He swore. He still wasn't sure he'd lost his pursuers and he couldn't give into exhaustion until he was sure they wouldn't find him.

Kullen shrank back and turned his eyes eastward once more. He knew from past experience he could only safely call upon Umbris's power once more, perhaps twice, but he wouldn't chance it.

"Just once more, friend," he said to Umbris.

"Take care, Kullen Bloodsworn, the shadows are hungry."

With that, Kullen was darkness once more, drifting on the open air from shadow to shadow. The feeling of dizziness and nausea continued, even grew, but he hadn't much farther to go.

When, at last, he made it to his desired destination, far enough away from the stone mill that the Orkenwatch and their Sniffer were sure to have lost him, he relinquished his grip on the Shadow Realm.

But it did not relinquish its grip on him. Invisible bonds tightened around him, dragging him deeper, deeper, and deeper still into the vacuum. Biting cold seeped into his limbs, sapped the strength from his muscles. Shrieks echoed faintly—not in his ears, but in his *mind*—wordless voices crying out in endless hunger.

Kullen fought to break free, to pull himself loose from the bonds encircling his soul. With every shred of his willpower, he compelled himself to return to the Mortal Realm. It felt as if something tore, and suddenly, he was back in reality. All vigor fled his numb, chilled muscles and he collapsed.

The moment he fully manifested, a terrible stench struck him like a blow to the face. It was a combination of potash, manure, blood—both fresh and old—stagnant water, and alchemical ingredients so foul-smelling they made his eyes water. He was glad he hadn't eaten since the morning—he'd have vomited if his stomach wasn't so empty. Acid surged to his throat and he barely managed to choke it back down.

But the stink flooded him with relief. It was bad for him; how much worse would it be for a Sniffer's keen nostrils? There was a reason the Orkenwatch gave this part of North Dimvein a wide berth. Indeed, few Imperial Scales ever entered the five-square-block section where all the city's tanneries were grouped together.

It was the perfect place to escape any pursuit. A horrid-smelling place, certainly, but one of the safest places in all of Dimvein to hide out.

In the middle of an alley, darkness forcing his dragon-eyes to activate, he struggled to his feet. His legs nearly gave out beneath him. He barely managed to stay upright, but somehow, he mustered the strength to stumble down the street—albeit like a drunk after a particularly heavy night of boozing. His eyelids already felt heavy, and his body cried out for rest. He shivered with every step as if chilled from winter's fiercest nip, even though the night was no more than cool.

This was the consequence of over-bloodsurging. The power he wielded was derived both from his bond with Umbris—using some of the dragon's life force granted him by the Shadow Realm —and from Kullen's own reserves of energy.

The Emperor had warned him that he'd lost one of his Black Talons to greed and addiction to the bloodsurge. He'd used it too much and disappeared into the Shadow Realm forever. Even when asked, Umbris would never talk about the man called Heshe.

The world spun around him, the experience made worse by the slow come-down from the stim-pop. Kullen considered taking another but knew if he did, he'd be hard-pressed to find sleep—something he desperately needed.

He could have wept when he drew within sight of the back alley that was his destination. He clung to the wall for support, barely coaxing his legs the final fifty steps to a small stone staircase that descended to a basement beneath one of the tanneries. His hands shook with violent tremors as he worked the gears and levers to input the right combination. It felt like an eternity before he finally heard the *click* and the door swung open.

He had just strength enough to dodder inside, heel the door shut behind him, and hurl himself toward the narrow rope-frame cot set along one wall of the tiny underground chamber.

Even as his body collapsed, his vision blurred and the world went dark.

30
NATISSE

The sun had nearly risen by the time Natisse returned to the Burrow. Her stomach tightened as she approached the common room, dreading what she'd see there. She was relieved to discover Garron had been moved and someone had cleaned up his blood.

Most of it, that was. No amount of scrubbing could get rid of the blood that now stained the table where he'd lain and the surrounding chairs. But at least the floors had been cleared and all crimson spatter wiped off the stone walls. It was a start.

Natisse hurried toward the War Room. Uncle Ronan needed to know what she'd uncovered. Instead, a roar and repeated thudding impacts drew her attention to the training room. There, she found the grizzled Crimson Fang leader pounding away at one of the weighted punching bags, growling his fury with every blow.

Natisse hesitated, uncertain whether she should disturb him. She hadn't seen him like this in... years, perhaps? Not since the Embers had burned to the ground and thousands of citizens died in flames. He'd never told her who he'd lost in the fire, but for weeks after, he'd thrown himself into a frenetic effort of sifting through the ashes in search of survivors, then helping rebuild.

She'd never forget the day he'd pushed himself so hard he'd collapsed from sheer exhaustion.

Now, it looked like he was beginning down the same spiral. Natisse couldn't blame him. He'd lost Baruch and Ammon in less than a week, and Garron had come within a hair's breadth of following the brothers into Shekoth's pits. He was grieving in his own Uncle Ronan sort of way.

Her hesitation lasted only a minute. The news was too monumental to wait. Uncle Ronan could resume taking his pain, sorrow, and anger out on the punching bag after she'd informed him of Magister Branthe.

"Uncle Ronan!" she called out as she hurried toward him across the high-ceilinged training room. "I found out—"

Uncle Ronan spun at the sound of her voice. His eyes locked on her, and his expression contorted in a rush of emotion: fear, relief, joy, then dark, hard anger.

"What in Ezrasil's blood-covered fist were you doing?" he roared. His face flushed a furious red and he stalked toward her, eyes blazing. "Taking on Magister Onathus all on your own?"

Natisse flinched, startled by the intensity. "I went to get answer—"

"You went to get yourself killed, that's what!" His shout rang off the walls and set the ground beneath Natisse's feet trembling. "I taught you to be smarter than that, to think before you act. But this, this was sheer—" He seemed at a loss for words, torn by outrage. "—sheer goddamned recklessness!"

Natisse's jaw muscles clenched. He wasn't wrong. Over the years, he'd hammered home the necessity of always working with others, having someone to watch her back no matter what she was doing. But all that aside, though she called this man Uncle, she was no child to be scolded.

"Maybe it was reckless," she snapped, "but it bloody well worked!" Instead of being cowed by his anger, she stepped closer, squared up before him. He'd taught her never to back down, and she wouldn't, not even from him. "Magister Onathus spilled his bloody guts, gave me the name of the person they're in league with."

"Gave you those bruises, too!" Uncle Ronan's gaze darted to her neck and the many other wounds she'd incurred. "Damn it, Natisse, you knew how dangerous he was even before you went in, but you still decided it was worth the risk to go alone."

"Yes, I damn well did." Natisse stared back at him defiantly.

"And you came away almost entirely empty-handed," Uncle Ronan spat. "Or did you already deposit the valuables and documents you purloined elsewhere?"

For the first time since narrowly escaping death at Magister Onathus's massive hands, Natisse realized that she'd forgotten to steal anything in her flight. No jewelry or items of worth that the Crimson Fang could fence to feed the poor of the Embers. No papers that could link the aristocrat to the slave trade, or his fellow conspirators. Nothing but the word of a dead man to tie Magister Branthe to the operation.

Uncle Ronan removed his gloves and tossed them aside, then took a swig of water.

"Now," he said, like she was an infant, eyes blazing, "when the Orkenwatch dig into his death, what do you suppose they'll think? That it was a theft gone awry, or a targeted assassination attempt? How long do you think it'll take them to connect him to Magister Perech, Magister Estéfar, and all the others we've recently eliminated? And when they find that, where do you think that'll lead them?"

"Not back here!" Natisse snapped. "No one saw me. I was damned careful. Like you taught us. Taught me."

"That's not what I'm worried about!" Uncle Ronan roared. "The minute the Orkenwatch start sniffing around this slave trade, the people running the operation are going to disappear."

"Yes!" she said. "They'll get the justice they deserve!"

"Goddammit, Natisse. Have you ever seen a noble get what

307

they deserve? Have you ever seen justice dealt to anyone on those hills? No. You've not. None of us has. Their misdeeds will be buried and forgotten and all will go on as normal but for them being quietly sent off on some business trip or another in some far off land."

"And we'll find them."

"Natisse," Uncle Ronan said, his voice softer. "We won't. Even now, our numbers dwindle by the day it seems. If we lose this chance now, everything we've worked for these last few years will be wasted. Baruch and Ammon's deaths will mean nothing because we'll lose the one lead we've found in months."

Those words struck Natisse with the force of a blow to the gut. She wanted to write it off as Uncle Ronan's anger getting the better of him, but at the moment, his tone so soft, the accusation stung too much to ignore.

"Be angry all you want," she snarled, "but at least I'm doing something! I'm the only reason we know who's behind this."

Uncle Ronan opened his mouth, but this time Natisse over-rode him before he could retort.

"Onathus told me that it was Magister Branthe running their operations," she shouted. "And if I hadn't been so *reckless*, we'd never've known that. So you're welcome!"

She spun on her heel and stalked from the training room, pulse roaring in her ears, anger swirling bright and hot in her belly. She refused to glance back—too furious to even look at Uncle Ronan right now—but slammed the door to the training room behind her. Stomping her way down the passage, she burst into her room and set about stripping off her rumpled, torn, and bloody clothing, fuming all the while.

How dare he lecture me? She pulled the tunic over her head with such force she tore one sleeve halfway off and nearly ripped the neckline. *I'm not some child like Sparrow!*

She hurled her lashblade, daggers, and climbing gear onto her bed, but still it wasn't enough. Anger blazed—by Ezrasil, it blazed!

Her legs trembled and her fists clenched so tightly her forearms screamed. She wanted to lash out, to hit something with every shred of strength, to let out the fury building within her.

She heard his words again, but this time, they echoed different in her mind.

"Baruch and Ammon's deaths will mean nothing because you've lost *the one lead we've found in months."*

"I almost jeopardized the mission," she said aloud.

"The mission above all," she heard Ammon say. She turned, searching the empty room. The voice was so real, she'd expected to find the man standing in her chambers.

In that moment, Uncle Ronan's outburst made terrible sense. He was as angry as she was. He'd lost as much as she had—perhaps even more. For it was his decisions as the Crimson Fang's leader that had put Baruch, Ammon, and Garron in harm's way. He'd simply taken it out on the most convenient targets—first the punching bags, then her.

With that realization, her rage drained away, albeit slowly. It took her a full ten minutes to cool down enough to let out a calm breath and unclench her fists. By the time she'd changed into a fresh set of clothing and donned her weapons once more, she'd regained control of her temper. Hopefully, Uncle Ronan would have as well.

She stepped from the room, but before she could go in search of him again, she caught sight of Jad emerging from Garron's quarters. The big man looked tired, his face lined, deep bags beneath his eyes. He tried to smile a greeting, but Natisse saw the worry beneath the façade.

"How's he doing?" Natisse asked quietly.

"As well as can be expected," Jad answered. "He'll mend, but it's going to be a long road."

Natisse glanced toward the door. "He sleeping?"

"Too stubborn to rest," Jad said, shaking his head. Though, this time, his smile held a faint trace of genuine humor. "Might be he could use a few minutes of company until I can rouse Sparrow and get her to sit with him."

"Healer's orders?"

Jad nodded. "Friendly faces go a long way toward speeding up the recovery process."

"I guess mine will have to do." Natisse squeezed the big man's hand, and he returned the gesture before turning away and heading for Sparrow's room at the end of the hall.

Natisse pushed the door opened and entered the room. The stench was almost as overpowering as the one in the sewers had been. Blood and pus and salves and ointments. Natisse was careful to avoid the look of disgust on her face.

Garron lay on his bed, his entire upper body wreathed in bandages, some bloodstained. His face was pale, his complexion just on the alive side of deathly wan, but he was awake, his eyes sharp as ever.

"You look like shit," he croaked.

Natisse couldn't help a bark of laughter. "I was just about to say the same to you."

"And the smell, right?"

"You or me?"

Garron managed a faint grin, though it was tight with pain. Laconic as ever, he watched her cross his room. She took the chair next to his bed. For a moment, Natisse thought he might speak, but he seemed content to simply share the silence.

She couldn't look at him—at the bandaged stump where his left arm had been—for fear the turmoil of emotions would over-whelm her. So, she stared at the bed, the walls, the door, anywhere except for the rangy, terrifyingly weak-looking figure lying beside her.

"It's not so bad, you know?" Garron's voice surprised her.

Natisse's head snapped toward him. "What's that?"

"The arm," he gestured toward his stump with his chin. "It's

going to heal, and I'll still have my right hand. I'm not dead, just…
a bit less useful."

Natisse sucked in a breath.

She turned to face him. "I'd never think you were anything
less just because you're short an arm."

Garron's face was tight with pain—physical, and, she saw,
emotional. "Just thought… you weren't looking…" He trailed off
weakly.

"Hey, now. Lose the other, and maybe I'll change my mind."

The joke fell flat.

"It's all…" The emotions washed over her, and she could fight
them back no longer. Her shoulders slumped and her eyes burned.
"It's too much, too close together. First Ammon, then Baruch, and
now…" Her voice cracked, and as if a dam had been broken. A tear
tore down her cheek and she rushed to wipe it away. "I just think
of how close we all came to losing you, and I ca-can't bear it."

"I'm fine," Garron said. "I mean, not really fine. But alive.
That's gotta count for something, right?"

Natisse swallowed, tried to stop the flow of tears. "If I'd
known you were hurt—"

"But you couldn't have known," Garron insisted. "And if you'd
tried to help me, you'd have been captured or wounded, too. You
got away. That's all that matters."

"But you—"

"Are alive." Garron's eyes gleamed with determination,
strength of spirit even if his body was weak. "I'm alive, Natisse. So
are you. And while we are, the mission is what matters."

Natisse rubbed the back of her neck. "Look at this." She
laughed mirthlessly.

"What?"

"This. Here you are, lying in recovery and *you're* consoling
me."

Natisse was about to say more, but at that moment, the door

opened and a yawning, sleepy-eyed Sparrow entered the room. The young girl startled at the sight of Natisse sitting next to Garron's bed.

"Oh, sorry," she mumbled. "Jad sent me, but I can come back later."

"No." Natisse shook her head. "Lazybones here is all yours." Rising to her feet, she turned to Garron. "I'll be back to check on you soon. You heal up."

Garron grunted and gave a little nod. Evidently, he'd expended what few words he had to say.

Natisse paused as she passed Sparrow. "Take good care of him."

"I will." Sparrow's expression held that same fire and grit Natisse had seen earlier. "He'll be back on his feet and talking our ears off in no time."

Natisse chuckled, patted the girl's arm, and left the room. She closed the door behind her, leaned against it, and breathed a sigh of relief. It felt good to know Garron would come out the other side of this—not just alive, but whole in mind and spirit, if not in body. The loss of his arm was a devastating blow, but if anyone could come back from such a hard hit, it was Garron.

She resumed her search for Uncle Ronan. Despite their clash, they'd need to work together to come up with a strategy for what to do next. The revelation about Magister Branthe was enormous. They had to be careful in plotting. How does one take out such a powerful aristocrat, one with close ties to the Imperial Palace?

Her first stop was the War Room, but it sat empty. Next, she checked the bathing room, but there was no sign of Uncle Ronan there, either. She was about to search his private quarters when she caught sight of movement through the open door of the training room. Lamplight shone on Uncle Ronan's solid, compact form. He wore a dark cloak—the sort they all used when traveling inconspicuous around Dimvein—but instead of heading toward the passage that led up into the warehouse, he was moving deeper into the training room.

Natisse frowned.

"Where are you going?" she whispered. She was about to call out when something stopped her. Something about the furtiveness of Uncle Ronan's movements and the way he glanced over his shoulder, as if searching for watching eyes.

She pressed herself against the wall, out of Uncle Ronan's view. Only after a few seconds passed did she dare look again.

He approached one of the many wooden racks that held both wooden training blades and sharp steel weapons. Reaching between two dusty swords, he fumbled with something beneath a shelf at chest-level.

Natisse's jaw dropped as an entire section of blank wall next to the rack slid aside to reveal a hidden opening carved into the stone.

31

KULLEN

Kullen awoke to thundering misery drumming in his skull. He couldn't remember the last time he'd drunk to blackout—while grieving Prince Jarius and Princess Hadassa years earlier, perhaps—but the torment in his head was far crueler than the worst hangover.

He managed to pry his leaden eyelids open, and found light streaming through the tiny window set high into the wall of the underground room. He'd lost consciousness shortly after midnight, meaning he'd slept through the rest of the night and at least some of the day.

Rising from his cot required every shred of willpower Kullen possessed. Had it been up to him, he would've buried his head beneath his pillow and remained in the quiet, painless darkness forever. But vicious headache or no, he couldn't afford to linger in bed. He needed report the previous night's events and discoveries to the Emperor.

He found it more difficult than expected to shrug off the lingering effects of overusing his bloodsurge. He couldn't remember the last time he'd come so close to being trapped within the Shadow Realm. The memory of the icy threads binding his limbs and the feeling of quicksand dragging at his soul sent a shiver down his spine. He'd be damned careful in the future. He *never* wanted to feel that again.

Finally, he shook off the last of the chill and set about the task that had gotten him up. Pawing through the pockets of his cloak, he was relieved to find that he still had Magister Issemar's leather-bound notebook. It wasn't evidence enough to convict the Magister in a court of law, but that would no longer be an issue. Magister Issemar was standing judgment before Ezrasil's judgment seat, answering for his sins even now.

Yet Emperor Wymarc would want to know that Magister Issemar had, indeed, been defrauding him—in truth, stealing the supplies purchased to feed the populace. Though the aristocrat was beyond Imperial justice, his complicity could lead to the unmasking of further co-conspirators.

Among whom, Kullen fervently hoped, would number Magister Deckard. The aristocrat's presence at Magister Issemar's should be enough to convince the Emperor to allow Kullen free rein. This could very well be the excuse Kullen had awaited for years, ever since Magister Deckard's lust for the bloodsurge had led to the deaths of countless Imperial citizens and the only people in the world Kullen had truly counted as friends and the creation of the Embers.

That thought was enough to propel Kullen to his feet.

The room was about the size of a multi-prisoner jail cell in dungeons. It would be winning no awards for best decorated or cleanest, but it served his purposes. A bed, fully dressed with blankets and a pillow, a worktable made of rough wood, and a four-drawer chest, each locked with its own combination only Kullen knew. Each item was bolted to the ground.

He took a step and wobbled on legs that ached. Pins and needles coursed through his whole lower half. He resisted the urge to take another stim-pop—it had been partly to blame for his collapse the previous night, and his current miserable state.

Instead, he sought out one of the healing draughts he stored in every one of his many safe houses around Dimvein.

Though they were no Gryphic Elixir, there were a few potions mixed up by Serrod, a Brendoni alchemist and healer whose shop in the One Hand District was kept afloat by Kullen's many purchases there. Kullen chose one from his supply, a basic Navapash draught that had proven effective in the past. Serrod had the bedside manner of a hungry dragon, but only the Emperor's personal alchemists rivaled his skills at mixing up remedies and elixirs.

Kullen downed it in a single long pull, grimacing at the foul taste and oily film it left coating his teeth and tongue. Why did alchemists always have to make their brews so nasty? It seemed the more potent and effective the remedy, the more unpleasant it was. Kullen made a mental note to suggest a spoonful of sugar to be added to the ingredients list.

It didn't stop him from drinking a second, though. He had no desire to combat a pounding headache on his trek southward through Dimvein.

Within a minute, the throbbing behind his eyes diminished, at least enough that he no longer felt his brain would explode through his ears. That was about as good as it would get for now. His body required time to recover from the strain of overdrawing on his inner wellspring of magic. He'd be drained for at least another day or two, until after a proper night of rest to restore his full vitality. He would rest after reporting his findings to the Emperor.

He leaned over on the worktable. Last night had been the closest he'd ever come to suffering Heshe's fate of being stuck in the Shadow Realm. He ran a hand through his sweat-soaked hair, internally scolding himself for taking so many chances.

But what was he to do? Get caught by the Orkenwatch?

Kullen stripped out of his crimson-stained clothing. A small pipe ran from the street above to a basin that was currently half-full with rain water. Kullen drank his fill, then washed the crusted blood from his hands and face. Feeling much refreshed, he donned a fresh outfit from the drawer third from the chest's bottom. It was a simple affair—dull, faded gray tunic, sleeveless leather jerkin, and a pair of trousers ripped at the knees. The perfect outfit to blend in among the Dimvein's impoverished.

He turned his fine cloak inside out and rolled it up into a loose bundle, which he tucked under one arm. He made no effort to hide the weapons strapped to his belt—both were hunting knives with faded wooden handles and plain pommels that belied their blade of finest Imperial steel—and he knew the daggers sheathed in the tops of his boots and hidden in his leather arm bracers would be invisible unless anyone looked too closely. His faded, dull clothing all but guaranteed no one would be doing much looking.

Just to be safe, he knelt in the alley outside, scooped up a bit of mud, and rubbed it onto his face. The filth, together with the stooped posture he adopted, made him wholly unremarkable among the equally bedraggled and dusty Emberites.

"Clean but for a moment," he said under his breath.

Bundle under his arm, he shuffled south, away from the stinking tanneries, heading toward the One Hand District. He was surprised to find it was an hour away from sundown—had he truly been unconscious for the entire day?

The open square bustled with people. Most were of humble means, but the occasional well-dressed aristocrat did their best not to touch anyone or anything. A day among the people—how noble of them.

The throng was thick. Hundreds—if not thousands—of people moved among the stalls, carts, and blankets upon which were displayed every manner of wares—fruits and vegetables, fish freshly caught, tools, trinkets, jewelry, even weapons.

Women in drab garb carried twine-weaved baskets under their arms or on their heads, filled with their day's purchases.

Other, less savory women wore colorful and immodest dresses cut too deep about the chest and too high about the thighs, faces painted like lust incarnate. Kullen spotted one chatting up one of the visiting noblemen and she had him, hook, line, and sinker. She tugged him along through the crowd toward The Dewy Rose Petal where she'd bed him and feed her children for a week.

Kullen held no judgment for the woman nor the man, though that was not what he'd come for.

More than a few Imperial Scales patrolled, tramping along and barking out orders to citizens who—in Kullen's eyes—were doing nothing out of the ordinary. A few of the men appeared serious, intent on executing their duty with professionalism. Those were the ones with wary eyes that never stopped moving, always scanning the crowd for pickpockets, cutpurses, and swindlers. Most of the silver-clad guards, however, lounged in the shade of overhanging awnings or sampled the wares of merchants—rarely with the merchant's consent.

Of the Orkenwatch, Kullen saw no sign. Perhaps his slumber through most of the day had worked in his favor. The patrol he'd escaped last night had doubtless already given up the hunt for him after losing his trail. All the same, he'd have to be careful to avoid them even more assiduously than before. All of the Orken would have picked up his scent, and a Sniffer's olfactory memory could last a lifetime.

The rumbling of his stomach reminded him that he hadn't eaten in over a day and a half. Thankfully, the One Hand District was home to plenty of vendors selling foodstuffs.

Kullen told himself he was a man of simple tastes, believing that his time spent eating humbly at Mammy Tess's table defined who he was. However, when the carriage wheel hit the road, his years in the palace with Prince Jarius had done more to shape his palette than he cared to admit. He followed his nose to a meat stand where he purchased an auroch kebob and a cup of rockcrab broth.

The smokey flavor of the auroch washed down with the salty broth felt like life itself pouring back into Kullen's soul.

Between the hearty meal and Serrod's alchemical potions, Kullen felt much more himself. A craving for something sweet settled over him—a bit of honeymead, perhaps. He gave in and headed toward the Apple Cart Mead Hall at the western edge of the district. The sun hung low over the western rooftops and the evening had already begun to grow cool. After a quick drink of honeymead, he'd visit the palace, report his findings to the Emperor, then to catch a few more hours of sleep. After that, he'd venture outside the city for an early morning meeting with Umbris in the glade. He owed the dragon another pork shoulder in thanks for saving him from the onyx sharks—a thought that made Kullen shudder—and then his help earlier with Magister Issemar.

He was about to turn down the street that led past the Mead Hall, but movement on a larger street to the south caught his attention. A carriage clattered by—the same carriage he'd seen the previous day at Magister Issemar's mansion—surrounded by more than twenty mounted guards.

Kullen frowned. What was Magister Deckard doing here, and with such a large force of armed men? He clearly wasn't on his way for a drink of Dyntas's honeymead, but headed due west.

Toward the Embers?

Kullen's pulse quickened. *Toward the Refuge!* He tried to come up with another reason for the aristocrat to be this far away from his roost in the Upper Crest, to enter the filth so close to the Embers with so many armed men at his side. Yet he could think of none. Mammy Tess's words from days earlier echoed in his mind.

"He's trying to buy the building."

Fear rippled through him. If Magister Deckard had grown tired of trying to purchase the property, he might simply have decided to take it by force. That would explain the guards.

Breaking into a run, Kullen barreled through the streets, racing through back alleys west toward the Mustona Bridge. He stayed within eyesight of Deckard, where Kullen could see the carriage but was sure no guards would see him. All the while, he hoped he was wrong, hoped Deckard was heading somewhere else.

But cold dread sank like a stone in his belly when Magister Deckard's carriage rattled over the bridge and headed due west. Through Thanagar's protective dome on a direct course toward Pawn May Avenue. There, it drew up in front of the orphanage, and the man himself emerged. Half of his guards remained seated in their saddles, lanterns in hand. The other half dismounted and flanked him as he strutted the few steps to the Refuge's open doors.

"Good evening, my lord." Mammy Tess's voice drifted into the street, and a moment later the woman herself appeared from inside. Her age-lined face was as calm as her voice, a serene smile on her lips, but Kullen knew her well enough to see the tension in her posture. "If you have come to make a donation to the needy, you and your men are—"

"You know why we are here!" Magister Deckard snapped. The man's florid face turned an angry shade of red, and he drew himself up to his full, less-than-impressive height. "We have come to make a final offer."

"I have heard your offers in the past, my lord," Mammy Tess said, her tone that of a patient mother speaking to a willful child.

She coughed a few times into the sleeve of her shirt, but that didn't stop Deckard from drawing back like he'd just been spat on. He pulled a handkerchief from his pocket and began wiping himself off at random.

"And, as I have told you," she continued once she'd brought herself under control, "the Refuge is not for sale. At any price."

"Yes, you have said as much." Magister Deckard sneered. "Which is why I come offering not gold, but a chance to live."

Mammy Tess frowned. "The power over life and death is reserved for Ezrasil alone, Magister Deckard."

"Not so!" Magister Deckard reached a hand beneath his shirt, and from his other hand sprang a sword of pure fire. It burned hot, casting Mammy Tess's face in orange terror. "I can kill you here and now. You, and every child within these walls!" He leveled the fiery weapon at her throat. "My offer is this: depart now, and take your brats with you, and you will all live. Refuse, and you and your Refuge will burn."

32

NATISSE

Shekoth's icy pits! Natisse stared in open-mouthed wonder at the secret passageway. To her knowledge, the the only way in and out of the Burrow was through the the front gate. There were tunnels aplenty running beneath Dimvein, allowing the Crimson Fang to surface in Heroes Row, the One Hand District, High Reach, even within the Embers. But all joined the one passage that ended at the heavy, trapped gate guarding the Burrow.

The hidden opening's presence was only half of what confused her. Perhaps less than half. For starters, why had Uncle Ronan kept it a secret from her? That was becoming more and more a question in the recent days. First, the elixir that had spared Garron's life—not that she would complain about that too strongly—and now this?

Furthermore, why would he depart via this secret door when he could just have easily walked out the front? No one would question him. None of the Crimson Fang would've even noticed —they were all either out on mission, resting, or tending to Garron. So why, then, was Uncle Ronan using this mysterious passageway that none of them even knew existed?

Then, a sick feeling seeped into her gut. What if they all knew but her?

The thought sat ill with Natisse. Uncle Ronan was a man of many secrets—all in the Crimson Fang knew that, and his past had been a subject of great speculation between Baruch and Ammon—but why keep this secret?

Natisse waited until the stone wall slid shut before entering the training room. She ran toward the shelf where Uncle Ronan had stood and bent to look where he'd been reaching. At first, she saw nothing out of the ordinary—blank stone, wooden shelf, and steel brackets supporting the weight of the weapons. Yet upon closer inspection, she noticed a small brass ring set into the wall just beneath the shelf's underbelly. Natisse slipped her finger through the ring and, after a moment's pause, pulled.

Something clicked within the wall and, again, the hidden door slid silently open. Natisse tensed, awaiting an angry shout from the hidden passage. She'd tried to wait long enough for Uncle Ronan to gain some ground, but she had no idea what awaited her within. If it was a single straight corridor, Uncle Ronan would be alerted by the sound and light.

No sound came from within. Natisse peered inside, and found an earthen-walled tunnel tall enough that even Jad could enter without ducking. Brass support arches held up a ceiling that even with her arm extended, her fingers barely grazed the densely packed earth overhead.

What is this? she wondered. It seemed this mysterious underground den they'd all called home for so many years still possessed secrets left to discover.

Like Uncle Ronan's past, the origin of the Burrow with its many stone-walled rooms, floors, and ceilings had been a source of discussion among Ammon and Baruch. Natisse, too, had wondered whose hand had carved the underground network from the ground beneath Dimvein. Eventually, when no answers proved forthcoming, she'd stopped wondering.

Now, however, she couldn't help her burning curiosity. Whoever—or whatever—had built it had also hollowed out a secondary means of ingress and egress. An escape tunnel in case the warehouse above was breached and their hidden entrance was found out, perhaps?

Natisse was so busy wondering about the tunnel's provenance that she nearly trapped herself in darkness. The door began to slide shut behind her. Only then did she realize that she had no source of light. Jumping backward just in time to avoid the wall's closing—which shut mere inches from her face and narrowly missed catching her cloak—she lifting a shuttered lantern off the wall before triggering the opening mechanism once again. With one last look behind her at the empty training room, she slipped into the tunnel a second time.

Now, as she scanned her surroundings in the lamplight, she saw another ring set into one of the brass columns. Sure enough, when she gave it a pull, the door slid shut behind her.

Ezrasil's bastard son! Natisse blinked into the darkness behind and ahead of her. It was amazing. Incredible. Magnificent.

And, she had to admit, more than a little worrisome. Again, the fear struck her that, perhaps, Uncle Ronan wasn't the only one aware of the tunnel's presence. Did the rest Crimson Fang also know—Garron, Jad, Dalash, or any of the others? Worse, did anyone outside the stone walls also know? If so, the stronghold they all believed was so secure might be terribly vulnerable.

Would the Orkenwatch or Imperial Scales one day come streaming down these passages and catch them all by surprise?

There was only one way to find out: she had to ask Uncle Ronan. No longer worried that he'd discover her, she hurried to catch up, keeping her lantern shuttered just enough to illuminate her way forward without casting too much light.

Natisse was relieved to find that, so far, the passage contained no forks or branches. Twenty yards ahead, it turned to the left, then to the right. Then, she reached an intersection with two paths branching out in both directions and her assurance vanished. Shuttering the lantern fully, she scrutinized the dirt floor. Boot tracks went in both directions and she could spot none as newer made than the others. Then, her heart leaped as she caught the merest flicker of light off to her left. Opening the lantern's shutters a crack, she hurried after the dim illumination.

The tunnel sloped gently upward for a hundred feet before turning sharply to the left. This time, Natisse slowed as she approached the turn. She lowered her lantern, leaving it well hidden behind the wall, then peered around the corner. There, barely thirty yards ahead of her, was Uncle Ronan, some strange light emanating from his upturned hand. Alchemical glowstones, perhaps?

He turned a corner and she retrieved her lantern. Maintaining her distance, staying far enough back that he wouldn't spot her creeping along in his wake, she stalked like she was on a hunt. She kept close enough that she wouldn't lose him at the various intersections they passed and fury spurred her to hasten her pace more than once. But she breathed steady, forced herself to slow. Sounds in the darkness caused her to right hand to stay ready by her lashblade hilt but she never drew it. She was reminded of Uncle Ronan's admonition to always travel in pairs with weapons and a light source.

She had no desire to meet anything clawed, fanged, or creepy-crawly. There were creatures within the main tunnels, vile ones without names. The Crimson Fang referred to them only as gnashers due to the unnerving sounds they made in the darkness.

A particularly loud sound—like bone or chitin scraping across stone—caused her to swing around and unshutter the lantern. The tunnel behind her was empty, no sign of whatever had originated the noise. Natisse swallowed the fear surging within her and returned to her pursuit of Uncle Ronan.

But the way ahead was empty, too. There was not so much as a glimmer of Uncle Ronan.

Cursing, Natisse broke into a run and sprinted the thirty yards to where Uncle Ronan had disappeared. To her relief, she found it was just another bend in the passage. Her relief proved short-lived. Around the corner, the passage ran for a few feet before splitting into four individual corridors. Natisse shuttered her lantern again, but this time, could find no trace of Uncle Ronan's light.

She scanned the darkness in vain, her pulse quickening. Had she lost him? She couldn't have! He'd been right there just a few seconds earlier.

Drawing in a deep, calming breath, she willed her heartbeat to slow, to still the blood rushing in her ears. She closed her eyes and listened. Straining to hear anything—everything—in the passages around her. Beyond the sounds of her own ragged breathing, the distant scuffing of whatever creatures lurked in the darkness. She was listening for—

There!

The sound that reached her wasn't the scrape of Uncle Ronan's boots on stone. Instead, it was the low murmur of voices.

Voices? Natisse's brow furrowed. Who is he talking to?

She listened at each of the passages, even moving a few paces down each to make certain she had the right one. Finally, she chose the tunnel farthest to her left. Her best guess proved correct. With every step up the corridor, the conversation grew louder. Again, she slowed as she approached at the far end of the tunnel, peering around the corner. Uncle Ronan stood with his back to her, his body blocking the light's faint glow.

Someone else was there. A figure shorter and slimmer than Uncle Ronan—a man, judging by the voice, though there was something peculiar about the way he talked. Natisse was too far away to hear their conversation clearly. She could barely make out a few snatches of the words that passed between them.

"… certain that he is the one who…"

"… the plan for how to proceed with…"

"… cannot know what you have found. Not yet. Not until…"

Natisse ached to edge nearer, but dared not. There would be nowhere to hide in the long, straight passage. She couldn't trust the darkness to shroud her, either. There was no telling what would happen if Uncle Ronan overheard her or the mysterious man he was meeting spotted her.

And so she was forced to stay put and strain her ears to make out their conversation. Much to her frustration, the men talked too quietly, their voices barely carrying in the earthen tunnels. Right up until Uncle Ronan snarled at full volume, "Not a damned chance! I'm not risking anyone else for your—"

The other man cut him off, albeit at a volume below Natisse's hearing. Their conversation continued for a few moments longer, then suddenly Uncle Ronan turned, lowering his hand. The light went out and he stalked toward her.

Natisse caught the barest glimpse of the other man before the tunnel went dark—sharp, black eyebrows, a slim, angular face she didn't recognize, and a neatly trimmed goatee. She ducked back around the corner, suddenly realizing that Uncle Ronan would likely be backtracking the way he'd come to return to the underground stronghold—which meant he was headed right toward her.

She purposely avoided every turn she'd made, hoping she'd be able to find her way back or out another way. It was dark and she'd kept the lantern shuttered. She made one final turn, sure she'd put enough distance and enough wrong turns between her and Uncle Ronan and stopped to breathe.

That's when she heard it. Teeth grinding, snapping… gnashing.

33

KULLEN

There was no doubt in Kullen's mind: Magister Deckard would carry out the threat without a second thought. No Orkenwatch or Imperial Scales patrols would come in time to save the Refuge, as guards generally considered the stench they were likely to pick up in the Embers not worth the simple lives they might save. Indeed, they rarely ventured into the slums, not even to investigate the rumors of Ember-dwellers vanishing without a trace.

Beyond Thanagar's protective dome, not even the dragon's magical senses would detect what was about to happen. What Magister Deckard had come here to do.

The bastard could claim ignorance of the fire—or, worse, could protest that he'd been on his way back from buying the property, leaving just before a "freak blaze" destroyed the building and killed Mammy Tess and everyone within. No doubt he'd make a grand spectacle of mourning the loss of so many innocent orphans and the woman who had done so much good for the poorest of Dimvein.

But like it was with any aristocrat, it would amount to little more than noise. At the end of the night, no one would refute his claims. He would be in possession of the property he'd been trying for years to acquire.

And Mammy Tess would be dead, along with all her children. Hadassa's plaque would be nothing more than melted slag among the ashes.

"Mammy Tess," came a small voice. The child it belonged to stood at the woman's side, eyes droopy with sleep. "What's wrong? Why's the army here?"

Kullen immediately recognized the boy as the one he'd been responsible for brining to the Refuge. In light of the situation, that name carried with it a cruel joke. *The Refuge.* Those two children would've been better off dying of starvation on the streets than burning to death.

Fury boiled in Kullen's chest, a raging inferno he hadn't even a desire to quell. He would suffer no caution or restraint here. The lack of patrols that Magister Deckard counted on would also be the reason he met Ezrasil this day.

"It's nothing, Sanjay," Mammy Tess said. "Go back to bed before your brother worries."

She scooted young Sanjay along.

"Yes, boy. We don't want the children worrying…"

Deckard's threat hung thick in the air.

"This is outrageous, Magister Deckard," Mammy Tess said. "I demand you leave my property at once."

Magister Deckard made a show of looking around the front porch. He touched Hadassa's plaque with a finger, then abruptly wiped it off on a handkerchief.

"Won't take much to burn," he said. "It's already damn near fallen over with neglect." He took a step closer to her. "I feel rather generous this evening. I'll give you one last chance to accept my offer. In fact, I'll raise it by ten percent. How does that sound? Think about how nicely you could finish out your life on that kind of money?"

"And what of the children?"

Deckard waved a hand dismissively. "Children are resilient, Tessaphania. We both know this. Fine. Twenty percent."

"Magister Deckard, you could offer me five-hundred percent over your initial offer and I would still decline you with a smile on my face."

That woman had guts, Kullen couldn't fail to admit.

Deckard shook his head as he turned to his guards. He sighed deeply and the first of his men stepped forward.

There were only twenty of them standing between him and the bastard who'd killed the Prince and Princess. A part of Kullen longed to rush in, to summon Umbris's power—or the dragon himself—and carve through the ranks of armed men like fresh baked bread. But he couldn't risk Mammy Tess being killed in the scuffle. He needed to distract Magister Deckard long enough for the woman to retreat inside and bolt her front doors.

He stepped from the growing shadows of dusk and raised his voice. "Barridas Decker!" he roared. "Back your peckerless ass away from the Refuge, or you die where you stand."

All eyes whipped toward Kullen. Magister Deckard's guards reacted first, spinning on their heels or turning their mounts to face him. Mammy Tess was next, her gaze darting to the corner where Kullen stood. Magister Deckard moved slowest. His head raised toward Kullen with a look of mingled surprise—which was replaced a moment later by outrage, as if he couldn't believe some low-blooded ruffian had dared threaten him.

"I don't know who you think you are," Magister Deckard snapped, swiveling to face Kullen, "I assure you, this is not something you want to do."

"I'd say the same to you." Kullen advanced slowly, his empty hands spread wide at his waist level. "Then again, I'm actually hoping that you're too pig-headed to listen to my warning, so you give me an excuse to carve your gizzards to little tiny pieces."

Magister Deckard's guards tensed, hands lowering to their weapons. Magister Deckard, however, appeared utterly bewildered—almost intrigued. He glanced between his men and Kullen.

"You and what army?" he sneered.

"I don't need an army." Kullen's voice was calm, his steps measured. His mind, however, was working at blistering speed, analyzing every one of the guards standing and sitting mounted in a semi-circle around the aristocrat and the front door of the Refuge. "And if you think this rabble can stop me from putting you down like the dog you are, then you're in for a rude—and very short-lived—surprise."

Some tiny voice in the back of his mind warned him that he was just making the situation worse. By insulting the aristocrat, he was guaranteeing a fight—one he didn't have the best odds of winning. But he was beyond caring, reminding himself yet again that Magister Deckard was the bastard responsible for Jarius and Hadassa's death. He'd come to the Refuge—the only place where Kullen had ever come close to calling home—to burn it to the ground and, if necessary, kill everyone inside. Every fiber of Kullen's being wanted nothing more than to rip Magister Deckard apart with his bare hands and hear the aristocrat scream for mercy.

The prick could scream all he wanted; there would be no mercy tonight.

"You insolent blaggard!" Magister Deckard fumed. His face turned a furious shade of purple. "I'll have you whipped where you—"

"Mammy Tess," Kullen shouted, drowning out the aristocrat's blather. "Get inside, and bar the doors. These men won't be troubling you any more. Not tonight, not ever."

Mammy Tess' eyes went wide.

Magister Deckard's gaze shifted from Kullen to the woman he'd come to intimidate—and kill. His sword hand, still wielding the blade of pure fire, began to move back to threaten Mammy Tess.

"I've said that I'm feeling generous tonight," Deckard said, that sword growing ever closer to Mammy Tess. "I'll offer you one last chance. If you know what's good for you, you'll walk away this instant."

"Thing is, my Magister," Kullen said, voice still steady as Lake Poplen on a calm day, "I very rarely do what's good for me."

In an instant, both of his hands tore throwing knives from their places hidden in his belt, and the two blades shot like darts toward the assembled men. The first buried into the shoulder of the nearest horse. The second hurtled right at the side of Magister Deckard's exposed neck.

The wounded horse reared up on its hind legs and kicked out with its forelegs. Its metal-shod hooves crunched into the head of a dismounted guard, crushing his helmet and head and sending his body careening into the four guardsmen next to him. All five went down in a tangle of flailing limbs and spraying blood.

The rider atop the rearing horse lost his grip on both reins and the lantern he held. The lantern crashed to the street and shattered, spraying its liquid fuel all over the cobblestones. The rider followed it a moment later. He flipped ass over tea kettle to land on his head in the puddle of oil and glass shards. Kullen couldn't hear the man's neck snap, but the guard didn't move even as the oil caught alight and he was engulfed in flame.

Pandemonium consumed the street.

But Kullen had eyes only for the second dagger, aimed at Magister Deckard's neck. The aristocrat would never see it coming. He'd be dead before he drew another breath.

One of Magister Deckard's guards, however, moved with impressive speed, raising an armored forearm to intercept the thrown weapon. The blade skittered off his steel vambrace and spun away to clatter harmlessly to the cobblestone street. With his other hand, he reached for the sword still sheathed at his belt. Those of his companions still standing did likewise.

But Kullen had not counted on the daggers finishing his work.

Even as the throwing knives spun through the air, he'd drawn his two long hunting knives and charged the guards. He hit the first cluster before they could unsheathe their swords. His knives flashed out, then in, and three men fell with slashed faces and throat wounds that gushed blood.

Rushing through the throng, deflecting attacks as he went, Kullen angled himself toward the one who'd reacted, saving Magister Deckard's life. He was up the stairs to the porch in a breath. Deckard shrank back and out of harm's way, but his soldier stepped forward to meet Kullen's attack.

The military precision of the guardsman's posture was obvious. As was the worn hilt of the sword hanging in a well-oiled sheath at his side. Kullen recognized the mark of a soldier when he saw it. Almost a shame the man had to die, really. He'd simply chosen the wrong loyalties and taken part in an act so vile that Kullen had no choice but to send him to Shekoth's pits alongside his master.

The guard managed to clear his sword and swing a blow at Kullen's head. Kullen interposed his right-hand dagger in a cross-body block that stopped the swinging sword short, then drove his left-hand dagger straight outward. As expected, the guard blocked the attack with ease. Then, the man's eyes betrayed him—rather, they betrayed his fellow sneaking up behind Kullen.

Kullen's booted foot thrust back and found the man's head even as he charged up the stairs. He didn't bother to look, never taking his focus off Deckard's personal bodyguard.

"You're took good for this," Kullen told the man.

"So are you."

"Touché," Kullen said, stabbing forward again.

The guardsman slapped the blade aside with his bracer and brought his sword down in a diagonal slice from right to left. Kullen fell into a roll that brought him up just behind the man's attack and jabbed his other dagger into the guardsman's unarmored throat.

Razor-sharp steel punched through gristle and cartilage, snapped bone, and severed the spinal nerves. Even as the guardsman dropped boneless to the deck, Kullen released his grip on his left-hand dagger. He did two things at once. He snatched the sword falling from the dying man's limp fingers and kicked the falling dagger. It soared through the air and found its mark buried in the guard Kullen had just kicked down the stairs.

Kullen tested the sword's feel in his hand. It was a good weapon, well-balanced and free of nicks and rust. A soldier's blade. Kullen may have been partial to daggers and short knives, but that didn't mean he was untrained with swords.

He cut down the first of the guards rising from amidst the pile brought down by the horse-kicked corpse, deflected a blow from a mounted guard, and dragged his dagger along the horse's flanks. The horse reared up, lashing out with its hooves, and Kullen had to throw himself backward to avoid getting head-bashed.

The horse's agonized trumpets added to those of the already-wounded mount. The two stamped and plunged, kicking out at anything around, the smell of blood, no doubt, thick in their sensitive nostrils. Their roars of pain startled the other horses, and a handful of the riderless horses took off in a mad panic. The two mounted guards who'd been holding their reins were dragged from the saddle and crashed to the cobblestone street with force enough to knock them senseless.

Fortune had smiled on Kullen, his enemies' number diminished in the space of seconds, but he was still vastly outnumbered and his foes weren't entirely incompetent. Two more of the downed guards managed to struggle out from beneath the corpse of their dead comrade and their flurrying attacks drove Kullen back with wild, furious swings of their short swords. Kullen momentarily took the defensive—a position he didn't particularly favor—and had to parry with every shred of speed to keep the blades away from his unarmored flesh.

He spared a single glance for Magister Deckard. The aristocrat stood riveted in place, his expression a mix of horror, shock, and fear. The blade of fire had guttered out, leaving him empty-handed and open-mouthed in the middle of a rapidly thinning handful of guards.

To Kullen's relief, the front doors of the Refuge had been thrown shut, Mammy Tess vanished within. His swift actions had bought the orphanage a few moments longer. Now he just had to finish tearing the rest of Magister Deckard's men apart and bring the aristocrat himself to the ground. Only once the bastard was dead could Kullen rest easy knowing the Refuge was safe.

One of the attacking guards attacking overextended and lost his balance, just for a split second—long enough for Kullen to cleave his head from his shoulders. The second guard watched the body crumple in abject horror, giving Kullen the opening he needed. He slid his dagger around and up the man's arm. The blade found flesh and bit deep into the crook of his elbow, between the vambrace and rerebrace on his upper arm. The man screamed and lost his grip on his sword, the tendons and muscles of his forearm severed. Kullen hacked open his throat with a vicious swing of his hunting knife.

For a heartbeat, he stood alone, surrounded by corpses, an island of calm amidst a sea of shouting men, stamping horses, and fires burning on the street where lanterns had fallen. Magister Deckard—the man's florid face ashen, all trace of his outrage vanished—stood deathly still with only utter panic etched into his expression.

Kullen saw the man's courage break. A moment later, Deckard turned to run. Kullen raised his dagger to hurl it at the aristocrat's back, but the clatter of hooves to his left snapped his attention away. He had just a split-second to register the charging horseman and the saber swinging for his head. Desperate, he dove forward, out of the path of the descending sword. He couldn't quite clear the horse, however. The beast slammed into his diving feet and he flew in a whirlwind.

Somehow, he turned his off-balanced tumble into a somersault that brought him back up to his feet. He slammed into the orphanage's wall, felt the solid stone and cool brass of Hadassa's plaque against his back. Shaking his head to clear his whirling vision, he waded back into the fray with a roar and a furious chop of his stolen sword. The blade cut deep into the thigh of the horseman who'd charged him, and the man let out a terrible shriek of agony. Kullen carried through with the blow and scored a hit on the flanks of the man's steed. The horse reared up, throwing its wounded rider off. Kullen followed it up with a swift jab of his blade and the threat was no more.

All the destruction around him, and Kullen's sympathy, above all, went to the horses. For all his wealth and power, Magister Deckard possessed little in the way of courage. The aristocrat was already halfway into one of his dead guard's empty saddles and turning his horse away. The half-dozen guards left to him closed in, forming a solid wall of steel and flesh that blocked any hope Kullen had of reaching the man. Within seconds, they'd galloped off and vanished around a corner.

Kullen stood, prepared for any number of things—more guards appearing from the darkness of night, already downed soldiers proving to only be stunned or injured—but none of those things happened. After a moment, his battle fury subsided and it felt as if he were coming down off a stim-pop. His heart raced, lungs burning almost as hot as the fire sizzling in his gut. Yet, with those sensations, came awareness of his body. New pains coursed through his arms, legs, face, and stomach.

Looking down, Kullen found he was covered in blood— including some of his own. His left arm had taken a deep gash along the biceps, and his right leg bled from a shallow cut just above the knee. He pressed a hand to the stinging pain in his cheek; it came away red, and not only from his enemies' gore.

He groaned, one part pain, one part anger. A cocktail fit for the moment.

A metallic thunk from behind him brought him spinning in time to see the front doors of the Refuge swing open. Mammy Tess stood there, a cast iron frying pan in her hand. Her eyes widened at the sight of him. She stared. as slack-jawed as Magister Deckard had been mere moments earlier.

"Ku… llen?" She struggled to form the words and not just due to the coughing.

"I'm okay," he said. "The wounds are worse than they look." He moved toward her, but she stepped back. Was that fear?

"What…happened to you?" Mammy Tess's eyes filled with horror. "What did they…" She swallowed, looked him over from head to toe. "What did they do to you ?"

He knew she didn't mean Deckard's men. It was the first time she'd seen him act as the Black Talon. The first time she would have the scantest suspicion that he'd been brought into the Emperor's palace as anything more than Prince Jarius's royal companion.

That look of horror, paired with the shock in Mammy Tess's eyes, drove a dagger into Kullen's gut. All these years, it had pained him to keep the Emperor's secret. But he knew it was to protect her as much as him. Now, she was seeing the truth with her own eyes, and it filled her with revulsion.

Kullen felt as if a sword had been thrust into his heart. The pain of his wounds was nothing compared to the ache that formed in the pit of his belly at her horrified expression.

Yet he steeled himself.

"They made me into a weapon to protect the Empire," he said, his voice calm yet hard as cold iron. "And that's exactly what I did tonight. What I'm going to do."

Darkness shrouded Mammy Tess's face as she took a step back. Whether it was his words, bloodstained visage, or the intensity of his voice, Kullen didn't know. He could worry about that later. For now, he had bigger things to fret over.

"Bar this door, Mammy Tess," he said. "Don't open it until

sunrise." Dropping his stolen sword, he strode to retrieve his throwing knives from where they lay in an ever-widening pool of blood and ripped his hunting knife free of the dead guard's neck.

"What will you do?" Mammy Tess asked. "Will you…"

Kullen glanced over his shoulder, found her gaze fixed on the corpses strewn around the street in front of the Refuge.

"I'm going to make sure Magister Deckard never bothers you again," he said, wiping his blades on one of the dead guard's cloaks. "And, in the process, get justice for Jarius and Hadassa. If anyone asks, you didn't see my face. Understood?"

Mammy Tess nodded and Kullen went hunting.

34
NATISSE

The gnashers were only real to a select few people. Mostly, they were monsters in tales told to scare children around the campfire. She and the Crimson Fang had heard faint sounds for years, suspecting them to belong to rats, but they'd always joked they might be gnashers. It was humor wrought from fear. But nothing could've prepared her for the creature that loomed from the darkness before her.

Five feet tall and propelled on four powerful legs, the monstrosity had two enormous copper eyes on the front of its hairy head and six smaller black eyes surrounding it. Venom dripped from four elongated fangs protruding from the horrifying aperture that was its mouth, and a stinger-tipped tail extended nearly three feet back from the rear of its bulging body.

A scream rose to Natisse's lips, but she had no time for terror. Rumors of gnashers told of people vanishing without a trace in the darkness beneath Dimvein, no trace of their corpses found. Now that she knew the tales to be fables to be fact, she had no desire to be one more morsel for this hideous beast.

The gnasher hissed, and Natisse swung the shuttered lantern up in front of the its enormous eyes. With her other hand, she reached for the lashblade strapped to her back. With a tug and a whip, the sword unhinged in several sections. She snapped the razor-sharp tip at the creature's face. Steel bit into hairy flesh and bright yellow ichor oozed from the gap.

The gnasher let out a terrible screeching whine and recoiled, both from the pain and the light. Hope surged within Natisse. She brought the lashblade back for another strike, and again waved the lantern between her and the creature. She needed to fling the shutters wide, let the light drive the hideous thing back, but she didn't have a free hand, not if she wanted to keep her sword at the ready. She wasted a split second contemplating her options, then settled on a second attack with the lashblade. This time, the tip punched straight into one of the gnasher's copper eyes. Again, the pus-like liquid gushed forth, spattering Natisse. Another scream issued from the creature, and this one rang with terror and fury.

The monster's mouth opened wide, revealing two rows of teeth and a snakelike tongue. With blinding speed—especially for something its size—it thrust itself at Natisse. She barely managed to evade by leaping backward. The creature's fangs closed on empty air but its ensuing tail-whip smacked into her with the force of a runaway stallion. It sent her bodily into the earthen wall, causing a thin layer of dirt to explode into the air. Knowing she had no time to spare, she rose and retracted her lashblade, then brought it to bear, hacking at the scorpion-like stinger. Try as she might, even her steel couldn't cut through the veneer of chitinous armor protecting the appendage. She was once again forced to scramble backward as the tail lashed at her once, twice, three times.

The last attack struck the lantern, battering it from her hand. Metal crumpled against the stone and the glass within shattered, spraying oil everywhere and snuffing out the flame. Instantly, the tunnel was plunged into terrible, all-consuming darkness.

The only thing she could imagine being worse than fighting this terrifying and heinous beast was doing so blind. Panic gripped at Natisse's heart. Though she couldn't see it, she had no doubt it could see her. Desperate, she hacked at the air about her. Desperate, she hacked at the darkness around her. She struck only empty air time and again She stopped, bringing her sword up in a defensive position.

"Where are you?" she taunted, though she felt no courage behind her words.

The creature answered with that terrible gnashing of its teeth. In response, Natisse flicked out the blade's whip-form in a frantic attempt to keep the gnasher at bay. More than once, she felt the lashblade sink into monstrous, hairy flesh. The creature's screams of pain echoed loud around her and the smell of its ichorous blood thickened the already stagnant air within the passage.

Yet Natisse fought a losing battle, she knew. A war of attrition, Uncle Ronan would've called it. The moment her arm tired and her lashblade faltered, the creature would charge in. She cursed herself for a fool. She'd been so determined to follow Uncle Ronan, she hadn't prepared for whatever she'd find within the underground. Worse, she'd ignored his training and come on her own.

Her heart beat faster, the gnashing grew louder and just as she was about to consider herself dead, a bright light seared, lighting the beast in brilliant warm blue.

Uncle Ronan stood at her side, sword drawn with a magical globe of light held high. Natisse caught a glimpse of the gnasher mere feet from where she stood, its tail poised to strike, fangs bared and ready to sink through her supple flesh. Yet, it didn't. Instead, the creature recoiled from the sudden brilliance, and its scream rang with terror so all-consuming it sent a chill down Natisse's spine.

"Back!" Uncle Ronan waved his sword at Natisse, gesturing for her to retreat. "Get back!"

He raised his hand, and for the first time, Natisse saw the light for what it was. Not glowstones, nothing so easily explained.

She nearly fell over, but not from the fear of the gnasher.

The Gryphic Elixir had been a shock. The secret passage too. But this...

Uncle Ronan was a... Lumenator?

Just the idea of him having powers said to be imbued by Thanagar and the Emperor made Natisse's limbs go numb.

He spared the smallest glance Natisse's way before stabbing forward with his sword and making the beast retreat ever so slightly. The Lumenator's globe flared, and the gnasher screeched.

Yet another secret Uncle Ronan was keeping from her. And this one was massive.

Natisse's stomach clenched and her heart hammered a staccato beat against her ribs. She'd already been angry at Uncle Ronan. But now, every new revelation only compounded that anger.

However, she didn't have time for the shock rooting her in place.

"Quickly, behind me, Natisse!" Uncle Ronan shouted. "Shield your eyes, before it decides that you pose a true threat to its younglings."

At that, Natisse spotted several dozen smaller gnashers planted upon what would be the mother's back. They dug their claws into their protector's fur, hissing along with her.

It was enough to kick Natisse's mind into reason. She scrambled backward, nearly tripped over a loose rock, and had to catch onto the tunnel wall beams for support. When she straightened, Uncle Ronan was backing toward her, keeping the glowing light between him and the screeching gnasher.

"Dammit, Natisse!" Uncle Ronan urged. "Cover your eyes!"

Natisse did as Uncle Ronan instructed. No sooner had her lids shut than she saw through them a light so bright it would've rivaled that of the sun. The gnashers, all of them, screeched and roared.

"Go!" Uncle Ronan shouted.

Natisse turned and opened her eyes. Little spots impaired her vision, but she fumbled her way along the tunnel, using the wall and the glow of Uncle Ronan's magic to guide her back to the first bend in the corridor. If she weren't so terrified, the prospect of Uncle Ronan wielding magic would have paralyzed her.

Around the corner, she flattened herself against the wall and fought to regain control of her hammering heart. Her breath came in great gasps.

A few seconds later, Uncle Ronan came careening around the corner.

"Run!" he shouted. "And stay close to me if you value your life."

Natisse didn't need to be told twice. She ran for all her life was worth, staying close on Uncle Ronan's heels as they charged through the Lumenated, twisting tunnels. She had no idea where he was going, but when they arrived, she'd damn well confront him. About everything. He demanded their trust yet kept secrets of this magnitude from them?

Through the darkness she followed the man who'd been leader to the Crimson Fang—and, in a way, the closest thing to a father she could remember. Since before she'd even blossomed, he had been her mentor, guide, caretaker, trainer, taskmaster, and commander. And now… a Lumenator?

The feelings of betrayal grew with every thundering beat of her heart, every frantic moment they retreated along a secret tunnel she'd only discovered by accident.

She fought every urge—and there were many—to scream at him. Attack him even. But that would do no good. She needed to understand fully. He might've been lying, but he'd never been a liar.

She had no idea how long they ran—it could have been a minute or an hour—but finally Uncle Ronan slowed, then stopped and turned to glance back the way they'd come.

Though he, too, was breathing heavily and sweat dripped

down his face, his voice was calm as he said, "I don't think she'll follow us anymore. Not if it means abandoning her nest."

Natisse's mind boggled. She'd seen no nest—no younglings of any sort—only the enormous monstrosity trying to kill her. And how did Uncle Ronan know anything about gnashers and their habits?

He rounded on her. "What in Shekoth's pits are you doing here, Natisse?" he demanded, an angry flush in his cheeks. "And how—"

Natisse cut him off. "I could ask you the same!"

Thankful as she was for Uncle Ronan's help, she was angry, too. She'd nearly died, all because Uncle Ronan had kept this a secret. From her!

"What in Ezrasil's name are these tunnels, and who was that man you were talking to?"

The red in Uncle Ronan's face deepened, the lines around his eyes and mouth tightening. "You... saw him?"

"Of course I did!" Natisse snapped. "Are you going to answer me with truth this time, or add to your ever-growing list of lies? Who is he and why were you meeting with him?" Then, another question—the question she truly wanted to ask—tore from her lips. "And why the hell are you keeping secrets like this"—she gestured to the tunnels—"like him from us. From me?"

Uncle Ronan's expression hardened. "Natisse, you know what we do is dangerous. That operating the way we do puts us all in peril every moment of every day. Keeping secrets—"

"Don't you dare say that it's to protect us," Natisse snarled. "We're not children, Ronan. Not anymore." The way his face twisted into shock and hurt told her he'd noticed that she hadn't called him Uncle. She didn't care. That's what she wanted. She squared up in front of him, glaring straight into his face. "You trained us to be fighters, to carry out the Crimson Fang's mission—the mission you said you needed our help to carry out. You ask us to put our faith in you, to trust that you're making the smart choices, and yet you keep secrets like this?"

"To me, you still are," Uncle Ronan said quietly.

She had plenty more to say—to shout, really—but Uncle Ronan's soft words threw her off-balance.

"What?" she demanded.

"You said you're not children." Uncle Ronan's face grew sad, his eyes dark. "You're not, but sometimes, to me, it feels like you still are." He let out a long breath. "I still see the little girl I found on the road, a child lost, scared, and in pain, who needed me to protect her. I still see the two young brothers one day away from starving on the streets. I still see the smith's apprentice beaten to within an inch of his life, yet still forced to swing a hammer." He fixed her with a piercing stare. "You have no idea how difficult it is to not see the children and youths you once were."

The response somehow both calmed Natisse and made her angrier at the same time. She opened her mouth to say something —she didn't know what, but her boiling temper wanted to hurl something back at him—yet no words came to her lips.

"I know this looks bad," Uncle Ronan said, his voice heavy. He stretched his hand toward her and she pulled away. "And yes, I have been keeping secrets from you. Some bigger than you'll ever know." Whether he meant to or not, he raised his hand and the glowing orb grew brighter. "But I am doing it to protect you."

Natisse slid away from the magic. "We don't need you to protect us like you did when we were children!"

"I know, I know." Uncle Ronan nodded slowly. "And in truth, much of the time, I keep these secrets because it's necessary for operational security. Like these tunnels." He gestured to the dark tunnel in which they stood. "The more people that know these tunnels exist, the greater the risk that others will learn of them." His eyes narrowed. "What if Ammon had known about them? Would he have revealed them to Arbiter Chuldok?"

"Have you so little trust in us?" she said. "Are we just pawns in some sick game where you're a goddamned Lumenator and you couldn't bother to tell us?"

Natisse had fought the urge to slap him, but he still looked struck.

"No," she continued. "He never would have. Ammon was strong. Strong to the very end!"

"He was," Uncle Ronan agreed. "But even the strongest men and women break under torture." His jaw muscles clenched. "Information is a currency, Natisse. A blessing as much as a burden. In the right hands, it can save lives. In the wrong hands, it can end them just as easily. Keeping certain information to myself ensures that I am the only one who has to carry the burden."

"And you just expect that to be good enough?" Natisse's anger was far from diminished. "You expect me to keep my mouth shut and trust you because you're *Uncle* Ronan?"

"Yes," Uncle Ronan said simply. "That's exactly what I expect. That's how I trained you."

Natisse opened her mouth to retort, but Uncle Ronan continued before she could speak.

"The mission above all," he said, no doubt expecting her to repeat it.

"Even above trust? Honesty? Loyalty?"

"We cannot put the entire operation at risk," Uncle Ronan said, shaking his head. "Natisse, you must promise to keep this… all of this… a secret. The fewer people who know about this place, about me, the safer we will all be. And not only because of the Arbiters—how well do you think Sparrow would have fared against that gnasher. Or Dalash?"

That shut Natisse's mouth. In truth, she doubted any of the others—save perhaps Garron before his current wound—would still be standing.

"As for the man I was meeting, he, too, is a secret that must be kept safe," Uncle Ronan's mouth twisted into a frown. "Some of our information has to come from places and people that…" He hesitated, seemed to be thinking for the right word. "...I'm not sure I can fully trust. But we need that information anyway. So I choose to put myself in the path of danger for the sake of our cause."

"What a martyr," Natisse said under her breath.

"Natisse, I am not trying to paint myself that way. But as it stands, I'm the only one that can be linked to the Crimson Fang, which means that all the rest of you are able to continue operating in anonymity. Believe it or not, this *is* for your protection, and for the sake of the mission."

Natisse wanted to argue, but couldn't. Ezrasil take him, he was right.

"The mission abo—"

"No. No. None of that. You're right, too." Uncle Ronan reached for her again, and this time Natisse didn't move away from his outstretched hand. He gripped her shoulder and gave her the paternal smile that had always seemed so out of place on his grizzled face. Yet, as always, it made her love him all the more. "I know you're not children. You're adults, fighters, fully competent. And that..." He sighed. "That can be terrifying. Your lives are in constant danger. I must accept that. But for some of you, it's harder to accept than for others."

Natisse nodded. "I know." She'd never heard him shout at any of the others the way he had at her. But they'd never lost two of their number in the space of a week before. "And I understand why you were angry at me for going to Magister Onathus's mansion alone."

"But it's good you did," Uncle Ronan said. "What you discovered about Magister Branthe—that changes a great deal. And what my contact just told me backs up your findings. Turns out, he's been spending far more than his fair share of time in the palace. My contact says he's caught him snooping but Branthe always has an excuse. And the Emperor loves him."

"All the easier to stab him in the back."

"You did well, Natisse," he said. "You always do well."

Her gaze fell to the floor.

"Uncle Ronan?"

His hand fell upon her shoulder and she looked up. His head tilted, urging her to continue.

"Can you promise me something?" He was already shaking his head when she said, "No more secrets?"

"Do you trust me, Natisse?" he asked.

"I do," Natisse said, without a moment's hesitation. And it was the truth. She might not like the fact that he kept secrets from the Crimson Fang—from her—but she could understand it. And accept it, for the sake of the mission. The mission came above everything else, that was what he'd taught her.

"I can't make that promise but I can promise you, when the time is right, I will explain this further. In the meantime, know that I care very deeply for you."

That wasn't exactly enough, but for now, it would have to be.

"So what now?" she asked.

"Now, we do a bit more digging, see what we can turn up about Magister Branthe and his businesses in Dimvein and around the rest of the Empire." Uncle Ronan's expression grew pensive. "If we can link him to Magister Onathus and Magister Perech, with real, concrete proof, then we can present the evidence to the Emperor and get the whole ugly business shut down."

"And if there's no evidence to link them?" Natisse asked. "We've still got those slaves being held at Magister Perech's caravan yard."

"I know," Uncle Ronan said, nodding. "And Haston and Athelas will keep watch on the shipyard and caravan yard. If anything happens there, we'll know."

"I've got Leroshavé digging into the caravan yard, seeing who's taken over operations after Magister Perech's death."

"Good thinking!" Uncle Ronan grinned at her. "We're on the

right track, Natisse. All we need now is to figure out how we're going to nail the bastard Magister Branthe—either proving his crimes, or stringing him up ourselves." His smile faltered. "But we're going to have to be careful about it. Magister Branthe's got a private guard force twice the size of Magister Perech's, and after the recent deaths, he'll be on high alert."

"Magister Perech's guard didn't keep him alive," she quipped.

Uncle Ronan laughed. "Don't get cocky, now."

She laughed too, but the mention of Magister Perech's death brought back the face of the man who'd also killed that night. Twice.

"So we're going to play this smart," Uncle Ronan said, breaking the memory. "We're going to make sure Magister Branthe never suspects a thing until it's too late. By the time he knows we're coming, we'll have our blades at his throat and all his gold and power won't be enough to stop us from getting justice for his crimes!"

35

KULLEN

There was only one place a coward like Magister Deckard would run, only one place he'd feel safe: within the walls of the fortress he'd built to hide his shame.

After Golgoth—Deckard's Ember Dragon—had burned the poorest district of Dimvein to the ground, Magister Deckard had feared that public outcry would turn against him, that the riots that had led to the murdering of Prince Jarius and Princess Hadassa would spill over into the Upper Crest and a bloodthirsty mob could demand his head. Worse, he'd been terrified that the Emperor wouldn't be content to stop at levying enormous fines—but would settle for nothing less than his execution.

He'd sunk what little remained of his fortunes into fortifying his mansion. Gone were the ornate lawns, marble sculptures, glass windows, fluted columns, and flying buttresses that his fore-fathers had used to beautify the estate; in their place were stone walls thirty feet high topped with battlements upon which guards were eternally patrolling, hideous bulwarks of brick and sharp-ened iron, and heavy steel bars over every window and door. Arrow slits were carved in almost any place imaginable, giving

Deckard's own private army the advantage over any approaching foe.

In short, Magister Deckard had built for himself a stronghold that not even the Orkenwatch could easily breach. Had Emperor Wymarc truly wanted the aristocrat's head, he would've had to call out the entirety of the Imperial Scales to break down the steel gates barring the entrance. Even Thanagar's mighty magic would be limited—Magister Deckard had cleared away every living plant and tree, ordered his entire estate paved with stone or covered in clay. He'd shrouded the place in darkness, allowing no open courtyards or garden where Thanagar's light could prove a boon for the Emperor.

It appeared like a wasteland, void and desolate, the mark of a man terrified.

However, the days of his fearing for retaliation had passed and Deckard once again moved freely throughout the city, had even regained his position within the court. But after tonight's blood-bath, the aristocrat would once more be running scared for his life.

Kullen could only imagine the memories stirred up within Magister Deckard by the sight of fire in those streets. That fateful day, Golgoth's fires had stopped just short of Pawn May Avenue and, ultimately, the Refuge. He wondered what sickness had possessed the man to be so desperate to own land so close to the world he'd destroyed.

Kullen knew he had no chance of catching up to the panicking Magister Deckard before he reached the safety of his gates and the small army patrolling its high walls. But from the day he'd discovered that Magister Deckard had been behind Jarius and Hadassa's deaths, he'd prepared himself to infiltrate the aris-tocrat's stronghold. He'd interviewed every architect, engineer, and stonemason involved in the construction, paid vast sums to obtain information on any weaknesses the structure might have. With a fervor bordering on madness, he'd been determined that when the time came go after Magister Deckard's head, he would be ready.

Now, that time had come.

Tonight.

Emperor Wymarc hadn't given explicit permission, but Kullen couldn't stand down. Not now. Not after Magister Deckard's recent visit to the traitorous Magister Issemar's office and his intended attack on the Refuge. Kullen would simply have to make certain that he extracted intel from the aristocrat before killing him, prove beyond any doubt his complicity in some treacherous plot. And if there was nothing implicating the man? Kullen would endure whatever tongue-lashing or censure Emperor Wymarc heaped upon him. No price was too high to pay in the name of avenging the deaths of his only friends in the world.

There was a time when Dimvein had entertained the idea of mixed cultures, of the possibility that other gods mattered apart from Ezrasil. Now, it was more likely the city believed no gods mattered, but still, enough of Ezrasil's followers remained to make his the sole remaining faith in the city.

However, the old temples still cast their shadows, if only in a state of disrepair beyond hope. One such building stood on the outer fringes of the Upper Crest, a shrine to Yildemé, the goddess favored by the Brendoni and the people of the far west.

Kullen stood behind the temple, in a narrow path between the building itself and a steep cliff atop which housed the noble mansions. He pulled back a frayed, dirt-stained sheet to reveal a door carved from a single piece of hard wood. After a quick glance to make sure he wasn't being watched, he dug through a pile of broken bricks and wood that would've gone unnoticed in a back alley such as this, and retrieved a rusted brass key. He pushed his way inside, slammed the deadbolt home and re-locked the door behind him.

The building was an eyesore—one that Magister Deckard had been complaining about for years, as it was his property which looked down upon the place. However, with so many Brendoni still in the city, despite their distinct disinterest in honoring their goddess by worshiping in her temples, the Emperor refused to tear down nor would he spare the expenses to repair any one of them.

The inside was decidedly worse than the exterior. Like so many of the older buildings in Dimvein, the roof was all but gone, its tiles shattered all over the floor. The magnificent statue of Yildemé, however, rose the full height of the temple, watching over the place where her people had once gathered.

The onyx effigy wore the culturally accurate sarong—though left something to be desired for the lack of color. The Brendoni were flamboyant people, full of life and vigor. Her neck was adorned with many rings. Her ears, lips and eyebrows were pierced, as were her nipples, which the artist had clearly outlined under the sarong.

They were also a people unashamed of their sexuality, often giving into passionate throes in the very streets of Dimvein. Though not explicitly illegal, the Orkenwatch tolerated none of it.

Kullen strode through puddles of rainwater, past cracked and broken pews toward one particular pile of rubble beneath the only section of roof still intact. He kicked aside clay tiles until he found what he sought: a small bronze ring set into the ground, invisible beneath the layer of dust and the debris he'd used to cover it. He hadn't created the tunnels, but he'd damn sure used them over the years.

Kneeling, he pulled on the ring. Something clicked in the floor to his right, and the solid ground seemed to split apart. The fissure widened until the opening was broad enough to see a stone staircase descending into the ground.

One thing that the Emperor had never warned him about before his official christening as the Black Talon was how often he'd find himself in the shit-infested sewers below the city and just how awful they smelled. Wading through a few feet, he made it to a roughly built stone wall. It didn't look like the ones surrounding it, the rock another shade and texture.

He hefted a pickaxe he'd had waiting for just this moment from its place leaning against the western wall. Bringing it to bear, he struck the wall several times. In mere minutes, a dam burst open and sullage and sewage poured forth. The pipes and tunnels slowly began to fill with the putrid mixture.

The first part of his plan had been set into motion. The architect who'd upgraded the mansion had, at Magister Deckard's request, blocked off any connections from the city. Yet it had been shoddy work done by unscrupulous builders. Kullen had also spent years slowly hastening the decay of the clay stoppers that sealed it off. The dam had been Kullen's handiwork. Deckard's plumbing had been constructed to dump directly into Blackwater Bay, bypassing the city sewers entirely. Instead, the slope had accumulated an enormous backlog of sewage that, when unleashed, would burst up through Deckard's plumbing, flooding the lower levels and filling his grounds.

Kullen retreated from the river of stench, hurrying up the stairs that led aboveground. He pulled the bronze ring again, and the stone floor slid shut, concealing the hidden staircase once more.

Next, clambering onto the pile of debris, he approached what was once Yildemé's priestesses's pulpit, the very place at which grand sermons had been preached over the centuries. Now, it was just like any other mound of rubble. In Kullen's mind, that spoke great volumes about religion in general.

He located a long wooden chest he'd stashed there years earlier. It was covered in a thick layer of dust, the metal rusted by exposure and repeated rain, but the Trenta-crafted lock still held solid and clicked open when he twisted the right combination of gears. No one built mechanical contraptions like the diminutive, tunnel-loving Trenta.

Lifting the lid, Kullen stared down at its contents. Two swords still in enameled white leather sheaths—a gift from Hadassa, the last she'd given him—lay atop a folded pile of dark fabric. Removing the weapons, Kullen then lifted the garment and let it fall, revealing a rich, black riding cloak with an inner lining of rich crimson velvet. It had been a gift to Jarius from Hadassa on his twenty-third birthday. He'd taken the damned thing everywhere, called it his 'lucky cloak.'. He'd forgotten it the day he and Hadassa went to the Embers and were killed in the riot. Kullen had spent these last many years wondering if it had, indeed, been lucky.

Other items: alchemical tricks, rings of value both magical and monetary, and weapons of varying styles and types lay within. All were brand new, never-before used, forged for him by the finest smith in Dimvein using pristine Karmian steel.

But all paled in comparison to the blades. Hadassa had called them the Black Talons. Two identical curved swords, black as night and sharp as an eagle's eye. The pommels bore the likeness of Umbris's head, curved horns and all. They'd be as wicked a weapon as the pointy end.

He'd never had a chance to use them before that day when Jarius and Hadassa were torn apart by the very people they aimed to aid. It was then that Kullen vowed that they would never spill blood until they'd tasted Deckard's. Kullen was far from sentimental, but from the moment he'd decided that bastard deserved to die, he'd prepared himself for this night.

He replaced his smoke spheres from the small stock he had hidden on hand, as well as other tricks and trinkets. Though he had a few throwing knives already, he took more—some on his belt and other slid into a sheath under his left arm—easy to grab at a moment's notice. It was always better to be over-prepared than find oneself lacking.

The cloak fit like it was made for him, though he knew it was not. A sword hung from each hip. Once finished, he replaced the near-empty box and jumbled the lock. Only one thing remained.

"*The time has come, my friend*," Kullen said. "*Tonight, we move against the one who killed my Heartbound.*"

Dragons didn't mate, nor had they siblings or friends—at least not in the mortal realm. Umbris, especially, alone in the Shadow realm, had no one like him. They did, however, understand the love shared with their Bloodsworn.

Kullen had used that as a means to explain the love shared between himself and Jarius. He'd done the same with Hadassa, though he'd chosen not to expound upon how much she'd truly meant to him.

"*It is good*," Umbris said through their mental bond. "*I can feel your rage—it, too, boils within my chest.*"

Settled dust and detritus burst upward in a violent torrent as Umbris stepped into the temple, seemingly out of thin air. The dragon snuffed, expelling a gust of scorching smoke from his huge nostrils.

"*Let us bring vengeance for those you have lost,*" he continued.

Kullen grabbed hold of Umbris's neck furls, using them to pull himself up. Umbris shifted his weight to assist his friend. Once settled, Kullen patted his back, and braced himself.

"Upward," Kullen whispered into Umbris's ear.

The dragon's powerful hind legs shoved off the ground and with a burst of speed, thrust up and through the open rooftop. Yildemé's temple became a small blotch as they rose into the clouds.

Umbris's black scales immediately blended into the night sky and together, they soared in a tight circle above Deckard's estate.

"*Perhaps I could just tear through the place and make it indistinguishable from an abandoned temple?*"

Kullen laughed. "*If only, my friend.*"

From above, Deckard's place looked far less like the fortified stronghold he'd turned it into, and more like the vast sprawling mansion it once was. Though where every other Magister—other than Issemar's poison lawn—had beautiful gardens, even in darkness, Deckard's place looked brown and dead.

Kullen gave a cold, hard smile. It was now more brown than ever. The entire property was awash with the Magister's own shit. Below, guards slogged through waist-deep muck, struggling to escape the sludge flowing out of the mansion. The gate stood abandoned and the sentries nearest the estate's walls had run up onto the battlements to escape the foul, ever-rising tide.

Kullen was pleased with his handiwork.

The bulk of Magister Deckard's guards were cut off from the mansion itself. Those within would likely be too busy dealing with the mess on the lower level to realize that their master was in danger from above.

"Are you sure I can't lay waste to the whole estate?"

"Not today," Kullen said through his mental connection.

Reluctantly, Kullen could sense, Umbris swooped down until he was level with the rooftop. Just as he'd done at Magister Issemar's place, he did once more, allowing Kullen to slide off and land painlessly atop the fortification.

"So much for security," Kullen said.

He dismissed Umbris, who disappeared in a whipping wind, and was already running the instant his feet touched the roof. The building's original architect had pinpointed two vulnerable points: a single two-yard-wide skylight set into the domed roof above the atrium, and a door utilized by builders to provide frequent maintenance to the roof.

The skylight had been part of the re-fortification project, covered over to ensure Thanagar's presence would not be felt. That left only the latter.

There was a steep drop where a ladder must've once been, and Kullen was one floor down in a gully between two walls. A crawl space—more a grate or vent than anything else—would lead him unseen into what might've been the most secure building apart from the Emperor's palace in all of Dimvein.

After many years of disuse, the small door stuck, forcing Kullen to kick it open. Kullen had expected to find a dirty, dusty attic, but that was only because he'd forgotten the nature of the man who owned the place. The room he entered was spotlessly clean. Crates lined one wall while shelves lined another. Where many people would've stored their unused items haphazardly until the next time they'd needed them, Magister Deckard seemed to have a system.

The wood floor was without pit or creak. Polished almost to the point where Kullen could see his reflection, if that were possible.

"Ezrasil's bloody bastard son," he whispered.

At least he wouldn't have to worry about an old house giving him away.

He pressed forward, always ready to slide into the shadows but unwilling to use the bloodsurge unless absolutely necessary.

Last night's scare had him on edge.

Besides, there was so much commotion, so many echoing shouts coming from the ground floor that no one would be worried about the attic. As he descended the stairs, people bellowed orders, servants responded in kind, water—and other things—splashed audibly, and people frantically attempting to gain control over the rising tide of sewage.

However, not all of Magister Deckard's guards were occupied or trapped outside the mansion. The half-dozen who'd fled the Refuge just two hours earlier now stood outside the heavy oak door that led into the Magister's private study and bedroom. They were far from wary, their weapons sheathed and their stances relaxed. All that would change the moment Kullen showed himself.

Had it been anywhere else, his target anyone else, he'd have chosen the path of stealth. But tonight, Kullen felt in the mood to visit the same suffering upon Magister Deckard that the aristocrat had intended for the Refuge and all its inhabitants.

Reaching into his cloak—Jarius's cloak—he drew out two small glass bottles filled with acidic green liquid. He had the slightest concern the concoction might've lost some of its potency after being stored so long in Yildemé's temple, but it would still do the job.

He didn't bother pulling the stoppers, but simply stepped into view of the guards and, with a contemptuous sneer, hurled both against the door at their backs. Kullen spun, dropped into a crouch, and used Jarius's cloak to shield his eyes. The sound of glass shattering was followed by a deafening *whumph* and a billowing wave of heat that nearly knocked him to the ground. It faded a moment later, only to be replaced by brilliant light and horrible, agonized screams.

Lowering his cloak, Kullen stood and found the guards, door, and hallway in which they'd stood engulfed by brilliant emerald flames. The flammable alchemical mixture had ignited upon exposure to air, creating a blaze that burned as hot as dragonfire. The four men standing closest to the points of impact had died instantaneously, their armor liquefied and flesh charred by the explosive burst of flame. The two who'd been farthest away hadn't escaped the flames, but now lay on the floor, writhing.

Kullen couldn't summon even a shred of pity for them. They'd die fast—faster than Mammy Tess and her children would have if the guards had carried out Magister Deckard's command to burn down the Refuge. Indeed, their screams fell silent within seconds, and the blistering heat dissipated as the flames consumed the last of the alchemical fuel.

Only now did Kullen reach for the swords on his belt. The weapons slid free of their sheaths smoothly, the masterfully crafted blades still oiled and in pristine condition. It was fitting that the first blood they tasted would be Magister Deckard's.

Kullen waited a moment, hoping Deckard would try to run. But when no one exited the room, he strode forward, stepping over smoking bodies. Somehow, the remains of the door still hung on its hinges. He lifted his boot and drove his heel into the door with such force it tore from its frame. Splinters flew inward like little arrows. Only after he'd done it did he fear they might steal his joy and slay the man outright before he had the chance.

Luck was with him. The pitiful whelp of a man sat cowering behind his desk, his bald head sticking up, bobbing and shaking with sobs.

Kullen raised a sword toward the aristocrat. "Make a move, any move, and you die where you stand."

36

NATISSE

Uncle Ronan stopped at the blank stone wall at the
tunnel's end and pulled a small, thin wire Natisse
hadn't spotted upon entering. Torchlight shone through
two pinprick-sized holes in the wall. Uncle Ronan peered
through and into the training room beyond.

"Empty," he said a moment later, nodding. He released the
wire and the tunnel went dark, the holes once more covered.
Tugging on the brass ring triggered whatever mechanisms
opened and sealed the stone wall. Quickly, the two of them
slipped through the aperture.

"Not a word to anyone," he told her, closing the secret
entrance behind them.

Natisse wasn't fully calm yet. Between the encounter with the
gnasher and the revelation that Uncle Ronan was keeping secrets
as big as him being a Lumenator, she was shaken. Though, she
had to trust that the man who'd trained her, sacrificed so much
for her, had her best interests at heart.

She nodded. "Yes, sir."

It might've been a lie had Baruch been alive. She would've
been hard-pressed to keep from confiding in him—if nothing

else, just to see his eyes light up at the promise of a spilled secret. The man had loved puzzles and mysteries and riddles. Now, the knowledge that she had no one to tell about the passage brought sorrow welling within her. She trusted the rest of the Crimson Fang, even liked more than a few. But none of them had understood her the way Baruch had, and she didn't care for any of them as much as she'd cared for Baruch. He'd loved her, she knew. Loved her in the way only he could. She'd seen it in his eyes, heard it in every moment of silence between his words. And perhaps, one day, she might've allowed herself to feel enough to return his affections.

But that would never happen. Baruch was gone, and she still had the Crimson Fang's mission to drive her onward. Or, at the very least, distract her from the emptiness she'd begun to feel in the days since Ammon and Baruch's deaths.

"Ahh, there you are!" Leroshavé's voice echoed in the high-vaulted training room.

Natisse spun in time to see the small man entering the chamber, a shank of cold mutton in one hand and a heaping pile of mashed potatoes in the other.

"No clean plates?" Natisse jested.

"A custom I'm still not used to," Leroshavé said. He sank his teeth into the mutton and ripped off a chunk, speaking around a mouthful of food. "Been lookin' for you. Both of yous, in fact."

"Found out something of interest?" Natisse asked, making a point of keeping her gaze away from Leroshavé's open mouth. It seemed another custom that hadn't been important in Brendonia. His half-chewed was fully visible. He had the cunning and skills of a street rat, and manners to match. "About Magister Perech's operations?"

"Aye, that I do." Leroshavé swallowed the meat and took a bite of the mashed potatoes he held cupped in his other hand. He continued speaking, seeming not to notice the bits of food clinging to the corners of his mouth. "Had a few drinks with the strongbacks millin' about. Plenty of tongues waggin' after a few ales. None of them knew much, but puttin' it all together, I think I have an idea of what's what and who's who."

Natisse glanced at Uncle Ronan, who nodded at the little man and raised an iron-gray eyebrow. "We're listening."

"From what I gather," Leroshavé said, "no one's officially taken over Magister Perech's estates. Not officially. Things are still tied up in the courts. And though no one I talked to seems to know why, it's clear that the process is going slow. Like treacle in winter slow."

"Officially?" Uncle Ronan said.

Natisse's eyes narrowed. "If Magister Branthe's somehow putting his finger on the scale—"

Uncle Ronan snapped his fingers. "—he could be stalling the proceedings," he said, finishing her thought.

"Aye, that's what the boys at the caravan yard seem to think." Leroshavé nodded. "Magister Perech's got no heir, no wife, no family to pass his estates off to. Jad's the savvy one for legal whatsits, but even I know it should be, ah… What's it the apothecaries say? Cut and dried? Yes, that's it. Should be cut and dried. Should go to the Emperor, or to whoever's willin' to buy out his holdin's."

The knowing look in Leroshavé's eyes told Natisse that he had an idea of that "whoever's" identity. "They know who's making a play for it?"

"Like I said, officially? No." His face scrunched up. "Everythin' in that caravan yard is just continuin' operations as normal—no one wants to be out of a job, even if their boss is dead. But a couple of the strongbacks heard from a couple of others who heard it from a foreman that someone's already informed them that the business will be passed on to other noble hands instead of revertin' to the Palace. And that *someone* looked an awful lot like one of Magister Branthe's nephews, Baronet Ochrin."

"Wait, did you say Ochrin?" Natisse's eyebrows shot up, and her head swiveled toward Uncle Ronan. "Isn't that the name Jad found next to Magisters Perech's and Estéfar on the title deed for that abandoned property in Western Docks?"

Uncle Ronan frowned. "The property he found out is located dead-center between Magister Perech's caravan yard and Magister Onathus's shipyard, you mean?"

Natisse sucked in a breath. "Shekoth's pits!"

"I'll never understand that expression," Leroshavé said.

Natisse ignored him. "It can't be a coincidence."

Her mind raced. Baronet Ochrin was Magister Branthe's nephew and tied to a building located far close to where the Crimson Fang believed the slaves were being taken?

"No such thing as coincidences," Uncle Ronan said, stroking his beard.

Leroshavé appeared altogether pleased with himself.

"Thought you might figure out how it all matters," he said with a smug grin and a nod. "Now, while you two deliberate on our next steps, I must sleep." He gave a theatrical yawn. "Matchin' strongbacks drink for drink is tirin' work."

Natisse rolled her eyes, but Uncle Ronan just grunted. "Don't sleep too soundly or too long," he told the little man. "Athelas and Haston will need supplies. Fresh food and water, and a chance to relieve themselves."

Leroshavé groaned. "Never a moment's peace for us heroic savior-of-the-Empire types!" He stuffed the rest of the mashed potatoes into his mouth, licking the last traces from his filthy hand as he strode out of the training room.

Natisse turned to Uncle Ronan. "We've got—"

"—to see what's so interesting about that abandoned property?" Uncle Ronan asked. A grin spread across his face. "Course we do. If that many noblemen put their names down as owners, it means they're taking precautions to ensure it stays out of the wrong hands. That way, if anything happens to any of them, the rest will still be able to continue business as usual."

"The question, then," Natisse said, "is what exactly is that business?"

Hours later, Natisse still had no answer for her question. She and Uncle Ronan had spent the morning and early afternoon surveilling the property, and to all outward appearances, it fit the description of "abandoned" and "decrepit" to perfection. All except one thing that she was unsure was of any note at all. There, beside the building, was a pagoda with flowering blooms aplenty.

"You sure that's not important?" she asked Uncle Ronan.

He shook his head. "Doubtful."

"Who's tending it?"

"Who needs to?" He turned and looked over his shoulder.

Natisse knew what he was eyeballing: Thanagar the Protector, steepled high upon the palace, his magic practically oozing out of him.

"Right," she said. "All hail the king of dragons."

The building was two stories tall with the support beams exposed due to rot.

From their perch across the street, they had a clear view of anyone coming or going through the big iron gate.

"And Jad's sure this is the right place?"

"It's the place," Uncle Ronan said, a bit more sternly than Natisse had expected. "I'm sorry, Natisse." He placed a hand on hers. "We are both growing impatient. However, just because we're not seeing anything, doesn't mean there's nothing to see."

Natisse's jaw muscles clenched. "You're right," she said, standing. "I am growing impatient. Time to break in."

Uncle Ronan's hand gripped her arm and pulled her back down out of sight of the street below.

"Not yet." He shook his head. "Wait until nightfall, then slip in under cover of darkness."

Natisse frowned. "You really want to wait that long?" The sun wouldn't set for hours. "Sunlight's wasting, and we're nowhere closer to the truth than we were two days ago."

"Not true." Uncle Ronan's lips pressed together, deepening the lines on the corners of his mouth and eyes. "We've tied Magister Branthe to the mess, which is far closer than before. And if this really is connected to what's going on at the caravan and ship yards, then we're better off waiting and watching. As Leroshavé says, 'See what's what and who's who.'"

Natisse grimaced. "We'd see a lot better from the inside."

"Natisse, stand down," Uncle Ronan's voice never rose in volume, but the intensity cracked like thunder, and fire blazed in his eyes. "Stand down," he said more softly. "Not until after dark."

"This is absurd," she said, but she obeyed—ever the good soldier.

"I already told you," Uncle Ronan insisted. "You and I are the only able-bodied fighters the Crimson Fang has left. I won't risk either of us getting captured, killed, or incapacitated unless there's no other choice. If that means sitting on our hands a while longer and biding our time, I'm willing to shut my mouth and sit my goddamned ass down. I expect you to do the same, As. I. Trained. You!"

That last bit was said in a whisper-scream, but it carried a tone that clearly said "this conversation is over."

Natisse looked up at the sun, still high in the sky but starting its inevitable descent. If waiting a while longer meant getting answers, she'd have to learn to be patient. She was letting her anger from earlier cloud her judgment.

"Right," she said. "As you've trained me."

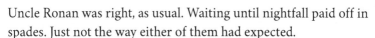

Uncle Ronan was right, as usual. Waiting until nightfall paid off in spades. Just not the way either of them had expected.

Uncle Ronan wakened her from a light doze just before sunset, and motioned her to silence and to stay low. When she joined him at the roof's edge, she'd been surprised to see movement around the abandoned property. Two guards now stood behind the tall wall, all but invisible to the surrounding streets. Even from their vantage, they could barely be seen. The fading daylight made it impossible to identify the insignia on their armor, but they wore the blue and green like the guards patrolling Magister Onathus's shipyards.

A quarter-hour later, a plain, drab-looking carriage pulled up in front of the property. The three cloaked figures who emerged from within were quickly hustled into the building by the two guards. For a moment, Natisse caught a glimpse of lantern light filling the building, and the flash of metal marking the presence of at least one more armed guard within.

Over the next hour, nearly two dozen carriages and two-wheeled hansoms came and went, with more than fifty cloaked and hooded figures being ushered inside by armed guards. Though she hadn't seen a single face or identifying feature—the people were careful to remain covered up—the vehicles conveying them and the quality of their clothing marked them as wealthy.

Judging by the frown on Uncle Ronan's face, he'd come to the same conclusion. But they would need a closer look to be certain.

"I'm going to slip down to the street," she whispered. "See if I can find somewhere to get a better look at the people beneath those cloaks."

Uncle Ronan chewed on his upper lip. It was dangerous, they

both knew, but from their current position, they wouldn't see anything useful.

Finally, he nodded. "Let's go."

Natisse raised an eyebrow. "Let's? One of us should stay here and keep—"

"Fine," he said. Then Natisse went to rise and he finished. "You stay."

"What? No way."

He smiled. "Then we both go."

Natisse sighed.

"After what happened at the caravan yard," he said, "it's better we stick together, close enough to help each other out in case things go sideways."

Natisse's face tightened along with her gut. If she'd have heeded those words, Garron might not have been lying in a recovery bed with one less arm.

"It wasn't your fault," Uncle Ronan said.

She was shocked by the words. Did she betray her emotions so easily?

Choosing to ignore the comment, she cleared her throat. "And if an Imperial Scales patrol comes by? Or, Ezrasil forbid, the Orkenwatch?"

"Then we'll be far less interesting than whatever's going on in that building," Uncle Ronan said.

Natisse scowled. "But we won't know they're coming until it's too late."

Uncle Ronan shrugged. "It's the chance we've got to take." He held up a hand to forestall any further protestations. "This isn't up for discussion, Natisse. You want to get a closer look, then I'm going with you. End of matter."

Natisse ground her teeth. It wasn't like Uncle Ronan to be protective—Jad was the mother hen of the Crimson Fang. But could she blame him, after all they'd lost in the last weeks? Or perhaps he felt guilty after all the lies? Either way, she saw there would be no changing his mind on this.

She sighed. "Let's go."

It took just a few minutes to reach the ground circle around the lookout building. Silently, they approached the front gates where so many nobles had just entered. Though, it proved difficult to find a place where they would remain hidden from the two guards —especially now that she couldn't see them either. If they hadn't moved, they were still just beyond the wall on the right side. She had to settle for the shadows behind a crumbling brick wall twenty yards south of the guards' position. It didn't give her the best vantage, but it was as good as they could manage for the moment.

Waiting for the next carriage to arrive, she scanned the neighboring structures. This part of Dimvein never saw much action. The guards rarely patrolled—Scales or Orkenwatch—and for there to be so many from the Upper Crest present said something was going on. Curious at best, nefarious at worst.

Across the street from her, beside the building they'd spent the last several hours atop, was an old mason hall no longer in use. Beside it was a large storage facility. Both were in disuse and in far better condition. The walls were solid, the roofs still appeared mostly intact, and the front gates were made of iron that had mostly escaped rust. If Magisters Perech, Onathus, and Branthe— through his nephew—had purchased the property for the building's sake, they'd been ripped off. Any one of these would have been better.

However, Natisse suspected the building mattered not at all. Her mind was once more drawn to the ramp in the caravan yards that led into the underground passage where the slaves had been taken. A passage she suspected was connected to the shipyards— as indicated by Magister Onathus's guards drinking and chatting with Magister Perech's.

What if Magister Branthe and his conspirators cared nothing

for the building, but what lay beneath? The excitement that had been steadily simmering within her since discovering Magister Branthe's connection to Magisters Perech and Onathus now rose to a roiling bubble. What if that abandoned building concealed yet another entrance to the underground tunnels?

If that was the case, there was a chance those tunnels could lead her to slave pits they'd been seeking for so long. The only way to know for certain, though, was to get inside. Here and now, while the guards were ushering these cloaked, hooded figures into the building. If, as she suspected, they were Dimvein's wealthy nobles—who else could afford such fine clothing and conveyances?—then she had a decent chance of getting inside. She just had to know for certain before risking it.

Her pulse quickened as the clopping of horse hooves echoed down the street. A few moments later, a small two-wheeled hansom appeared from the shadows and pulled up alongside the gates. Leaning forward, ears straining to hear voices, eyes locked on the figures emerging from the vehicle, she strove for anything to help identify them.

Ezrasil smiled on her. The last of three dismounted from the hansom and tripped over the hem of their long cloak and stumbled into one of their companions. The collision caused the second figure's hood to flop backward, revealing long, golden hair pulled back in a turquoise headscarf and a woman's soft features.

Natisse stifled a gasp. She'd seen the woman at Magister Perech's party. She didn't know the woman's name, hadn't bothered speaking to her, but she recognized her as one of those who'd surrounded Perech himself.

Elation coursed within her chest. Her suspicions had been confirmed.

"I can go in," she whispered to Uncle Ronan beside her, voice pitched low so it didn't carry. "Disguised as Lady Dellacourt."

Uncle Ronan's mouth halfway opened to protest, but he

stopped himself, seeming to think better of it. After a moment's contemplation, he grunted.

"Not a bad idea. You have everything you need?"

"Won't need much," she said. "A nice cloak and a bit of lace and frill should sell the charade. Doesn't look like the guards are checking for weapons or asking many questions."

Again, Uncle Ronan took a moment to consider. This time, however, he looked ready to argue.

"If that's what I think it is," Natisse pushed on before he could speak, "then there's a damned good chance the building has some form of access that leads down. Which could very well mean that we've found the slave fighting pits. We just have to get in, get down there, and make sure."

Uncle Ronan scratched his chin.

"Unless you can think of a better plan," she said, "then I'm going."

Steeling herself, she waited for his response. This time, she was right. And if he didn't understand that, then he wasn't as smart as she'd believed all these years. Pulling off an infiltration in such a haste was an enormous risk, but one she was willing to take.

"The mission above all, right?" She couldn't be turned back now, not so close to success.

Uncle Ronan sighed, then nodded. "Do it. I'll stay here, keep watch, and if I feel anything off, I'll shut the plan down. But for now, it's a go."

Natisse breathed a sigh of relief. "I'll be back in a quarter-hour."

She rose and slipped through the shadows, circling around to head north. She knew exactly where to go—Gaidra, an elderly seamstress who ran a small shop in the One Hand District, owed the Crimson Fang both her business and her life.

For one of Uncle Ronan's "training missions," he'd dispatched Natisse, Baruch, Ammon, and Garron to eliminate an upstart gang of bone-breakers plaguing the city's market district.

What they didn't know was the bone-breakers weren't just everyday street thugs. They worked for the noblemen directly, encouraged to stir up trouble in order to drive the tenants away so they could buy up the block. The four of them had dispatched the dozen or so brutes handily, and in the process, liberated the businesses they'd been extorting in their protection racket. A percentage of the coins earned fencing valuables the Crimson Fang stole from the nobility still went into the pockets of Gaidra and other shopkeepers in the vicinity. In return, the people had been more than grateful. Gaidra would gladly provide her with the garments she'd need to pass as Lady Dellacourt.

She'd barely traveled two streets south when the sounds of a commotion caught her attention. It was coming from the west, in the direction of Magister Perech's caravan yards. She could hear shouting, but not what was being said.

Grimacing, Natisse slowed to a stop and crouched within the shadows of an alley. She wasted a single moment wondering what was happening, but the knowledge of what she'd set out to do banished her curiosity. Haston would tell her what the fuss was later—for the moment, she needed to focus on infiltrating that secret gathering of noblemen and women.

But before she could take a step, a flicker of movement in the shadows set her on full alert. A shadowy figure burst into view from a side street, running with a speed clearly born of desperation. The shouts pursued the fleeing person, and the street behind them grew suddenly bright with lantern light.

Natisse's heart leaped into her throat. The figure's face was still cast in silhouette, but she instantly recognized Haston's cloak and the compact frame beneath.

She had no time to cry out a warning; a moment later, a guardsman appeared not ten paces behind Haston, sword in hand. From behind the man came a shout. "Stop him! Double rum rations for whoever captures the spying bastard!" More guards followed, six in total, three carrying lanterns and all wielding an assortment of clubs and short swords.

Haston risked a glance behind him—a mistake. His boot caught an uneven cobblestone and he went down hard, tumbling head over heels and landing in an ungraceful sprawl on his belly. Air whooshed from his lungs and for agonizingly long moments, he didn't move, didn't even stir. Natisse feared he'd been knocked unconscious in the fall.

Haston gave a little groan, then pushed himself up onto one elbow. He tried to climb to his feet—too slow.

The first guard reached him a moment later and drove the pommel of his sword into the back of Haston's skull. Haston flopped to the ground and, within seconds, he was surrounded by House Perech's orange-and-mauve-clad guards.

"Got him!" said the first man, panting for breath. He snarled down at the prone Haston and lowered his sword to point the tip at the unconscious man's back.

"Joakim'll make quick work of loosening his tongue," another said. "Once he tells us who sent him, we'll throw him in the pit with the others."

37

KULLEN

"**M**ake a move, any move, and you die where you stand."

Magister Deckard took Kullen's threat literally—he froze in place, fingers hovering mere inches from the dragonblood vial hanging at his neck. One corner of his mouth twitched, and his eyes darted between Kullen and the expanse of carpeted floor between them.

Kullen had no doubt the man was sizing up his chances of activating his magic before being cut down. It was possible Magister Deckard's panic-numbed mind hadn't yet recognized him as the same person he'd just faced a couple of hours earlier. Clearly he was still grappling with the notion that someone had managed to penetrate his stronghold.

Kullen had no intention of letting the man regain his wits. He took a threatening step closer, the sharp edge of one Black Talon aimed unwaveringly at Magister Deckard's throat.

"I will not hesitate to cut out your tongue, rip off your shriveled manhood, and stuff it down your throat," he snarled. "But answer my questions, and you may yet live through the night." It was a lie—he had no intention of leaving the aristocrat alive. But Magister Deckard needn't know that.

"Wh-who are you?" Magister Deckard stammered. The hand that had been reaching for his dragonblood vial rose to wipe a bead of sweat from his florid forehead.

"You misunderstood," Kullen said, taking a step forward and letting the blade draw blood from Deckard's cheek.

The Magister whimpered like the dog he was.

Kullen saw something spark in the aristocrat's eye, like he was about to rise up and grow a pair. But that vigor passed like a cloud.

"What m-manner of questions?" he said instead, gagging as his own blood trickled into his open mouth.

"Simple ones." Kullen gave the man a feral smile. "Such as 'what treachery do you have planned against the Emperor' and 'who are your conspirators in this treason?'"

Magister Deckard's red face went bone white, the color of death. "I-I don't know what—"

"Do not take me for a fool!" Kullen thundered, his voice ringing off the study's stone walls. "I know you paid a visit to Magister Issemar yesterday afternoon, and that he was involved in a scheme to defraud the Emperor and destabilize peace in Dimvein."

A feigned look of shock washed over Deckard's face. "Magister Issemar? The shame!"

"Yes, quite," Kullen said. Kullen crossed his blades in an X formation, resting the flats of each on Magister Deckard's shoulders. Blood from the man's open cheek now stained his pristine robes. "What remains to be seen, Magister Deckard, is what your part in the plot was. How much you tell me now determines whether you face the Emperor's justice here and now, or in an Imperial court of your peers."

Magister Deckard's mouth fell open. "Y-You wouldn't! Killing an aristocrat—"

"Is my duty and privilege as servant to the Emperor." Kullen tightened the scissor-like threat until two more lines of blood deepened the sanguine stains. "I am the Black Talon, the left hand of the Emperor, the blade of shadow." That sounded suitably ominous, enough to terrify the already-fearful aristocrat. "Justice will be served, but whether you live to see the sunrise... that depends on what you say next."

Magister Deckard's eyes crossed and he stared down at the swords menacing his throat. He licked his lips, swallowed, and opened his mouth. Before he could speak, however, a sound echoed from the hallway behind Kullen: a shout of surprise, accompanied by thudding bootsteps.

Kullen took his eyes off Magister Deckard for a split second, just long enough to glance over his shoulder. Three guardsmen with drawn swords of their own were rushing past the charred and blackened corpses of their comrades, gazes fixed on Kullen's cloaked form.

He returned his attention to Magister Deckard—he'd seize the man, make him a shield, press the edge of his sword to the aristocrat's neck, and threaten to open his throat unless the guards backed off—only to find his blades menacing empty air. Magister Deckard's retreating figure was just vanishing into a deep patch of shadow between a pair of bookshelves on the southern end of the room.

Cursing, Kullen gave chase. Too slow. Just as he reached the spot where Magister Deckard had vanished, a door slammed directly in front of him. He leaned forward and drove his left shoulder into it, but the wood—solid sepher—held fast.

"Halt!" one guard shouted.

He had no time for a second try. Despite the pain flaring through his shoulder, he had to turn and face the three guards. They charged into the study and were courteous enough to come at him in a line rather than flanking out to encircle him.

"Friends, let's work this out," Kullen said. "You asked me to halt and I've done so."

"Who are y—"

The moment the forward-most guard opened his mouth and lowered his blade, Kullen threw his right Talon straight up and, with his hands now freed, whipped one of his throwing knives out from the sheath beneath his arm. In the same motion, he sent the blade flying to lodge itself through the man's Adam's apple. Blood gurgled from his lips and the others stared as their fellow died.

"Murderer!" cried the next in line, and now they attacked in a reasonable formation.

Kullen knocked aside the first guard's blow and caught his second sword as it fell. He spun, slashing both across the man's belly. The guard gave a half-grunt, half-scream, dropped his sword, and clutched at his insides as they cascaded to the floor.

Kullen then darted to the right and swung his left-hand sword in a rising cross-body blow that tore out the second guard's throat and parried his wild chopping attack. The two guards fell in unison, one spitting blood, the other shrieking in pain. Kullen ended his cries with a quick downward thrust that drove the tip of his sword into the man's chest.

With his enemies down, he turned back to the door, intending to give chase, when Magister Deckard's voice echoed through the same hallway the guards had just entered through.

"Intruder!" the aristocrat shrieked. "Assassin!"

Kullen broke into a run, sprinting up the hallway, past the burned bodies and blackened carpet. The corridor led to another that ran to the south, which, in turn, connected to the atrium at the center of the mansion. There, running for dear life and screaming bloody murder, was his prey.

Magister Deckard was twenty yards ahead of Kullen, but he ran like a man with the demons of Shekoth's deepest pits on his heels. Fear spurred him to near-superhuman swiftness. He reached the atrium and vanished around a corner before Kullen had covered half the distance between them.

Bursting free of the hallway, Kullen barreled around the same corner where Magister Deckard had turned. Ahead and below him, the aristocrat fled down the broad marble staircase. Kullen took the steps two and three at a time, trusting to his instincts, balance, and innate speed to keep him from tumbling.

Magister Deckard, however, was neither as agile nor as fortunate as Kullen. He was halfway to the ground floor when his foot twisted on a marble step and he fell hard, tumbling head over heels until he sprawled ungraciously on the shit-soaked, carpeted landing.

Servants cried out. Some took the opportunity to run away, while others stayed, stuck somewhere between a desire to help the man up and a need to watch what happened next.

Kullen covered the distance to the man in the space of three heartbeats. Too late. Magister Deckard didn't try to rise or flee. Instead, he rolled onto his back and his hand reached for the dragonblood vial at his neck.

Ice rippled through Kullen's veins. He felt the moment the man bloodsurged. It was like a million frost-coated spiders crawling the length of his spine, vibrating in the pit of his stomach. He braced himself for a burst of fire or a desperate swipe of the fiery sword Magister Deckard had summoned at the Refuge.

But he was utterly unprepared for the sudden rush of magic that infused the world around him. It felt as if he was running through mud, the very air growing thick, blistering hot. One moment there was empty air and darkness; the next, a pillar of flame burst upward. The atrium became a furnace, the fecal matter burning up and creating a noxious gas.

Kullen shut his eyes and fought to breathe.

When he opened them again, the enormous form of a red dragon stood at full height before him.

Golgoth was a mass of rippling red scales that seemed to glow with their own inner light. The cracks between gleamed like rivers of lava, and the dragon emanated such terrible heat that sweat immediately broke out along Kullen's entire body. Golgoth's hind legs were planted on the ground floor far below, but her forelegs gripped the marble columns of the staircase. Two thin horns rose upward like swords and the length of her neck was lined with razor-sharp spines.

Shocked, Kullen stumbled and nearly fell. He managed to catch himself on the wall, to slow his descent before he followed Magister Deckard's ungainly tumble.

The dragon's head lowered toward him, bright, fiery eyes fixing him with a malevolent glare. Kullen swiveled toward her, his swords coming up to a defensive guard, but even as his body moved, his mind registered the impossibility of his situation. He was still half a floor below the corridor that led away from the atrium, to relative safety. But even if he could somehow ascend the steps, one burst of dragonfire would instantly incinerate him. The moment she opened her mouth, he was a dead man.

"Golgoth!" screamed Magister Deckard. "Kill him!"

Every muscle in Kullen's body tensed, ready to spring into action. If he could reach Magister Deckard, he might be able to use the man as a human shield as he'd intended to do upstairs. He'd have to be swift to evade the enormous talon that gripped the marble column mere feet from where he stood, or to avoid the snapping jaws and teeth nearly as long as he was tall, or the horns, or...

The beast was death incarnate, able to send him plummeting to Shekoth's depths with barely a thought.

Yet to his surprise, the dragon did not move. The fire burning in her giant golden orbs brightened, and the heat radiating from Golgoth's enormous form increased. Yet the dragon didn't lash out at him or open its boundless maw to bite off his head.

Kullen didn't dare move either. He had no idea why Golgoth hadn't yet attacked—was she toying with him, savoring his mounting fear?

"Kill him!" Magister Deckard screamed again. "Now, damn you!"

And still, Golgoth remained motionless—all save her eyes, which shifted toward the pathetic figure now sitting up on the landing. Kullen sensed more than saw her reaction. He couldn't explain how he knew—the dragon gave no outward expression—but it was as if he could feel the scorn emanating from the dragon among the waves of blistering heat.

No, not scorn. Anger. Hatred.

Kullen had no time to contemplate the strange response. The dragon's immobility bought him the split second he needed to make his move. He threw himself down the staircase, charging toward the spot where Magister Deckard sat.

The aristocrat's eyes went wide.

"Kill him, Golgoth!" he shrieked. "I command it!"

Kullen didn't glance at the dragon, but he heard the metallic shifting of scales, felt the heat, and saw the light of Golgoth's mouth opening in the reflections in the marble as he ran. He had mere seconds as the dragon stoked its inner fires—magical or physical, he didn't know—to generate a pillar of flames powerful enough to immolate him, reduce him to cinder in the blink of an eye.

But those mere seconds were enough.

He shouted for Deckard's servants—the foolish ones who still waited around— to run for cover as he leaped the last five steps. He landed hard enough to stumble and careen into the wall. Piss splashed under his boots, the ground squishy. The impact nearly knocked the swords from his hands, but he managed to retain his grip on the weapons and spin back toward Magister Deckard. The aristocrat's gaze flashed between Kullen and the gaping jaws of the dragon.

Kullen seized Magister Deckard's collar and dragged the man to his feet, interposing the aristocrat's body between him and the dragon.

"Call her off!" he shouted. "Call her off, or you die, too!"

Surprise tied Magister Deckard's tongue in knots, and he

could only stammer out incoherent words that might have been plea, command, or neither.

Kullen gave up trying to get through to the aristocrat. He simply gripped Magister Deckard's robes tighter and lifted his gaze to Golgoth's towering form.

"Your flames may kill me," he called to the dragon, "but not before it turns your bondmate to ash."

Again, the fire burning within Golgoth's eyes brightened, and this time, Kullen noted the dragon's reaction. Its mouth opened wider, baring its enormous fangs, and the glow deep within its belly brightened but her gaze said something entirely different.

Impossible...

Kullen shoved Magister Deckard forward and dove aside, putting himself firmly behind a thick, marble column. Just in time. Behind and above him, a brilliant gout of flame washed across the landing. The wet ground boiled.

"Noo!" Magister Deckard's shriek was cut off in an instant, fire overwhelming him.

Nothing could be heard over the blaze.

Kullen gritted his teeth, braced himself for the searing, burning agony of dragonfire that would end him along with Magister Deckard.

It never came.

His eyelids cracked open just as the torrent of Golgoth's fire slackened. Smoke emanated from the dragon's mouth, filled the atrium, and rose from the ruins of the landing. What could be charred and blackened was. The carpet was gone, leaving nothing but exposed stone. And Magister Deckard was nowhere to be found.

The dragon's huge mouth slowly closed, and her bright eyes turned toward Kullen. In that moment, another look passed between them. Kullen thought she'd been trying to tell him to move aside just moments earlier, but he hadn't been entirely sure.

Now, somehow—perhaps because of his bond with Umbris—Kullen understood clearly.

Golgoth had despised the man who had been her "blood-sworn," yet because of their magical union, she could not visit her rage upon Magister Deckard. Until now, until his command had given her permission to unleash her unholy fire upon him in an attempt to destroy Kullen.

The dragon bowed her head, a sign Kullen had come to know from Umbris as well.

"No," Kullen said, his voice trembling. "Thank you."

Kullen had done her a service by liberating her. For that, she would let him live but he had no doubt she would do the same to him should he misstep.

Kullen went to speak again, but the spot where she stood became a blinding pillar of flames, leaving Kullen alone—and more than a little shaken—on the sewage-filled ground level of Magister Deckard's mansion.

Pain flared sharp through Kullen's shoulder as he clawed his way up the wall and to his feet. He still couldn't believe he was alive. He'd stared into the fiery eyes and fanged maw of Golgoth herself, but instead of torching him, she'd shown him gratitude. Well, as much as a dragon could show by not incinerating or eating him alive.

Yet here he was, alive and breathing—albeit with difficulty, his lungs stinking from the sulfuric smoke that still filled the house.

His eyes strayed to the blackened landing where Magister Deckard had stood mere moments earlier. Nothing remained of the man himself, not so much as a pile of ash or a speck of charred clothing. A few scraps of still-bubbling molten gold flecked the burned walls. And there, lying on the burned marble, was Magister Deckard's dragonblood vial.

Kullen climbed the stairs, stooped, and scooped up the vial. The simple-looking bottle of glass with its gold cap showed not a hint of damage. Not a scratch from falling to the stone landing, the glass not discolored by the terrible heat of dragonfire. The magic inherent in the vial—in the deep crimson dragon's blood within—shielded it from any and all damage.

Kullen kept his fingers well away from the hair-thin needle set into the golden cap. He dared not risk activating the magic by mingling his blood with that of Golgoth. He doubted the dragon would spare his life a second time. Nor did he believe she would be willingly bonded to another so soon after earning her freedom, and Kullen had no desire to match himself in a battle of wills to subjugate such a fiery, powerful creature. Carefully, he slipped the vial into one of the hidden pockets within Jarius's velvet robe.

Shouts from all around finally pierced the ringing in his ears. He had no idea if more guards would be coming to investigate, but Kullen couldn't linger to find out. Struggling to ignore the pain in his shoulder, he jogged up the stairs and back through the hallways that led him to Magister Deckard's study.

The room was quiet, silent. Kullen once again stepped over the dead guardsmen, careful to avoid the puddle of blood encircling them, and slipped toward a writing desk. He hadn't even realized it had gotten so dark that he'd needed his dragon eyes. He rifled through the drawers, looking for anything to prove Deckard's guilt. His hand rolled over something smooth—the same scrimshaw carving he'd seen in Issemar's office.

That was proof enough they were receiving the same kind of payment, but not enough to nail him to the wall.

He turned his attention to the rest of the room. He'd just resolved himself the checking the pages of every book on Deckard's many shelves when something in the fireplace caught his attention. Among the cold, gray ashes of a fire that had clearly gone out hours earlier, Kullen spotted a small piece of parchment lying beneath the metal grate. Magister Deckard had likely not realized it had slipped out of the flames in which he'd attempted to destroy it. Curious, Kullen knelt by the hearth and picked up the palm-sized scrap.

Burned edges flaked away as Kullen touched the parchment. He moved gently and with exaggerated caution to prevent the rest of the scorched scrap from crumbling away. Only a few words had escaped the fire, and they made no sense to him.

"...with all speed,"

the note read,

"... haste in this matter... preparing for our next... could be our undoing... dealt with once and for all."

Kullen had no idea what the message was about, but it could not ported anything good. Two more words had escaped the fire. Written in the same neat, precise handwriting was what he guessed to be a name.

Red Claw

Kullen frowned. Red Claw? He'd never encountered it before in all his dealings. With as much care as he could muster, he wrapped the scorched parchment in a handkerchief and tucked it carefully into the pocket containing Magister Deckard's dragonblood vial. Those two would be presented to the Emperor—the vial for safekeeping and ultimately bestowing on a worthy aristocrat, and the latter to determine if Wymarc recognized the handwriting.

He had just risen and begun to inspect the office one last time, when the sound of bootsteps echoed in the corridor beyond.

Kullen cursed—he'd run out of time.

He raced toward the empty doorframe of Magister Deckard's office, but instead of drawing a weapon, he reached for one of the alchemical surprises he'd tucked into Jarius's cloak. Even as the guards came charging around the corner, he hurled the two knuckle-sized glass orbs at the wall immediately behind them.

Glass shattered, the alchemical mixture within exploded with a thunderous *crack*, sparks sprayed, and a pillar of thick, choking white smoke engulfed the guards and the hall. Kullen gulped in air and held his breath as he charged through the outer edges of the smoke. He clung to the northern wall, darting around the guards coughing, choking, and staggering into the hallway. One of the men swiped at him half-blind, but Kullen just raced on and left the disoriented guards behind.

"*Umbris*," Kullen said within his mind.

"*I will await you on the rooftop.*"

Kullen traversed the attic, then shoved his way through the grate and onto the roof. But even as the chill wind whipped past his face, his mind was hard at work analyzing what he'd found. It was precious little—just a missive that reeked of urgency and a name that meant nothing to him—but it was more than he'd had when he walked in. That, together with Magister Issemar's connection to the Blood Clan pirates, was enough to report to Emperor Wymarc.

Perhaps the Emperor, together with Assidius and Turoc, would be able to piece together more of this perfidious plot to destabilize the Empire and remove him from power. Even if there were no assassins wielding knives in the Palace, the threat was no less dire.

With every new name Kullen added to the list—Magister Iltari, Magister Taradan, Magister Issemar, and now Magister Deckard—they tightened the noose around the necks of whoever was truly guilty of the treasonous plot.

Red Claw.

38

NATISSE

Natisse acted without hesitation. The mission was important—the lives of an unknown number of slaves hung in the balance—but she couldn't stand idly by while her friend was in danger. She'd been unable to help Ammon, and Baruch had died to give her a chance to run. Garron was in terrible condition because he'd come to her aid. She couldn't lose any more of her comrades.

Springing to her feet, she charged. The lashblade slipped from its sheath with a whisper of steel on leather, and Natisse's arm whipped forward to strike at the back of Perech's guard threatening Haston. The steel tip punched into his neck, just above the collar of his breastplate, and severed the spinal cord. The guard flopped into a limp heap on the ground next to the dazed Haston.

Natisse retracted the lashblade into sword form and hammered a blow into the guard to her left, shattering his arm and knocking the club from his grip. A third strike cut down another guardsman, tearing open his throat. The man dropped to his knees, fumbling at his neck in a desperate attempt to stanch the gush of blood. His rusty orange and mauve jerkin became a splotch of red.

Spinning, Natisse lashed out at the next guard, but her lash-blade struck solid steel. She refused to be put on the defensive, but instead surged forward with a flurry of lightning-fast blows. The unpredictable barrage of high-and-low attacks overwhelmed the guardsman's defenses and he fell bleeding from two deep wounds in his left leg.

A curse echoed from behind her, and Natisse spun to find one of the last two guards standing rushing her, club raised and lantern swinging for her head. She bent backward, and the lantern flew not two inches past her face, so close it singed her bright red hair.

The brilliant flame, heat, and angry shout triggered something in her mind. She was ripped from the present, and suddenly she was no longer in the darkened streets of Dimvein, but instead surrounded by roaring flames. Fire seared her hair and flesh, ravaged her clothing. Again, she heard the woman's cries of terror and the bellowing laughter. But now, she saw them. Saw the slim woman struggling in the grip of an enormous brute. Their faces swam slowly into focus before her eyes. She could almost make out their features, the details of their faces, hair, clothing.

She desperately wanted to see them—to see who these people were who plagued her past—but she hadn't the time. With an enormous effort of will, she slammed shut the door in her mind to block out the memories. The next breath she took was a gasp as she ducked a swinging club on the streets of Dimvein.

Natisse threw up her lashblade, barely managing to block a short sword coming for her throat from the second guard. The force of the block sent her staggering backward. She gave ground just long enough to recover her composure, to regain full control of her wits. The two guards attacking with sword, club, and lantern served to ground her in reality. Within seconds, she had her momentum back and her mind was clear.

She ducked, parried a club strike, flowed out of the way of the short sword thrust, dodged, strafed, and blocked her way back into the offensive. Her sword snapped out and cut the lantern from the club-wielding guard's hand before he could swing it at her head again. Glass shattered and bronze buckled as the lantern slammed the street. The guard's bloody fingers followed a moment later. The man was too stunned to scream. He stumbled back, clutching his wounded hand to his chest.

Natisse let the man be and focused all her attention on the sword-wielding guardsman. The blood pounding in her ears had drowned out everything, but suddenly, she realized that he'd been shouting curses at full volume the entire time. At the sight of his comrade wounded, the guard's expression changed—eyes going wide, face paling—and he looked on the verge of calling for help.

So she raised her lashblade level with his head, and pressed the release trigger. The word had just left his mouth when the many-thonged whip shot forward and through his gaping maw. It punched through the back of his head before quickly retracting again, pulling a whole mess of skin, flesh, bone, and brain matter with it. For a moment, he stood there wide-eyed, as if held up only by sheer disbelief. In that instant, Natisse recognized the man—Four Teeth. She'd marked him the previous night, one of the five marching the chained slaves down the ramp. What remained of Four Teeth's brain finally informed the rest of him that it was over and he slumped to the ground in lifeless heap.

"Help!" The shout pierced the thundering of Natisse's heart-beat. The last guard standing had turned to flee, trailing blood and crying out loud enough to wake the dead. "Get over here and help us!"

Natisse's hand darted toward one of her throwing knives, pulling it free smoothly. Her arm whipped back and forward. The blade flew from her fingers, spinning end over end, and buried itself into the guard's back.

He went down with one final, shrieking cry of "Over here!"

Natisse cursed. They were only a few streets away from Magister Perech's caravan yard, close enough that the shouts could've easily reached the other guards on duty. If any had been in pursuit of Haston, they might've heard the cry for help. Kneeling at Haston's side, she gripped the man's shoulder and shook him hard.

"Haston, can you hear me?"

For answer, Haston gave a little groan. His normally bright eyes were shrouded behind a thick film of weariness and confusion. Blood and sweat dampened his golden hair.

"You've got to get up!" Natisse seized his left arm. "We need to get you out of here now. There could be more coming any second."

Haston stirred, tried to rise, but his right arm couldn't support his weight. Natisse glanced at the wound where the guard had struck him. Blood leaked from the gash on the back of his head. There could be serious damage to his brain. He needed a healer now. There'd be no time to get him to Jad, and there was likely to be more guards on the way.

Growling, Natisse sheathed her bloody lashblade and slid both arms under Haston's shoulders.

"Get. Up!" She pulled with all her might. The man was lean but solidly built and surprisingly heavy. She managed to get him up to his knees, slung his right arm over her shoulder, and hauled him to his feet. "Lean on me, but we've got to move fast."

"Move… fast," Haston mumbled.

Natisse took that as a good sign and half-dragged, half-carried the man up the street, heading farther south and east away from the caravan yard. Gaidra's next-door neighbor was an alchemist and healer. Serrod could patch Haston up, give them a place to hunker down to evade pursuit. They just had to travel a quarter-mile before—

"Burrest's shout came from over this way!" echoed a shout from behind them. "Hurry!"

Natisse cursed.

The caravan yard's guards had heard the cries. Within

seconds, they'd find six corpses and spot her and Haston fleeing the scene. Any intention of capturing Haston would melt away like a snowflake amidst dragonfire and the guards would fight to kill.

"Come on!" she said through gritted teeth. "We've got to move."

She scanned the road ahead, looking for any alleyways or side streets down which they could disappear. But the closest was fifty yards south, much too far for Haston to reach in time. Instead, she hauled him toward a stoop on the east side of the road.

"Gonna have to let you sit here while I deal with these bastards." She tried to keep the worry from her voice—no telling how many guards were giving chase. If things got truly bad, she might be able to lead them away from—

"Natisse!" Uncle Ronan's voice called behind her.

She craned her head to glance over Haston's shoulder. Uncle Ronan raced up the street toward her. His gaze darted to the fallen lanterns and the corpses littering the cobblestones, taking in everything at a glance—including the shouts that grew everlouder and the lantern light brightening the darkness to the west.

With no time to question why Uncle Ronan had left his post, she was just relieved that she wouldn't have to fight alone.

"He's hurt bad," Natisse said. "I just need to put him down, and we can face them tog—"

"No!" Uncle Ronan's voice cracked like a whip. "Keep going. Get him out of here. I'll deal with them!"

Natisse's eyes widened. "Alone? Uncle, you—"

"Child, would you stop questioning me at every turn?" Uncle Ronan's voice was firm. "If I'm the only one they see, I'm the only one they'll chase. I can lead them away from here, give you a chance to get him help."

Natisse felt like telling him he deserved to be questioned. The memory of what had happened the last time they split up remained fresh in her mind.

But Uncle Ronan didn't give her a chance. "That's an order, Natisse," he snapped. "Go, now, before it's too late!"

"Let's… go," Haston mumbled. His voice was still thick with pain but a bit less slurred. That was potentially a good sign—the blow to his head might've simply jarred him, but hopefully failed to inflict any serious damage. She'd still need to get him to a healer, and soon, just to be certain.

Though every fiber of her being rebelled, Natisse forced herself to obey Uncle Ronan. He was her leader, and if he gave an order, it was her duty to comply. She hurried Haston up the street, her mouth clamped shut so tightly her jaw muscles ached. The alley seemed so far away—there was no chance they'd make in time.

The sound of bootsteps rang out behind her, but instead of growing louder, they drew farther away. Natisse glanced over her shoulder and found Uncle Ronan had drawn his long sword and was now charging toward the oncoming guards, his shout ripping through the night.

"Come and get me, you bastards!"

Natisse couldn't bring herself to watch. Uncle Ronan was a skilled and ruthless fighter, the one who'd taught her most of what she knew about combat. If anyone could survive this clash, it was him.

Worried for his safety as she might be, she had to worry more about the man who currently bled all over her.

"We're going to have to toss these clothes. Both of us," she said, hoping to just keep Haston awake and engaged.

He didn't respond.

"Haston. Come on, stay with me. We are almost there."

"Almost… there…"

Haston slumped to the ground with a groan. Then, awareness sparked in his eyes. "Go… help him!" he mumbled. "I can manage the rest of the way."

Natisse didn't need to be told twice. She spun away from

Haston and sprinted back the way she'd come, drawing her lash-blade. She'd only made it a few yards before she spotted Uncle Ronan leading the guards in the opposite direction, sword streaming blood.

Cursing, Natisse backpedaled and flattened her back against the alley wall. She fought to calm her racing heart, to take slow, measured breaths. It wasn't long before she no longer heard the chase at all.

Uncle Ronan would be fine. He'd fight his way clear or lose the pursuing guards in the maze that was Dimvein. He didn't know the streets like she did, but he knew them well enough.

"All right, you dumb bastard," Natisse said to Haston. "Let's get you to a healer."

Silently, she prayed that Uncle Ronan wouldn't end up needing one too.

39
KULLEN

Kullen was bone-weary by the time he reached the secret door that opened into the prisons. Arbiter Chuldok was hard at work earning his pay tonight—the screams of the latest victim on his torture table rang off the stone with such ferocity they set Kullen's head aching. Bile rose to his throat at the smell. Bodily odors, excretions, and stale air assaulted him as vigorously as any foe. But he fought back, keeping the meager contents of his stomach in place.

The bruises earned in Magister Deckard's mansion—many of which he was still discovering—still throbbed with every step. Compounding it all was the exhaustion that came from overusing his bloodsurge the previous night. Though he'd slept much of the day, his body still felt sluggish, heavy, his wits dulled.

To his relief, the Emperor's private study was blessedly empty of useless princelings and persnickety Seneschals. No sign of Emperor Wymarc, either, but Kullen allowed himself a few moments to recover after his trek across Dimvein, through the secret tunnels, and up more flights of stairs than he cared to climb in his current state of fatigue.

He poured himself a goblet of dragonfire rum from Emperor

Wymarc's personal stash—tucked well behind the bottles of wine, whiskey, partruk, opulence, and other lesser spirits he kept to offer the few guests he permitted into this room.

Kullen raised the glass to his lips and prepared to down the contents in a single pull, but the memories brought on by the smell hit him like a blow to the gut. He'd hated dragonfire rum the first time Jarius had made him taste it. And the second, and third, and every other time after. By Shekoth, he couldn't remember when he'd stopped hating it. One day, he'd just downed the liquor without feeling like his mouth was on fire and his insides would turn to slag.

That had been the day he learned of Jarius and Hadassa's deaths. He'd have welcomed that fire—wished it burned him alive, if only to end the pain of his loss. In one senseless act of violence, he'd lost his best friend, the only woman he'd ever truly loved, and any hope that he might've had a future beyond his service as the Emperor's Black Talon.

Since that day, he hadn't touched the stuff, hadn't had to face the images of his past that came flooding back with it.

Training with Jarius under the stern, watchful eye of Swordmaster Kyneth. Sneaking through the Palace, hunting Jarius in their never-ending game of hidden-to-find. Riding through Dimvein at Jarius's side—and, eventually, with Hadassa joining them. Visiting their secret glade in the Wild Grove Forest. Hiding out in the Emperor's garden and evading the army of tutors and servants sent to track down the mischievous prince.

So many happy memories, yet they felt like a lifetime ago. Or a different lifetime altogether. Since that day in the Embers, Kullen's life had felt hollow. His only sense of purpose came from his service to the Emperor, the only meaning to protect the Empire and its citizens, people like Mammy Tess and the orphans under her care. Everything he'd done had been to execute his duties for the Emperor. He'd forgotten what it meant to be Kullen because, in a way, Kullen had died alongside his Prince and Princess.

Closing his eyes, Kullen thought back to the last time he'd seen the Prince and Princess. They'd been preparing to ride out of the Palace on their mission to care for the people of the Embers, dressed in simple clothing and laden with a fortune in supplies: blankets, clothing, food, tools, everything else they could gather— not to mention enough marks to feed the whole district for weeks. Hadassa had kissed her young son farewell, insisting Jaylen wasn't quite old enough to accompany them.

"Soon," she'd promised, with that motherly smile that seemed so natural on her beautiful face.

Even then, Jaylen was insufferable, crying and pouting the whole time. Finally, Kullen had managed to get the boy to wave goodbye, then returned to his training without a second thought. Never knowing that they would be ripped away forever by an angry mob incensed over Magister Deckard's failures to keep his dragon under control.

The men who'd murdered the Prince and Princess—or at least the ones who took the fall—had long since been found and executed. Now, with Magister Deckard dead, Jarius and Hadassa had been avenged.

Kullen raised his glass of dragonfire rum.

"May you know peace in Ezrasil's embrace," he told them almost silently. "You are loved and missed."

He didn't even know if he still believed in the God, but hope for something more than utter blackness when this life had passed was all someone like Kullen had left. Then again, perhaps blackness was all that same someone deserved.

He swallowed the rum in a single pull, savoring the fire that burned its way down his throat.

At that moment, the door to the study opened behind Kullen. Kullen swung around, expecting the Emperor, but it was only Prince Jaylen. The prince had an armload of books—no doubt taken from the study's private shelves—which he nearly dropped as he spotted Kullen. To his credit, he recovered quickly and managed to keep his grip on the tomes.

"Is that grandfather's best dragonfire rum?" Jaylen asked, eyeing the glass in Kullen's hand.

A mocking retort rose to Kullen's lips, but to his surprise, died unspoken. In that moment, the young man's face reminded him so much of his parents. Jaylen had Hadassa's eyes and smile, but Jarius's strength and upright carriage.

Guilt stung in Kullen's mind. He'd treated Jaylen poorly all these years, and why? Because he was a pampered princeling? Jarius had been much the same, yet Kullen had loved and respected him. Emperor Wymarc had been far more involved in Jarius's training, education, and development after the death of his wife, Jarius's mother. But Jaylen was growing up without either of his parents, only a grandfather haunted by the memories of his dead son and daughter-in-law. That couldn't be an easy upbringing, yet, reluctantly, Kullen had to admit Jaylen had grown up to be a decent young man.

Perhaps it was the dragonfire rum, the exhaustion, or the memories, but Kullen found himself ashamed at his attitude toward the Prince. He owed it to the man and woman who had been his best—and only—friends to treat their son better. He might never love Jaylen as he'd loved Jarius, but, from that point forward, Kullen swore to himself he would do what he could.

And so, instead of a retort that would have mocked or insulted Jaylen, Kullen just shrugged and said, "He's the one who told me where he stashes the bottle. Had he not wanted me to drink it, he'd have stayed quiet."

Jaylen set the stack of books down on the small table next to Emperor Wymarc's favorite stuffed armchair and turned to Kullen with an indignant look.

"By that logic," he snarked, "does that mean you can take gold from the Imperial treasury simply because you know its location?"

Kullen gulped the last of the dragonfire rum and set the empty glass on the wooden bar.

But Prince Jaylen seemed determined to test Kullen's newfound resolve to treat him better.

"I take it you've come to explain how Magister Issemar wound up lying dead in the streets?"

"To your grandfather, yes," Kullen said. "Where can I find him?"

"In a meeting..."

Jaylen began fidgeting with the books. It was his way to provide just enough information to require a follow-up question to be asked. Kullen wondered which strategist had taught him that so he could slap them with the cold, flat edge of a blade.

"With?" Kullen could play the game if it got him answers.

"I don't believe who We meet with is any of your concern."

"*We* are meeting with no one," Kullen said through clenched teeth.

Jaylen came to stand in front of Kullen, staring up at him with that bug-eyed look of his. For a moment, Kullen half-expected the young man to demand an apology as he had the last time they'd spoken in this room. However, Jaylen just turned and beckoned for Kullen to follow.

"I'll take you to him."

Kullen unclenched his jaw. He didn't think he'd be able to keep a hold on his tongue should Jaylen get all imperious on him again. The princeling was on his way to being a half-decent ruler—at least in contrast to most of the Imperial nobility—but he had a long way to go to earn Kullen's respect on his own merit. And Kullen's restraint out of love for Jarius and Hadassa could only endure so much.

They strode through the halls. Kullen noted the boy's gait ahead of him and also noted that this was no child any longer. So long had Kullen thought of him as Jarius's son that he simply hadn't considered that he was a man in his own right.

And then the Prince went and ruined the moment by speaking.

"Can't you keep up? I swear you move slower than my grandfather."

"Sure thing, Your Grace," Kullen said, doing his best to keep the sarcasm from his tone.

Jaylen stopped and turned. "Watch your mouth, Assassin."

Kullen raised both hands in surrender. "I meant no disrespect, son of Jarius."

Jaylen eyed him suspiciously but ultimately decided upon a small scowl and got on his way once again.

They took a turn that led them past the training room where Kullen had spent years learning the ways of the sword and knife. He could almost picture Jarius in there, throwing sharpened blades at Kullen, not holding back one bit. He could almost feel the times when he hadn't dodged in time to avoid a slice.

Before he knew it, two wide ivory doors were being opening by two burly-looking Scales, and thick wet air slapped him across the face.

"Ah, Prince Jaylen, we were just speaking of you." Magister Branthe's face brightened as he spotted Prince Jaylen.

He and Emperor Wymarc were fully emerged in a long rectangular bath on the eastern balcony, arms spread over the edge as steam rose around them.

"Truly, my lord?" Jaylen asked, his expression perking up. "I am equal parts honored and curious."

Magister Branthe threw back his head and laughed, a full-bellied soldier's laugh. "Come, come," he said, beckoning for Jaylen to join him and the Emperor in the water. "It's the perfect temperature. There's no bath like an Imperial bath."

Prince Jaylen moved to obey, and Kullen slipped into the room behind him. Magister Branthe was one of the few in the Empire who ever saw Kullen in the Palace, and Emperor Wymarc had explained away Kullen's presence as an unobtrusive minder to shadow Jaylen, an added security measure for the prince's protection.

"Emperor," Branthe said with a tone far more condescending than most could get away with, "isn't Jaylen a bit old to still need... him?"

"Yes, grandfather," Jaylen agreed. "Aren't I?"

The Emperor sighed. "One can never be too careful with the royal heir, now, can they?"

"I suppose. I suppose. Ah, yes, Prince Jaylen. Don't be shy. Nothing we've not seen before."

Branthe laughed again as Jaylen undressed and slid into the water.

Kullen took up a position just inside the room with his back to the door, hidden from any potential threat.

Not that he had much to fear in the Palace. Between Thanagar's ever-present shield, the Imperial Scales patrolling the grounds, and the two serious-looking men guarding the door, Prince Jaylen was as safe as could be expected. And Magister Branthe was no slouch with the sword he wore at all times—the sword he'd wielded during his years of service of Dimvein and the Emperor.

Though, looking at the man now, naked, top half sticking up from the water. He'd gone soft. His flabby arms and chest spoke of a man who'd spent too much time being pampered and not enough time training.

"We were just speaking of recent events," Magister Branthe said, giving Jaylen a fatherly smile, "and how it could very well be time for you to become more visible to the citizens of Dimvein."

Kullen's eyes narrowed. That sounded diametrically opposite to the stance Emperor Wymarc had taken only days earlier when Jaylen had begged for freedom. His gaze went to the Emperor, and found Wymarc's face broadening into a tight, tense smile.

"Carritus has made a convincing case for increasing your duties beyond training and education." Emperor Wymarc's tone was calm, but Kullen recognized the unspoken hesitation beneath the words. "You are, in fact, my heir, and will rule the Empire in my stead."

"Grandfather!" Jaylen sounded shocked. "Surely you cannot—"

"I don't mean today, Jaylen." Emperor Wymarc gave a little chuckle. "When I am gone, which, hopefully, will not be for many more years to come."

"Many, many years," Magister Branthe said, with a mocking wink for the Emperor. "But when that day comes, we will need a ruler who is more than just educated, but has real-life experience to match his learned knowledge." He gestured to Prince Jaylen. "Such experience can only be gained by getting your hands dirty, so to speak."

His gaze turned to the Emperor and he nodded, as if granting the ruler of all the Karmian Empire permission to speak.

Emperor Wymarc gave Magister Branthe a flat look, then turned back to Jaylen.

"After some consideration, I have come to believe that it is time for you to become more involved in the day-to-day runnings of the Empire." He drew in a long breath.

"Grandfather, I am absolutely thr—" Jaylen began.

The Emperor continued speaking as if he the Prince hadn't opened his mouth. "You will spearhead Turoc's investigation into the recent deaths of Our nobility. Starting with Magister Issemar's death two nights past, and investigating all the others to find who is behind the killings."

Prince Jaylen's spine went rigid. He glanced Kullen's way.

"Why are you looking to him?" Branthe said. The Emperor himself is talking to you."

"Yes. I just… Truly, grandfather?"

It was initially unclear how Jaylen felt about this assignment, but when Emperor Wymarc nodded, he leaped to his feet, splashing water everywhere, grinning from ear to ear. "You do me a great honor, Your Grace. And you, Magister Branthe." He gave the aristocrat a bow from the waist. "Whatever you said to aid my cause, you have my thanks."

"No thanks necessary." Magister Branthe dismissed the Prince's words with a wave. "Now, please, sit. You're scaring away the livestock."

Jaylen's face went red and he lowered himself into the water again.

"Thank you. Yes. Wow." Jaylen continued muttering similar things under his breath.

Magister Branthe leaned forward to fix the Prince with an intense stare. "I am—and always have been—considering how best to serve the Empire. A ruler must be wise as well as strong. You have your father's strength in you. Now, it is time to see if any of your grandfather's wisdom has rubbed off."

The mention of Jarius from Branthe's lips brought curses to Kullen's. But he bit back a retort. How wise could a teenager be? Especially one who'd lived a life as sheltered as Jaylen's. But he wisely kept that to himself and held his tongue.

"Come, young Prince." Magister Branthe said, rising and reaching for a towel. "I have already drained your grandfather's best brandy and taken up enough of his time." He shot a grin and a wink over his shoulder at the Emperor. "I will escort you to Tuskthorne Keep on my way out."

"The Orken barracks?"

"Where else do you suppose we'll find the Orken leader?"

"Ah, right. Of course," Prince Jaylen said. "How stupid of me."

Branthe stopped patting himself with his towel and eyed Jaylen seriously.

"Don't ever say that about yourself, Prince," he said. "You have the mind of Kings."

"You honor me, Magister Branthe." Prince Jaylen also dried off and fell into step next to the aging aristocrat, exuberance visible in every quivering muscle of his body. "Are you certain there's nowhere else you need to be?"

"Call it an old man's desire to spend more time with the godson he has been neglecting for far too long," Magister Branthe said, chuckling. "Now, tell me, how goes your training with Swordmaster Kyneth? Have you mastered your barehanded combat skills yet, or has he still got you drilling with dagger and…"

Magister Branthe's voice faded into the hallway as the door closed behind him and Prince Jaylen.

A long moment of silence elapsed before Kullen spoke.

"How long did it take to convince you that was a good idea?"

Emperor Wymarc's forced smile—adopted for Jaylen's benefit —vanished immediately, replaced by a scowl. "I'll let you know when I am convinced." He huffed through his nostrils, cupping water and rubbing his face. "The only reason I'm even willing to allow it is that he's as safe at Turoc's side as he could be anywhere in Dimvein."

Kullen couldn't argue that. The Orken's Tuskigo made a damned fine bodyguard. And better Jaylen was irritating the rigid Turoc than playing imperious with Kullen.

"What news to report?" Emperor Wymarc asked, reaching for a snifter half-filled with rich golden brandy.

"Are you planning on staying in there throughout the conversation?" Kullen asked.

The Emperor sighed and rose. "Now I can't even have a bath and a moment's peace and quiet."

"Such are the woes of leadership."

"Truer words… Okay," he said, wrapping a towel around his waist. "Tell me."

Kullen filled the Emperor in on everything that had happened since last they'd spoken in the rooftop garden—his surveillance of Magister Issemar's mansion, Magister Deckard's visit, and uncovering the evidence of Magister Issemar's dealings with the Blood Clan pirates. Emperor Wymarc thumbed through the dead aristocrat's notebook with a frown, listening as Kullen told of Magister Issemar's late-night journey to the seemingly abandoned factory, and his subsequent murder as he left the scene.

"So that was you," the Emperor said, looking up with a sly smile for Kullen. "Turoc was on the verge of ordering his Orkenwatch patrol strung up for drinking on duty—he was certain no one could simply vanish into thin air, and could find no other rational explanation."

Kullen chuckled. "Had to outrun a bloody Sniffer. Damned hard to shake without resorting to a few tricks."

"Not the first person to do so," Emperor Wymarc said, frowning. "Evidently there was another incident a few nights back where an Orken patrol was attacked, and their assailants managed to lose them by slipping into the shit tunnels."

Kullen raised an eyebrow. "Not a bad plan." He resolved to try it next time he was fleeing the Orkenwatch.

Emperor Wymarc gestured for him to continue.

Kullen detailed the attack on the Refuge, and was glad to see the Emperor's face turn red, his nostrils flare in anger.

"Magister Deckard has gone too far!" His hands clenched so tight around Magister Issemar's notebook that he half-ripped one of the pages. "He must be dealt with at once."

"I couldn't agree more." Kullen smiled. "Which is why I knew you wouldn't mind that I paid him a little visit."

Kullen told him of the outcome of his "little visit"—including Magister Deckard's fiery death, Golgoth's odd behavior, and the discovery of the scrimshaw in the aristocrat's office—proof that he, too, was conspiring with Magister Issemar and the Blood Clan pirates.

The Emperor shook his head.

"But this is what I found most interesting," Kullen said, digging into his pocket and pulling out scrap of half-burned parchment he'd recovered from Deckard's hearth. Unfolding the cloth, he carefully presented it to the Emperor.

Emperor Wymarc read it, frowning, then looked up at Kullen.

"Red Claw? Does that name mean anything to you?"

Kullen shook his head. "I was hoping you'd know it."

Emperor Wymarc's lips pressed together into a tight line.

"It is not known to me. This script, however..." He stared down at the parchment. "I have seen it before, but where, I cannot remember."

Kullen was about to say, "Perhaps Assidius would recognize it", but stopped himself. He still had his doubts about the Seneschal's loyalties. Something about the lean man sat ill in his gut—he was too damned persnickety and fussy, even more so than his role as administrator demanded. That didn't mean he was a traitor or a spy or secretly in league with these other nobles, but it didn't have to be anything so severe for Kullen to want to keep him far away from this.

On the other hand, if the handwriting did belong to Assidius, the Emperor would have doubtless recognized it immediately. Kullen would have, too. Assidius's handwriting was obsessively neat, his letters so tiny they bordered on cramped. The Seneschal hadn't written the missive.

Reluctantly, he resolved to voice the thought aloud. "Would Assidius be able to identify the sender by the handwriting?"

"Perhaps," Emperor Wymarc said, nodding thoughtfully. "Or one of his scribes." He folded the note up and handed it back to Kullen. "You will find him at Tuskthorne, awaiting my grandson."

Kullen's stomach sank. "And you want me to take it to him?"

Emperor Wymarc nodded. "While you're there, you can ask Turoc what he's uncovered about the missing vials."

"Speaking of," Kullen said, plunging his hand into his pocket. He handed the Emperor Deckard's dragonblood vial.

The Emperor held it up to the light, then handed it back to Kullen.

"Keep this for now. At least in your care, I know it will be safely out of the hands of whoever is stealing them from the noblemen."

"You want me to keep it?" Kullen asked, incredulous.

"What better, safer place?"

"I could think of many," Kullen said softly. Then he realized what that implied. "You believe it's someone inside the palace walls."

"Right now, I'm worried it could be anyone." Emperor Wymarc's jaw muscles clenched, his face growing hard. "Until Assidius and Turoc uncover the identity of whoever is behind the thefts, I'm going to have to be extra cautious."

Kullen stuffed the vial back into his pocket, careful to keep his thumb clear of the needle.

It appeared the Emperor was even more concerned than Kullen had originally thought. If Kullen didn't do something soon, there'd be no nobility left in the court.

Though, he could think of worse things.

40

NATISSE

Natisse kept a close eye on Haston as she helped him limp south through the Western Docks. She lacked Jad's skills or knowledge of the healing arts, but she'd sustained enough injuries to know a thing or two about dealing with wounds. Head wounds, in particular, could appear mild but end up being more serious than expected.

So, when Haston's eyelids began to sag again, she knew she had to keep him awake.

"Haston. Haston, focus!" Natisse shook the man.

"W-What?" Haston blinked, struggling.

"Stay awake, Haston," Natisse said. "At least until Serrod takes a look at you."

"Hurts to stay awake," Haston mumbled.

"I know it does." Natisse's stomach clenched. They had barely gone a half-dozen blocks, and still had a great deal more ground to cover and she was sweating heavily from supporting most of Haston's weight.

She needed to keep him talking.

"What happened back there?"

"What?" Haston mumbled.

"Magister Perech's guards," Natisse said. "How'd they find you? You're the stealthiest of us all, you should never have been spotted, much less caught. So what happened?"

"Oh, that. Was stupid." Haston blinked again, his eyelids fluttering.

"What was stupid?" Natisse pressed, shaking him again. "What did you do?"

"Didn't do anything," Haston muttered. "Just stupid... unlucky." He said no more and his chin hit his chest.

"Wake up!" Natisse jabbed the heel of her hand into his short ribs.

Haston's eyes snapped open.

"Ow!" He shot a glare at her. "What was that for?"

"For your own good," Natisse retorted. "You've got to stay awake until we can get you to Serrod's. And until you tell me what in Shekoth's icy pits happened. What was stupid unlucky?"

Step. Drag. Step. Drag.

Natisse wasn't weak, but she was growing more tired by the second.

When Haston didn't respond, she prodded him again.

"The guards were just... there," the man mumbled, as if he hadn't just nodded off after her question. "Same place as me. Same time. Just... unlucky."

Natisse frowned. "What place?" She hunched to look into his eyes, trying to assess his faculties. "Start from the beginning. Tell me everything."

"Beginning," Haston echoed. His mouth twisted into a pensive grimace.

Step. Drag.

"I've been stuck on that roof for a couple of days now. Everything's been business as usual in the caravan yard—strongbacks... hauling cargo, wagon trains coming and going, guards... guarding, the typical. Without anyone to spell me on watch, I figured it was quiet enough that I could take a short walk. Stretch my legs. Piss."

Natisse nodded. Under normal circumstances, there would be two pairs of eyes surveilling any location of interest. However, the Crimson Fang's personnel were stretched dangerously thin at the moment. With Nalkin, Tobin, and L'yo on business in Half-vale, Leroshavé digging into Magister Perech's operation from the inside, Dalash still waiting for an opportunity to extricate himself from the dead aristocrat's household, and Athelas monitoring Magister Onathus's shipyard, there was no one to share the burden. Eventually, even the most long suffering man's patience would crack.

"While I was… doing my business," Haston said, "two guards showed up. Same place. Same time. Started to engage in…" He hesitated. "… amorous pursuits away from prying eyes."

Natisse raised an eyebrow. "While on duty?"

Haston shrugged.

Telling the story seemed to have him more aware than he'd been in the last quarter hour. It was working. Just a little longer.

"Looked like," he continued, even starting to take a little of the weight of Natisse. "They were all over each other, right up until they spotted me. One look at my clothing and the dagger on my belt, and they got suspicious. Thought I'd lose them, then double back. Get up to the roof, but…" He winced and rubbed at his leg. "Damned cobblestones hurt. Ain't broken, but I won't be running anywhere for a few days."

Natisse winced. He'd been running at full speed when he tripped. With a fall like that, he was lucky to limp away with only bruises.

"That one guard called you a 'spying bastard' and was going to have you tortured to find out who sent you," she said. "Any idea what that's about?"

"No." Haston gave a little shake of his head, and instantly

appeared to regret it. He groaned, his eyes wobbling, and his legs grew weak again.

"Easy, easy." Natisse grunted beneath Haston's weight and fought to keep the man upright.

Haston eventually managed to regain his balance, and nodded his thanks to her.

"Don't know why the guards thought I was spying or that I was spying for anyone, but by the way they instantly drew weapons, I got the feeling they had orders to keep whatever's going on inside the caravan yard secret—no matter how much blood has to be spilled."

That fit with Natisse's suspicions. Men like Magister Perech would kill without compunction to protect their secrets, power, and wealth. Though the aristocrat himself was dead, his operation continued in effect. Whoever was running things from behind the scenes—at the moment, Magister Branthe was the chief suspect—would want to maintain the status quo and preserve the confidentiality of their illicit operation.

For awhile now, Natisse had considered the lack of Lumenators within the caravan and ship yards to indicate that the respective Magisters were trying to keep the Emperor's nose out of things. But what if he was somehow involved? What if he commanded the Lumenators be kept far away so as to not implicate him in the dealings?

No. As much as she hated the man, there was no reason he'd play a role like this. He had all the riches, authority, and holdings any man could desire. What was there to gain from any of this? He may've been above worrying about the little people of the Embers, but he'd never shown outward hostility toward any of them. Had he?

Finally, they entered the One Hand District and Natisse led the way straight to Serrod's shop. A wooden sign hung emblazoned with faded painted letters that read "Serrod, alkemyst and heeler." Another thing the people so close to the Embers lacked:

literacy. Likely, most of the people who came this way wouldn't be able to read the words anyway, but they'd recognize the Brendoni healer's emblem: intertwined blue and white sparrows flying above a pair of cupped hands.

Instead of approaching from the front, however, Natisse helped Haston limp around to the rear of the shop. There, she pounded on the rickety wooden back door.

"Serrod! Serrod! Wake up."

She waited for a few seconds, then hammered and called out again. This time, a small window on the shop's second floor banged open and an older man with long, stringy, gray hair—none of which resided on the top of his pate—poked his umber-skinned head out.

"What is it?" Serrod mumbled in a voice halfway between sleepy and furious. "What do you want?"

"It's Natisse." She turned her face upward, letting moonlight illuminate her features. "Haston took a nasty head wound, and he needs your help."

"Haston?" Serrod asked. "Don't know no Haston."

"Just come down, Serrod!" Natisse called. "He's in bad shape. Maybe even dying."

It was exaggeration. The gash on Haston's head no longer bled, and any traces of malaise had fled. But if she was going to wake Serrod up in the middle of the night, he'd grumble unless she had a damned good reason. Then again, he'd probably still grumble anyway.

"All right, all right!" The Brendoni vanished from sight and the window banged shut. A few moments later, the shop's rear door swung open to reveal Serrod, clad in a faded yellow nightshirt, holding a lit candle.

"Come on in," he muttered, beckoning them to enter. "Just try not to bleed everywhere, will you?"

"I'll do my best," Haston said, giving the man a grin.

Serrod led them a few steps down a narrow hallway. Each wall was covered in paintings that appeared to be done by a child.

"Who painted these?" Haston asked. "Daughter? Grandson?"

Serrod stopped, turned, and stared.

"I did," he said, then quickly spun and kept walking.

Natisse gave Haston a look that said, "Good job."

The hallway opened into his examination room. Every square inch of the place was occupied by what, to Natisse, appeared mostly bric-a-brac. He had magnifying glasses of all sizes, both handheld and mounted, shelves upon shelves of potions, elixirs, and oils. Tucked into one corner of the room was a statue of carved ebony wood depicting the naked, bedangled figure of Yildemé, the Brendoni's favorite goddess. Nearest the door stood a table covered with skulls and bones that could've been from any animal, but looked distinctly human.

"Are those... real?" Haston asked, swallowing audibly.

Serrod stepped over to them, knocked on a skull with his knuckles, and said, "Appears so. Now, get on the table."

He snapped his fingers and pointed to a long wooden board in the middle of the room that looked like it would inflict more pain by splinters than anything else. Dark stains marked it in several places. The Brendoni set the candle down on a table, lifted his butcher's apron from where it hung behind the door, and pulled it on over his head.

By the time Natisse had Haston seated on the table, Serrod had donned his round, wire-rimmed spectacles and a pair of parchment-thin calfskin gloves.

"Now, what seems to be the problem?"

Haston shot a glance Natisse's way.

She couldn't blame him. There was blood everywhere and it was clearly stemming from the back of his head.

"Took a nasty wound to the head," Natisse said anyway. "Cut deep, but I don't think it broke bone."

"Hmm," Serrod mused, pulling his thin lips together in the

way he always did, which made his already small mouth almost vanish amidst the tangle of his wispy white beard. "Let me see, let me see." He hustled Natisse out of the way and squinted down at the back of Haston's head. "Nasty, indeed."

Haston let out a hissing breath as Serrod prodded the area around the wound. "Ezrasil's bloody bastard!" he swore.

Serrod seemed not to notice—or simply didn't care. He was focused entirely on inspecting the wound by the light of the candle, which he'd ordered Natisse to bring over and hold up for him. His tongue shot out and did a loop around his lips. A nervous tick Natisse had noticed on many occasions. After a few seconds, he straightened and turned to Natisse with a frown.

"Don't see no break in the skull, but I can't be too sure. Better he stays where I can keep an eye on him overnight."

Haston's expression tightened. "Is that really necessary?"

"Necessary?" Serrod snorted. He tapped Haston's forehead with a finger three times. "If you want to make sure you've got all your brains in the morning."

Haston gave Natisse a questioning look.

"He's the healer," Natisse said, holding up her hands. "He says you stay, you stay."

Haston raised an eyebrow, his expression filled with meaning. "Can we…"

"Afford his rates?" Serrod asked. "Of course you can. I don't charge nothing for friends of Natisse." He stepped back and cocked his head. "Trust me? About as much as you can trust any dumb bunker in the One Hand District."

"Serrod's as good a man as I've ever known," Natisse said. The alchemist's face filled with pride. "May not look like much—this little shop—but there ain't a better healer even in the palace. Nor in all of Brendoni!"

Natisse knew it wasn't arrogance, either. Kooky as the man might've been, he was the best. Where many outsiders had received a less-than-friendly welcome in Dimvein, the Brendoni had prospered enough to afford a *two*-story building when most of his neighbors had single-floor dwellings. He even had two working doors and a window with a single pane of glass—testament to his much sought-after skills.

"And after what Natisse and her friends did for us all here," Serrod said, his tone and expression softening, "ain't enough gold in the coffers to convince us to turn on her."

All of Serrod's grumpiness had now passed, and he regaled Natisse with a nearly toothless grin. The umber-skinned healer was far from handsome, but every time Natisse saw him, she was struck by how that hideous smile transformed his face. Not all beauty came from without.

"You can trust him," Natisse said, nodding to Haston. "His bedside manner leaves a lot to be desired, though."

Serrod rolled his eyes. "You want someone to fluff your pillows and whisper sweet nothings in your ear, you go to a brothel. You want to get better, you come see Serrod."

"And endure his chivvying and scowling," Natisse said. She gave the bald Brendoni a grin and gripped his shoulder. "Thank you, Serrod."

"Always." Serrod rested a callused hand atop hers. "I'll look after him, get him back to you in one piece. You get back to saving the Empire for the rest of us."

"Always." Natisse repeated. She grinned, squeezing Serrod's arm before pulling her hand away, then turned to Haston. "When you're back on your feet, go find Athelas, and if he's not there, come back to the Burrow, got it?"

"Got it." Haston nodded. "And Natisse?"

Natisse had already turned away, but Haston's voice stopped her.

"Thanks," Haston said. A little flush rose to his cheeks, and he gave her an embarrassed but grateful smile. "For saving my ass out there."

"It's what we do." Natisse inclined her head.

"And maybe we don't tell Athelas or Garron about this, yeah?" His cheeks reddened even further. "They'd never let me hear the end of it."

"Better you stay on my good side, then." Natisse chuckled. "Piss me off, and—"

"Enough, enough." Serrod waved her away with one hand, his other filled with bandages for Haston's head. "Get out of here already!"

"Get better," Natisse said. Then, she complied and started off down the hallway toward the back alley. She was just glad to escape without too much lecturing from Serrod.

But she hadn't escaped completely. Her hand was on the rear door when Serrod's voice bellowed from behind her.

"And for the love of Ezrasil, learn not to wake good, hard-working folk in the middle of the bloody night!"

41

KULLEN

No one who'd laid eyes on the Tuskthorne Keep could
have any doubt as to its true purpose. It looked as
fierce, rough, and brutal as the Orken who inhabited
it. Ten stories tall, built of black stone, every level bristling with
enormous ivory tusks, the tower was eternally patrolled by the
huge sallow-skinned Orken in full battle gear. A single gate
opened into its base, and set high upon the spike-rimmed, flat-
topped crest of the tower were four gargantuan Orkenhorns.

Those mammoth instruments had been blown once in
Kullen's lifetime: the day Golgoth had destroyed the Embers. It
was said only Orken lungs could generate breath enough to make
them sound. It was also said that when blown, their deep bellows
carried across all of Dimvein to the depths of the Wild Grove
Forest and far out to sea… even as far as Hudar and the southern
provinces.

Kullen had never been foolish enough to break into Tuskthorne, but suspected that even the Shadow Realm would fail to
get him inside that ferocious stronghold. It was the only structure
in Dimvein that he'd deemed impregnable. He wasn't looking
forward to the day he had to put that belief to the test.

The Orken were loyal to a fault. Though Wymarc's long line had been kind to them when others weren't. They were also a bit of a mystery, even to Kullen. He'd always assumed the Watch made their beds here in the tower, though he had very little in the way of proof to make such a claim.

There wasn't a day that passed where enormous Orken of all genders and ages were seen walking the streets. The Orken women towered nearly as tall as their male counterparts, though their musculature was far less pronounced and they lacked the coarse, bristling beards. Even Orken children stood as tall as a man of average height.

But where they went at night, to sleep, Kullen assumed the Emperor alone knew. People tended to fear what they didn't understand, and very few—if any—understood the Orken people. Besides that, the Orkenwatch weren't well liked by any, even those who need never feel their blades or tusks. They were known to be crass and crude and chose to act upon animal instinct more often than strategic planning. If they even thought a crime against the Emperor was being carried out, blood would spill—and Kullen had rarely seen an Orken bleed.

He stared up at a narrow walkway suspended above the portcullis, glad for the Emperor's letter in his pocket.

"Here on the Emperor's business!" he shouted up.

A moment later, an Orken leaned over the black stone wall.

"Name," he growled.

"Kullen."

"Last name?"

"Kullen."

"Yer name's Kullen Kullen?"

Kullen nodded curtly.

"Sounds made up," the Orken said.

"Fine. What's your name?"

"Garg."

"So does yours."

The Orken did something akin to smiling. "Stay there once the gate opens." He flipped a lever and the gate slowly began to rise.

Kullen had no patience for dealing with Orken procedure or submitting to a thorough questioning. Not after the exertions of the last few days. His earlier exhaustion had increased with every plodding step across Dimvein. The bloody Tuskthorne dominated the eastern section of the city, within sight of the enormous Northern Gate, a full hour's trudge northwest from the Palace.

Had it been night, Kullen would've summoned Umbris to carry him across Dimvein. Unfortunately, with the sun now reaching its zenith, he had no shadows to conceal the dragon's bulk. He was sure that news of the stone mill, where he'd been forced to shadow-slide in front of the Orkenwatch patrol, had traveled quickly throughout the ranks and all of them would be on the lookout for anyone behaving with strange magic. Turoc, Assidius, and every other Orken within would find his arrival on dragonback far too fascinating.

As it was, he'd been unfortunate enough that Verar—who he'd known as "Hiccup" during his youth—had been manning the stables this morning. Though Kullen had managed to coax him into loaning out one of the Emperor's horses, the groom, no doubt out of spite for some slight imagined or real, had given him the slowest, orneriest of the mounts in the Imperial stables. Kullen had expended more energy trying to keep the horse under control than he'd have spent walking on his own two feet.

Which, eventually, he'd chosen to do. A silver coin had hired a local urchin to return the horse—who had grown suddenly docile and placid the moment Kullen dismounted—to the Palace. Kullen had been all too willing to make the remaining journey on foot, fatigue be damned.

Yet now, as he stood, arms crossed, watching the guard descend the stairs, he pushed aside his fatigue and focused his full attention on the Orken lumbering toward him. There were few places in Dimvein where he would be in greater danger—if Turoc or any of the other Orken had even the slightest suspicion that he was more than he appeared to be, they'd clap him in irons and haul him off to some deep, dark hole for interrogation. An interrogation where fists and truncheons would ask some damned pointed and painful questions.

Kullen's pulse quickened as Garg drew nearer. The gate guard's black eyes locked on him, and shining steel weapons were ready to attack if need be.

Garg stopped mere feet away.

"Why you here?" Garg was a giant even among his own kind. Kullen very rarely had to look up to meet eyes with anyone, but here, now, his neck ached for the effort. Hints of gray peppered the Orken's bristling beard and cracks traced his tawny, leather-like skin. Age had begun to gnarl his fingers and swell his knuckles, yet he held his ten-foot-tall spear leveled at Kullen without a hint of tremor. He wore silver rings in his beard that marked him as a mid-level grunt. Had he been an officer, his would have been gold like Turoc's. Even still, they were pitted and black, tarnished from repeated stroking.

Kullen reached into his pocket. Garg thrust his spear forward threateningly.

Kullen raised both hands in a placative gesture. "Whoa, now." He moved a little slower, but the guard steadied himself. Once Kullen pulled out the burned parchment, Garg seemed to settle. "Here to show this to the Seneschal."

Garg reached for it and Kullen pulled it away.

"His eyes only," Kullen said for emphasis.

Garg grunted. "Wait here."

As the Orken turned to leave, something caught Kullen's eye. A company of six Orken were marching from the south, heading straight for Tuskthorne as if at the end of a long patrol. Yet one of them, the smallest of the group, stopped and half-turned toward him. Kullen's gut clenched as the broad-nosed Orken lifted its head and drew in a deep breath, tasting the air.

"Ezrasil's ass," Kullen swore under his breath.

"What's that?" Garg said, stopping and facing Kullen.

Thirty yards separated him from the Orken Sniffer who had picked up his scent when he fled the scene of Magister Issemar's murder. There was no wind to blow his smell toward the Sniffer, but that could change at any moment. If the Sniffer caught a whiff of him, he'd be forced to flee. In broad daylight, with few shadows to slide between, he'd have no escape.

"It seems—foolish me—I've grabbed the wrong parchment."

Garg eyed him with suspicion.

"I know. Quite embarrassing."

Garg turned his massive head, eyes fixing on the returning company. Before the Orken could voice any more concern, Kullen swept a little bow.

"I'll return shortly," he said. "And please, don't mention this little kerfuffle to Turoc. Your Tuskigo has a low enough opinion of me already."

He quickly turned on his heel, hurrying his steps away from the Orken. With his excuse, the guards would write off his urgency as needing to retrieve the correct letter rather than trying to evade them.

Sweat flowed like fountains down his face and back. His heart sounded like a drum within his chest and ears. He dared not glance over his shoulder—nothing drew more suspicion than a fleeing man looking back. Indeed, it almost screamed "guilty" to any trained eye.

Just ahead, a rather sizable Church of Ezrasil stood atop a hillside littered with grave markers and tombs. He headed for a small pocket of darkness between the building itself and a smaller gravedigger's shack.

Once he was safely within the shroud of darkness did he chance a peek around the corner. To his relief, he saw no sign of the Sniffer. Likewise, neither was Garg looking his way, and there were no pursuers preparing to hunt him down.

He let out a long breath and rubbed his face free of sweat.

In the wake of all that had happened over the last day, he hadn't even considered the likelihood of that same Sniffer who'd come dangerously close to catching him being inside Tuskthorne. That was careless. Something Kullen prided himself in *not* being. Was it the lack of sleep? The overuse of the Shadow Realm's power?

Kullen shook his head. He'd just accused himself of foolishness to Garg, and now he feared it was true. To enter Tuskthorne would risk him being found out. He'd have to wait until Turoc and Assidius returned to report to the Emperor—knowing the fastidious, meticulous Seneschal, he'd be back at the Palace before nightfall with an update on their progress into the investigation, or lack thereof.

Kullen turned his head toward the graveyard and spotted two figures beside a tall oak tree. One was clearly an Orken, though from his position, he couldn't make out any features. The other was much smaller, a man. They stood close, speaking in what appeared to be hushed tones. Moments later, they parted, the Orken walking away from Kullen's hiding place but the human headed right toward him.

With another look back at Tuskthorne, sure there was no one in pursuit, Kullen slipped back onto the street and slowly strode away. He found a seat on the church's rough, stone steps and pulled the hood of his cloak over his face. To any passerby, he'd seem like any other vagabond or street-sleeper.

Finally, the figure emerged and started down the street away from Tuskthorne. Kullen gazed from beneath the shadow of his hood.

Magister Branthe?

The foppish Magister walked with purpose, entirely ignoring Kullen.

What was he doing talking to that Orken? Kullen knew the

man had offered to escort Prince Jaylen to Turoc, but what business could he have had in secret within the cemetery?

Perhaps he was being paranoid. Hadn't Kullen recently heard that Magister Branthe was planning to travel south to Hudar? Yes, indeed. That would have to be it. It wasn't entirely out of the ordinary for a Magister to hire Orken on the side. They were robust, powerful warriors that often accompanied Magisters on long trips where they would require security. And such acts were often done in secret. Though it wasn't illegal, it was a show of weakness on the Magister's part and someone like Branthe could never been seen as weak.

Kullen estimated he would have a few hours before Assidius and Turoc found their way back to the Palace. A few hours' delay wouldn't change anything. The dragonblood vials would still be missing, and there would still be traitors scheming to undermine the Emperor.

"Looks like I've got enough time for a short rest and a visit with a very important someone."

Kullen actually smiled as he slipped into the empty Embers building he'd purchased for the occasions when he needed to visit with Umbris but couldn't escape the city to visit him in the Wild Grove Forest. Days like today, when his service to the Emperor kept him too busy to find time for a quiet getaway.

The sun had begun to set, and in the fading afternoon light, the interior of the building was mostly shadowed—save for the red-gold glow streaming through two windows set high into the eastern and western walls.

Kullen pulled the vial from within his shirt and pressed his finger to the tip. Blood flowed from his thumb into the vial. Just a small drip. It mixed together with Umbris's and Kullen focused his efforts upon his friend.

With a powerful gust of wind, Umbris appeared as if from nowhere. Where there was once shadow, now stood a dragon that nearly filled the entirety of the building.

Kullen unslung the sack from his shoulder. It thudded when it hit the ground.

Umbris sniffed the sack, and his gleaming yellow eyes brightened.

"*Is that...*" Umbris's words felt nearly human, a child anxious for a gift on their birthday.

"Your favorite." Kullen bent and unclasped the bag, pulling out two smoked pork shoulders, as promised.

Umbris, quick as a leaping cat, snatched the meat in his huge jaws, chomping through bone, gristle, and flesh alike. Kullen was struck by the blinding contrast between Umbris and Golgoth. The enormous red dragon had been a creature of majesty, every move ponderous and mighty, her very presence emanating a sense of power and menace that could not be ignored. Umbris, on the other hand, was compact, lithe, built for speed. Kullen had no doubt the dragon's muscles could manage immense power, yet Umbris doubtless relied on cunning and his ability to move between shadows should he find himself locked in combat.

It was a strange and terrifying thought. He'd only ever witnessed one clash of dragons before—the day Thanagar had battled Golgoth into submission over the Embers. The two enormous beasts had wrecked hundreds of buildings and caused extensive damage with the ferocity of their conflict.

How would Umbris fare against either the white or red dragon? It would doubtless be a battle akin to Kullen taking on Turoc in hand to hand combat—he'd have to be damned smart, fast, and vicious to take down the larger foe.

"*Your thoughts are troubled,*" Umbris said through their mental bond once the pork was fully devoured.

Umbris already knew of Kullen's encounter with Golgoth. As part of the bond between them, Kullen's thoughts were never private. It would work both ways, if Kullen had been better at focusing. Umbris had assured him that only one of his bloodsworn had been able to read the dragon's thoughts beyond the words it spoke.

"I've never come so close to being eaten alive or burned to ash by a dragon before," Kullen said. "It's pretty damned troubling, truth be told."

"*I would never harm you in that manner,*" Umbris said, as if Kullen needed the reassurance.

"You remember the day we met?" Kullen reminded him. "Came pretty damned close then."

Umbris lowered his head apologetically.

"I jest. That was a difficult day for all of us."

Kullen reached into his pocket and pulled out Deckard's dragonblood vial.

"This belonged to Magister Deckard," Kullen said. "The bastard went too far."

"*Golgoth,*" Umbris said.

"Indeed. At least now there's a chance of the dragon bonding with someone with a shred of decency."

Kullen considered how easily things back at the Refuge could've gone if Deckard had chosen to summon the dragon instead of his flaming sword.

"*He was too frightened,*" Umbris said, reading Kullen's thoughts. "*The last time Golgoth had been released...*"

"I lost some people very dear to me."

Kullen then thought of Mammy Tess—of the look she'd given him after watching him cut down Magister Deckard's guards.

"*Go, speak to your Heartsworn,*" Umbris said. "*If she truly is as you say—bound to you by cords of love—then she will understand. If not...*" The dragon left the rest unsaid.

Kullen's gut churned at the thought of speaking to Mammy

Tess. The horror in her eyes at the realization of who—what—he now was... That was a wound that still felt far too raw. How would she look at him now? She'd had time to process the events of the previous night, but that didn't necessarily mean her heart would be settled.

"What did they make you into?" Those had been her words. As if the man who'd stood there in front of her was a total stranger, a monster wearing the face of the Kullen she'd known. He'd hidden the truth from her out of necessity. And now that she'd seen a fraction of the true Kullen, could she bear to know the rest?

In the end, the answer was simple: he owed it to her to find out. After what she'd done for him—taking him in when he was too young to remember his own parents or even his own name—he owed her the truth, come what may.

"You're right, friend," Kullen said. "Until next time."

With that and a nod, Kullen dismissed Umbris back to the Shadow Realm.

The burden on Kullen's shoulders grew heavier with every ponderous breath. He'd felt so rested and refreshed just minutes earlier. Now, it was as if the weight of reality came crashing down onto him, as it had the day he'd learned of Jarius and Hadassa's fate.

But he'd have to bear it, at least long enough to look Mammy Tess in the eye and tell her the truth.

His determination hardened, his jaw muscles clenched, and he exited the building. Quick steps took him toward Pawn May Avenue. But before he arrived, the sky filled with white, fluttering... snow?

No, it wasn't snow.

A dark cloud billowed in the sky. The smell of burning wood and smoke...

Kullen broke into a run, barreling through the streets and careening around the last corner. Just in time to see a column of armed and armored men charging into the burning Refuge.

42

NATISSE

"**O**h, dearie, you look marvelous!" Gaidra pressed her hands to her lips and beamed brightly. "I swear you grow more beautiful every time I see you."

"You're too kind, Gaidra." Natisse smiled, but it was entirely for the white-haired seamstress' benefit. She loathed the gaudy mountain of lace, ribbon, sequins, and pearlescent buttons that some overweening noblewoman would call a dress. The corset squeezed too tightly around her midsection and the train... well, that horrible mess of silk could go straight to Shekoth's pits and rot for all eternity. How was she to turn with so much fabric dangling on the ground behind her?

She was only too glad for the simple cloak to throw over the elaborate costume, for it was a garment that made her feel at least fractionally more comfortable.

"I promise I'll bring it back in one piece. This won't be like last time."

"Oh, pish posh!" Gaidra gave a dismissive wave. "What good is a seamstress if she can't fix up a few tears here and there?"

This time, Natisse's smile was genuine. The last outfit she'd borrowed from Gaidra—an aristocrat's velvet jacket, vest, and stockings for Baruch to wear—had been returned with a number of new dagger holes, mud stains, and a missing sleeve. Luckily, the Crimson Fang had come away from the villa of their target—a wealthy merchant by the name of Dazaq—with enough coin to more than repay the seamstress for the damaged clothing.

Natisse examined herself one last time in the full-length mirror. She had no idea what the courtly Imperial ladies saw in such torturous extravagance, but she couldn't help but admit to herself that the royal blue dress complemented her fiery red hair beautifully. A moment later, one of the corset's whalebones dug painfully into her rib—a reminder of just how ridiculous these outfits were. Give her a suit of leather armor or her usual comfortable street clothing any day!

"Ezrasil's bones," Natisse said. "You'd think something this uncomfortable would provide protection against a ballista!"

Gaidra chuckled. "The price of beauty, my love. This outfit will dazzle even the noblest of nobles."

"If it doesn't kill me first."

Gaidra made a few more tucks and offered another pat or two. Then, still smiling, she said, "I think it's perfect."

Natisse swayed in the mirror one last time. Satisfied that everything was in place, she turned back to Gaidra. "Right. I'll see you in a few hours."

"If I haven't kicked the bucket yet!"

"Don't even joke!" Natisse playfully slapped the seamstress.

Gaidra pressed Natisse's hands in hers. "I suppose an old woman could only hope. These old bones get harder to live with each day. I'll see you soon. And you'll find these clothes of yours freshly washed, pressed, and mended when you return."

Natisse loved the old woman. She was the closest thing to a grandmother she'd ever known. She made certain that the Crimson Fang slipped a few extra coins into the purse dropped into Gaidra's hands after every haul.

Much as she wished she could stay for a cup of tea or one of

Gaidra's famous lace cookies, she hurried toward the door and out into the night. It had been more than an hour since she'd left the nobles' meeting place. Unless she was fortunate enough to cross paths with a hansom or carriage traveling through the Western Docks at this hour of night—about as likely as sprouting wings or wielding dragon magic—it would take her nearly an hour again to return. She could only hope that whatever the cloaked noblemen and women had entered that building to see would still be there when she arrived.

Fumbling with her dress, she ran as fast as the cumbersome attire would allow. She did her best to avoid the muddy puddles plaguing this part of town, but it was useless. Before she knew it, the dress was soaked to above her ankles.

A noise in the distance set Natisse's heart pounding—something like running feet, the whisper of cloth on skin, or perhaps whispered voices. Her right hand darted toward her hip where her dagger would normally be and then she remembered the dress.

Swearing, she pushed aside the fabric of her frilly left sleeve of her dress, gripped the hilt of the dagger hidden there. This wasn't the Embers, where people just went missing without a trace. This was the Western Docks, and if anything, *she* was the true danger here.

She fell into a stalk, using the cover of the buildings to hide her. When she say the source of the sound, she found herself caught somewhere between laughter and tears. It turned out to be an alley hound rustling through a pile of debris for any scraps of food. The malnourished dog turned mournful black eyes on her, but slunk away a moment later.

Natisse drew in a deep, calming breath. It was certainly unusual to find a woman in such rich clothing wandering alone through the Western Docks, especially at this late hour, but if anyone dared to accost her, they would find her no wilting noble, no easy target ripe for fleecing.

She hurried through the empty, quiet streets, her mind wandering back to the fragment of her past she'd glimpsed during the fight to rescue Haston. Or what she'd almost glimpsed. She'd banished the memory before any details could crystalize, but she knew for certain that she had begun to see the faces of the woman who'd cried out and the man with the cruel laugh.

She tried to reach into the vaults of her mind, to tap into the memories she'd, until now, believed lost. But it was in vain. There was no great epiphany. None of Ezraisil's brilliant light from above making clear something once obscured. She still saw the blurred outlines of the frail woman struggling in the enormous man's grip, but no more details. No faces, no hair color, not even a hint of clothing to give her an idea of who they might've been. She was certain that those two had been with her the day she survived the dragon attack, but try as she might, she could not recall any more details.

Frustration mounted within her. She cursed quietly—why had the memory returned at that exact moment? Why couldn't she have remembered it in the darkness and quiet of her quarters, or at any other time when she could've explored the depths of their meaning? No. No light from Ezrasil. Just his mocking laughter through the mouth of the brute in her memory.

All was quiet when she reached her destination. The street was empty of carriages and hansoms. No sign of anyone guarding the front gate, either. Though from her vantage point north of the building, she wouldn't be able to see the men on watch.

She smoothed down her ornate dress and checked her outfit one last time. To her relief, the streets here were just as wet and mud-covered. No one would find fault in a lady having a mishap when disembarking her coach.

Plastering on a haughty expression, she pulled the cloak up higher around her head and strode free of the shadows. It proved a surprisingly difficult act to slink through the night while still carrying herself like a self-important noblewoman. Thankfully, the guards at the gate either didn't notice or didn't suspect anything amiss. Indeed, the pair made no appearance until she strode right up to the gate and rapped her knuckles against the steel.

"I say, this is a poor way to treat a lady of the Imperial court," she said, her voice quiet, yet ringing with disdain. "I haven't ridden all this way to be ignored!"

At the accusation, the guards' eyes went wide, their expressions both showing a mixture of curiosity, bewilderment, and chagrin.

"Where's your ride?" asked one, a bearded fellow with salt-and-pepper gray hair.

"How dare you ask such an impertinent question!" Natisse drew herself up to her full height, though she was careful to keep the hood pulled forward just far enough that her face was mostly hidden in shadow. Her dress, however, was on full display, the sequins twinkling in the light of the lantern in one guard's hands. "Perhaps I should ask who you are. If only so I can tell your master what dreadful disrespect one of the men in his employ demonstrated."

"I—I meant no—"

The other guard, a younger man with a handsome, sunburned face, cleared his throat.

"Forgive my companion, my lady," he said, giving her a small bow from the waist. "He's had a long night, and is far from gracious on the best of days."

"Indeed." Natisse gave a dainty sniff and turned pointedly away from the older man, facing the younger guard full-on. "My good friend Baronet Ochrin would be awfully displeased to hear that all the men of Dimvein are so ill-mannered. It is good to see that at least someone recognizes quality breeding and shows it the respect due."

The name of Baronet Ochrin had the desired effect on both men. The older man's suspicion vanished instantly, and the younger man nearly fell over himself sweeping an apologetic bow.

"Forgive us, lady…?" He raised an eyebrow.

"Dellacourt," Natisse said. "Lady Dellacourt of Elliatrope."

"Of course. Lady Dellacourt." The young guard beamed up at her. "We simply didn't hear your carriage approaching so—"

"Carriage!" Natisse snorted. "These ladies of the capital and their disdain for exercise!" She leaned forward and dropped her voice to a conspiratorial whisper, making certain to breathe directly into the younger man's ear. "It makes them soft, you know, in all the wrong places. We ladies of the outer reaches, however, we prefer to occasionally walk on our own two feet."

She'd concocted the lie to explain why she'd come walking when all the others had arrived in vehicles. It was a simple fabrication, one the city-dwelling guards would have no reason to disbelieve.

"Your apology is accepted, young sir," she said, waving her hand dismissively. "Now, if you'd be so kind as to escort me inside—"

"I'm afraid that's not possible, my lady." The young guardsman blushed.

"What?" Natisse didn't need to pretend surprise. "Are you telling me that my personal invitation from Baronet Ochrin is not enough to gain me admission?"

"N-No, of course not!" The color on the young man's face deepened, and he began to stammer.

The older guardsman came to his rescue. "What he means, my lady, is that the night's festivities have ended. Cut short, I'm afraid."

"Cut… short?" Natisse let outrage trickle into her voice. "Whatever could that mean?"

"A few of the… contestants came down sick," said the guardsman. "Too sick to provide proper entertainment."

"But don't worry!" put in the younger man, trying heroically to recover his composure. "A healer has been summoned and rest assured that tomorrow night, the spectacle will take place as planned." His eyes brightened and he adopted a smile that looked far less confident than he doubtless hoped.

"A spectacle the likes of which have not been seen in Dimvein for years!" the older one added like he was trying to sell tickets.

Something about those words unsettled Natisse, though. They'd all but confirmed her suspicion that this was, in fact, the slave fighting pit the Crimson Fang had been seeking. Yet what manner of "entertainment" could be so unique to warrant such a proclamation?

"I do apologize for the inconvenience, my lady," the younger guard said, sweeping a deep bow. "If you would like a carriage to be fetched—"

"No, that won't be necessary." Natisse gave a dismissive wave. "A midnight stroll should suffice to dissipate some of my irritation." She spoke the last word in a pretense of barely controlled anger, and allowed the corners of her mouth to droop into a genteel frown.

"Perhaps I could accompany you?" the young man put in. "The streets of Dimvein could be dangerous for one such as yourself."

"A kind offer." Natisse patted the guard's shoulder, then ran a fingernail up the side of his neck and brushed his ear lightly. "Perhaps another night?"

She hid a smile at the little involuntary shiver that ran through the young man's body. The longer she appraised him, the younger he appeared—perhaps no more than eighteen or nineteen, and clearly inexperienced in all the ways of the world. Far easier for her to manipulate than the older, graying guard at his side.

"Good night, gentlemen!" Natisse called airily as she turned and flounced up the street, back the way she'd come. "I expect when I return tomorrow, I will be treated with the respect due Baronet Ochrin's personal guests."

"Of course, my lady!" the young man said. "And a good night

to you, too. May your dreams be sweet and your sleep—ow!" His honeyed words cut off in a sharp cry, followed by a hissed, "What was that for?"

Natisse didn't hear the older guard's muttered response, but she had already pushed the pair from her mind. They'd bought her Lady Dellacourt ruse, and though she'd arrived too late for whatever "spectacle" had taken place tonight, the guards had given her valuable information.

Tomorrow night, she would be back, and nothing would stop her from getting inside that door to find—and, if Ezrasil willed it, destroy once and for all—the slave fighting pits.

43

KULLEN

Kullen had no swords. Having already dispatched Magister Deckard, the Black Talons had done their job and were put to rest once more. But that didn't stop him from rushing through the Refuge's front doors in pursuit of the invading guards. His hunting knives slipped free of their sheaths with a hiss of steel on leather, and drove into the base of the nearest guardsman's skull before the bastard could register the threat. Kullen's gave a savage twist and ripped his blades free in a spray of blood, no small amount of which bathed his own face. The guardsman slumped to the ground at his feet, body lying across the orphanage's threshold.

Leaping over the corpse, Kullen charged after the next pair of guards. So intent were they on setting fire to the wooden shelves lining the front hallway that they too failed to notice him until it was too late. The first of the pair died with Kullen's hunting knife buried in the side of his neck. The second managed to half-turn and raise his flaming torch in a pitiful defense. It did him no good; Kullen simply dropped low and slashed the guard's inner thigh. Blood sluiced down the man's leg and he fell, screaming, clutching desperately at the wound. His dropped torch landed at

441

his feet, only to be extinguished when the guard collapsed atop it a moment later.

But the screams had alerted the other guardsmen already inside, which also triggered the screams of the children upstairs. Kullen had just time enough to wrench his blade clear of the dead guard's neck before three armed men barreled around the corner. They froze at the sight of his bloodstained blades, dark cloak, and the bodies littering the ground around him. Only for a moment, but that split second was all Kullen needed. He leaped toward them, blades flashing, and all three fell with throats sliced wide open.

Black smoke thickened the air within the Refuge. The orphanage's humble wooden furniture burned—tables, chairs, shelves, wardrobes, everything that could be set to the torch was now being consumed by fire. A terrible wall of heat slammed into Kullen's face as he charged toward the rear of the house, forcing him to retreat. The kitchen and small pantry were engulfed in flames, the dining room where he'd shared so many meals with his fellow orphans was equally ablaze. He caught sight of a corpse lying beneath one of the burning tables —too large to be a child, it had to be one of Mammy Tess' helpers.

"Quelly!" Kullen shouted, running for the cook. He knelt, instantly hoping he'd be wrong. But he wasn't. Quelly was dead. He'd never taste her potatoes and gravy again.

She hadn't just been the cook, either. Kullen had grown up with her, played in the yard with her. They'd even shared a small kiss one day when they thought no one was looking. They hadn't expected Mammy Sylla to be watching them from the doorway, curious as to what two little ones were doing sneaking around near the storage rooms.

Anger rose within Kullen, an inferno that raged as hot as the blaze now running rampant within the Refuge. He rose, clutched his bloodstained hunting knives tighter, and stalked down the hallway that led toward the sleeping quarters. There, the sounds of shouting, cursing, and a woman's scream echoed loud.

"Mammy Tess!"

He charged up the rickety stairs, lowered his shoulder, and burst through the door into the first room, colliding with a pair of guards charging the opposite way. The two fled the blaze that they'd just finished setting, which now consumed the rickety bunkbeds, sagging straw-filled mattresses, and ragged blankets.

Where were the children?

The two guards rebounded off Kullen's bulk"

"Watch yersel—"

The guard stopped when he saw Kullen's face—no doubt expecting him to be a comrade. The man's features went from shock to fury at the sight of him, then fear at the blades that gleamed in his hands like tongues of fire. He didn't give them a chance to call out, to even draw in another surprised breath. Like twin serpents, the knives drove forward and punched into the two guards' throats. Their jaws went even slacker as they dropped their torches and fought frantically to stanch the blood gushing from their necks.

Kullen didn't wait to watch them fall, nor did he try to advance further into the bedroom. It was a lost cause, the flames already devouring every source of fuel they could find. He raced out of the burning room and advanced on the next where the screams had apparently originated.

Kullen kicked the door in to find five guardsmen surrounding a shrieking, struggling woman. Two of the guards held torches, another pair had the woman by the arms and were pinning her to a plain wooden cot while the fifth unbuckled his belt.

"Come on, then!" roared the guardsman. "Ain't you supposed to be all about helping the needy?" He leered down at her. "I've got needs right enough, and you—"

He never finished his filthy words.

Kullen stalked forward, the roaring flames covering the

sounds of his movements. In one motion, he tore one of the guard's longswords free of its sheath and sheared through the bastard's neck.

"What the bloody—?" another guard cried as the decapitated head rolled onto the wooden cot.

Kullen went to work, hacking down one of the remaining four before his fellows could draw swords. He drove a savage kick up between the legs of the next-nearest guardsman. Air whooshed from the man's lungs and he fell to his knees with a pitiful, mewling cry. The torch fell from his numb fingers to clatter onto the stone-tiled floor, rolling beneath the bed upon which the woman was still held down. Kullen slashed open the kneeling man's throat as he passed, then was upon the first of the two men trapping the woman. His punch caught the guard square in the face, snapping his head back, and the guardsman crashed against the nearby stone wall.

Kullen whirled to face the other two. The man with the torch had recovered from his shocked surprise, at least enough to swing his fiery brand at Kullen's head like a club. Kullen ducked and drove the hunting knife he still held in his off hand through the man's groin, just beneath the hem of his leather vest. The man squealed, and squealed again when Kullen twisted the knife and ripped it free. Kullen kicked the falling guard backward into the final man.

The one Kullen had punched rose, blood covering his face. He charged forward, sword slashing. Kullen slapped aside the first attack with his stolen sword and kicked out with a heavy boot. The guard's knee shattered with a snap and the man screamed. As the guard dropped, Kullen plunged the sword through the man's eye and redrew his second hunting knife.

Now, the other two had made it to their feet. They looked to each other, each hoping they wouldn't need to be the first to attack. Kullen made the decision for them by hurling one of his throwing knives. The force of his throw drove it through the simple leather armor to bury to the hilt in one of the guard's chests. The dying man stood there, stupefied while his comrade sprinted for the exit.

Kullen stuck out a foot, causing the fleeing guard to stumble and fall. On his way down, the man smacked his head on a chest of drawers and clattered to ground onto his back. Groans rose from somewhere deep in the pitiful fool's belly. Kullen walked over and stamped hard on the man's throat. The cries cut off with a wretched gurgling cough. Wheeling away from the dying man, Kullen stalked back to where the guardsman now sat on a cot, still staring down at the dagger in his chest.

"Who sent you?" Kullen snarled. "Magister Deckard is dead. Who is giving you orders now?"

The guardsman managed to lift his eyes to Kullen. His mouth worked soundlessly, then his head slowly toppled forward and lolled on his chest.

"Damn it!" Kullen tore the dagger from the dead man's chest. He looked at the corpse—really looked—for the first time. The guard wore only plain boiled leather armor, the sort utilized by street toughs or men-at-arms hired by the poorer noblemen of Dimvein. The men Kullen had just killed were far below the caliber of the guardsmen he'd faced the previous night, or the assailants who'd murdered Magister Issemar.

But they weren't just thugs or brutes on a mission to destroy for cruelty's sake. No one in Dimvein would dare raise their hand against the Refuge, not after everything Mammy Tess had done for the Embers. No one, that was, except someone who had no fear of reprisal. Who could hire men to carry out their dirty work for them.

Had Magister Deckard still lived, Kullen would have believed the man responsible. But the aristocrat had been turned to ash the previous night. Someone else was behind this—but who?

Kullen coughed. The smoke filling the room made it difficult to see the woman who still lay rigid as a board on the bed. A small whimper escaped her lips. Kullen's approach startled her upright. She scrambled, fumbling at the shreds of her torn dress, her face white and eyes wide. Kullen recognized the signs of shock and panic—she hadn't even thought to flee the room or escape the burning Refuge, so paralyzed she was by fear.

"You need to run!" he called over the crackling fire. "You need to get out of here before this whole place comes down."

At the sound of his voice, she cried out and clawed her way backward along the bed, desperate to escape him.

"I'm not here to hurt you," Kullen said, trying for a tone somewhere between gentle and firm. It was a difficult task with the entire building ready to collapse. "I'm here to stop them." He swept a bloodstained dagger toward the corpses lying on the ground. "It's too late to stop the blaze now."

Not without the water-wielding powers of Magister Perech, or the ability to channel an ice-dragon's magic as Magister Iltari had.

"You need to get out while—"

"Mammy Tess!" The woman surged to her feet and sprang forward with speed born of terror. Her fingers clutched at Kullen's cloak and she seemed to be struggling to get out words. "She... and the children... barricaded in the chapel!"

"Go!" Kullen ordered. "I'll get to them."

Shaking himself loose from her grip, he stalked from the room. He didn't check to see if she obeyed—he had greater problems to occupy his mind.

The chapel was devoted to no specific god or goddess. With so many children from so many walks of life, Mammy Tess always believed it right to allow them freedom to follow their hearts. It stood at the rear of the Refuge, on the far side of an open-air atrium that had served as the orphan's playground since Kullen had lived here. That part of the building was made of old, weathered stone but had a roof of tile rather than thatch. The only door into the chapel was solid and could be barred from within. There was a chance that Mammy Tess and the children she'd gathered were still safe.

But not for much longer. If the men had orders to carry out the threat Magister Deckard had made the previous night and burn the Refuge and all its occupants to the ground, they'd be finding a way to break down the doors to the chapel. It was only a matter of time.

Not if Kullen had anything to say about it.

He raced through the hallway, passing two more bedrooms engulfed in flames. He refused to look at the unmoving lumps on bed that could very well be corpses, told himself they were just pillows and blankets. He let the smoke and heat block out everything around him, all but the path ahead where the flames were thinnest. The invaders might not be elite soldiers, but even they wouldn't be stupid enough to cut off their only means of escaping the blaze they'd set.

At the end of the hall, the staircase led toward the exit into open-air gathering hall. Sure enough, a repeated thud, thud, thud echoed through the open door at the end of the hall's far end, just behind the raised platform Mammy Tess used to address the orphans each morning.

Kullen raced out into the cool, dark courtyard. There was nothing to burn out here—the benches and columns surrounding the open-air space were all made of stone—so the only light came from the burning Refuge and the torches held by leather-clad men clustered around the chapel. There were fifteen in total—nine carrying burning brands and bared weapons, with six more attacking the chapel door with a battering ram they'd made from one of the various statues of some worthless god or goddess.

Fifteen against one, Kullen thought, a wry smile on his face. *Against these peckers, I'll take those odds any day.*

He sheathed his bloodstained hunting knives—he wouldn't need them just yet.

"What a bunch of whoresons and cowards!" he roared.

"Attacking defenseless women and children, laying waste to a bloody orphanage."

At the sound of his voice, the battering ram stopped its thudding, and all of the bully boys whirled to face him.

"Tonight," Kullen snarled, "every one of you will rot in Shekoth's deepest, darkest pit, where Binteth's teeth and Ulnu's claws will never cease their violence upon you. But before you die, you will answer me one thing: who sent you?"

Kullen didn't believe a single one of those fairytale creatures existed, but faced with death, these men might.

They looked past him at the door leading into the Refuge, as if prepared to see an army charge out behind him. Yet when no reinforcements arrived, cruel smiles broadened their faces.

Perhaps they wouldn't.

One laughed at the threat. He spit on the statue as if to emphasize his disbelief.

"We won't answer a goddamned thing!" sneered another, a brutish fellow with a thick beard that even Turoc would have envied. The man was tall, taller than Kullen, with shoulders like an ox and dark eyes. He stepped forward, waving his sword in the air. "Only thing that'll happen is you dying slowly, screaming as you drown in y—"

Kullen moved, far too quickly for the loudmouth to react. One moment his hands were empty, the next, two throwing daggers spun from his hands and sunk through the man's open mouth, cutting off his words. He stumbled backward, crashing into his fellows, dropping his torch and sword to paw at his throat.

"I ask again," Kullen said, holding his empty hands wide. "Who sent you?" He fixed the fourteen remaining men with a baleful glare. "Tell me, or I kill you all slow."

They all exchanged glances. Then, all at once, they dropped the statue and drew weapons.

"Ye can kill one but not a—"

Once again, Kullen fired off a throwing knife as the new

speaker began his threats. It slashed a deep gash on the right side of his neck and throat then continued to strike the shorter sellsword behind him in the forehead. They both dropped unceremoniously to the floor.

Men swore, words Kullen knew and others that were far more creative in nature. They rushed him, no doubt hoping to overwhelm. But Kullen had no lack of throwing knives and took out four more of them before the first reached him and swung a blade.

The slash was wild, further proving these men weren't trained soldiers. Swordmaster Kyneth would've given the man a month of latrine duty for such a foolish display of swordsmanship.

Kullen looked into the man's bloodthirsty eyes and didn't feel the least bit sorry for grabbing his arm, flipping him onto his back, and twisting his wrist until it snapped and his sword fell free. He somersaulted over the man, making no effort to spare him the full weight as he drove his shoulder into the man's stomach.

He leaped to his feet, raising the fallen man's sword to parry a hasty attack. Using the force of his momentum, he spun and bashed the sword's pommel into the attacker's lower back. The man stumbled forward, tripped over his downed ally, and flopped. Kullen stabbed the sword downward. It sank into the first bully boy's gut, relieving him of his wrist pain.

"Who sent you?" Kullen roared.

A longsword came down toward his head and Kullen locked blades. They slid to the hilt, but Kullen didn't let the entanglement stop him. He ducked low, directing the man's sword into the stone floor. Then, with his offhand, he hamstrung another. Blood fountained upon the gray stone. Once again, Kullen rose. This time, he dropped the sword and knife and drew two more throwing daggers. He cast them one to each side and downed two thugs on their way toward him.

"Who sent you!" he bellowed again.

He drew his second hunting knife and a stiletto.

A fist caromed into his face, sending him sprawling into two men who held him by the arms.

"We're gonna kill you, you foul prick," the man whispered in his ear. "And then, whoever's in that room is gonna pay for your sins. Slowly… like you threatened."

They both laughed. Kullen struggled, but they were both strong. A third stepped toward him. Kullen got the impression that the first man he'd killed was the highest ranked amongst this rabble, and with him gone, this one probably filled his shoes.

He was blonde, blue-eyed and looked like he would've fit in on Perech's pleasure barge had he been dressed differently.

Kullen waited. Waited…

When the man was close enough, Kullen spit.

It plastered the bully boy's face.

"Think you're funny, do you?" the man said, wiping it off.

Kullen spit again.

At this, the man charged. Exactly what Kullen wanted. He kicked up, then planted both feet against the rushing sellsword's chest, using it like a wall to flip himself over his captors.

The momentum of his flip dragged the two down and Kullen further used his own strength to smash their upper bodies into the cold stone. He still held in his hands a stiletto and his hunter's knife. Those two drove down into the stunned thugs' faces, splitting them wide.

"Who sent you?" Kullen asked.

Finding them still disinclined to answer, he hurled a throwing blade at the blonde with the same deadly precision. Blood gurgled from the man's mouth and throat and he dropped to his knees. He wasn't dead, but it wouldn't be long.

By Kullen's count, five remained. Then he heard the raised voices of men urging each other to run. Three remained as two cowards fled the gathering hall.

He rose and set his feet, shuffling backward while putting the remaining three men squarely in front of him.

"Who sent you?"

One feigned an attack, stepping forward swiftly and pulling back all the same. Another on Kullen's right, came in at the same time. His sword flung out to strike but met only Kullen's hunting knife.

"You should run too," Kullen teased.

The three exchanged glances and Kullen thought for a second they were considering it. But then, in unison, they attacked.

Blades blurred before him but Kullen had learned from the best Swordmaster the Karmian Empire had ever seen. Kyneth's training had Kullen facing an onslaught of attackers without end until finally one struck him. By the time his training had completed, Kyneth's men had tired out before Kullen had taken a single strike.

Kullen strafed aside, and nicked one bully boy on the cheek. He considered it a warning strike. The man didn't take the hint.

"Fine," Kullen said.

The same thug struck out with his longsword and Kullen used both of his weapons to deflect the wild strike to his left. Before the man could react, his sword drove into the neck of his fellow standing beside him.

"Who sent you?" Kullen asked quietly.

"Your mother," sneered one of the remaining sellswords.

Kullen gritted his teeth and kicked the man hard in the chest, sending him reeling backward and onto his back.

"Who sent you?" he growled as he plunged his stiletto through the side of the standing one's head, right through the temple.

Kullen then spun on the last living bully boy, the one he'd just kicked.

When Kullen arrived to stand beside the downed man, he spotted a sword sticking out of the man's belly. Blood pooled around him and fear filled his eyes.

"You have one more chance to answer before I start removing body parts ." He placed the dagger to the man's groin to make it utterly clear which part he'd sever first. "Who sent you?"

The man opened his mouth, blood bubbling on his lips. No words came out.

"Who sent you?" Kullen pressed a throwing dagger to the corner of the man's eye.

"Magister—Magister Branthe!" the man spat. "Magister Branthe!"

Ice slithered through Kullen's veins, freezing him in place. For a heartbeat, he was certain he'd misheard the bully boy's gravelly words.

"Did you say Magister Branthe?" he demanded. "Magister *Carritus* Branthe?"

"Don't know the Carritus part," the dying man wailed. "But sure as shit, it was Magister Branthe. I seen him a few times out in public. Hangings, ceremonies—"

Kullen shook the man. He had no time to hear all the places where this fool had laid eyes on Magister Branthe.

"Why?" he demanded. "Did he give any explanation as to why he wants the Refuge?"

"He don't explain himself to the likes of me," the hired blade protested. "All's he said was get the job done. Tonight. Was very specific 'bout that. Said it had to be done, that everything else…"

The man stopped and coughed, gagging on blood.

"Keep going," Kullen said, threatening to use the knife again on the thug's eye.

"It all hinged on burning this place before sunrise."

Kullen scowled, confused. He couldn't begin to fathom why Magister Branthe had such an urgent need to burn this insignificant-seeming building to the ground, or why anything beyond the lives of a few orphans hinged on it.

Yet there was another part of the man's answer that had caught his attention.

"What is 'everything else'?" he snarled. "What else is happening tonight?"

"I don't know!" the man protested. He winced from pain. "All's I know the big Orken bastard with him insisted they had to go before 'it began'."

Orken, Kullen thought, his mind taking him back to the graveyard.

"What did he look like?"

"Like an Orken." The man's voice was growing weaker by the second. Kullen didn't have much time left to get his answers. "Big… ugly… beard…"

"Is that it?" The man was quiet. Kullen slapped him. "Is that it?"

"He had… gol…"

"Hey!" Kullen snapped.

"Gold bands… beard."

A cold chill ran down Kullen's spine.

He wanted to ask the man more. But it was too late. The guardsman's eyes rolled into the back of his head and he went limp in Kullen's arm. With a last, rattling breath, he expired. The bully boy had succumbed to his wound and lay dead on the floor of the Refuge.

44

NATISSE

The sun had all but risen by the time Natisse extricated herself from Gaidra's company. Upon Natisse being practically peeled out of the dress, the kindly old seamstress had declared her "too thin by far" and proceeded to sit her down for a feast of tea, biscuits, preserves, and cold sliced ham. Twice, Natisse denied subsequent helpings only to be told "I'm not asking" before Gaidra shoveled more onto her plate.

Natisse had wanted to depart sooner but had, apparently, fallen asleep while Gaidra stoked the fire and boiled the kettle for their third round. Unlike most nights, she'd slept soundly, untroubled by dreams of fire and haunting memories. By the time she'd awoken, dawn was just an hour off.

Still, the rest and food Gaidra had pressed upon Natisse came as a welcome relief. The woman wasn't wrong, Natisse had been sleeping and eating far too little over the last few days—since Ammon's death, really. There had simply been too much to do and it had fallen to her to do it.

She woke with a start, the sound of Gaidra *tap-tap-tapping* her spoon against the rim of her tea cup.

"Oh, I'm sorry to wake you, dearie," Gaidra said. "You were sleeping like a princess."

Natisse wiped her cheek.

"I don't know if princesses drool."

Gaidra laughed. "Would you like some tea? I just brewed some fresh."

"What time is it?" Natisse asked, still rubbing the sleep from her eyes.

"Just after dawn," Gaidra said. "Slept straight through. Suppose you need—"

"Dawn?" Natisse rose and hurriedly gathered her belongings. "I've got to go. I'm sorry. Thank you. Thank you for everything."

Without another word or glance back, Natisse rushed out the front door and into the busy marketplace. The sun burned bright in her eyes, creating little glowing orbs and distorting her vision. She silently cursed herself for not at least taking some tea to go. She would need something to wake her.

Suddenly, her wish was granted. She was wide awake and staring up from the ground at a member of the Orkenwatch.

He was big... and hairy, even for his kind. A thick beard, typical of the race, hung to his belly, clasped together by silver rings. The Orken had all black eyes, no white to be seen at all, which made it especially difficult to tell where they were looking at any given moment. But not this one; he glared down at Natisse with hateful venom.

"Watch where you go," he growled. "Unless jail you want."

Natisse stood, dusting off and looking around for any sign of a sniffer. She didn't recognize this particular Orken, which meant it wasn't likely he was one that had accosted her and the others the other night.

"No," she said. "I'm sorry. I was careless."

The Orken stared at her a moment, then grunted and walked away.

Natisse sighed deeply.

Awake and somewhat reinvigorated, she hurried through the One Hand District toward the first place in the Western Docks she would search for Uncle Ronan. With every step, worry gnawed its way deeper into her belly. How could she have slept without knowing for certain Uncle Ronan was out of harm's way? It didn't matter that she'd passed out, unable to keep her eyes open—she should've been out tracking Uncle Ronan's movements like a hound.

Had it been any other occasion, she would've immediately dismissed the anxiety. Uncle Ronan could more than look after himself. But Ammon, Baruch, Garron... too much loss and hurt had befallen them of late. Haston's injuries were just the latest in a string of bad luck that had started the night of Ammon's capture by Magister Estéfar.

Natisse frowned. Could this be Magister Oyodan's bloodsurge magic somehow affecting them all these weeks later? Had the aristocrat's uncanny luck somehow turned against them, poisoned everything the Crimson Fang attempted to do?

With effort, she pushed the thought aside. She had little understanding of how the strange magic worked, but from everything Uncle Ronan had told them, the effects ended upon the possessor's death. No, this wasn't magical misfortune, just the dangers that the Crimson Fang had accepted upon taking up their mission to balance the scales of justice in Dimvein. They'd all known the high price they might pay in their war against the Imperial nobility—she just hated that it was her people who ended up hurt while the rich and wealthy continued to live lives of excess.

Then a sickly sweet joy flooded her at the thought of all those nobles who had died recently. It wasn't a fair trade, but it would have to do for bolstering.

As she approached the building where Haston had watched Magister Perech's caravan yard, she slipped through the alleys that led to her target, silent as a shadow, clinging to the lingering darkness beneath overhanging roofs and narrow-set walls. None of House Perech's guards appeared from the streets around her, no rusty orange and mauve jerkins. She managed to slip in unnoticed.

The knotted rope still hung from the roof, and Natisse made quick work of scaling it. The rooftop was empty, no sign of anyone having been there in hours. Frowning, Natisse slid back down the rope and retreated eastward, away from the caravan yards and any of the guardsmen on patrol. She retraced Haston's steps toward the spot where he'd fallen in his flight from the guards.

Her skill at tracking might not match Haston's, but even she could read the heavy bootprints in the spots where the mud was deep. Blood spattered a nearby fence post, and a sanguine trail marked the path of a body being dragged toward the caravan yards. Yet the muddy bootprints led away from this spot, heading south. The direction where Uncle Ronan had run as he led the guards away from Natisse and Haston's hiding place.

The bootprints only led a few score yards before the Trade District turned into the loose stone streets of the Embers. There, they soon faded from view completely. A few blood droplets hinted at combat—someone had sustained a wound, though Natisse couldn't tell whether it was Uncle Ronan or Magister Perech's guards. She followed the trail of crimson until it, too, vanished.

Knots tightened in Natisse's shoulders as she scanned for further signs. A few minutes spent searching turned up no more blood trail or muddy bootprints to indicate Uncle Ronan's flight or Magister Perech's guards giving chase. The part of the Western Docks was deadly quiet. Not even a cat stirred within the debris piled against the walls, nor dogs scavenging in the refuse.

Natisse's stomach began to churn. She tried to ignore the sensation, but she couldn't fully push it away. She hurried across the district to the spot where she and Uncle Ronan had watched the nobles pile in for their secret meeting, then, finding it empty as well, moved toward Athelas's place watching Magister Onathus's shipyards.

She was both relieved and worried to find Athelas alone on his rooftop perch.

"Have you seen Uncle Ronan?" she demanded the moment she reached his place at the roof's edge. "Has he come here since last night?"

Athelas shook his head. "No sign of him. Why?"

Natisse explained what had happened with Haston, the flight from Magister Perech's guards, and Uncle Ronan's distraction. Athelas's youthful, dirt-stained face tightened, but he tried to put on a brave expression.

"I'm sure he's fine," he said, his voice only wavering slightly. "It's Uncle Ronan, for Ezrasil's sake. He's probably back in his quarters napping, or sitting in the common room, sharing a meal with Jad."

Natisse couldn't bring herself to feel the young man's confidence and she suspected his was false as well. The nagging feeling in her gut told her that something was amiss... she just didn't have the proof of it yet.

"But Leroshavé should be back any time," Athelas continued, "and I'm sure he'll bring word that Uncle Ronan is safely underground."

"Back?" Natisse asked.

"I sent him to report to Uncle Ronan or Jad on last night's events," Athelas said.

Natisse narrowed her eyes. "What events?"

"Not really sure." Athelas ran a hand through his long blond hair. "It was certainly weird, but I figured someone higher up the chain of command might make better sense of it. Maybe you'll know."

Natisse cocked her head. "Tell me."

"So, a couple of hours after sundown, a whole bunch of

carriages showed up at the shipyard." Athelas gestured to the stockade-encircled property he'd been tasked to watch. "The guards let them in no muss, no fuss, and they just sort of sat at the northern end of the stockade for a couple of hours."

Natisse's eyebrows shot up. "The northern end? You're sure?"

Athelas nodded. "Didn't see what exactly happened or what they were doing, but a little before midnight, all of them just took off at once, in a big long procession. Less than a quarter-hour and everything was quiet again. Weird, huh?"

Natisse's mind raced. She hadn't even thought to question how the noblemen and women attending the "spectacle" in the abandoned building would depart. Evidently, Magister Branthe's conspirators had figured out an elegantly simple solution. The slaves were brought in via the tunnel in Magister Perech's caravan yard, while the spectators entered through the seemingly abandoned building. Anyone who left—those not enslaved in the fighting pits—departed through Magister Onathus's shipyard. It was the perfect way to avoid suspicion at any one of the three locations. The underground tunnels that connected the properties facilitated the enterprise.

"It gets weirder." She explained what she and Uncle Ronan had discovered the previous night, along with the information gathered during her conversation with the two guards. His eyes grew steadily wider, his jaw slackening.

"So, that's it!" he hissed, his voice harsh. "We found it?"

"I'm certain of it," Natisse said, nodding. "As certain as I can be without seeing it for myself. Which I will, tonight."

"And I'm going with you," Athelas said. "I'm no Baruch, but I can play Baronet Charlati well enough."

Natisse didn't immediately squelch the young man's enthusiasm. Athelas was young and, for all his thief's skill and enthusiasm, lacked experience in the subtle arts of deception. He was no fighter, either. If Natisse brought him with her, she'd spend too much time worrying about him.

No, with Garron out of the fight, there were only two people she'd consider bringing with her. Uncle Ronan was her first choice, if she could find him.

At that moment, Leroshavé's head poked up over the rooftop wall.

"Could bring some rope next time," he complained, wiping his hands off on his pants. "You people might love scalin' brick, but my little legs struggle." Then he saw Natisse. "Oh, good, you're here. Jad was getting worried that—"

"Jad?" Natisse cut him off. "What about Uncle Ronan? Tell me he's back!"

"Not yet." Leroshavé shook his head. "He ain't been back since you both left ye—"

But Natisse was no longer listening. She swore. Something was wrong. She could feel it all the way to her bones, but she'd forced herself to remain calm and not to worry. But with her suspicions confirmed, fear for Uncle Ronan wormed deeper into her gut.

She climbed over and down the wall on the rear side of the building, and raced back to the spot where she'd lost Uncle Ronan's trail. It was a short run, but her insides quaked. Try as she might, tucking down the worry wasn't something easily done. Her eyes darted about, scanning every side street and alley for any hint of what had happened. As it had been, the cobblestones showed no muddy footprints, and there were no blood trails to guide her. What had she been expecting? That she'd missed a clear clue? There was nothing here to lead her another step further.

Her heart hammered faster with every frantic breath.

Where was he? Were the rumors of people vanishing from the Embers true? But this was the Western Docks, not—

A clatter behind her set Natisse spinning around. Her hand dropped to a dagger tucked beneath her cloak, but she stopped as she recognized the source of the noise. One of the piles she'd believed was just debris and rubbish shifted, and a human head emerged from the reeking, filthy mess. The person was covered in head to toe with the bloodstained bandages of a leper, but atop it, he wore a long woolen coat that appeared far too clean for someone of his apparent station.

Natisse's heart leaped into her throat. She recognized that coat: it belonged to Uncle Ronan. Its many adornments could not be mistaken. He always wore that coat. And he'd *been* wearing it the previous night.

"Where did you get that?" she demanded of the leper. Her eyes took in the rips on the left arm and shoulder, along with blood-stains that couldn't have come from its new wearer.

The leper shrank back.

"Please!" pleaded a man's voice from beneath the layers of bandages. "I didn't steal it!"

"Then where did you get it?" Natisse forced her voice to calm. She reached into her own coat, earning another flinch from the man, but instead of a weapon, she produced a silver coin. "Tell me where you got the coat, and this is yours."

The leper's eyes flicked to the coin, and he swallowed hard. "Y-You won't h-hurt me?"

"No, I won't." Natisse held the piece of silver out to him. "Just tell me where you found that coat. And what happened to the man wearing it."

"They took him," the leper said. "Took him, but left the coat." He reached out a bandaged hand, but Natisse snatched the coin back.

"Who?" she demanded. "Who took him?"

"Armed men," the leper said, his tone pitiful. "Wearing orange and red or pink—"

"Mauve."

"Sure, mauve," the man agreed. "The man they were after, h-he managed to get free, slide out of the coat. But there were too many. They brought him down just over there." He pointed a finger toward the street fifty yards south. "Took him, said something about throwing him in the pit. But they didn't say nothing about the coat, didn't seem to want it. So I t-took it." He began to fumble at the coat, pulling it off his shoulders. "B-But if you want it—"

"No, keep it." Natisse said gently. She tossed the coin to the leper. "Thank you for your help."

She turned to go, but the leper's voice stopped her.

"I seen others go in there!" the man called. "People like me. Nobodies that nobody will miss." His voice was mournful. "They go in there, and they don't never come out!"

Natisse's stomach clenched. The rumors *had* been true, then. Citizens of Dimvein vanishing without a trace.

But she knew the truth, now. Out of this leper's mouth.

"That ends tonight," she growled, fists clenching.

She marched determinately out of the alley. Perech's men had made a grave mistake taking Uncle Ronan, and they were about to find out why.

45

KULLEN

K ullen stared down at the corpse as if willing the man to awaken and tell him more. But the piece of shit remained silent—he'd speak only when begging Ulnu or Binteth to spare him pain.

Kullen's mind whirled.

So it *hadn't* been a chance meeting in the graveyard, nor had Branthe been hiring private security. This was something more. Far more. An Orken alongside Magister Branthe. Magister Branthe's urgency in burning the Refuge down. The hints of "everything else" and "before it began"—something was terribly wrong.

Suddenly, pieces began to click into place. Magisters Deckard and Issemar lacked the cunning to contrive a proper plot against the Emperor on their own. Though Kullen hadn't found any clues to indicate they were connected to anyone else, he doubted the pair could've devised a scheme to defraud the Emperor without help. That sort of thinking was far too grand for them.

But not for Magister Branthe, who had, once upon a time, been General Branthe of the Karmian Army. A general had to understand things like logistics and supply. Just as an army ran on its stomach, so, too, an Empire flourished—or withered—according to how well it cared for its populace.

Magister Branthe was in the perfect position to destabilize the Empire from within. Indeed, he had the Emperor's ear, not to mention his trust—an honor few alive today could claim. How easy it would be for the aristocrat to avoid Thanagar's watchful gaze and keep the eyes of Emperor Wymarc, his confidante and friend, turned away from his seditious activities.

Oh, he could never be directly involved in the schemes of men like Magisters Deckard and Issemar, but he could run their treason from the shadows. As an enigma called "Red Claw," perhaps?

Kullen couldn't figure how the Refuge mattered to Magister Branthe, but he had no time to contemplate it either. If the aristocrat was planning treachery—if "everything else" would "begin" tonight—Kullen had to get to the Emperor and warn him of the danger Magister Branthe posed. Even now, the bastard could be sharing a dram of fine dragonfire rum in Wymarc's study, ready to drive a dagger into the Emperor's back. Emperor Wymarc would never see the danger until it was too late.

He'd half-turned away and reached for his dragonblood vial to summon Umbris, but stopped as he remembered why he'd come. Spinning on his heel, he rushed toward the chapel. The makeshift battering ram had splintered the door, the wood one or two solid blows from giving way. Yet it had held just long enough for Kullen to save the occupants barricaded within.

"Mammy Tess, it's me. It's Kullen!" He pounded a fist against the door.

"K-Kullen?" Mammy Tess's voice echoed through the cracks in the door. "What are you doing here?"

Kullen ignored the question.

"The men who attacked won't trouble you, but the Refuge is still burning. You all need to get out now while you still can."

The fire might not spread to the chapel, but the thick, choking smoke could still do serious harm to the orphans—and the aging Mammy Tess, for all her fiery spirit, was still prone to those coughing fits.

A few seconds of silence elapsed, then Mammy Tess's voice returned. "We can't get out! The bar…" Her coughing fit lasted only a few seconds, but to Kullen, it felt like a lifetime. "Too damaged… to lift." She gasped, regaining her breath.

Kullen's pulse quickened.

"Stand back!" He sheathed his weapons and hurled his shoulder against the chapel door. It shuddered beneath the impact but did not give. Kullen knew it was futile—he could throw himself against that door, but it had held out against a crude battering ram.

He glanced down at the stone statue. It had to weight nearly twice as much as he did. No way he could lift it alone.

Suddenly, he realized: he wasn't alone.

"Stay away from the door!" he shouted into the chapel. "I'm going to break it down."

"How?" Mammy Tess called.

"Just trust me and get as far away from the door as you can," Kullen said, reaching into his cloak. He jammed his thumb onto the golden cap of the dragonblood vial.

Come to me, Umbris, he said. I have need of your strength.

In the blink of an eye, the Twilight Dragon appeared in the gathering hall.

"Help me!" Kullen told the dragon. "I need you to break down this door."

"Who are you talking to, Kully?" Mammy Tess asked.

Kullen didn't respond, just stared into Umbris's golden eyes. The beast lowered his huge head to regard the door. His lips pulled back into what Kullen knew was a grin and he gave a little snorting huff.

"*With pleasure.*"

The dragon's claws clacked on the paved courtyard as he

turned his back on the chapel. His huge black tail curled up along the left side of his long body, then suddenly whipped out and crashed into the door. Wood splinted and disintegrated beneath the immense force of the strike.

Through his mental bond, Kullen instructed Umbris to hide in the shadows. But remain close, he told the dragon. I have need of your swiftness.

"*As you will, Bloodsworn,*" Umbris responded.

Kullen darted inside before the flying door finished crashing to the stone floor. Inside, he found thirty orphans huddled around Mammy Tess and two of her fellow ministrants. She gave a cry of joy at the sight of Kullen and bounded toward him the best she could, arms outstretched. Kullen drew her into an embrace and held her tight. Only now did it sink in how close he'd come to losing her... again. Having lost so much already, he didn't think he could have endured her death.

Mammy Tess pulled away quickly, glancing at Kullen's bloody clothes and face. Her expression tightened and for a moment, Kullen feared she would react as she had the night he fought off Magister Deckard's guards.

Instead, she just lifted her eyes to meet his. "Are you hurt?"

Kullen shook his head.

"Not badly." His jaw hurt from having been punched, and it appeared he'd been stabbed at least once, as evidenced by the stinging sensation along his side, but it wouldn't put him down. "How about you? Are you all unharmed?"

"A few bruises, maybe a splinter or two," Mammy Tess said, giving a dismissive wave. "Plenty of tears and fears all around, but what matters is that we still live."

"You need to get out now," Kullen insisted. "You need to leave the Refuge."

"But—"

Kullen knew what she would say even before she said it.

"I know it's your home, Mammy," he said, gripping her hands, "but right now, it's an inferno, and it's too dangerous for you all to stay here. No. Don't argue, please. I promise that the Refuge will be rebuilt. I'll make sure the Emperor takes care of it personally."

Her eyes widened a fraction at that.

"You can do that?" she whispered.

"Yes," Kullen said. It wasn't exactly a lie. Emperor Wymarc had promised to ensure Assidius sent more coin. Now, "more" simply meant enough to cover the cost of a brand new building—along with temporary housing for Mammy Tess and her orphans while the Refuge was being repaired. "But if you don't leave now, you won't be alive to rebuild the Refuge." He squeezed her hands tighter. "Please, Mammy."

Mammy Tess eyed the place with tears. The look on her face was enough to break Kullen's heart. This place, now in flames, black smoke rising to greet the clouds in the nigh sky above... it was all she'd known for longer than Kullen had been alive. He knew there was nothing more he could say and hoped she saw reason.

She nodded.

"I will." She turned to the women and children sheltering in the chapel. "Come, come, little ones. We must leave now."

Kullen waited until everyone had found their way out. He was glad to see Groundskeeper Voyles was there as well. The man gave him a hearty shake and a thank you on the way out.

"Thank you, Mister," said another small voice.

"You're welco—" Kullen started to say, turning away from Voyles.

He found himself staring down at the young boy he'd introduced to Mammy Tess.

"Sanjay, is it?" Kullen said. Then his heart sank. "Is your brother..."

"He's over there, with Mammy Kana." He pointed ahead where Kullen had just sent the survivors.

Kneeling down, Kullen placed a hand on the boy's shoulder. "Great. Now why don't you get up there as well?"

Sanjay smiled and ran off as if he hadn't just almost died.

When Kullen emerged from the chapel a few seconds later, the dragon had vanished from sight. He herded Mammy Tess, her fellow ministrants, and the orphans out of the chapel and across the gathering hall. He led the way through the burning Refuge, carrying a child in each arm and using his cloak to shield their bodies. When all were safely outside, he turned to race back into the building.

"Kullen!" Mammy Tess called after him. "Where are you going?"

"To do my job," he told her. He gave her a smile. "My job of protecting the Empire. I know what it looked like, the other night. It may not be what you expected—or wanted for me—but just know that I will always look out for you, just as you looked out for me all those years."

He knew she'd shed tears over the place, and so would he. He turned to run inside, but stopped at the front door. He wrapped his hands in his cloak and firmly gripped Hadassa's plaque. One good pull tore it off the wall, taking chunks of wood along with it. He shoved it away and entered the Refuge.

The fires raged all around him the walls collapsing, ceiling caving in. The place he'd called home was soon to be a distant memory. One that had fallen to the same fate as the Embers.

Kullen thought he'd put an end to this kind of thing by taking down Deckard. Who was to know there'd be a greater foe still out there?

He did one last sweep of the place, ensuring there was no one left alive within. Once satisfied, he pushed his way through tinder and cinder until he reached the gathering hall.

"May I come out?"

"Come, Umbris," Kullen said.

The dragon materialized before him. It was as if he'd always been there, the shadows themselves shielding him from view.

Kullen hopped onto Umbris's back and together, they soared upward into the darkness of night.

Kullen looked down upon the place.

It was gone.

Forever gone.

It would be rebuilt, even if the funds came from his own purse. But it would never be the same.

One thing was certain. Kullen would deliver Branthe to justice. He'd burn him alive, perhaps in front of the whole world.

But first, he had to warn the Emperor that his most trusted and loyal friend was the traitor behind all of the problems plaguing Dimvein.

46

NATISSE

"I can't do it, Natisse." Jad's eyes darkened, his huge face pulling into a frown. "I...won't."

"But you have to," Natisse insisted. "With Garron out of commission, there's no one else. Unless you think Athelas or Leroshavé could handle it?"

Jad's wince told Natisse he'd come to the same conclusion as she. Athelas and Leroshavé had their skillset, but Natisse needed a true fighter beside her. At the moment, Jad was her only option.

"If there was any other choice," she pressed, "you know I wouldn't ask this of you. But Uncle Ronan needs us." She stepped closer, placed a hand on Jad's huge arm. "He needs *you*."

Jad's jaw muscles worked, but he didn't outright refuse a second time. His expression grew pensive and Natisse knew he was thinking it over.

"It has to be you," she said quietly, her voice barely above a whisper. "You're the only one I can trust to have my back in there."

"That's not fair, Natisse," Jad said. His expression grew sorrowful. "You know what you're asking of me."

"I do. But I have no choice." She gripped his forearm. "For Uncle Ronan."

Jad sat heavily in a chair next to the makeshift infirmary bed where Garron lay sleeping—the chair where he'd spent most of the last twenty-four hours. His shoulders slumped and he leaned forward, burying his face in his huge hands.

Natisse didn't press him further. He was struggling inwardly, she knew, but he'd already come to the decision of what needed to be done. That was ever the way with Jad, always striving to make the right choice, no matter the personal cost.

And this choice... well, it came at a greater cost than anyone except Natisse and Uncle Ronan realized.

"I don't want to be *him* again, Natisse." Jad's voice was muffled, strained. "I can't be." He lifted his face, and tears streamed down his huge cheeks. "I still see them every night. Still hear them screaming for me to stop, hear Forgemaster Randyll roaring at me." A great shudder shook his frame. "I feel their blood on my hands, taste it in my mouth, smell it in the air. I can't—" His voice cracked. "I can't be that monster. Not again!"

Natisse swallowed the lump rising in her throat. She remembered the night she and Uncle Ronan had found Jad sitting in the smithy, weeping over a broken form. Petal, the puppy that had been Jad's only friend and companion. Forgemaster Randyll had been slumped over the anvil, unconscious. At Jad's side lay two dead youths, bullies who'd tormented the bulky smithy apprentice—until they'd gone too far and killed Petal. Their skulls had been crushed, pounded into unrecognizable mush, and their blood still stained Jad's fists, clothing, and face.

Since that day, Jad had refused to raise a hand or weapon in violence. Instead of forcing the issue, Uncle Ronan sent the boy out to learn skills that would serve the Crimson Fang: healer, alchemist, tailor, butcher, accountant, scribe, and more. Ever since, Jad had cared for his companions with the same tenderness he'd shown Petal during the three weeks the puppy had been his.

"Jad, look at me." Natisse knelt in front of the huge man, placed a hand beneath his chin, and tilted his head upward to face her. "I know what I'm asking of you. I know what you're afraid of. And you know what *I'm* afraid of."

Jad's eyes darted to the right side of her neck, to the scars he knew marred her flesh.

"But for Uncle Ronan's sake, we've got to put that aside." Natisse's eyes bored into his. "We've got to fight through our fears and be strong. Ammon and Baruch aren't here. Garron won't be out of this bed for days yet. There's no one else."

Jad's eyes grew mournful. He'd always reminded her of a giant Owlbear, fiercely protective and loyal but gentle.

"I need you," Natisse whispered. "I need you to protect me and the others like you have all these years. Can you do that?"

A long silence passed between them. Jad alternated between staring down at the ground and watching Garron breathing steadily. Finally, his gaze turned to Natisse.

"I can," he said, his voice a rumbling whisper. His hands closed around hers, fully enveloping them. "I've got your back, Natisse."

Natisse smiled, but inwardly she breathed a sigh of relief. She'd hoped she could convince Jad, but hoping was far from being certain. Though she would've proceeded anyway, with or without him at her side, the knowledge that he'd be there for this dangerous mission filled her with confidence.

"Thank you." She smiled and kissed his craggy forehead. "Now, here's the plan I have in mind for you and the others…"

"Lady Dellacourt!" The young guard's eyes brightened as Natisse dismounted from the carriage she'd hired to convey her to the abandoned property. "I trust this evening…" His congenial smile faded momentarily as Jad emerged behind her. Despite his surprise, the guard quickly regained his composure. "…finds you well?"

The carriage shook from side to side, creaking as Jad stepped down. He looked quite dapper, if Natisse were to be honest. He wasn't handsome by anyone's definition of the word, but he had a certain… appeal. His genteel nature was carried upon his broad shoulders. Shoulders that were currently wearing a black great-coat with gold-plated buttons. Though he wore a necktie, it didn't quite fit, visibly constricting his bull-thick neck at the collar.

There would be no more flirting from the guard this evening, even though it was clear the big man was accompanying her as her manservant as opposed to a love interest. That was the effect Jad had on men. And it was the desired effect this evening.

"Very well," Natisse said. Between the stunning black dress—sewn by Jad weeks earlier for the Lady Dellacourt persona—and the arch smile she lavished on the young guard, she looked every inch the well-heeled noblewoman. "I trust tonight's festivities have not yet begun?"

"Just getting started, milady," the young guard said, beaming. "I'd offer to escort you inside personally—"

"But my manservant here would grow rather upset at being deprived of his most important duty," Natisse said, dismissing the offer with a wave. "Your kindness—twice now—is noted, my good man." She leaned forward and dropped her voice to a breathy whisper. "Perhaps after the spectacle, you would consider paying my rooms at the Gilded Apricot a visit?"

Color rose to the young guard's cheeks and he stammered something incoherent, much to the amusement of his older companion.

Natisse took advantage of the young guard's discombobula-tion to flounce past him in a swirl of black lace and frill. She minced the short distance to the building's entrance and left the flummoxed man behind before he could regain control of his wits.

"Cruel woman," Jad muttered from his place behind and to her right.

Natisse chuckled evilly. "Just playing the part."

She resisted the urge to glance back at the carriage. Leroshavé sat in the driver's seat. He knew well his role in her plan, as did the rest of the Crimson Fang. She just had to trust that they'd follow her instructions precisely. The success of her scheme—and Uncle Ronan's life—depended on it.

The building's interior left much to be desired. Natisse couldn't imagine there was any value to the place apart from being torn down and rebuilt anew. Like many of the older structures in the Western Docks, the place had suffered from years of vacancy and lack of maintenance. Indeed, there appeared to be a fresh collapse in the roofing, raw wood showing lighter than its exposed neighbors. The walls, if they could be called that, were filled with holes covered by black tarpaulins.

But despite the number of nobles she was confident had already arrived, the room was empty save for another guard. Unlike Natisse's love-smitten admirer out front, who donned House Perech's orange and mauve, this one wore House Onathus's blue and green. He stood erect, hand firmly on the pommel of his sheathed longsword.

"Approach," he said at their entrance.

"I am Lady Dell—"

"Names don't matter here," the guard said. "Follow me."

He turned on his heels and led them down a short hallway. Very short. Just a few steps before ending at a set of stairs that descended into the ground. Natisse and Jad shared a furtive glance, then followed the guard down two full stories beneath street-level before the staircase ended at a set of doors fabricated out of solid steel.

The guard banged three times. They waited a few seconds, then he banged twice in quick succession as if fulfilling some agreed upon sequence. A small peephole slid open and a bright blue eye peered through at them. After a moment of examination, the peephole closed and the *click* and *clank* of sliding deadbolts and turning locks echoed.

"Stand back, please," their escort said.

Before they'd even had a moment to respond, the two doors swung out wide and toward them.

Following their escort, Natisse and Jad stepped through into a room with no other doors, only three solid earthen walls. A guard stood within. The only other thing in the room was a small chair placed against the wall. Natisse's curiosity burned. She knew there was no way this was the end of the line—already, they'd seen close to two-dozen other noblemen and women entering the building in the last half-hour. There had to be another way out of this room. A secret door, perhaps, like the one that Uncle Ronan had used?

Sure enough, once the steel door been shut and barred behind them, the guard strode toward the wall opposite the entrance and pulled a small brass ring very similar to the one she and Uncle Ronan had used to enter the tunnels within the Burrow. The stone wall moved, controlled by some hidden mechanism Natisse couldn't see. Instantly, a seam split the earth and the entire wall slid aside.

The moment the door began to move, a solid wave of sound hit them. Shouts, cheers, the shuffling of boots. It was excitement unbound, and that made Natisse's skin crawl and her stomach curdle.

Natisse and Jad shared another look.

The din grew louder as they traveled the dark corridor toward brightening light. Dust billowed from the ceiling in response. When the reached the light at the end, it revealed itself to be a corner. But when they turned that corner…

Men and women of the court sat in a round room on long, wooden benches in some cases, plush velvet couches in others. All of the seats faced toward the room's center where a pit of sand rested.

Everyone carried goblets filled with wine or mead or some other expensive alcohol. Men dressed in fine suits, silk or velvet top hats. The women—all, no doubt, hoping to outdo their peers —had spared no expense or time. Their hair was perfect, despite having covered it with hoods to enter. Necklaces and bracelets of cut gems hung wherever possible. And rings sparkled from the fingers of each, many wearing more than a couple.

Natisse walked slowly, watching as bets were placed, money was exchanged, carousing and reveries participated in. Such lavish lifestyles these people led, even underground.

On one end of what could only be a fighting pit, a gated tunnel led to where Natisse knew people were being held against their will. Slaves. People forced to fight for other's pleasure—most likely to the death.

As the grew closer still, the sand upon which those poor souls fought was covered with blood and even small bones. Weapons hung strategically on posts dotting the sands.

Natisse's blood ran cold. She'd pictured this place a thousand times before, but it was so much worse than she'd ever imagined.

She'd finally found the slave fighting pits. Now, she just had to find and free Uncle Ronan, which felt like odds as insurmountable as slaying Thanagar.

47

KULLEN

Urgency set Kullen's taut nerves thrumming and his heart pounding. He had to get to the Palace and bring warning of Magister Branthe's treachery before it was too late—before the duplicitous aristocrat used his proximity to Emperor Wymarc to put a knife in the Imperial ruler's back.

Umbris soared high above the city, blending into the night sky. The moon was full and bright. Below, the Lumenators' bright lights glowed, but none reached so high. Kullen often wondered if Thanagar's eyes spotted the wide shadows they cast over the city as clearly as his magical senses felt their energy, but never did the great white dragon give the slightest hint that he had. From here, Kullen could see the Upper Crest and the Palace growing larger, but not fast enough. Magister Branthe's mansion was easy to spot, even in the dark. He employed more of the Emperor's Lumenators than anyone alive.

However, as Kullen examined the property, he noted something. The lights within Branthe's estate were amber and flickering... not the warm, steady blue of the Lumenators' globes.

"*Bring us lower,*" Kullen ordered Umbris.

"*We may be spotted,*" Umbris replied.

"I'll take the risk."

Umbris dipped and Kullen's stomach floated within his body.

Magister Branthe maintained the largest private force of guards in Dimvein, and put his experience as General of the Imperial Forces to good use training them. The hired muscle sent to burn the Refuge had been toy soldiers by comparison to the drilled, strictly disciplined army under Magister Branthe's command.

Emperor Wymarc had never questioned Magister Branthe's reasons for collecting such a large force. He'd never had cause to, for he trusted the aristocrat who'd served as his father's general— and his own commander during his years of service. Too, Magister Branthe had always maintained that the force was at the Emperor's disposal should it ever be needed. Furthermore, Magister Branthe's men had been the first among those laboring to clear away the rubble of the Embers after Golgoth's attack.

Kullen's eyes widened. And they'd been there the day the mob murdered Prince Jarius and Princess Hadassa. Indeed, it'd been Magister Branthe's guards who carried back the grim news—all of the Palace guards sent to protect the Prince and Princess had died in defense of their charges.

Horror rippled down Kullen's spine. Had the Prince and Princess's deaths been orchestrated by Magister Branthe? Had the Emperor's most trusted friend and loyal subject been behind the murderous mob? It wouldn't have taken much to inflame the tempers of the already angry crowd of dispossessed Ember-dwellers. They'd lost their homes, meager belongings, and loved ones in the blaze. A few words whispered into the right ears was all it would've taken to redirect the anger away from Magister Deckard and aim it squarely at the Emperor.

Kullen found it impossible to believe, yet even more impossible to shake the notion. Magister Branthe had learned the art of tactics and strategy during his years in the military. He'd know the value of demoralizing and destabilizing his enemy through attrition, leaving them too weak to defeat a direct assault at precisely the right moment.

But what made this the right moment? Kullen had no idea why Magister Branthe insisted that it had to be tonight. There was nothing special about this night, except—

The new blood moon! His gaze darted up to the star-filled sky, where the moon was visible despite the cloudless night.

"Umbris, tonight is the start of the cycle, is it not?"

"Yes," the dragon said. *"Tonight, my brothers and sisters shall submit themselves to new bonds, should there be need."*

Kullen swore. It was all becoming clearer. The stolen dragonblood vials…

If Magister Branthe had all nine missing vials as Kullen suspected, he could use those to empower anyone he chose. And with such an endless supply of willing agents, it would only be so long before the dragons would break.

Magister Branthe's wealth, position in the Emperor's court, and private army already made him powerful enough. With an army of dragon-bonded loyal to him—both those who he'd recruited to his cause and those newly bound to the dragons of the slain noblemen—at his side, he could storm the Palace in force. Thanagar the Protector was mighty, but even the enormous white dragon might fall beneath the assault of so many enemies.

Nine missing vials, he thought grimly.

Nine dragons to combat Thanagar, plus Isaxx, the acid-spitting bronze dragon who had been bound to Magister Branthe for nigh on four decades. Though none of the dragons could rival Golgoth in sheer size and ferocity—much less Thanagar—together, they could overwhelm the great white dragon. Even the protective dome over the city would fail to shield from a threat that came from within, and Thanagar's mighty magic was bound to fail against so many foes.

Normally, Kullen would've utilized the passages himself, finding his way in silent secrecy to the Emperor's study. But now, there was no time. Kullen hated to rush anything, but what was he to do when the Emperor's life was at risk?

Despite Branthe's gathering masses—something Kullen had to admit wasn't out of the ordinary for the man—all was quiet as he and Umbris approached the Palace.

"That's low enough," Kullen said.

Umbris pulled level.

The torches within Branthe's walls were innumerable. The mass of men, armed to the teeth, countless. But not a single Lumenator in sight. They were still too high to trace the army's movements. Even now, Kullen feared he was too late. Who knew how many more soldiers Magister Branthe employed? Even now, half of them might be sneaking into the Palace using one of the many secret passages—about which the aristocrat had likely learned over the long in Emperor Wymarc's confidence.

The skies above the Palace were dark and quiet, but at any moment, the forms of enemy dragons could appear and fill the night with their thunderous roars, flashing claws, and potent magic.

Could Magister Branthe have become unsatisfied in his position? Might this be an attempt at the throne itself, or was he working for someone as well? What if all of the Upper Crest were in cohort with one another?

"Back up, Umbris."

Umbris immediately obeyed, soaring upward again, getting as close to Thanagar's magical barrier as possible without touching it and prematurely alerting the white dragon to their presence above. It was a dangerous adventure regardless. Even if they were high enough to avoid the gaze of the Palace guards, there was one glowing pair of ruby eyes he could not evade.

The prismatic white dragon's enormous body was curled around the two tallest of the Palace's towers, wings furled tight against his side. Though his massive eyelids were closed in the appearance of sleep, Kullen knew better. Thanagar watched

Dimvein not through his eyes, but through his magic, which sensed the energies of every living thing.

The energies of an approaching dragon—even one as stealthy and compact as Umbris—would be impossible for Thanagar to miss. The moment Kullen and Umbris drew within a mile of the Palace, Thanagar would have his full focus locked on them. Too close, and the white dragon would rouse from his apparent slumber and confront them head-on. Whether with magic or with claw and fang, there was no doubt in Kullen's mind that the white dragon could prevail over them with ease.

And yet, he did not instruct Umbris to turn away. He kept his dragon flying directly toward the Palace, soaring high above the city to be invisible to the watchers below. Through his mental bond, he relayed to Umbris his desperate plan.

"The risk is great, Kullen Bloodsworn," the dragon told him. Kullen felt a deep, unsettled rumbling shudder through Umbris's body. *"But for the sake of your* honorsworn, *I will do as you ask."*

Closer and closer they drew, Kullen's pulse quickening with every great beat of Umbris's wings. His gaze locked on Thanagar, ready for the moment the white dragon stirred. Like his dragon, every muscle in Kullen's body tensed in anticipation of what he knew to come.

Suddenly, Thanagar's enormous head lifted from its tower-top perch, and two eyes of deepest red fixed on Kullen. Fear shivered down Kullen's spine—only a fool could meet that baleful gaze and not feel a twinge. Slowly, the dragon's great wings unfurled and its body coiled, prepared to leap into flight. Kullen could almost feel the air around him rippling as tendrils of Thanagar's magic reached toward him.

Recognition sparked in Thanagar's eyes, but he rose nonetheless.

"Steady, friend," Kullen said to Umbris, sensing his trepidation. *"He will see reason."*

As planned, Umbris rose above the Palace. There, they waited, hovering in place with but a few flaps of his massive wings.

A force like gale winds nearly sent Kullen reeling from Umbris's back. The Twilight Dragon reared back as Thanagar met them in the sky.

"*You dare cross these walls?*" Thanagar bellowed. His voice boomed in Kullen's head like a million drums. It made it hard to think, much less return speech.

"*Friend Thanagar,*" Kullen began.

He knew his mistake before he made it, yet it was too late.

"*Friend?*" Thanagar said, tone harsh. "*Never have I given myself to your friendship. At this moment, you are a threat to the Karmian Empire and my* bloodsworn."

"I am here to save the life of your bloodsworn," Kullen said, struggling to make words. "*My* honorsworn."

Thanagar was silent. Kullen took that as permission to continue. He explained to the dragon as succinctly was possible what they'd uncovered these last weeks. Several times, Kullen thought Thanagar was going to speak, but merely puffed air through his massive nostrils. When he was done, Kullen awaited the dragon's reply.

"*You think me a fool?*" It was not the response Kullen expected. "*Do you believe me so ignorant that I could miss such a gathering force?*"

Kullen had to watch his next words.

"*All I ask is that you turn your gaze upon Magister Branthe's estate,*" he said.

Together, they looked and though the men and their torches were still there, it seemed far less compelling an argument in light of Kullen's current predicament. It was true that Magister Branthe always had men aplenty at the ready. But something about this time—and Kullen hoped it wasn't just paranoia—seemed off. Perhaps it was the lack of Lumenators. Perhaps...

He cursed himself inwardly. What proof did he have that

Magister Branthe had anything to do with this? The words of a dying man? A scoundrel and sellsword at that. Had Kullen been duped?

"*Magister Branthe is a loyal servant of the Empire,*" Thanagar said. "*His army stands at the beckoning of my* bloodsworn."

"*This is not working,*" Umbris said into Kullen's mind.

Though Kullen was sure Umbris knew better, he didn't have the proper understanding of the dragonbond to know how Thanagar would not hear Umbris's words. Kullen chose not to respond for fear that he would not have such control.

"*If you would just let me see the Emperor—*"

"*You've always thought yourself special, Black Talon, As if such a meaningless title would carry weight with one such as me. My* bloodsworn *may trust you, but it is my job to ensure his safety, even from those he trusts.*"

Frustration mounted in Kullen's mind.

"*I respect your stance on the matter,*" Kullen said through gritted teeth. "*For it is my own stance as well. The Emperor trusts Magister Branthe and will, therefore, grant him audience at his own risk. If you care about your* bloodsworn *as you claim to, you will let me—*"

"*That was a mistake, Kullen,*" Umbris said at the same time Thanagar roared.

"*You question my loyalty?*"

Thanagar struck out and his giant paw slammed into Umbris's side. The impact hurled Kullen off his dragon's back and sent him plummeting. Heart springing into his throat, wind whistling by, the ground rushed up dizzyingly fast. Despite every instinct screaming at him to look down—look *bloody* down!—at the inevitable and fatal end to his fall, he spun to face upward, to watch the two mighty dragons. Umbris did his job, keeping Thanagar occupied.

The Twilight Dragon was aware of the potential complications to Kullen's plan, though neither of them hoped for this outcome. The goal was to get Thanagar to agree to let them pass, but either way, Kullen would achieve his goals.

Behind and below Kullen, the Palace loomed larger, his fall accelerating to disorienting speeds. Though he wasn't looking, he was cognizant of his surroundings. His timing had to be swift and perfect.

Seconds before spattering against the stone roof of the Palace, Kullen dismissed Umbris. The Dragon disappeared into the Shadow Realm just as Kullen pressed his thumb into his vial. Thanagar's attention shifted moments too late.

Kullen fought back an instinctive ripple of fear—the memory of what had *nearly* happened the last time he'd bloodsurged remained visceral and fresh in his mind—and became one with the shadows, his form shifting, finding the closest patch of darkness. He slid into it, just feet above the Palace gardens. Thanagar roared behind him, and the mighty flapping of his wings sent ripples of energy cascading throughout the city. Kullen slid again through the shadows and landed in his solid form behind the broad, blackish leaves of the karodine bushes. He emerged once more into the Mortal Realm, leaving behind the icy chill and wordless shrieks of the Shadow Realm.

Back in solid form, he shouldered open the hidden door, barreled down the stairs, descending three floors at a dead run. Thanagar roared, angry behind him. But as the door shut, his presence became a memory. No, the dragon wouldn't relent, but hopefully, Kullen would reach the Emperor before he could do anything about it.

Kullen's dragon-eyes turned utter darkness into a mass of grays, blacks, and whites, filling the twisting spiral staircase. Somehow, he managed to reach the Palace's ground level without shattering his ankle or stumbling. There were two places he'd expect to find the Emperor at this time of night: in his bedchamber, or sitting in his private study, enjoying a quiet drink after the end of a long day. Kullen chose the latter—with every passing year, the aging Emperor had begun to sleep less and spend more time reading or basking in the silence of what little solitude he could find.

Despite Thanagar's uproar, the palace was quiet, a shroud of calm blanketing the darkness filling the vaulted halls and carpeted corridors. For the first time in his life, Kullen was relieved to see guards patrolling the halls. Though it forced him to take a circuitous route to evade their watchful eyes, it assure him that Magister Branthe's attack—if there was one—had not yet occurred. Peace reigned within the Palace.

But for how much longer? How much time remained before Magister Branthe made whatever next tactical move he had planned? He hadn't destroyed the Refuge with such urgency without reason. However, what reason he might've had mattered not at all to Kullen at the moment.

Kullen stuck to the shadows, but didn't call upon Umbris's magic. He couldn't afford to waste his bloodsurge without knowing what was to come. Finally, he arrived. Four guards stood outside the Emperor's private study—proof that Wymarc was, indeed, within.

Kullen didn't slow—on the contrary, he pushed all the harder, rushing the guards at full speed. Cloaked in shadow and Jarius's black cloak, he was nearly on top of the four Imperial Scales before they spotted him. These were no mere grunts. Not if they were tasked with the Emperor's safety. Though neither was Kullen.

His hand swept forward, hurling one of his glass spheres. The orb shattered at the guards' feet and instantly, a pillar of hazy gray smoke erupted in the hall. Kullen had taken care when choosing. This smoke held none of the nauseating properties that the one he'd thrown at Magister Deckard's guards contained. This would serve only as a screen to conceal his movements.

To their credit, the Emperor's men reacted with impressive speed, closing ranks and standing back to back directly in front of the door. Yet Kullen knew how they'd react—he'd expected it after watching them training for years under Swordmaster Kyneth, the same man who'd trained him in the art of stealth and deception. He was ready for their defensive maneuver. Instead of barreling into the tightly packed knot of men, he dropped into a low forward slide that carried him around the legs of the guard farthest to the right. He was on his feet and reaching for the door handle before the Scales had even registered his presence.

Kullen had the door open and was halfway into the study when he was violently yanked backward. Apparently, he hadn't fooled them as well as he'd thought. One of the guards had seized his cloak and now fought to drag him away from the Emperor. Kullen knew he had a second, perhaps two, before a sword cut him down or a dagger slit his throat.

There was only one thing to do now.

"Emperor Wymarc!" he shouted as loud as he could. "Your life is in danger!"

48

NATISSE

N atisse studied the room through the analytical mindset Uncle Ronan, Garron, and Haston had each hammered into her over their years of training. She examined each ingress and egress, studied everyone around her in search of enemies, scanning for possible places of advantage and danger areas to avoid should the situation turn violent.

Twelve guards wearing the colors of Magister Onathus and Magister Perech—six from each aristocrat's retinue—held the room's perimeter. Two flanked the doorway through which she and Jad had just entered, with another three apiece holding the doors on the northern and southern ends of the circular chamber. No doubt those were the passages that connected to the caravan yard to the north and the shipyard to the south.

Three more stood at attention around a raised wooden platform that occupied the western edge of the fighting pit. There, Magister Branthe sat in an ornately carved chair, leaning on a plush velvet armrest and sipping from a silver goblet.

Natisse studied the man closer. She'd heard a great deal about the most powerful aristocrat in the Karmian Empire, but never seen him in person. He was... plumper than she'd imagined though not totally gone to fat. She'd always been told great tales of the man's military exploits. However, the Magister before her, shoveling pastries down his gullet hardly resembled anyone who had, at one time, "cut down a dozen men within a single breath."

Though she knew that particular anecdote to be one of extreme exaggeration, the implication still remained. Which meant Magister Branthe had grown soft.

That was especially true when compared to the giant by his side. The figure was almost fully cloaked, but he had broad shoulders and a thick black beard fell from beneath his hood, and...

An Orken? With gold bands?

It was unmistakeable, glinting in the torchlight. Those were gold bands, for certain.

A member of the Orkenwatch—and a highly ranked one at that—was at Magister Branthe's side. Natisse barely contained her shock to see such camaraderie between the two.

What was a such a high-ranking member of the Orkenwatch doing in a place like this beside a man like that?

Branthe looked, for all purposes, like an emperor sitting apart from and lording over his subjects. A self-satisfied smile played across his lips as he watched the noblemen and women cheering, shouting, and laughing on the wooden benches encircling the rest of the fighting pit.

At his other side sat a slim, nervous-looking younger man who bore a passing resemblance, though with much weaker features and a fretful disposition. Baronet Ochrin, Natisse suspected. He'd be no threat at all.

Magister Branthe on the other hand...

Despite his current condition, Natisse had no doubt the man he'd once been rested beneath. Retired from the Imperial army nearly two decades earlier, the sword that sat on his hip appeared well-used and a blade better-suited to combat than adorning an aristocrat's ornate ensemble.

The last two guards, both wearing House Perech's orange and

mauve colors over their hauberks, stood at a narrow stone staircase that descended into the fighting pit's northern side. Ending at the gated tunnel set into the stone wall beneath Magister Branthe's box, the path had no doubt been the same one she'd watched slaves dragged into days earlier.

Natisse scanned the crowd in search of additional threats. A few of the nobility filling the stands had brought manservants—a few, like Jad, clearly well-suited to protection as well as service. Those who'd come unaccompanied openly carried weapons: rapiers, short swords, ornate belt daggers, and fencing canes. She even caught sight of a pair of the newfangled and utterly unpredictable flintlock pistols tucked into one aristocrat's sash. Plenty of weapons, but how many of their wielders would actually prove able or willing to use them? Natisse suspected that the majority of those in the room would scatter at the first sign of peril. Much as they might revel in the thrill of the illicit sport, few would risk their lives to protect Magister Branthe's enterprise.

Natisse focused her attention once more on the guards. Her eyes narrowed as she recognized two of the men she'd marked a few nights earlier: Rat Face stood by the north-side door, and Flat Nose guarded the stairs into the pits. Natisse's jaw muscles clenched. When the time came, she'd make certain they, at least, didn't escape with their lives.

"What's the plan?" Jad's whispered question pierced the ruckus of the noblemen preparing for their blood sport.

Before Natisse could answer, Magister Branthe stood and raised his free hand, spilling wine over the rim of his goblet in the other. The effect was instantaneous—the cacophony died in the space between heartbeats, all eyes turning to the standing aristocrat.

"Gentlemen and ladies, nobles of Dimvein, I bid you welcome." He bestowed an imperious smile on the crowd, eliciting a cheer from his audience. After a moment, he held up a hand once more to restore the calm. "Last night's events were...

unfortunate, but I assure you that all is in readiness for this evening. What you will see here is a spectacle unlike anything witnessed in Dimvein for nigh on two hundred years, not since the days of Emperor Oriallis himself!"

Gasps and surprised whispers floated among the crowd. Natisse caught the mutterings of a pair of noblemen sitting directly in front of her.

"This had better be good," one said, a practiced tone of condescension ripe upon his words. "I've brought half my yearly stipend, and with the right wager, I'll walk away richer than our host himself."

"You're dumber than you look," the other sneered. "Everyone knows Magister Branthe always comes out the winner."

Natisse's fists clenched at her side. Magister Branthe had run a slave-trafficking ring in Dimvein right under Emperor Wymarc's nose. He certainly had come out the winner... until now.

She began edging her way around the room, circling to her left, along the room's southern perimeter. The chamber was vast —easily a hundred yards across—and it would take her time to draw within striking range of Magister Branthe's box. Time enough to figure out a way to kill the aristocrat before his Orken bodyguard could involve himself.

The stone walls and steel door wouldn't crumble, but the wooden benches with their velvet cushions and hanging tassels served as the perfect kindling. Stuffed beneath Jad's coat and Natisse's flowing dress were bottles filled with alchemical fire— more than enough to enflame the entirely of this wretched place.

Magister Branthe appeared to be quite the blowhard.

"However, as with any grand spectacle," he continued, "there must be a build-up, a mounting of anticipation to increase the pleasure of the crescendo." He raised his goblet to the crowd. "You have come for blood, and blood you shall have, in abundance!"

The crowd cheered and raised their own cups and goblets. Magister Branthe stomped his foot on the wooden platform once, a sound that rang out through the fighting pit. At that signal, the grille set into the wall beneath his box creaked open, and a trio of heavy-necked men wearing black hoods and spiked leather harnesses dragged two struggling figures out onto the blood-stained sands.

Natisse's gut twisted at the sight of the shackled men. They labored beneath the weight of heavy chains secured to their wrists, ankles, necks, and waists, and their bodies and faces bore the marks of a vicious beating. The taller of the two bled from a dozen cuts on his chest, while the other, a squat youth who looked barely older than Sparrow, had one eye swollen shut and counted a split lip among his various injuries.

The mismatched pair were hurled to the sand and held down by two of the guards. The third set about removing the shackles from their wrists, ankles, and waists. The chains connecting them by their necks, however, were left in place.

The three hooded guards then marched back into the tunnel, leaving the chained pair alone on the sands. The taller of the two rose first and thrust a hand down to help the younger man to his feet. At this, the crowd booed and jeered. If either of the men cared, they showed no proof of it. Both appeared exhausted, half-starved, and with skin pale from lack of sunlight. Natisse had no idea how long they'd been down here, but it could well have been weeks.

The two slaves stared in confusion at each other, then at the gated tunnel. They seemed not to understand what was meant to happen—ignorant to the fact that they were meant to fight each other.

A moment later, a figure swathed in bloody bandages stag-gered out onto the sands. More followed, a steady stream of cloth-bound people stumbling along behind them, eighteen in all. Acid rose in Natisse's throat.

The crowd's jeers turned to cheers. Natisse was not alone in her revelation of what was about to befall these pour souls. The two chained men, however, failed to comprehend until it was almost too late. One of the bandaged figures—a leper, Natisse recognized—stumbled toward the younger man and drew a rusty knife from within the folds of his tattered cloak. The youth leaped backward just in time to avoid being disemboweled, but the sudden movement dragged the taller man off-balance.

Natisse felt sick.

"I seen others go in there!" the leper who had worn Uncle Ronan's coat had told her that morning. *"People like me. Nobodies that nobody will miss. They go in there, and they don't never come out!"*

What cruelty—and inflicted upon those to whom life had already dealt the cruelest of hands. She turned away, having no desire to witness the bloodshed. Whatever the outcome, it would be terrible. Even if the two chained men somehow defeated the enemies that vastly outnumbered them, they would likely contract the wasting disease, falling to a slow death. Their triumph would be short-lived, the rest of their lives more miserable than they could possibly imagine. And Natisse had no doubt they'd eventually end up right back here on the other side of the battle.

What had these lepers been promised? A cure? How had they been threatened?

Natisse's hatred of Magister Branthe grew. The aristocrat reclined in his chair, watching the display with a cruel grin on his aged face. He, the Orken, and Baronet Ochrin sat alone in the box sizable enough for ten men—no doubt Magisters Perech, Estéfar, and Onathus had been intended to join him. Natisse felt a grim satisfaction at that sight.

She continued along the perimeter of the room. Though she hated the bloody spectacle in the fighting pit, she welcomed the distraction. All eyes, even those of Magister Onathus's guards, were fixed on the two chained men battling the lepers. None paid her or Jad any heed.

Natisse glanced up at Jad, normally salient man amongst any

crowd. The big man's face was tight, his jaw muscles tensed, a hard look in his eyes. Natisse recognized the look—she'd seen in only twice in her life, a sign Jad was on the verge of fury. He would keep his composure... but for how long?

She needed to do something to occupy his mind.

Reaching up, she pulled gently on his arm. He complied, placing his ears close to her lips.

"We're burning this place to the ground," she whispered. "Start pouring, and circle around to the north side of the chamber. I'll head south. When I give the signal, we set this place ablaze and hit Magister Branthe's box from both sides. Remove his and his Orken traitor's means of escape."

Jad gave her a tight nod, and did as he was told, reaching into his coat for the first of the little glass bottles.

Natisse did likewise, uncorking the first bottle and emptying its contents in a trickling line behind her as she continued to the south. Magister Onathus's guards didn't even glance her way, too busy shouting at the fighters in the pit and placing wagers with each other.

The odorless chemical was potent—colorless too. If anyone happened to spot the trail, they'd merely assume someone had drank too much and became clumsy with their goblet.

She made sure to splatter the contents beneath the many wooden benches, ensuring they would catch alight quickly—hopefully killing the noblemen and women crowding the seats in the process.

Natisse's progress was slow and careful. It took all her self-control to keep her movements steady, to avoid the notice of those she passed. A groan from the crowd drew her attention to the combatants in the fighting pit.

Fifteen beggars lay strewn around the sands—Natisse didn't know if they were unconscious or dead—blood leaking from fresh wounds. Of the three that remained standing, one cradled a broken arm, and crimson gushed from the bandaged face of another.

The two chained men, however, were down. The taller one's leg had been shattered, his chest crushed, and his neck snapped. The younger's face was pulp, his brains a bloody mess on the sand. Two of the surviving lepers bore deep crimson stains on the bandages covering their fists.

Magister Branthe rose to his feet. "Victory to the lepers!" He plucked a coin purse from within his cloak and held it up, its contents jangling. "Now, whichever of you slays the others walks way with the gold." He tossed the purse onto the sand between the three men.

The lepers hesitated for a moment, glancing nervously at one another, then threw themselves into a frantic, scuffling melee. A few seconds later, when Natisse glanced back, two of the lepers lay dead and the last sat atop their corpses, the purse raised high in his bandaged hand. A muffled cry of triumph rose from his mouth.

Something hurtled toward the leper and he was flung backward as if by an invisible fist. His body crumpled to the battlefield. Confusion settled in upon the crowd as the diseased man lay still, face up. Then light chuckles ensued, one after another, as the nobles noticed the shaft of a crossbow bolt protruding from his chest.

"A mercy," Magister Branthe said, with a cruel laugh. "His days would have been nothing but agony, but tonight, he dies a champion!"

Raucous laughter rang out among the gathered noblemen and women, and Natisse's fury only grew. How she wished she could kill them all. She fantasized about slitting their faces at the corners of their mouths, permanently scarring them with gruesome grins.

But she had to focus on the task at hand. To find Uncle Ronan, she needed a diversion to throw the chamber into chaos. Magister

Branthe's death would prove distraction enough—and the Crimson Fang would deliver justice to the innocents that lay dead in the fighting pit.

Blood for blood, she silently promised the chained men and the lepers around them. Magister Branthe's blood, and that of anyone who got in their way.

She scanned the room for Jad. He'd completed a quarter-circle around the fighting pit, but they both still had a lot of ground to cover, and more alchemical fire to pour if they wanted to be ready when the time came to set the fighting pit ablaze.

The gated tunnel ground open, the peel of rusty metal screeching throughout the chamber. A half-dozen hooded men emerged and set about dragging the corpses out of sight. The crowd of lords and ladies were too busy recovering the profits of their wagers or bemoaning their losses to care. As if following some pre-arranged signal, servants appeared from the door that led south to Magister Onathus's shipyard, bearing trays of refreshments and delicacies.

Magister Branthe would feed their bellies and satiate their bloodlust all at once. It was no wonder he'd risen to a place of such prominence. These feckless do-nothings whose coffers were so full they found use for their coin betting upon the deaths of those beneath their station... these would be his power base. He was buying their loyalty with blood.

Though, perhaps it was true, what Uncle Ronan had always said: Blood is cheaper than gold.

When the sands had been cleared, Magister Branthe stood and signaled for calm. Once again, the commotion in the room died down and all eyes focused on their de facto leader. Natisse's eyes roamed the box. Branthe and his nephew were there, but the Orken was gone.

Where'd you go?

"My friends," Magister Branthe said, a coy smile tickling his lips, "I promised you a spectacle the likes of which you've never seen, but what if I told you that tonight you would witness not one, but two marvels?"

Excited whispers ran through the crowd.

Magister Branthe's smile grew wider, more smug. "You all know the stories of General Andros, Hero of Blackwater Bay, Savior of Kollick, Conqueror of Hudar, and Defender of Dimvein. A man unlike any other, one of the greatest military commanders the Karmian Empire has ever seen. Indeed, a man beside whom I fought during my days in service to the Emperor."

"Aye, we know the stories!" shouted a voice from the crowd. "Stories about a dead man."

"A dead man, you say?" Magister Branthe affected an exaggerated look of surprise. "Certainly my eyes are mistaken, then!"

Murmurs coursed through the underground, making Natisse stop. She stood on her toes, and peered into the pits.

"Perhaps you should see and judge for yourself!" Magister Branthe said.

The gate slowly churned open once more. There were gasps, but Natisse could see nothing yet.

Everyone in Dimvein knew the stories—Baruch, in particular, had loved telling her the tales of the Great General Andros. One in particular had stuck firmly in her brain. After the recent events on Blackwater Bay and Magister Perech's pleasure barge, Natisse had to admit, she'd been thinking of it even more.

More specifically, she'd been hearing Baruch's voice excitedly telling of the time General Andros defeated the Hudar Hordes who, with the help of the Blood Clan pirates, had broken the Imperial Navy and assaulted Blackwater Bay. Thanagar's might had been fully evident that day, but the pirates had prepared ballistae and their own magic to combat the dragon's power. The true battle had been between the human armies that day.

While his men fought valiantly ship to ship and shore to ship, the General and a small battalion took to the waters, swimming beneath the Hudarian boats and blowing holes in the hulls using an alchemical compound the contents of which he'd supposedly never shared. All the stories agreed, though, that before anyone knew what was happening, the entire armada had been sunk.

It had been Baruch's favorite, and so, Natisse's too—the way his eyes lit up in the telling.

The grille creaked open, and from the shadows emerged an enormous figure, far larger than anything she'd ever imagined. The man stood well above seven feet tall, with a back broader than even Jad's and muscles that rippled with every movement. He wore the same spiked leather harness but no hood, carried no weapons. Only when Natisse saw the chains in his hand did she realize that this wasn't General Andros, but another of the jailers.

Yet not any jailor. The giant turned toward the crowd, and Natisse was struck by horror as she recognized the brutish features of Joakim—the flat-faced man she'd seen branding the slaves. He roared in laughter as he dragged a chained figure through the stone-walled tunnel.

That sound and the sight of the brute shattered something in Natisse's mind. Suddenly, she no longer stood in the dim, secret underground. She was surrounded by bright sun, yet she huddled in shadow, terrified, desperate. The sound of harsh laughter and a woman's scream echoed in her ears. Pain rippled through her, and the heat of fire engulfed her, driving her to panic.

Yet a new voice reached her a moment later. A man's voice, familiar, yet so alien. It knew her name.

"*Natisse!*" the man cried within her mind. "*Run, Natisse! Now!*"

Natisse turned toward the voice. A man's face hovered before her—green eyes, hair a fiery red like hers, a strong jaw and masculine chin. In an instant, she knew that face, ashamed she'd ever forgotten it.

"*Run, Natisse!*" her father cried again. "*Get away from here!*"

The woman's scream came again. The man's head snapped toward the sound. "*Nyanna!*" he shouted. "*I'm co—*"

Fire engulfed the man, and Natisse was suddenly driven out of the past, back to the present. She staggered beneath the weight of the memory and would have fallen if not for the wall to her left. She clung to the cool stone and fought to regain control of herself, to drag her mind back to reality, yet still remember what she'd seen.

Her father! She'd known it was him the moment his face became clear. And the name he'd shouted—Nyanna—she knew it too. Her mother's name.

A collective gasp of shock from the crowd pierced the muddle in Natisse's mind. Still reeling from the memory, she managed to focus on the chained figure being dragged onto the sand.

Magister Branthe swept a grand gesture toward the fighting pit. "My friends, I give you the Great General Andros, back from the dead!"

Natisse pushed off the wall, steadied herself, and stared at the grizzled, graying man. She knew him... better than she knew anyone else still alive today.

"Uncle Ronan?"

49

KULLEN

"**Y**our life is in danger!"

Even as the words left Kullen's lips, he heard the rasp of steel on leather. Spinning, he lashed out with an elbow and cracked one of the guards in the side of their helmet. It didn't do much damage, but it had the desired effect of breaking the guard's hold. Continuing the spin, he dropped low to hook his heel behind another Scale's knee. The man landed on his back with the loud clunk of metal on wood. An instant later, a heavy boot flashed toward Kullen's head. He rolled backward, barely evading the blow.

His momentum carried him farther into the Emperor's study. He rolled to his feet, drawing his hunting knives and bracing for the rear charge of the bodyguards.

"Hold!" came the Emperor's voice.

Relief flooded Kullen. He'd been prepared to fight, but hoped Emperor Wymarc would react to his violent entrance with speed enough to call off his guards. With nothing more than his two hunting knives to face off against their long swords and heavy armor, even Kullen's skill would be sorely tested. And that was before the inevitability of summoned reinforcements.

"Stay where you are, Imperial Majesty!" barked the larger of the two guards. Kullen knew him. The blond-bearded Angban was captain of the Emperor's Elite Scales, and a powerful warrior in his own right. Kullen had watched him spar with Turoc a few weeks earlier and the man had given nearly as good as he got. Captain Angban had his twin curved swords out and his eyes locked on Kullen's hooded figure. "I'll cut this suicidal fool down before—"

"I said, hold, Captain!" Emperor Wymarc's voice cracked like a whip.

Kullen knew what was passing through Captain Angban's mind as he froze. In this moment, the captain was torn between his warrior's instincts, his fierce loyalty to his position, and his obedience to Emperor Wymarc. But what if Emperor Wymarc had been wrong? What if Kullen had been there to slit the monarch's throat and the captain stood by watching?

"I mean the Emperor no harm," Kullen said as if such a simple statement would convince anyone.

Angban took a step forward.

Emperor Wymarc appeared at Kullen's side, moving to stand between Kullen and Captain Angban.

"Fool he may be," the emperor said, casting a reproachful glance over his shoulder at Kullen, "but he is my agent, and here at my request. If he says my life is in danger, it is not he who I have to fear. I will hear what he has to say."

"With all due respect, Imperial Majesty," Captain Angban started, "he is armed and—"

"And as loyal to this empire as you are," Emperor Wymarc cut him off with a slashing gesture. He turned to Kullen. "Sheathe your blades. Now."

Kullen complied. He recognized the anger blazing in Emperor Wymarc's eyes—the man was furious at Kullen's choice of entrances, but he was too busy keeping Kullen alive to properly scold him at the moment.

When the Captain had gone, however, Kullen knew he was in for a sharp-tongued lecture. He didn't care—he'd weather the Emperor's wrath if it meant saving his life.

"You see?" Emperor Wymarc turned back to Captain Angban. "Now put up your blades, Captain, and return to your post."

Captain Angban made no move to sheathe his swords or leave the room. His gaze was locked on Kullen, as if trying to see the features hidden by the shadows of Kullen's hood. Kullen kept his head turned down—the last thing he wanted was to be recognized.

Until a few days ago, he wouldn't have suspected anyone within the Palace of treachery. But the fact that Emperor Wymarc had given him Magister Deckard's dragonblood vial for safekeeping, combined with his discovery of Magister Branthe's betrayal, had instilled in him a sudden suspicion of everything and everyone. He trusted no one except himself and the Emperor.

"At once, Captain," Emperor Wymarc said, his voice stern, a frown on his lips. "I will speak to him. Alone."

It seemed to take every shred of Captain Angban's willpower to obey, yet obey he did.

"Of course, Imperial Majesty." He didn't sheathe his swords, but backed out of the room, fixing Kullen with a hate-filled glare. Exiting, he slapped the arm of one of his comrades who was busy helping up the guard Kullen had tripped. "Let's go."

Emperor Wymarc rounded on Kullen, his mouth open in what Kullen knew would be a harsh rebuke.

Kullen forestalled the haranguing.

"Your life is in danger, Imperial Majesty." He spoke quickly, not giving the Emperor time to interrupt. "I've discovered the person I believe is behind the actions of Magisters Deckard, Issemar, Edrian, and Iltari. The person who is trying to undermine your rule, foment discord, and, more than likely, make a move against you. This very night, possibly! The night of the full moon with all the dragonblood vials he has collected over the last weeks."

"Yes," the Emperor said calmly. "I know."

"You know?" Kullen barely kept the incredulity from his tone. "What do you mean, you know?"

"Do you believe you could ride in here on your dragon, challenge my Thanagar, and him not deliver the news to me immediately through our bond?"

"I didn't think—"

"Too true," Emperor Wymarc said, still calm as the bay in midyear.

"Your Majesty, you must believe me."

"Must I?" Emperor Wymarc asked. "You barge in here brandishing weapons, threatening my guard, and accusing one of my oldest, most trusted and loyal friends of what exactly? Mutiny? An attempt to usurp the throne?"

"I just came from the Refuge, which was attacked again, even after Magister Deckard's death. This time, the assailants wore no noble colors or insignia, but when put to the question, they implicated Magister Branthe."

"And I am to believe the words of a brigand?"

"You are to believe the words of your Black Talon!" Kullen shouted, nearly forgetting his place. He lowered his voice. "Is this not what you asked of me?"

The Emperor's features softened. "Go on," he conceded. "Spare no details."

Kullen knew he'd have one shot at this. He quickly recounted what he'd gotten from the dying thug—about the urgency of Magister Branthe's assault against the Refuge, and the mention of the Orken. At that, Emperor Wymarc's face drained of color and his eyes went wide.

"An Orken?" he said, his voice a harsh whisper. "And you trusted this man's word?"

"Had it not been for what I saw in the graveyard beside Tuskthorne Keep, perhaps not. But I did, indeed, see Branthe speaking with an Orken."

"But you couldn't confirm his identity?"

"Not at such a distance. But the man, with his dying breath, said he was big, ugly, and..." Kullen hesitated, "... with gold bands." Kullen's jaw muscles clenched. "I know how ludicrous it sounds. The Orken have been loyal to the Empire since—"

"Unfortunately," came another voice from behind Kullen, "loathe as I am to admit it, your assessment is correct in this matter."

Kullen spun to find Assidius emerging from a dark corner of the study. He hadn't even seen the man there—likely hiding in the shadows, afraid for his life—but if he'd been here the entire time, he'd heard Kullen's report. That saved him from having to track down the Seneschal to fill him in on everything he'd uncovered. He wasn't fully certain he could trust the man—and was very certain he didn't like him—but he'd decided that Assidius hadn't been the one to pen the note from Red Claw to Magister Deckard. Disdain or not, he couldn't treat the Seneschal as a threat, not with real enemies as powerful as Magister Branthe to contend with.

"You're telling me you knew an Orken was working against the Empire?" Kullen demanded.

"Not for certain, no." Assidius's thin face drew into a pinched frown. "But I had my suspicions—suspicions I made certain to keep from Turoc, mind you." Few men in the world were less trusting than Kullen; the Seneschal certainly numbered among that handful. It was his job as the Emperor's spymaster to suspect everything and everyone. Including, it seemed, the Tuskigo of the Orkenwatch.

"What do you mean by suspicions?" Emperor Wymarc asked. "What have you not told me, Assidius?"

"Nothing, Imperial Majesty," Assidius replied hastily, then amended. "At least nothing that I could prove." His frown deepened. "For the last three or four months, I've been receiving reports from the Imperial Scales and my assets around Dimvein that... shall we say, differ slightly from the reports kept by Turoc. At first, I wrote them off as oddities, but they continued piling up until I could no longer ignore them."

"Differ how?" Kullen demanded.

Assidius shot Kullen a look that left no doubt as to how he felt about Kullen's tone—only one person in the room commanded the Seneschal, and it was certainly not Kullen. Despite himself, he did answer the question.

"Minor details, really," Assidius said. "Things that could be easily overlooked by anyone without an eye for precisely those minor details." His voice held a tone that, on anyone else, might have sounded self-deprecating, but which Kullen recognized as Assidius's way of boasting. "Orkenwatch patrols avoiding certain parts of Dimvein, despite the routes being pre-arranged in coordination with the Imperial Scales. Reports going missing or being oddly vague. As I said, minor details—"

"But enough that they raised your suspicions," Emperor Wymarc finished.

"Yes, Divine Majety." Assidius bowed. "I have quietly been conducting my own investigation into the matter, and have thus far come up empty-handed. Indeed, I was on the verge of concluding that I was mistaken—until now." He looked to Kullen, his expression decidedly sour. "If the report of golden bands is true, this confirms my belief that it is someone high in the Orkenwatch ranks who might be behind whatever double-dealings and duplicity are occurring."

"How high?" Emperor Wymarc asked, eyes narrowing.

Assidius hesitated, as if unwilling to speak. "I don't know," he said. "But, gold bands means only one thing."

"Command," the Emperor said.

Kullen bit back a curse. That was a problem, indeed. Turoc led the Orkenwatch, with Ketsneer Bareg as his second-in-command. Additionally, six other Orken—the Arbiters—wore bands of gold, all of them powerful and well liked amongst their brethren. It could be any one of them.

But it wasn't just the Orken who had a powerful traitor in their midst. Kullen had come to warn the Emperor about the even more powerful threat facing them.

"Emperor," he said quickly, "based on my findings, there is a very real possibility that Magister Branthe will be coming here even now with his army. And if I am right, with the moon high, the cycle beginning, he will have many dragons under his command. You have to mobilize the Scales, call out the Imperial Army—whatever it takes to prepare for battle."

"Unnecessary," Assidius snapped. "If any force of any size was marshaling in Dimvein, I would have been made privy to it."

"Just as you were *made privy to* Magister Branthe's treachery?" Kullen demanded.

"Yes, in fact." Assidius drew himself up to his paltry height. "That was, in fact, what the Emperor and I were just about to discuss when you so rudely barged into the room."

Kullen's jaw clenched. "Is that so?"

"It is, indeed," Assidius retorted. The Seneschal turned away from Kullen, frosty as ice, and fixed his gaze on the Emperor. "Yesterday, I received word from one of my assets that Magister Branthe, in league with Magisters Onathus and Perech and his nephew, Baronet Ochrin, have been trafficking slaves through Dimvein for the better part of two years. Not only that, but I have credible reports of an underground slave fighting pit in the Western Docks. I am still waiting to hear back from my agents, but through my own independent verification, I have concluded that Magister Branthe has, indeed, been conducting clandestine business using Baronet Ochrin as a front to conceal his dealings."

Emperor Wymarc was quiet for a moment. "I tire of these games between you two," he finally said.

"I'm sorry?" Assidius said.

"You should be!" the Emperor roared, slapping a hand onto the table. "How much more quickly could this have been resolved if you two shared this information with one another."

"But how was I to know he could be trusted?" Assidius said, pointing at Kullen.

"Because I have commanded you to trust him!" The Emperor's face was red hot with fury. He turned to Kullen, who was doing his best not to smirk. However, it seemed he was unsuccessful. "And you wipe that smile off your face. Flying dragons, attacking guards... this is all—"

"My apologies, Emperor, but this isn't helping," Kullen said.

"You watch your tongue," Assidius said with a hard glare.

With a heavy sigh, Kullen turned to leave the room.

"Where are you going?" Assidius asked.

"Carritus Branthe is stirring up forces to overthrow this throne," Kullen said. "I intend to stop it, even if I am the only one."

The Emperor's face grew deathly pale as if the accusation was just now hitting home in his heart. He slumped into a chair.

"Carritus," he whispered. His eyes were hollow, his stare vacant. "I can't believe it. And yet…" He looked between Kullen and Assidius. "How could I have missed it?"

"Because Magister Branthe is a superb liar, Divine Majesty," Assidius said. "There have been rumors circulating for years now that some of his vaunted military achievements are either greatly exaggerated or, in some cases, outright fabrications." His lips pressed into a thin line. "During the skirmishes in Kollick, where he was the sole survivor, there are whispers that he lived only because he cowered beneath the corpses of his fallen soldiers until the King Kallias's men moved on. He returned, claiming responsibility for their victory, taking credit for many of General Andros's achievements."

"And he framed the man," Kullen said, his voice low.

"Yes," Assidius confirmed. "He accused General Andros of treason. Accused him of desertion."

"But he was acquitted of all charges," the Emperor said.

"Indeed," Assidius said, "but when a man like Andros's loyalties are questioned, they often… break."

"I heard he hanged himself in Halfvale," Kullen said.

"Speculation at best," Assidius said, waving his hand in dismissal.

"Blessed Ezrasil!" Emperor Wymarc buried his head in his hands. "Carritus."

Kullen knew he ought to tell the Emperor about his suspicion that Magister Branthe's guards might've played a hand in Jarius and Hadassa's deaths, but wasn't certain now would be the right time. Emperor Wymarc had just come to terms with the knowledge that his most trusted friend was a coward, liar, and traitor. That was a blow that would rock even the strongest man to his core.

"None of those rumors can be substantiated, of course," Assidius continued. "Lord Branthe is a man of great means. It would've been no trouble at all for him to keep quiet any man who threatened to reveal his secrets—whether by coin or by blade. Or, perhaps he simply hired them into his guard force to buy their loyalty."

At that, a memory flashed through Kullen's mind—the memory of military tattoos inked into the flesh of killers sent to murder Magister Issemar. Had Magister Branthe been behind that, too? Had he sent his sellswords to kill Magister Issemar? He couldn't know, couldn't figure out why, but that made a great deal more sense than soldiers-turned-muggers-and-robbers who just happened to attack an aristocrat as he left some secret meeting.

That factory...

Kullen frowned, but before he could speak, Emperor Wymarc rose abruptly and strode toward the study door. He hauled it open, to reveal Captain Angban standing with swords still drawn and facing the door, ready to rush into the room at the first sign of threat.

"Captain, rouse your men, and seal off this section of the Palace," Emperor Wymarc commanded. "Close the Palace gates, bar them quietly, and prepare for a possible attack."

"Attack?" Captain Angban's eyebrows shot up, and his gaze darted to where Kullen stood. "From who, Imperial Majesty?"

"Just make ready, Captain," the Emperor said, his tone curt. "And bring Prince Jaylen to me. If we are threatened, I want him at my side."

"At once, Emperor!" Captain Angban pressed a fist to his chest and, with another suspicious glare at Kullen, turned and hurried off to obey his Emperor's command. His shouted orders rang out in the hallway, growing louder as his Elite Scales rushed off to execute their duties.

Emperor Wymarc closed the door and turned to Kullen. "Have you shown him the message from Red Claw?"

Kullen shook his head. "No, sir. I was unable to get inside Tuskthorne Keep earlier. Ran into a Sniffer who might've recognized my scent, and couldn't risk it."

"Note?" Assidius asked, his slim, perfectly plucked eyebrows rising. "Red Claw?"

Kullen dug into his cloak and pulled out the cloth-wrapped scrap of parchment. Unfolding the cloth, he held it out to show Assidius. The Seneschal lifted the parchment carefully, handling it with surprising delicacy, and frowned down at the missive.

"I do not recognize the handwriting," he said after a long moment. "And this name 'Red Claw,' it is not known to me."

Kullen's brows knit. "Are you sure?"

"Yes, but it's possible that Magister Branthe is, in fact, this 'Red Claw.' I assume that is your belief? Yes, I thought so. Hmmm. He might've simply hired a scribe to write the letter for him." Assidius handed the parchment back to Kullen. "That would be a simple way of covering his tracks, removing any chance of connecting this note to him."

"Damn effective," Kullen muttered.

Magister Branthe might be a coward, liar, and traitor, but he was clearly no fool. He'd have to be smart to manipulate events so deftly, to keep suspicion away from him while using the recent spate of noble deaths to increase his standing. He could have spies planted in every noble house in Dimvein, feeding him information and secrets to give him leverage over his business and political rivals. That, in addition to his fabricated status as Survivor—as he'd been dubbed—which made him beloved among the people, the military, and the royal palace, had enabled him to make this move against the Emperor tonight.

"Odd." Emperor Wymarc's words pierced Kullen's thoughts.

Looking up, he found the Emperor staring at his desk with a pensive frown on his face. His right hand was clasped around the dragonblood vial at his neck.

"Sir?" Kullen asked.

Emperor Wymarc looked up, his gaze focusing on Kullen. "I've just spoken with Thanagar. Thus far, the only thing out of place in the Palace and its surrounding environs has been your arrival. He's cast out his senses, and nothing seems amiss. No sign of enemy troops massing outside the Palace gates, no one moving through the Orken-built tunnels. Nothing."

Kullen narrowed his eyes. "How is that possible?"

"According to Thanagar, there is no threat at all, Kullen. None."

That made no sense. Kullen hadn't known for certain what Magister Branthe intended, but he'd made an educated guess based on what he knew of the aristocrat's capabilities and background. Had he been so wrong? Magister Branthe was the one who'd attacked the Refuge—or was he? Had the hired blade lied? It wasn't the first time Kullen had considered it. Could Magister Branthe's meeting with the Orken have been something more innocent?

Kullen wasn't sure of the meeting's purpose, but Branthe certainly wasn't innocent. He couldn't be.

But was he Red Claw?

There was no other explanation—was there?

Even so, if he wasn't mounting an attack or trying to overthrow the Emperor, what in Ezrasil's name *was* he doing?

50

NATISSE

N atisse felt as if the wind had been sucked from her lungs. Her mind, still battling to return from the haunting depths of her past, struggled to make sense of what was taking place before her. Who was this man in the pits?

Magister Branthe had called Uncle Ronan "General Andros?" How could that be?

Yet, the look of triumph on Magister Branthe's face was undeniable. Gasps of surprise rose from the crowd around her—many of those present today were old enough to remember the Empire's most famous general. Had any of them actually met General Andros? Judging by the reactions of those filling the chamber, the answer was a resounding yes.

Natisse stared at Uncle Ronan, as if seeing him for the first time. She didn't understand—how could she?—but at the moment, she couldn't let the confusion stop her from carrying out her mission. Despite the serpent of fear and doubt constricting her insides.

With effort, she pushed the swirling emotions down deep, locked them away in the recesses of her mind. She focused on the calm, on the shadows around her, the stone wall at her back, the ground beneath her feet. These things were unchanging, immutable, a constant. They served as the focal point for her as she expelled all other thoughts. She had to stay focused, like Uncle Ronan—or whoever in Shekoth's icy pits he was—had taught her.

She closed her eyes and let out a long breath. When her eyes opened again, her wits were clear, sharp. She knew what she had to do. She'd come all this way to free Uncle Ronan. And, if the gods were just, eliminate the aristocrat at the head of the slave trafficking conspiracy. She could worry about everything else later. For now, she had her work cut out for her, and that was all that mattered.

She sought out Jad's hulking frame, and spotted him on the far side of the fighting pit, opposite her. Even across the distance, she could feel the tension radiating off the huge man. His face was tight, his eyes narrowed, and his sloped shoulders were bunched as if ready to fight. Jad was staring at the two figures in the fighting pit, and Natisse had a good idea what he was thinking.

Come on, Jad! She mentally willed the man to look at her. She needed to catch his eye, to make sure he knew that their plan hadn't changed—yet—just because of the latest development. They were still vastly outnumbered, which meant they still needed the diversion to throw the fighting pit into chaos. Only then could they make their move.

"My friends," Magister Branthe crowed from his elegant box overlooking the fighting pit, "I know how implausible this may seem. General Andros himself, back from the dead? It cannot be. No doubt many of you believe this is a charade." His smile broadened. "Perhaps a demonstration will help!"

Magister Branthe snapped his fingers, and the giant secured Uncle Ronan's chains to a ring set into the pit's eastern wall. Uncle Ronan had been beaten badly, his face a mess of bruises, cuts, and lumps. Yet he refused to allow exhaustion or pain to drive him to his knees. He stood tall, head held high, defiance in his eyes.

That was when Natisse spotted the black band around his neck. It glowed the color of a Lumenator's light. It had to be a dampener of some sort. Otherwise, why wasn't Uncle Ronan just doing to these men what he'd done to the gnasher back in the tunnels?

"Were this any ordinary champion," Magister Branthe said, leaning over the edge of his box to leer down at Uncle Ronan, "I would set Joakim to tear him apart. But what I have planned for you all tonight..." He licked his lips eagerly. "...such pleasures cannot be rushed."

He snapped his fingers again, and the gate creaked open. From the opening emerged three men, all wearing boiled leather armor and carrying short swords. The trio were hard-looking, well-muscled, and moved with the lithe grace of street fighters. They gave the giant Joakim a wide berth as they advanced on Uncle Ronan.

The fight was ugly, bloody, and over almost before Natisse realized it. The first of the trio rushed ahead of his companions, only to be brought down by a kick to the throat. Uncle Ronan disarmed the slumping man with ease and cut the remaining two down in the space of a few heartbeats. All three hit the sands at the same time. One lay gurgling and gasping, clutching at his crushed trachea. The second whimpered and pressed an open palm against the deep gash in his gut, from which his intestines spilled through his fingers. The last one made not a sound, but blood pumped from the wound where Uncle Ronan had stabbed him in the heart.

A gasp of surprise and bloodthirsty delight arose from the crowd.

"Can there be any doubt?" Magister Branthe crooned. "What other man could put on such a marvelous display of skill?"

The crowd cheered.

Uncle Ronan spat onto the sands.

"It is over for you, Carritus!" he shouted over the cacophony. "By sunrise, your blood will join that of your conspirators. Onathus, Perech, Estéfar, and Oyodan await you in Shekoth's pits, and it will be a cold greeting indeed!"

Magister Branthe just smiled more grandly, and the crowd's cheering rose.

Natisse tore her gaze from Uncle Ronan, and to her relief, found Jad staring at her. She read the question in the big man's eyes and gave a little shake of her head.

"Wait for my signal," she mouthed.

A tense moment passed, then Jad nodded his head. Natisse heaved an inward sigh of relief, and continued along her torturously slow circumnavigation of the round chamber. When the vial she held was finally empty, leaving a thin trail of liquid behind her, she slid it into her pocket and reached for another.

The crowd was riveted on the exhibition within the fighting pit. The three bodies had been dragged away, and now five newcomers strode out onto the sands. One carried a trident and net, another a sword and shield, while a third wore only spiked cestus gloves on his ham-sized fists. The last two, who had the look of twins, darted back and forth, swinging flails in wide arcs around their heads.

Natisse's gut clenched. Five warriors against a battered Uncle Ronan. He still carried the short sword, but his hands were bound and the chain limited his freedom of movement. He'd trained her to always be on the move, always attacking, never giving her enemies an opening to strike at her. But here, he was at a clear disadvantage, and he could not fight as he had in the training room.

Her heart leaped into her throat as the trident-wielder stabbed at his throat. Uncle Ronan swept the attack aside, dodged the net, but nearly died from a sword cut aimed for his head. He barely darted back in time to avoid the swing, taking a nasty cut that opened his cheek to the bone.

A roar rose up from the crowd. Noblemen and women surged to their feet, shouting, jeering, clapping, laughing. For a moment, the throng blocked Natisse's view of the fighting pit.

Suddenly, a hand gripped her arm and spun her harshly around.

"You!" A black-bearded guard in the blue and green—House Onathus—loomed over her, his face a glaring mask. "What are you doing?"

Caught off-guard, Natisse was torn between warring instincts. One screamed at her to bury a dagger into his belly, cut him down before he attacked. The other, however, warned her to remain unnoticed. She was so close to her objective, she couldn't risk calling attention to herself now.

With effort, she regained her composure and wrenched her hand free of the guard's grip.

"Unhand me, you boor!" she snapped. "You dare lay a finger on a member of—"

The guard stepped closer. "I dare to do whatever I bloody want! I'm being paid good coin to make sure nothing goes wrong, and you've all the look of 'wrong' to me!" He leaned closer, his hand dropping to his sword. "So tell me, *Lady*." The word dripped scorn. "What. Are. You. Doing?"

Natisse forced herself to keep her hands far from the blades hidden around her person.

"Trying to get a better view." She gestured to the backs of the people between her and the fighting pit.

"Bullshit." The guard's dark eyes blazed, his face creasing into a frown. "Ain't nothing wrong with the view a second ago, yet you ain't taken a seat since the moment you walked through the door." He half-drew his sword. "So either you're in the wrong place, or you're the wrong kind of person. Either way—"

"Fine!" Natisse hissed. She reached up, gripped the guard's

neck, and pulled his head toward her—so close her lips nearly brushed against his ear. "I'm trying to get close enough to our host's box for that handsome dolt, Baronet Ochrin, to notice me."

The guard stiffened, though whether from her touch or her words, she didn't know.

"If you unhand me this instant," she said, her voice sharp, "I will forget that you had the gall to embarrass an Imperial noble by forcing her to reveal her womanly wiles."

She released the guard, and when he straightened, she held before his eyes a silver mark she'd pulled from within the heavy purse she carried as part of her Lady Dellacourt disguise.

"And there will be plenty more good coin to join those you are already receiving once I have the Baronet's affections," she said in a much softer tone.

The guard's eyes went a fraction wider. He needed only a moment to contemplate her offer, then his huge hand engulfed hers, plucking the coin from her fingers. Stuffing the silver into his pocket, he nodded.

"Of course, noble Lady." With a weak grin, he marched back to his post beside the door that led south toward Magister Onathus's shipyards.

Natisse made a show of smoothing down her skirts, straightening her hair, and wrestling her displeased expression under control—all for the guard's benefits. He'd be watching her, she knew. She'd have to be extra cautious to avoid doing anything that might arouse his suspicion.

The good news, however, was that he'd expect her to approach Magister Branthe's private box. What happened when she got there... well, he'd realize the truth too late to stop the inevitable.

A loud groan rippled through the crowd, followed a moment later by another resounding cheer. The throng of people found their seats once more, giving Natisse a clear view of the fighting pit.

Impossibly, Uncle Ronan still stood, though he bled from

three deep scratches along the left side of his face, a puncture wound to the left shoulder, and a cut to his leg on the same side. His opponents, however, were in far worse sorts, all sprawled out on the sands.

The twins' flails were embedded in their skulls, their faces mangled and crushed. The trident had been turned on its owner as well. He lay still on the sands, wrapped up in his own spiked net. The sword-and-shield-wielder lay in three pieces—shield arm hacked off at the shoulder, head removed from his neck. The last warrior, the giant with the cestus, still knelt before Uncle Ronan, the short sword buried to the hilt in his guts. Uncle Ronan stood empty-handed, chest heaving. Blood trickled from fresh wounds. He swayed, staggering a few feet forward and then back again. His back arched, hunching over and gripping what Natisse expected to be broken ribs. But his eyes blazed with a battle fire Natisse had rarely seen.

"Marvelous!" Magister Branthe was on his feet, applauding with a mocking smile. "Truly, the passage of years has not dulled your skills nor sapped your cunning, Andros!"

"Nor have they diminished your cowardice, Carritus!" Uncle Ronan snarled the name as a curse. "I would challenge you to join me on the sands, but we both know that you always preferred to let others do your killing for you."

"True." Magister Branthe inclined his head. "But perhaps that is why I am sitting up here, and you are down there, yes?"

Laughter rippled through the crowd. Natisse's anger blazed, but she kept a tight rein on her emotions. She would do Uncle Ronan no good losing her cool when she was so close. She had just another ten yards or so to cover before she reached the southern edge of Magister Branthe's box. Uncle Ronan just had to keep the crowd occupied for a few minutes more.

She drew out the last vial of alchemical fire, uncorked it, and began pouring its contents on the ground beneath the rearmost row of wooden benches. With her other hand, she plucked out her firestarter—a cleverly built contraption with a steel gear wheel that, when turned, would strike a spark against the incorporated flint—and prepared to set the blaze.

"And speaking of letting others do my killing," Magister Branthe said, "allow me to bring out your next and final opponent of the night."

The gate creaked open and the giant Joakim appeared once more, carrying a figure slung over his shoulder like a sack of potatoes. Joakim barely even noticed the weight of his burden, but strode with ease to the center of the pit. There, he dropped the figure to their knees in the sand. A hood had been thrown over the man's head—for a man it was, his bare back and chest a mess of angry welts from a lashing—and his wrists were bound at his waist.

"The rules of this fight are simple, Andros." Magister Branthe said, grinning down at Uncle Ronan. "Kill him, and you walk free."

Uncle Ronan stared up at Magister Branthe with naked contempt etched into his face. "Like you let that leper walk free?"

Boos and jeers rose from the crowd—aimed both at Magister Branthe and Uncle Ronan.

Magister Branthe raised a hand for quiet, but some continued. "A fair accusation," he said, inclining his head, trying his hardest not to let the disobedience of the crowd shake him. "Perhaps this will satisfy you, then." He placed his right hand over his heart. "I swear by my honor as a noble of the Karmian Empire and by my eternal soul that if you should win this fight, you will be permitted to walk away from this place unharmed."

Uncle Ronan scowled up at Magister Branthe, studying the aristocrat as if searching for any sign of deceit. Natisse had no faith that Magister Branthe would keep his word—the man was clearly disloyal to the Empire, or else he would never have enslaved its subjects for his own pleasure and enrichment. As for his eternal soul, Natisse suspected its potential loss in the afterlife would faze him not at all.

"And if I refuse?" Uncle Ronan snarled. "You'll set your pet boar to tear me limb from limb?" He swept a disdainful gesture toward Joakim.

Joakim bristled and bared crooked yellow teeth, his close-set eyes alight with cruel bloodlust.

"No," Magister Branthe said simply, ignoring the brute. "I will simply order my men to shoot you where you stand."

As if to emphasize his words, two crossbowmen appeared at the opening into the tunnel from which the prisoners had been dragged. Both leveled loaded weapons at Uncle Ronan's chest.

"So be it," Uncle Ronan said, his voice cold. "He will die first." He stabbed a finger up at Magister Branthe. "Then you will follow him, no matter how many bolts your men put in me."

Magister Branthe lifted his gaze to the crowd. "General Andros, ladies and gentlemen!" He was playing to his audience, and the noblemen and women loved it. They cheered, roared, stamped, and shouted.

Natisse struggled to maintain her calm. She didn't know what manner of enemy Magister Branthe would hurl at Uncle Ronan, but she knew he'd keep his fiercest warrior for the final bout. This was all a game to him, murder for the sake of entertainment and profit. He didn't care that people were dying—so long as his life wasn't in danger, there were no consequences for his actions.

Yet.

Natisse was close now, just three yards away. She could almost reach out and touch the wooden railing of Magister Branthe's box. Jad, too, was approaching opposite her. They'd hit Magister Branthe from both sides, moving so fast the aristocrat couldn't bring his dragon magic into the fight. He would die and Dimvein would be cleansed of House Branthe's taint. Then, Natisse would slit the Baronet's throat while everyone watched before they all turned and ran.

Slavery might still exist in the Karmian Empire, but tonight, it would take a nasty hit.

"But who shall face our mighty general?" Magister Branthe shouted to the crowd. "Who is worthy of fighting a foe of such renown?"

A cruel grin broadened his face, and he nodded to Joakim. The giant stooped, seized the hood, and pulled it off the head of the man kneeling at his feet. Natisse caught a glimpse of a young man, his face sharp but handsome.

Triumph blazed in Magister Branthe's eyes. "Who other than the fearsome Prince Jaylen, son of Emperor Wymarc himself?"

51

KULLEN

At that moment, the door to the study flew open and Captain Angban burst into the room.

"Apologies for the disturbance, Imperial Majesty," he said. "But I've just learned that Prince Jaylen rode out of the Palace this morning and have not been seen since."

Emperor Wymarc leaped to his feet. "Rode out?" he thundered. "To where?"

"Unclear." Captain Angban's face darkened, his eyes flitting away. "Lieutenant Dorrin at the gate just informed me that he left shortly before noon, in the company of his protective detail. But neither the Prince nor his assigned guards offered any explanation." He opened his mouth, but seemed to think better of whatever he'd intended to add.

"Speak, man!" the Emperor commanded. "What are you not telling me?"

Captain Angban winced. "Lieutenant Dorrin confided in me that he didn't recognize the Scales riding at the Prince's side. At the time, he considered nothing amiss, but—"

Emperor Wymarc ground his teeth. "Lieutenant Dorrin has no

need to fear reprisal," he said, his voice thick with barely restrained fury. "He was merely doing his duty. There was no reason to suspect anything was amiss. No one did."

"Thank you, Imperial Majesty." The tension in Captain Angban's posture relaxed a fraction. "I will immediately send word to Tuskigo Turoc and Commander Peridott. Within the hour, both the Imperial Scales and the Orkenwatch will be scouring—"

"No!" Emperor Wymarc cut the man off with a slash of his hand. "Word of this does not leave the Palace. Is that understood?"

Clearly it wasn't, for Captain Angban's face creased into a bewildered frown. "Majesty?"

"You heard me," Emperor Wymarc said. "Continue with your preparations, but make no mention of my grandson's absence until such a time as I tell you otherwise." He stepped closer, and though he was shorter than Angban, he seemed to loom over the captain. "Understood?"

"Yes, Majesty!" Captain Angban saluted, whirled on his heel, and marched from the room.

Emperor Wymarc didn't wait for the door to close. He spun toward Assidius. "Every asset and agent you have within Dimvein, get in touch with them and find out where he went. Now!"

"Of course, Divine Majesty," Assidius said. "But, as you know, these things take time—"

"Time Jaylen might not have," Kullen snapped.

Wymarc's face paled, suddenly appearing haggard and lined with age.

Captain Angban's report had set his mind racing, and a terrible thought had just occurred to him. If Magister Branthe had been responsible for the deaths of Jarius and Hadassa, he might very well repeat the assassination with Prince Jaylen. The unfamiliar Imperial Scales could've been Magister Branthe's soldiers in disguise. Jaylen had been so taken by the man earlier that it would've been nothing for the trusted aristocrat to slip his own people into position in the Palace and wait for the right moment to strike. That moment would come as soon as Prince Jaylen left the safety of the palace's walls and Thanagar's watchful eyes.

"Thanagar," Kullen said thoughtfully. Then again, more forcefully as his mind landed fully upon the idea. The Emperor eyed Kullen and a moment later, clarity passed over his features. "There's still hope, Majesty," Kullen insisted. "If Thanagar can locate the Prince—"

Emperor Wymarc's hand flashed toward the dragonblood vial at his neck and his eyes glazed over. For several long moments, silence brewed thickly, then he sucked in a sharp breath. "Thanagar's found him! He's somewhere in the northern city! His presence emanates weakly, as if from deep underground."

"The tunnels?" Assidius asked.

"Perhaps," the Emperor said. "To search them would take days —maybe weeks."

"The north?" Kullen said to himself aloud. Pieces began to fall into place. He spun toward Assidius. "You said you have credible reports of an underground slave fighting pit in The Embers? One linked to Magister Branthe?"

"Indeed." Assidius nodded. "My sources tell me—"

"It's beneath an abandoned factory beside the river?" Kullen finished.

"That's the one," Assidius said. "How did you..."

"Then that's where we'll find the Prince!" Kullen whirled toward the Emperor. "Magister Branthe wouldn't get his hands dirty killing Jaylen himself, just as he didn't directly involve himself in the attack on the Refuge, just as he's kept himself removed from all the plots against you. Above all, he's a General. He orders other men to spill blood for him. If he wants Jaylen dead, all he's got to do is drop him into that fighting pit and let someone else do the killing."

"Then we have to get to him!" Emperor Wymarc insisted. "I'll send the Captain and his Elite Scales, or Thanagar can—"

"No," Kullen shook his head. "Magister Branthe's smart enough to have people watching for any trouble. The moment they spot Palace men or Thanagar, they'll kill Jaylen—no doubt about it." He thumped his fist against his chest. "I'm your only hope, Majesty. I can get in and get to Jaylen without anyone knowing."

"Majesty," Assidius started, "you have an army. You cannot trust something so important to—"

"No. Kullen is right. And you will help him," Emperor Wymarc said, pointing to a seemingly empty wall. "Kullen, go. Now!"

"I need to get to the roof," Kullen said, looking to Assidius. "I need Umbris."

"Through here." Assidius was already moving toward a nearby wall. A panel in the wood wall slid back to reveal a dark passage with a circular staircase. "Take this. It leads directly to the upper-most flats where Thanagar rests. It is supposed to be used only when the Emperor's life is in danger. Though, now seems prudent. Go!"

Kullen raced up the stairs, taking them two or three at a time.

Emperor Wymarc's voice pursued him up the twisting stair-case. "For the love you bear me, and that you bore his parents, save my grandson!"

"Umbris, I have need of you," Kullen said in his mind before he even reached the top.

The staircase ended but Kullen saw no door. Even with his dragon-eyes, nothing stood out as an escape route.

"Above you," came a voice in his head that was not that of Umbris. *"The ceiling opens,"* Thanagar said.

Sure enough, Kullen stretched his hands up and gave the

ceiling a push. A panel cracked open, allowing the pale moonlight to illuminate the secret shaft. He pulled himself up onto the roof top and found himself staring directly into one massive ruby eye.

"I am here," Umbris said.

Kullen turned to see Umbris waiting on the other end of the space. He half expected Thanagar to snap out with his giant maw and swallow him whole, but Thanagar just blinked. Umbris bent as Kullen darted toward him and climbed onto the Twilight Dragon's back.

"Black Talon," Thanagar said, causing Kullen to stop and look to the Great White Dragon. *"Should you ever challenge me again, I will do just as you fear."*

With that, Thanagar swallowed hard and let out an exaggerated and satisfied breath of steamy air.

Kullen nodded, then gave Umbris a light tap on the neck. In a blaze of wind and fury, Umbris shot off like an arrow.

"The Western Docks," Kullen said. *"The same place we went two nights past."*

Kullen's heart thundered in his chest, adrenaline blazing through his veins. He'd never liked Prince Jaylen much—partly the Prince's fault, for certain, but Kullen couldn't truly blame the young man for being largely useless and clueless. After all, he had sheltered his entire life by his doting grandfather. But Jaylen was all Emperor Wymarc had left of his beloved son and daughter-in-law—and all Kullen had left of his best friends in the world.

All thoughts of the Prince, whether good or bad, were pointless. The only thing that matter was he couldn't let Jaylen die. He owed it to the Emperor and the memory of Jarius and Hadassa to protect their son.

The abandoned building came into view and Kullen urged Umbris upward. Once over the building, Kullen stood and dove, heading straight for the rooftop. He drew his hunting knives as he did so. The roof grew ever closer. Nearly upon it, he slid into the shadows becoming one with the Shadow Realm and drifting through the very hole he'd made only two days before.

He landed inside, crouched. Raising his hooded head, he immediately sprang into action, leaping toward the only two guards visible in the dilapidated piss-hole that served as a front for a bunch of too-rich-for-their-own-good pieces of shit who took pleasure in others' pain and death. One wore House Perech's colors while the other was garbed in unfamiliar jerkin. But both were armed and, judging by their presence here, complicit in everything Magister Branthe intended tonight.

Kullen's first attack was deflected, his hunting knife slapped down by a longsword. The impact sent reverberations coursing up his arm but he took the parry in stride, rolled, and rose so close to the first guard that the man didn't know how to respond. His right-hand hunting knife buried deep in the man's belly, then as the he folded over, Kullen used his other knife to open the throat of Magister Perech's guardsman.

One down. One remaining.

Spinning away from the fountaining blood, he darted close to the other and drove his left-hand blade up under the man's chin. Razor-sharp steel punched through the roof of the man's mouth and drove deep into his brain, killing him instantly.

Kullen tore his dagger free, then retrieved his other knife from House Perech's guard's abdomen. The corridor the men had been guarding led to a set of stairs that Kullen raced down at a full sprint. At the end of the hall, a door of solid steel barred his passage.

Cursing, Kullen slowed. He'd never be able to break through the door, and in the narrow confines of the underground hall, he couldn't summon Umbris for a repeat performance of the Refuge's chapel door. He racked his brain, urgency thrumming within him. The door had no keyhole he could see, no handle to open it from outside. Which meant it would be opened by someone within, as evidenced by the peephole set at eye level.

Stepping close, Kullen hammered the hilt of his left-hand dagger against the steel door, then dropped into a low crouch, beneath the view of the eyehole. Nothing happened. Long seconds passed, and all remained silent.

He banged again. If there was some sort of secret knocking code he didn't know, he could be alerting whoever was within that doorway to trouble without. It could be too late for Jaylen. The Prince might even now be—

The eyehole slid open with a clank of metal. Kullen froze, willing his thundering heart to beat quieter. Silence hung thick in the corridor, and for a moment, he feared he'd made a mistake.

"Ezrasil damn you, Emmyth!" came an angry voice from within. "You feckin' with me again? I told you last time, it ain't funny! Here I am stuck babysitting this damned stuffy room while you and Lyesh get to enjoy the fresh night air. And don't get me started on Dannol and Kyton. They get to watch the goddamn show. And now you pull this? Well, I promised I'd give you a thrashing, and so I will!"

A series of *clicks* and *clanks* informed Kullen that the door was about to open.

The instant it did, Kullen leaped to his feet and drove his boot into the door. The impact slammed the heavy steel into the face of the guard inside, sending the man crashing into the earthen wall behind him. Bone crunched and the man collapsed into a senseless heap on the floor.

Kullen entered, prepared for another guard or two, but found none. The room was barely four paces square, with three plain earthen walls and a chair and candle placed behind the steel door. For a moment, Kullen feared he'd reached the end of the road. But why? What good was an empty guarded room? Kullen knew the tunnels were rife with Orken-built secrets, as was the Palace, but he saw none of the telltale signs. Then he spotted the small brass ring, so well hidden it was almost invisible.

He slipped a finger into the ring and give it a tug. Sure enough, the stone wall cracked open, sending dust billowing into the air. Kullen fought the urge to cough, unsure if he was alone. He pulled the secret passage open. Shouts, cheers, and roars slammed into him like an invisible wall. His dragon-eyes lit the tunnel like noonday, but there was nothing special about it. Kullen pulled his cloak tight about him, hid the knives inside his sleeves, and hurried toward a light at the end. The tunnel turned and not far off, opened up into a massive chamber.

Arranged in a circle, men and women Kullen recognized as Magisters and their ladies sat, fixated on a sand pit in the center of the room. Three figures stood within. One, a greying, grizzled man bleeding from a half-dozen wounds, was in rough shape. He staggered, facing a behemoth wearing only a leather chest harness and breeches. The giant man had a whip dangling from his right hand, and in his shadow, a third, smaller figure stood. A tunnel on the far end—is gate was currently raised—was guarded by two men with crossbows leveled at the grizzled warrior in what could only be a fighting pit.

"General Andros, ladies and gentlemen!" Magister Branthe's voice echoed through the underground chamber. He stood above the raised gate on a skybox not dissimilar to the one at the Court of Justice. From there on his perch overlooking the fighting pit, a foppish young man his only companion, Branthe owned the crowd. They roared and cheered, hanging on ever word he spoke as if the man were Ezrasil himself.

"But who shall face our mighty general?" Magister Branthe shouted to the crowd. "Who is worthy of fighting a foe of such renown?"

The leather-clad giant seized the prisoner's hood, and yanked it off

Branthe was gloating still, but Kullen heard none of it. A chill descended over him—not fear, but burning, ice-cold fury. Prince Jaylen knelt in those sands, looking more pathetic than ever, snot and tears wetting his face. One look at the man leering down at the Prince, and Kullen had no doubt that Magister Branthe had orchestrated the deaths of Jarius and Hadassa. Everything he'd done had been to destabilize the Empire, weaken the Emperor's rule, and accumulate wealth and power for himself. With Prince Jaylen's death, Emperor Wymarc would have no heirs. It would be a simple matter to arrange the Emperor's demise—poison that killed him slowly and quietly—while Magister Branthe used his influence in the Palace, with the Scales, the military, the Orkenwatch, even. The nobility of Dimvein already suckled at his goddamn teat. The day the Emperor died, whether by man's hand or Ezrasil's himself, Magister Branthe would assume the crown.

A plan as cruel as it was cunning. Magister Branthe had spoken with the Emperor on a near-daily basis, had played the role of loyal friend and confidante, lying through his filthy teeth with every word.

For a heartbeat, Kullen was torn between conflicting desires. A single shadow-slide was all he'd need to get behind Magister Branthe unnoticed, within easy striking distance. Yet the crossbowmen and giant in the fighting pit wouldn't hesitate to kill Prince Jaylen the moment their master fell. Kullen wasn't willing to risk that the grizzled fighter facing off against the Prince wouldn't seize the opportunity to kill him, either. The man carried no weapons, but blood staining the sands around him made it clear he was a fierce fighter. He could probably—no, he could—kill Jaylen with his bare hands.

Despite Kullen's hatred for Magister Branthe, he knew he had just one choice. Sheathing his knives, he reached into his pockets for the alchemical smoke spheres.

"In the name of the Emperor, my grandfather," Prince Jaylen shouted as Kullen hurled the knuckle-sized orbs, "I order you to—"

But no one heard Jaylen's command. Kullen sprang forward and tore through the crowd even before the smoke pellets struck the stone floor. Glass shattered, and the twin *pops* of the sparking alchemical mixture drowned out Prince Jaylen's words.

A moment later, Kullen was hit by a wave of heat not usually caused by his tricks. He turned to see a brilliant and impossibly large pillar of emerald green alchemical flames bursting in a circuit around the room.

The chamber was on fire.

52

NATISSE

The chamber was on fire.

Natisse never saw what started the inferno. One moment her world was dark, the next everything was awash with blazing heat and brilliant green light. The alchemical fuel she'd been pouring on her trail caught alight so quickly, the wall of fire nearly engulfed her. Only a desperate backward leap had carried her out of the path of the flames.

Panic seized Natisse's mind in a fist of iron. Confronted by the blaze, the smell of scorched cloth and singed hair thick in her nostrils, she found herself falling, slipping back in time through her memories. The darkness of the underground fighting pit vanished, replaced by intense daylight and the glow of devouring fires all around her.

She cried out, recoiled from the flames, but she could find no escape. Fire burned everywhere, blocking her path to freedom. Her eyes latched onto the darkness beneath the only wagon not yet consumed.

"Go!" a man's voice shouted at her. "Under there!"

A hand shoved her, hard, to the floor, and she rolled under the wagon.

"Don't stop!" shouted the man. "Keep going, and whatever you do, Natisse, don't look back!"

The sound of her name sent Natisse reeling back to reality. It was the first time she'd heard it in her memories. Her father speaking her name...

Somehow, it was strangely comforting—there had been life, of a sort, before the fire. People who knew her. At least one person who cared that she escaped and survived.

Yet she had no time to dwell on that past. The fire was all around her once more, and fear pushed all other thoughts from her mind. Her breath came faster, sucking in great breaths of scorching hot air, and panic froze her in place. She stepped back, struck the wall, and could go no further. Again, there was no retreat from the flames!

It felt as if a boulder had been dropped on her chest. Her head was light, dizzy. She felt herself falling over. But then, through a gap in the flames, her blurred eyes caught sight of Uncle Ronan still inside the fighting pit, facing off against the enormous Joakim. The giant's whip was raised high over his head, ready to strike. Uncle Ronan had squared off, fists raised, yet he was bleeding heavily and his face betrayed the immense pain he was in after the beating he'd taken at the hands of his previous opponents. There was simply no way he could defeat Joakim in his current state.

In that moment, Natisse knew what she had to do. Though it took every shred of willpower, she slammed the door shut on her fear, untethered her mind from the paralyzing emotions rendering her helpless. She had no time to be afraid, no time for panic. Uncle Ronan would die without her.

Summoning her courage, Natisse shoved off the wall and sprinted along the wall of flame. The alchemical fuel burned hotter than dragonfire, searing hot even through the cloak Natisse held up to shield her face. Her ornate dress caught fire, the lace and frills consumed in the blaze. Her cloak, too, burned.

But she made it to the fire's edge, to where she hadn't yet poured the alchemical fuel. Only two yards separated the flames from the wooden railing of Magister Branthe's viewing box, but Natisse dove through that narrow opening and barreled down the rows of seats, past panicking noblemen and women.

She spared a single glance for Magister Branthe—the aristocrat stood transfixed and stupefied by the flames, as if unable to believe what he was seeing. Her hand dipped into her sleeve. Her fingers closed around the hilt of a throwing knife, and she hurled the weapon at Magister Branthe.

Yet there was no time to see if it struck home. She lurched for the fighting pit and leaped over the stone lip, dropping three yards to the sands below. Landing in a forward roll, diminishing the impact, she came to her feet smoothly. Her hand reached for the hidden opening in her dress, closing around another hilt.

But instead of a dagger, her hand whipped forward and snapped the lashblade at the giant's upraised arm. Razor-sharp steel carved a deep furrow into Joakim's bulging left biceps and tore into muscle. The giant roared in fury and pain, the whip fell from his fingers, and he staggered back, clutching his bleeding arm.

Natisse planted herself between Uncle Ronan and the giant.

"Run!" she shouted over her shoulder. "Get out of here before—"

Joakim moved, impossibly fast, leaping forward and throwing a vicious punch at her head. Natisse went down, hitting the ground hard. She rose slowly, spitting sand and blood. Standing, she barely managed to stagger out of the way of another blow, her heels dragging in the sand. Dizzy yet again, she whipped her blade. Her desperate slash carved a shallow wound across Joakim's left cheek, yet it did little to deter the giant. Joakim waded after her with blow after blow of his huge fists. His eyes gleamed with a terrible fire and his mouth bared in a feral smile of yellowed teeth. In that moment, Natisse had no doubt that he'd snap her in half or tear her apart the second he got his hands around her.

She took each blow, blocking with her forearms. Long shards of bone armor laced the interior of her long gloves, but each impact still hurt and caused her to stumble backward. She gave ground as fast as she could manage, but she was too close to the edge of the fighting pit and her back slammed against the wall, jarring her to the spine. She ducked a punch that would've shattered her skull, and Joakim's fist slammed into the stone wall. The giant howled and retreated, clutching his hand to his barrel chest.

Beyond the giant, Natisse caught sight of Uncle Ronan. He'd fallen to one knee, leaning heavily on the sands, his shoulders slumped. With one hand, he weakly attempted to remove the dampener around his neck. The two crossbowmen had taken aim at him and Prince Jaylen, but before they could lose, a huge figure clad in a long gold-trimmed black coat roared a challenge and barreled toward them. Jad tackled the two crossbowmen and the three of them hit the sands in a tangle of limbs.

That was all the attention Natisse could spare. Joakim had recovered and now waded back into the fray, his punches only fractionally less powerful but far more controlled. His right-handed blows lacked conviction, but backed by his enormous frame, Natisse had no doubt they'd break bones or knock her unconscious if she let her guard down. And they served as a vicious distraction for the wild swings of his left hand.

Natisse's lashblade was the only thing keeping the giant at bay. She wielded it in sword-form, its keen edge hungry for Joakim's bare flesh. The brute blocked her strikes with the metal-bound bracers armoring his enormous forearms, forcing her continually on the retreat.

Uncle Ronan's lessons pounded in her mind. Attack, advance, force your enemy always on the defensive! Yet she could not find an opening in Joakim's impossibly fast and powerful blows to strike back. It was all she could do to stay upright, but the giant pursued her, refusing to let her get far enough to lash out at him with the whip-form.

Natisse changed tactics. Instead of retreating from Joakim's next punch, she ducked and closed in on the giant, punching the lashblade's hilt into his stomach. It felt like striking stone, with just as much effect. Joakim's fists rose high above his head and he brought them crashing down toward her. She barely managed to backpedal to evade the next devastating blow, which would have crushed her skull or snapped her neck. She used Joakim's momentary imbalance to skip quickly backward and open two yards between them.

With a snarl, she brought the lashblade up and over her head, snapping it forward like a whip. The segmented steel snaked toward Joakim and tore a deep, ragged gash along the right side of his barrel chest and the inside of his right biceps. The giant tried to wrap the lashblade around his armored forearm to trap the weapon, but Natisse hauled back on the handle with every shred of strength she possessed. The blades slid free of Joakim's grip, ripping open the back of his hand as it recoiled.

Joakim snarled a curse and shook his injured hand, spraying crimson droplets onto the sand. He now bled from multiple wounds, but none were serious enough to slow him. Indeed, the pain only seemed to make him angrier. His eyes narrowed and his lip curled up into a sneer.

"Come on, little girl!" he roared, flexing his huge fists.

With those words, Natisse was violently wrenched from her fight and hurled into the past again. She was once again there on that day of the fire. But for the first time, she could see clearly.

Brilliant scarlet-and-gold flames consumed her world, tongues of blinding heat licking at her clothing, her flesh, ravaging the air in her lungs.

A man's face loomed in her vision. Brutish features, a flat face, sneering smile, and enormous arms stained with blood. His laughter echoed in time with a terrified scream. A woman's scream. A voice she knew so well.

Natisse tried to cry out, but couldn't. Thick smoke choked and blinded her. Clawing at the flames, desperate to escape, frantic in her efforts to get to the woman. To her mother.

A hand closed around her arm, dragged her backward.

"Natisse!" a voice shouted to her. "Run, Natisse! Now!"

Stumbling, half-falling as the man dragged her, Natisse turned toward her father. That face—green eyes, hair a fiery red like hers, a strong jaw and masculine chin—that had always been so calm and confident now filled with panic.

"Run, Natisse!" her father cried again. "Get away from here!"

Natisse cried out, recoiled from a wall of flames that sprang up in front of her. Fire burned everywhere, blocking her path to freedom. Her eyes latched onto the darkness beneath the only wagon not yet consumed.

"Go!" her father shouted at her. "Under there!"

A hand shoved her, hard, to the floor, and she rolled under the wagon.

"Don't stop!" shouted the man. "Keep going, and whatever you do, Natisse, don't look back!"

The woman's scream came again.

The man's head snapped toward the sound.

"Nyanna!" he shouted. "I'm co—"

Then the pillar of dazzling fire closed in on the man, and Natisse was swallowed in agony and death as the wagon collapsed atop her.

No, not atop her. She'd been rolling and scrambling toward the other side, as her father had instructed. The burning wagon had crumbled atop her, but only caught a part of her. Fire seared the flesh of her arm and shoulder. Natisse cried out but managed to pull herself clear of the wreckage.

Weeping from pain, fear, and sorrow, she ran, away from the fires, away from the shouting and shrieking. She ran until she reached the stones bordering the road, and continued on over the sharp, jagged rocks until the cool embrace of a forest enshrouded her. Only then did she dare to look behind her.

Her parents' wagon burned, as did those of every other merchant in their train. Fifty carts and carriages laden with food-stuffs, textiles, and valuables—everything they'd owned and managed to carry with them on their arduous journey toward Dimvein—was up in smoke.

The giant still held Natisse's mother, but Nyanna no longer moved. She dangled limp in the brute's hand, her face a hideous, lifeless purple, her eyes white as death. Of her father, Natisse saw no sign. He had died, consumed by the fire that ravaged the caravan.

As for the travelers with whom she and her family had shared the road, the survivors of the attack now stood surrounded by armed men wearing shining metal armor and cloaks of gold and silver—the colors of House Branthe.

"Come on, little girl!" came the flat-faced giant's shout from among the armored men. "There's no running from us! Don't make me come into the forest after you."

High above the giant's head, a powerful bronze dragon cut the air with broad sinewy wings. A man sat upon the beast's back, too small for Natisse to make out.

Yet she could feel his eyes—and those of the dragon—fixed on the forest around her. Natisse shrank into the trees, fearing being seen.

Then a red dragon—the one she now knew had caused the fire that'd taken her father's life—came swooping back around, circling in high, lazy arcs around the caravan, its gaping maw open as if preparing to disgorge more flames. The rider atop the red dragon's back shouted something Natisse couldn't hear to the man mounted on the bronze dragon, who gave an equally indis-cernible answer. Together, the two dragons turned away from the wreckage and flew off into the bright sun.

"Find her!" came the giant's roar. "Find her, or I'll strip the skin from your backs!"

Natisse didn't wait for the men to pursue her. She turned and ran—away from the burning caravan, away from the bodies of her parents, away from the horror that had shattered her life forever.

The breath caught in her throat.

But it wasn't just the pain of memory constricting her throat. She blinked, and suddenly she was back in the underground fighting pit. Her feet were off the ground, and she hung dangling in the grasp of the giant—the same giant who'd been there that day. The one who'd killed her mother, just as he was killing her now.

Joakim snarled something incoherent in her face, spraying spittle. Natisse tried to strike out at him with her lashblade, but found her wrist trapped in the giant's grasp. He'd taken advantage of her momentary stupor to lunge at her. Now, she would die—not in fire, but in the hands of her mother's murderer.

She kicked at Joakim, aiming for his groin, but her boot struck only his rock-hard belly. Joakim's smile grew and the menace burning in his eyes grew as bright as the fires consuming the underground chamber.

"You're a fool, little girl," he rumbled, his voice deeper and crueler than she remembered. The face, too, had changed, the evil etched forever into the lines around his mouth and eyes. Yet it was the same face, the same voice. There was no doubt about it.

Fear welled within her. The same fear she'd felt that day—which she'd all but forgotten, except in her dreams—came flooding back, threatening to paralyze her. She could no more save herself now than she'd been able to save her parents all those years ago. Now, she would join them in death, killed in the same manner as her mother.

Darkness encroached around the edges of her vision. Blood thudded in her ears.

No! a small voice screamed in the back of Natisse's mind. *This is not how you die!*

That voice, wherever it had come from, shattered the mounting fear. Natisse felt the cold calm washing over her, felt her mind slipping into that place where emotion had no hold on her.

She'd trained her entire life for this very moment, had spent countless hours working with Ammon, Baruch, Uncle Ronan, Garron, and Jad to sharpen her skills. Every day had been a trial of courage and determination. She'd faced a damned gnasher, a creature of nightmare, and survived. She'd nearly been paralyzed by fear then, too, just as she'd been all those years ago.

But she wasn't that terrified child any longer. She was Natisse of the Crimson Fang, warrior and killer. Joakim would not break her—not now, not ever.

She summoned the last of her strength and swung her legs up, wrapping them around Joakim's arm. Planting both feet against his shoulders and face, she shoved off with all the force of leg muscles. The kick shattered Joakim's nose, split his lip, and broke his grip on her throat.

Natisse fell to the sand, landing hard, the breath bursting from her lungs. Yet she fought to scramble to her feet, to regain control of her oxygen-starved body before Joakim came for her again.

And with a roar, he did. The giant reached out a massive hand toward her. He wanted to break her—she could see it in his eyes —and wouldn't stop until she lay shattered at his feet.

Suddenly, the hand reaching for her spun away, severed at the wrist. Natisse caught sight of a figure in a dark cloak, and her breath froze in her lungs.

She recognized this man too. Scruffy beard, hair about his shoulders, visible even beneath the hood.

How was he alive? She'd seen him fall overboard, dragged into the depths of the Blackwater Bay by Baruch—her friend's final gift to her.

And he'd just saved her life.

Joakim's agonized roar dragged her out of her surprise, and she scrambled to her feet, lurching away from the bleeding giant. Before the bastard could recover or pursue her, Natisse flung her lashblade out in a wild, desperate strike, but it punched home into the meat of his left shoulder. Bone snapped and muscle tore beneath the blow, and Joakim staggered backward.

Natisse pulled the lashblade back, whirled it once around her head, and sent it flying toward the giant again. Instead of carving its target, the lashblade snaked around Joakim's throat, segmented thongs of steel pressing into flesh.

The giant fumbled for the extended lashblade with his one remaining hand, no doubt intended to pull it from her grip, but Natisse didn't give him a chance.

"This is for my parents, you bastard!" she snarled, and hauled on the lashblade with all her might.

Joakim's head spun away in a violent spattering of blood. It landed on the sand a few yards away. The body stood there a moment as if unconvinced of what had just taken place before it finally collapsed.

The headless corpse of the man who'd plagued Natisse's nights rested at her feet.

It hadn't been her intention this evening, but her parents were finally avenged.

53

KULLEN

The sudden ferocity of the blaze sent Kullen into an unsteady lurch forward. He recoiled from the brilliant wall of emerald green fires in confusion. Alchemy, here? It certainly hadn't been his smoke pellets that started the fire.

But his bewilderment lasted only a moment. Shouts and screams erupted all around him as the noblemen and women registered the blaze. Instantly, what had just been orderly rows of bench seating descended into chaos, people rushing frantically about to escape the fire that encircled them. Someone crashed into Kullen, rebounding and collapsing against the benches, toppling over. The was a loud crack that might've been the man's skull, but Kullen didn't see it. The impact sent him stumbling backward to collide with a woman whose ornate hairstyle and elaborate dress were in a state of utter disarray. Kullen caught them both before falling, but quickly spun away from the terrified noblewoman. He didn't care if she survived the fire—his one priority was Prince Jaylen.

His eyes locked on the prince, who still stood proud and tall, shouting his defiance up at Magister Branthe, seeming not to notice the fire consuming the world behind him. The two crossbowmen still held their weapons trained on the older man in the center of the ring, but Kullen knew that they could swing toward the prince at any moment.

Gritting his teeth, he shouldered his way through the throng of panicking aristocrats. He was jostled and jarred from all sides, and he had to fight to keep his balance. Barely ten yards and six steps separated him from the fighting pit's perimeter, but it seemed to take an eternity to cross that distance through the mass of terrified fops.

Finally, he pushed free of the crowd and hurled himself over the lip, dropping onto the sand. His eyes quickly registered all they could: Magister Branthe standing in his box, shouting incoherent fury to his guards, a young man beside him, panicking, the two crossbowmen suddenly on their backs, buried beneath a snarling, roaring brute raining vicious punches onto the pair. Prince Jaylen stood stunned in the center of the ring, and the gray-haired, bleeding man who'd been set to kill him had fallen to one knee, pale-faced and visibly in pain from his wounds. The bare-chested giant who'd dared to lay hands on Prince Jaylen was now locked in battle with a red-haired noblewoman in an elegant black dress.

Surprise jarred Kullen to the core, so much so that he hit the sands at the wrong angle and fell hard. He managed to tuck into a haphazard roll that reduced the impact on his aching shoulder and knees. Even as vaulted to his feet, he sought out the black-garbed woman.

"Ezrasil's bloody bastard," he swore at the sight of the assassin he'd locked blades with at Magister Perech's party. She was Perech's killer, no doubt about it—the same red hair, the same strange whip-like weapon that had come so damned close to killing him. And even in the haze of the moment, he was sure there was no other woman in Dimvein so beautiful who fought so well.

His mind raced. What was she doing here?

A roar from his left brought him whirling around. Two guards wearing the House Perech's colors barreled down the stairs and into the fighting pit with swords raised, their eyes fixed on Prince Jaylen and the grizzled fighter kneeling in the sand. Kullen had no idea which of the two they intended to kill—and he didn't want a chance to find out.

His hands darted inside his cloak, closing around the hilts of his hunting knives. He intercepted the onrushing guards before they'd taken three steps. His daggers flashed out, severing a throat, opening a guardsman's forearm, slicing deep into an inner thigh. The first of the two fell with a gurgling, gasping croak, jugular vein ruptured and spewing. The second wailed, dropped his sword, and collapsed to the sand. Kullen kicked the wounded man in the face before turning away—the bastard would bleed out in a matter of seconds.

Sheathing his right-hand hunting knife, Kullen scooped up the fallen guard's sword and raced toward Prince Jaylen. The young man stood, rooted in place by shock and surprise. His eyes were huge and round, and his face was only fractionally less deathly in tone than the wounded man kneeling not three paces away.

Before he could reach the prince, the flat-faced giant stumbled nearly into his path, forcing Kullen to leap backward to avoid being crushed. The brute was bleeding from his nose and throat, but his eyes burned with a cruel intensity. Two huge hands reached out toward the red-haired woman, who now lay gasping in the sand a few paces away. She was trying to climb to her feet, but she appeared dazed and confused. She'd be too slow, he knew.

For some reason he couldn't understand, he changed course— just a fraction, just enough to carry him within striking range of the giant. His sword flashed, hacking cleanly through the brute's wrist. Kullen's charge carried him past the man before his bellowing shrieks exploded like dragonfire. In five steps, Kullen stood next to Prince Jaylen.

"My Prince!" he shouted to get the young man's attention. "Come with me, now!"

Jaylen gawped at him, mouth agape and jaw slack.

Kullen fought the urge to slap the young man. Instead, he thrust the hilt of his stolen sword into Jaylen's chest, hard enough to stagger the prince. "Take this. Anyone comes close, you kill them quick and clean. Got it?"

That seemed to snap Prince Jaylen out of it. His hands fumbled until, finally, he managed to grip the hilt.

"K-Kullen?" he stammered. "What are you—"

"Saving your ass!" Kullen snapped.

He passed the dagger to his right hand, seized Prince Jaylen's cloak in his left, and set about dragging the young man toward the stairs that ascended from the fighting pit. Magister Branthe's box hadn't yet caught alight, though guards were rushing to protect their master.

A roar of rage ripped through the fighting pit, and Kullen spun to see the big man in the black coat barreling toward him. A berserker light shone in the man's eyes, and his fists and face were spattered with the blood of the crossbowmen he'd just pummeled to death.

Kullen threw himself into the man's path, dagger coming up in a low thrust that would eviscerate his enemy before he could launch a blow of his massive fists. But, to Kullen's surprise, the man evaded his attack with surprising agility.

No, Kullen realized a second later, he hadn't dodged. He'd simply angled past Kullen rather than charging directly at him. Spinning, Kullen found the big man wrapping an arm almost tenderly around the wounded, graying man. With a motherly care that seemed so strangely at odds with the hulk's enormous size, he helped his bleeding friend to rise.

Kullen had no time to contemplate his good fortune. More guards stormed down the stairs into the fighting pit—nearly a dozen of them, all wearing either orange and mauve or blue and green. Some carried drawn swords, and others clubs. But they were all armed, and all ready to fight.

Half of them leveled their attacks on Kullen and Prince Jaylen. The other half split off to engage the other three still occupying the fighting pit. The red-haired woman leaped into the fight with that strange whip-sword of hers flying in all directions. The black-coated brute snatched up a pair of cestuses that had fallen to the sand—doubtless in a previous fight—and waded into the guards with ferocious punches.

Blood flowed like wine from that serrated whip and Kullen was relieved to not be facing her again. Instead, he drew his second hunting knife and braced to meet the attack, but suddenly, Prince Jaylen was at his left side.

"Damn it, Jaylen, get back!" Kullen shouted.

"I can fight too, you know!" Jaylen protested, twirling his sword before bringing it up into a defensive guard.

Kullen had to admit, Swordmaster Kynneth would've been proud—if for no other reason but the prince's bravery in the face of unfair odds. Before Kullen could argue further, the guards were upon them, and his mind was occupied solely with dealing death.

He spun, dipped, slashed, and hacked like a twisting sand-storm, his blades darting in and out with speed that not even a well-trained Imperial Scale could withstand. Prince Jaylen, too, fought with surprising skill. His sword moved slower than Kullen's blades, but it still formed a solid wall of steel to guard Kullen's left flank. Three guards died in the initial clash, and Kullen killed the fourth a moment later.

The last two, however, proved far from incompetent. Unlike their comrades, they didn't rush Kullen or the Prince like stam-peding aurochs, but took their time, circling like pit-fighters accustomed to the sands. Kullen spotted a military tattoo on the forearm of the man facing off against him, and suspected the guard attacking Prince Jaylen bore one as well. More of the former soldiers loyal to Magister Branthe.

His opponent lunged in, swiping with his sword, forcing Kullen back a step. Kullen deflected the next attack, parried a follow-up, and tried to counter with a quick stab of his hunting knife. The sellsword was clearly expecting it and stepped back, out of range of Kullen's shorter blades. A slashing strike at Kullen's head covered his retreat, buying him a moment to re-center himself and regain his composure.

Kullen gritted his teeth. This one wouldn't be easy.

A cry sounded from behind him, and Kullen's head instinctively snapped toward the Prince. Blood leaked from Jaylen's left arm and he staggered back, barely holding off his enemy's sword.

That moment of inattention cost Kullen dearly. Pain flashed through his side, the sellsword's thrust biting deep into the flesh of his torso. Instinctively, Kullen twisted his upper body to keep the sword from carving through anything vital. What followed was a vicious tearing of flesh and a ripping of cloth as the blade pulled free. His cloak—the last gift from Prince Jarius—hung in tatters.

Unexpectedly, Branthe's hired blade faltered, blood streaming from a tear in the side of his neck. So stunned was Kullen that his mind barely registered the flicker of steel recoiling from the attack.

The red-haired woman pulled back her whip-sword, its tip red with blood. For a moment, their eyes locked. Hers showed equal parts hatred and gratitude. Kullen gave her a nod of silent thanks, but his muscles coiled in anticipation of an attack. After what he'd done to her friend on the boat, she had good cause to want him dead.

"My debt is paid," the woman said, then raced past Kullen toward the big black-coated man and the prisoner they'd rescued.

The fire was growing all around them, closing in, and the smell had become overwhelming, burning his lungs.

Another cry echoed behind Kullen, sending his heart leaping into his throat. He spun back toward the Prince. To his relief, he found the young man had gotten the better of his opponent and driven his sword into the sellsword's chest. Jaylen seemed stunned at the sight of a man dying in front of him. He stood, frozen, staring into the wide eyes looking back at his, until the life drained away and his enemy slumped to the sand.

"Branthe!" Kullen shouted, but even as he glanced up, he found the aristocrat attempting to flee, surrounded by his armed men. The idea of letting that traitorous piece of shit flee made him sick, but at the moment, Kullen had bigger problems.

More men raced down the stairs. Kullen met the first before his boot touched the sand, driving both daggers to the hilt in the guardsman's neck. His fallen body clogged the narrow staircase—Kullen knew it would buy them a few seconds, but that had to be enough.

He turned from the onrushing guards, raced back toward Prince Jaylen, and seized the young man by the collar.

"We need to go, now!" he roared.

"Where?" Jaylen asked. "There's no way out!"

Sure enough, the Prince was right. Alchemical fire consumed everything except Branthe's box. The heat was brutal, burning through all available oxygen, the smoke and fumes suffocating.

Had it just been him alone, he could have used Umbris's magic to shadow-slide toward the patch of darkness behind Magister Branthe's box. He'd be within striking range of the treacherous Magister and have a straight shot toward a way out.

But not with Jaylen to protect. He'd never tried shadow-sliding with someone else—didn't know if such a thing were even possible. He'd used the Shadow Realm's magic already a few times, he would only have a few more left in him before needing to rest. What if having an additional person drained him even quicker? He couldn't risk getting the prince stuck with him beyond the walls of darkness. Furthermore, he needed to save his strength. He had to keep Jaylen alive.

"We've gotta—" he coughed, "—fight."

Kullen knew Jaylen was frightened but a sense of pride welled in his chest when the prince said, "For my parents."

"For your parents," Kullen agreed and then went to work like a surgeon with his blades.

54

NATISSE

N atisse didn't know why the dark-cloaked man had saved her—or why she'd saved him in return. She ought to have cut him down where he stood, after what he'd done to Baruch.

But much as she wished him dead, now wasn't the time to entertain such desires. He would not die easily; the bastard had faced off against the four of them aboard the boat, and might very well have walked away if not for Baruch's sacrifice. The fact that he stood here in front of her offered proof that he was no ordinary man. At the very least, he'd been well trained.

She could fight him—and, she gave herself decent odds of winning that battle, given that he wielded only long daggers—but that clash would cost precious time. More guards already raced down the steps and flooded into the pit, intent on killing the five people left standing on the bloody sands. She couldn't take them all on alone. Her main focus had to be getting Uncle Ronan out of here and to a healer before he bled out.

Leaving the man in the dark cloak alive would buy herself, Jad, and Uncle Ronan a chance to escape. At the very least, he'd split the guards' focus. If he could kill off a few, all the better.

Her eyes bored into his, imprinting his face into her mind.

I will see you again, she vowed silently, *and when I do, you will not walk away alive!*

But out loud, she said, "My debt is paid," returned his nod and raced past him to where Jad was helping Uncle Ronan to stand.

And that's how she wanted it. She would owe him nothing when the time came to slit his throat.

"Come on!" she shouted as she ran. "We need to get him out of here."

"Working on it," Jad grunted. He may've been huge, but Uncle Ronan was tall and solidly built enough to weigh even on the bigger man. The flow of blood seeping from his wounds left him weak, forced him to lean on Jad for support.

Natisse reached Uncle Ronan's side and slung his right arm over her left shoulder, leaving her right hand free to defend them with the lashblade. She wouldn't be able to wield it in whip-form, but she was still damned good with a sword after all those years spent training with Ammon and Baruch.

She and Jad set about dragging Uncle Ronan toward the staircase that led out of the fighting pit, only to find themselves facing a mass of guards rushing down in their direction. Natisse cursed and glanced over her shoulder. The far wall of the pit was sheer and towered nearly twice her height—no way out there.

A roar brought her attention swiveling around to the guards in front of her. The dark-cloaked man leaped, daggers weaving a deadly wall of steel that cut through the onrushing guardsmen like a scythe through wheat. The pale-faced Prince Jaylen hovered in his wake, looking utterly useless despite the sword clutched in his shaking hands.

Natisse dropped Uncle Ronan's arm and prepared to join the dark-cloaked man in battle. He'd need help putting these dogs down, and they'd have to fight to carve a path clear of the fighting pit.

"No!" A hand gripped Natisse's shoulder. She spun to see

Uncle Ronan staring at her, face drawn in pain but eyes resolute. "We can't leave yet. Not until we've freed the captives."

Natisse opened her mouth to retort, but Uncle Ronan drove on.

"This is why we're here!" he insisted. "This is why I allowed myself to get captured, so I could gain access to this place and find out what's really going on."

The word struck Natisse like a blow to the gut. He'd allowed himself to get—

"You knew I'd find your coat!" she said.

"If anyone would," his eyes fixed on hers, his expression deadly earnest, "I knew it would be you. I knew you'd put the pieces together. I couldn't let you—" His eyes lifted to Jad's face. "—any of you, risk yourselves any more. But it worked, Natisse! I found them." He jabbed a bloody finger toward the rusty grate. "All of the slaves, every last one of the people Magister Branthe and his underlings have been smuggling into Dimvein, they're in there!"

Natisse's bright blue eyes were drawn to the dark stone mouth. Beyond the still-open gate, she caught sight of two flickering torches illuminating a roughhewn stone chamber filled with iron cells. For the first time, she saw the people locked behind the bars—men, women, even children—peering at her with hollow eyes and terrified expressions.

Natisse wanted to argue. Uncle Ronan was in no condition to fight, and further fighting would be inevitable even if they left at that very moment. But she knew he was right. Everything they'd done had been about liberating the captives. It was the mission that drove the Crimson Fang, the bedrock that served as the foundation for every theft and assassination they'd carried out.

Gritting her teeth, she nodded to Jad. "He's right. The mission above all."

But Jad was already moving, slipping out from beneath Uncle Ronan's arm and charging toward the gated tunnel with a furious roar. Natisse caught Uncle Ronan as he swayed, and by the time she had him steady on her shoulder, the sound of Jad's shouts and the clash of steel echoed from within as Jad tore into the men who'd stupidly remained behind to guard the prisoners.

"Come on," Natisse said, adjusting her grip on Uncle Ronan's arm. "Let's get in there and help him."

"Wait!" Uncle Ronan's voice was tight with pain, yet rang with iron. "I need a sword." He knelt, slowly, to retrieve a blade dropped by one of the guards.

Natisse was about to help him stand when something caught her eye. A strangely soft, warm glow emanated from a hollow in the sand. Frowning, Natisse moved closer. It was a vial, and her eyes flew wide as she recognized what it was.

Gryphic elixir!

She bent and snatched up the vial, then spotted the pouch from which it had fallen. She had no idea where it had come from —one of the guards, perhaps, or the man in the dark cloak?—but didn't question her good fortune. She scooped up the healing draught. Another vial had fallen from the pouch, lying a hand's breadth away. This one was far more ornate, with a cap of purest gold and made from a glass that appeared as delicate as crystal. Within was a deep, red liquid that looked almost like blood.

Without hesitation, she scooped up the second vial. She might not know its purpose, but she could always ask Serrod about it. If nothing else, the gold cap would fetch a hefty price—enough to keep the Crimson Fang fed for a few weeks.

She stuffed the crimson-filled vial into her pocket and spun back toward Uncle Ronan.

"Look!" She held out the elixir. "Take it, drink."

Uncle Ronan's lips parted. He stared without words for a brief moment. He didn't question, simply popped the cork and drained half the vial in a single pull.

Immediately, wounds his body over began to heal, new skin being formed. The blood remained, however, staining his whole form.

Uncle Ronan straightened, the color returning to his face, his vigor renewed.

"Let's go," he said, waving his sword toward the prisoners. "Jad might need our help."

Natisse was already running. She spared a glance for the dark-cloaked man and Prince Jaylen, who were halfway up the stairs. The former hacked and sliced his way through the oncoming guards. The latter stumbled up the bloody stairs in his wake. Natisse couldn't help admiring the assassin's skills. He was a damned fine fighter, even armed with nothing more than just daggers.

Within the tunnel was a scene of blood and chaos far beyond anything she could have imagined. The corpses of the fighters who'd died in the pit lay unceremoniously heaped on a two-wheeled pushcart, their blood staining the wood and leaking down to puddle on the stone floor beneath. Theirs weren't the only bodies, either. Four more guards lay dead, skulls crushed, chests stoved in, faces pulped, and limbs smashed. In the circular antechamber in front of the cells, Jad drove vicious blows into the last two guards standing. The spiked cestuses on his fists ripped through flesh and fabric with terrible ease, raking the men's faces, arms, and denting their leather breastplates.

Jad finished the pair off before Natisse closed within striking range. His left fist hammered a straight jab into one's chin, snapping his head back and opening another gouge around his mouth. A savage haymaker punch shattered his neck and caved in the side of his head. Jad spun with the momentum of the blow and backhanded the other man straight in the face, sending the guard hurling backward to crash into a stone pillar. The stone and his skull gave a sickening wet crunch and he slumped, buried beneath the rubble, dead before he hit the ground.

Natisse recognized the man's face—or what was left of it. It was the guard she'd marked as Rat Face. Next to him lay Droopy Eyes, and Four Teeth was one of the corpses littering the path of

Jad's destruction. She felt no trace of pity for the dead guardsmen whatsoever. Their complicity had earned their bloody ending. They'd gotten exactly what they deserved for their role in this cruelty.

Above, the ceiling started to give way. Stone and dirt flaking off and peppering the ground.

"Shit," Natisse swore. "We've got to go!"

Jad and Uncle Ronan were hard at work. Jad tore cell doors from their hinges and bent bars, while Uncle Ronan, fully recovered from most of his minor wounds, aided the prisoners in finding their way out.

The prisoners stampeded a guard who'd just appeared at the entry to the cave, many of them stopping to deliver damaging kicks and blows.

Natisse went for the final cage. Large cracks in the ceiling told of the danger preparing to befall them.

The rusty cages looked like they could've held dogs or aurochs but not humans. Bones, whether from leftover food scraps or previous prisoners sat piled in one corner, shit and puddles of piss in another.

She stopped cold as she laid eyes on the prisoners within. These were no ordinary captives. Not random men, women, nor children rounded up from around the Karmian Empire. These had sallow and leathery skin, sharp teeth, black eyes and pointed ears. They were...

"They're Orken," Uncle Ronan said from behind her as Jad bent the bars to allow a woman and her two children to escape. "And yet not."

Natisse stood there, motionless, speechless, until she felt a hard clump of dirt pelt her on the shoulder.

"Get out of there!" Jad cried from the tunnel's entrance.

And as he did, the ceiling began to give way.

55

KULLEN

Kullen barely had time to leap out of the way before a charging throng of ragged-looking prisoners swept over the last of the guards barring his path. He'd fought his way to the top of the stairs, cutting down the enemies attempting to impede his escape, and now he dragged Jaylen clear of the mob stampeding up behind him. He stood aside and watched with cold satisfaction as the guards were trampled beneath the furious crowd. Judging by their torn and bloodied clothing, gaunt frames, and hollow faces, they had endured far worse than just captivity at the hands of Magister Branthe's conspirators. Now, the freed slaves—Imperial citizens locked in cages like animals—unleashed their rage on those who had enslaved them.

Except their true target was escaping.

Kullen scanned the crowd of jostling, screaming, panicking aristocrats still visible in the underground chamber. The alchemical flames had all but died, save for a few of the wooden benches still burning, but smoke thickened the air in a grim haze. Fully half of the spectators who had only minutes earlier been seated to watch the fight were now dead—trampled by their fellows or consumed by the fire that had seemingly sprung up out of nowhere. The rest were pushing and shoving their way toward an open doorway on the southern end of the chamber.

Magister Branthe, however, was escaping out another door on the room's northern wall. He had already run twenty yards up the stone tunnel that led away from the chaos. Six guards hustled him and the young man who'd been seated with him along the corridor, while six more held back the panicking crowd, shoving them aside or swinging swords at the frightened men and women trying to follow Magister Branthe's path of escape.

Anger bubbled deep within Kullen's chest. The thought that Magister Branthe would escape rankled, but he had no choice but to let the man flee. He couldn't risk Prince Jaylen's life trying to fight his way through those swordsmen. He'd have to hunt down Magister Branthe later. The Emperor's justice—or vengeance—could wait until after Jaylen was safely away.

"Let's go!" Kullen shouted, grasping the prince's arm. They waded into the thinning stream of people attempting to break free of the smoke-and-fire-choked room. "We've got to get you—"

"Wait!" Jaylen protested. He tried to pull his arm free, but Kullen held him in a grip of iron. So the prince tugged until Kullen stopped and glanced back. "He has Tempest. He has my vial!"

Kullen's blood ran cold. For the first time, he noticed the Prince's bony chest, visible beneath his torn shirt. The gold necklace that had once belonged to Jarius was gone, and with it, the dragonblood vial that had been passed down to Jaylen after his father's death.

For a moment, indecision rooted Kullen in place. But only a moment.

"Go!" He gestured with his bloody dagger toward the door through which the rest of the noblemen were stampeding. "Get out with the rest of them. Find somewhere safe to hunker down."

He'd almost commanded the Prince to find the nearest Orkenwatch or Imperial Scales patrol and get them to drag his ass back to his grandfather, but thought better of it. Truth was, Kullen no longer knew who he could trust. He could very well have been delivering the boy right into the waiting hands of the enemy.

"But Tempest—" Jaylen began.

"I'll go after the vial!" Kullen cut him off, fixing the young man with a look that brooked no argument, one he'd seen on Emperor Wymarc's face a thousand times. "I'll get Tempest back and bring him to the Palace."

Jaylen opened his mouth to protest, but Kullen shoved him hard.

"Go! That's an order."

The prince had no chance to argue even if he wanted to. A mob of magisters and their frazzled ladies swept him up on their way toward the exit. Kullen hoped Jaylen had the good sense enough to do as he was told—he might not be the prince's Imperial grandfather, but in a situation like this, he was as close as it got to Jaylen's protector. Jaylen was headstrong and brash, but not stupid.

"I won't be long," Kullen said although the prince could no longer hear him, and he hoped it was true.

Suddenly, the ground shook and a terrible rumble pierced the air. Kullen spun. The grated tunnel where the prisoners had just been was caving in, sending waves of dust and sand billowing outward. It would only be a matter of time before the rest of this chamber was buried and the streets above collapsed.

There was no time to worry about who may or may not've escaped. Kullen had to catch up with Magister Branthe before the old bastard went into hiding.

He kept his head down and his shoulders hunched as he waded through the press of people between him and the six armed and armored men barring his path. The guards were too busy shoving away the shouting, clamoring nobility to see him in his dark cloak until it was too late. He dropped to one knee and hacked at the exposed shins of the foremost guards. The men fell with a cry, and Kullen leaped over them to strike out at the pair next in line. His sudden appearance caught most of them by surprise, and they didn't even mount a defense before his hunting knives found their throats.

Even as the dying guards slipped off his bloody blades to collapse to the tunnel's stone floor, the last two men came for him, swords flashing in the lantern light. Kullen ducked beneath a strike aimed at his neck, twisted out of the path of a stab intended to open his belly, and extended his right arm into a neat thrust that buried four inches of steel into a guard's eye. His left-hand hunting knife came up to parry the follow-up slash from the last surviving guard, and, releasing his grip on his right-hand blade, drove a vicious punch into the man's throat. Cartilage crunched beneath the blow and the man collapsed, gagging and choking.

Kullen stooped, seized his hunting knife, and ripped it from the dead guard's eye socket. It pulled free plastered with bits of eye, brain, and nerves dangling off the tip. A contemptuous flick cleaned the blade, sent the eyeball spinning away. Without hesitation, Kullen raced after the guards hurrying Magister Branthe toward his freedom.

Had it been anyone else, he might have remained silent, might have kept the element of surprise. But the sight of Magister Branthe fleeing enraged him. The murderous, vile bastard deserved to know fear in the last few minutes left alive to him—fear that would follow him forever into Shekoth's deepest, darkest pits.

"Branthe!" Kullen's roar reverberating off the tunnel's stone walls, floor, and ceiling with the force of a thunderclap. "For your treason against the Emperor, you die tonight!"

Even as he spoke, his hands were moving toward a hidden pocket in his cloak, reaching for the last glass orb remaining. He hurled it with every shred of strength, and it shattered against the floor at Magister Branthe's feet as the aristocrat and his guards glanced back toward the oncoming threat.

The sparking *crack* and sudden puff of noxious smoke filled the air. Two more rushing guards crashed into each other and went down, only to be trampled by a pair racing along behind them. Magister Branthe tripped over the piled bodies and tumbled gracelessly head over heels. The last of his newcomers managed to evade their fallen comrades, but caught a face full of the foul smoke. Instantly, they began to cough, horrible, hacking coughs that had them staggering. Tears streamed from their reddened eyes and the pair fell retching to their hands and knees.

Kullen drew in a deep breath and, as he charged toward the pillar of smoke, swept his shredded cloak up to cover his own face. He dared not close his eyes for fear he'd collide with one of the guards or Magister Branthe, but braced himself for the sting.

When he reached the cloud of alchemical smoke, it felt as if two torches had been jammed into his eye sockets. Flames burned from within, tears poured, his mouth filled with saliva though it felt like acid searing his throat as he swallowed. He knew from past experiences that the effects wouldn't be long lasting nor would they have permanent repercussions, but that didn't help at the moment.

He put his head down and barreled through, his speed carrying him to the other side in only a handful of steps. Relief came when he entered the close, stale air of the tunnel beyond.

One of the guards was down, unconscious, and the other who'd fallen with him cried out at the pain of a shattered forearm. Sharp edges of bone jutted through torn skin—he was well and truly out of the fray for the moment. The guards who'd taken the brunt of the smoke still heaved and vomited, in no condition to fight. However, the two who'd trampled their fallen comrades were still on their feet and dragging a teetering Magister Branthe away. The aristocrat frantically pawed at his cloak, as if reaching for his dragonblood vial, but the guards' grip on his arms hampered his efforts.

Kullen had to hope it would stay that way. The power of Isaxx, Magister Branthe's bronze dragon, was truly devastating. One burst of the magically generated acid could kill Kullen where he stood. The blast would spatter the six guards in their immediate vicinity in the process, but Kullen suspected the aristocrat wouldn't mind. Anyone who could be so callous with human lives —Prince Jarius and Princess Hadassa, Prince Jaylen, and all the others he'd been responsible for killing in this fighting pit— wouldn't hesitate to kill others to save his own ass.

Kullen had no intention of letting the aristocrat use his dragonblood magic. He caught up to the fleeing men in three quick steps and buried his dagger into Branthe's spine, just below his shoulders. The knife slipped between the bones, cleaving through muscle on its way to slicing the spinal cord. Kullen could feel it stealing the man's life.

"You deserve a slow death," Kullen whispered.

Instantly, Magister Branthe flopped like a puppet with its strings severed. His guards were almost dragged down beneath the dead weight of his limp body. The sudden change of weight threw them off-balance long enough for Kullen to open the jugular of the man to his right. The last guard standing tried to bring his sword to bear, but Kullen was inside his guard, his fist rising in an uppercut that crashed into the man's jaw. The impact snapped the guard's head backward and he slammed into the tunnel's stone wall, then slumped to the ground unconscious.

Kullen glanced back. The man with the broken arm was still down, cradling the injured limb to his chest. The two who'd been coughing moments earlier had now joined their senseless comrade, lying face-down in their own vomit. No one would stand between him and Magister Branthe now.

Kneeling, Kullen slid his dagger free of Magister Branthe's neck slowly, cruelly. Magister Branthe gave a weak, strangled cry, but he was powerless to do anything. The damage to his spinal cord had been done.

Kullen gripped Magister Branthe's shoulder and pulled him roughly onto his back. Arms, legs, they no longer functioned, but Branthe wielded his eyes like weapons, fixing Kullen with a look that blazed hatred as bright as a Lumenator's globe.

"You!" spat Magister Branthe. "I always knew there was more to you than just the Prince's companion." His mouth twisted into a snarl. "I should have had you killed years ago."

Kullen grinned down at the man. "A mistake you will not live to regret, my lord." He held up the dagger, still stained with Magister Branthe's blood, in front of the aristocrat's eyes. "Or, perhaps, a mistake you will regret for the rest of your long, miserable days."

Magister Branthe's eyes widened. "What?"

Kullen's smile turned evil. "The damage to your spine. It's not fatal." He tapped the side of his own neck. "The wound is low enough to render your limbs useless, but the nerves that control your organs will continue functioning for years to come." He leaned closer, until his blood-flecked face hovered a foot above the aristocrat's. "The Emperor knows of your treachery. He will personally ensure that you live for decades still. I will personally see to it that every physicker, chirurgeon, and alchemist in the Emperor's service employs their skills toward keeping you alive. Alive, trapped inside your body, to spend the rest of your days like this."

Try as he might to hide it, utter horror streaked across Branthe's features. In that moment, he seemed older than ever. He struggled to breathe.

"You can't," he said, the words barely escaping.

He might've been a coward, liar, and traitor, but he'd also been a soldier once, a man of action and battle. This was a man who still wore a sword, donned his general's armor at every occasion of ceremony, and had not let his muscle go fully to fat despite his age. For him, there were worse things than death.

A fact Kullen had counted on to loosen the treacherous bastard's tongue.

"Despite your treachery," he said slowly, letting the words drag out, "I am not without mercy. I offer you a quick death, in exchange for answers."

"Answers?" Magister Branthe's expression grew hard, but Kullen saw the calculating look in his eyes.

"I understand you are a feckless craven," Kullen began. Branthe went to speak and Kullen sliced the Magister's ear, taking the lobe cleanly off. "Be silent. I talk now. You listen—or I'll make it so you can no longer do so. Understood?"

Branthe nodded.

Above, the tunnel threatened to cave in like the other one had, dust coming down in sheets.

"You are a coward, but why a *traitor*, too? I want to know the reason behind your treachery."

"That's all?" Branthe asked.

"To begin with," Kullen said, inclining his head.

"It's no great secret," Magister Branthe snapped. "Even a blind fool could see that the Empire is dying."

"Do enlighten a blind fool such as me, then," Kullen said, the threat still clear in his tone.

"The once-great Karmian Empire has withered, gripped by the decay brought on by peace. Surely you are familiar with the writings of the military historian Necrodotus: Peace breeds weakness, weakness breeds chaos, chaos breeds war—"

"And war breeds strong men, who in turn breed peace once more," Kullen finished the famous quote. "So you're doing this because you want to return the Empire to war to what—strengthen it?"

"The Empire will die if it does not change," Magister Branthe said, his voice oddly filled with zeal. "Emperor Wymarc is a good man, but his goodness cannot stop his lands from withering, his subjects from starving, his Empire from descending into lawlessness and evil."

"But you can?" Kullen snorted. "Emperor Branthe would somehow be a better ruler?"

"This was never about me taking the rule!" Magister Branthe's eyes blazed. "That is for another to take. My part was always to stir up unrest, weakening the Emperor's political stranglehold." Branthe's voice grew weak, as if he'd used up his store of strength. His breathing became labored, wheezy. It was then that Kullen realized the tunnel was nearly full of the billowing dust. "Chaos breeds war, even if that is civil war."

"Is that why you had your followers kill the Prince and Princess?" Kullen demanded. "Why you gave the order for Deckard to burn down the Refuge? For civil war?"

Magister Branthe's expression grew strangely guarded, his lips pressing together into a tight line. "What I did with the Prince and Princess was for the sake of the Empire, yes. But the Refuge..." A cruel, coughing laugh bubbled from his lips. "That is the key to everything, but you, like everyone else, will never know the truth until it is too late."

The Refuge, key? The words made no sense to Kullen. An orphanage? How could something so simple—

"Who is Red Claw?" Kullen asked, desperate for one last answer. "Who is he?"

"Who indeed?" Magister Branthe began to wheeze louder now, his breaths coming harder. Kullen's gut clenched as he realized the truth: the wound to Magister Branthe's spine was fatal, not just paralyzing. His body was shutting down, no longer able to tell his send his blood pumping. Soon, his lungs would stop drawing in breath, his heart cease to beat if the tunnel didn't crumble first.

The aristocrat seemed to realize the truth in the same moment. His smile widened, and he sneered up at Kullen. "You'll get no more answers from me, assassin. The twilight of the Karmian Empire is approaching. Soon, a new power—a terrible, all-mighty power—will rise, and with it, bring about... a new age the likes of which... this world has never seen." His final words came out slurred, like he was drunk. Blood bubbled on his lips. "And you... will be alive... to see it... to see the end... of all things." He laughed despite his condition and that of the tunnel around them. "I both... envy... and pity... you."

Kullen snarled down at the man. Then, remembering the words etched all over the Embers, he said, "Blood for blood," and drove his dagger through the Magister's throat.

56

NATISSE

J ad's shout shattered Natisse's momentary surprise. She sprang to the side, barely avoiding a chunk of falling stone. The ceiling had begun to collapse, and in mere moments, it would cave in atop her head. A deep rumble continued as if the streets above were barely holding on. Branthe's guards, too, were likely to descend upon her at any second. Curious as she was, she hadn't the time to stand gawping over the strange Orken-like creatures. They had to get out—and take the enslaved creatures with them. She could worry about who—and what—they were once they were all safely far away.

"Uncle Ronan, Jad!" She spun toward the two men, who were busy herding the last of the prisoners out of the cells and sending them down the tunnel. "I need help here!"

She stepped into the cell, but as she entered, two wizened-looking elders barred her path.

"You not take them!" one snarled, his voice guttural and Orken accent thick. His eyes appeared like bottomless pits, the whites barely visible beyond dark eyelids. Thick eyebrows, white as freshly fallen snow, stuck out wildly, contrasting against honey-gold skin. He bared jagged, yellow teeth, extended long, dirty fingernails like claws, and the look in those eyes made it clear he intended to use them on her.

She showed her hands, raising them palm outward in a placating gesture.

"You understand my words?" she asked, hurried.

The Orken gave no response, but Natisse drove on anyway.

"We need to move, now!"

"We not go!"

"We're not here to hurt you." She looked to the Orken, small and frail, still desperate to escape the underground and the few remaining within the cells. More of the ceiling collapsed to her right. Dust filled the air. "We're here to get you out of this place. We have to go. If you come with us, we can escort you someplace safe!"

The old Orken's eyes narrowed, and suspicion flashed across his leathery features. Natisse couldn't blame him—she'd be damned skeptical too if she'd been locked in a cell for Ezrasil knew how long by creatures not of her race. No doubt to him, she was as foreign and alien as Orken were to her.

But she didn't have time to wait for the Orken to make up his mind.

"I swear that you will come to no harm as long as my friends and I can protect you."

Jad approached slowly behind her, his breath sharp. Uncle Ronan's eyes, too, were wide, his face drained of all color. When he spoke, his words were in a harsh, discordant tongue Natisse didn't understand.

The Orken, however, recognized the language, for he answered in kind. Just a few words, but Natisse saw his posture relax and surprise replace his suspicion.

"Come!" Uncle Ronan said, gesturing for them to follow. "You are safe—" He finished his sentence in that unfamiliar tongue.

A loud *crack* reminded them of the imminent danger, one of the crossbeams above splintering in two.

"We need to hurry!" Natisse urged.

That had an instant effect on not only the old Orken, but the rest of the creatures within the cage as well. Instantly, those who could climbed to their feet, then stooped to assist those too weak to rise. Natisse backed out of the cell to make way for them to shamble out from their incarceration.

"Natisse, Jad, clear a path for us!" Uncle Ronan barked. He was like a new man, restored by the Gryphic Elixir, and once more in command. "Get us bloody out of here."

"On it!" Natisse swallowed her questions—so many questions about who in Shekoth's pits "Uncle Ronan" really was and how he knew the language of these creatures—and dashed back up the inclining tunnel toward the fighting pit. Jad ran at her side, his long legs eating up the ground with ease. More than once, Jad took heavy hits from falling debris, but he shielded as many as he could from the impacts.

Through the gate, Natisse led the way toward the stairs, ready to fight.

But there would be no fighting now. Blood and bodies littered the stairs in a gory trail that ascended from the pit, and no more guards stood between her and freedom. Natisse couldn't help a grudging admiration for the dark-cloaked man—he'd done a damned good job of carving his way through the ranks of Magister Branthe's sellswords and brigands.

However, she stuffed her approbation for the man who'd murdered Baruch down quickly and picked her way up the stairs, careful not to slip on the blood-slicked stone or trip over the corpses barring her path. The alchemical fires had died, leaving only a few lightly burning benches and thick smoke clogging the underground chamber. Dozens more bodies scattered the rising benches which encircled the fighting pit. Most belonged to the noblemen who'd met a fitting end beneath the trampling feet of their fellows. Others were charred, a victim of the fire. Though some were guards freshly slain.

Only a handful of people still moved within the chamber now, all pushing and shoving their way toward the exit on the southern end of the room, fleeing toward their waiting carriages in Magister Onathus's shipyards. Through the doorway that led north toward Magister Perech's caravan yard, Natisse caught a glimpse of the dark-cloaked man kneeling over Magister Branthe with a bloodstained dagger in his hand.

A grim smirk toyed at her lips. She didn't know why this stranger had cause to kill the aristocrat, but she was glad for it. Magister Branthe had gotten what he deserved.

"Nat!" Jad's voice brought her attention back. The big man pointed toward their way out and moved toward the door. "If the others have kept to the plan, we're still going to have to fight our way free of the shipyards. Uncle Ronan and those... whatever they were won't be far behind." He adjusted the bloodied cestuses on his huge fists. "We need to clear a path."

She raced across the room. "I'll lead the way," she told him. "You watch my back."

Jad stepped into her path, an argument forming on his tongue. Natisse ducked around him and slid through the open doorway before he had a chance to speak. She knew how much tonight was costing him. She couldn't let him lose himself in the battle fury, as he dreaded he might. She had no qualms about shedding blood, at least not the blood of those who they would be facing at the end of the corridor.

Jad ran behind her, his heavy footsteps echoing, accompanied by hissing curses. Natisse ignored them and sprinted onward. He was fast for his size, but Natisse was far fleeter and could make the hundred-yard dash down the tunnel without losing her wind. Still, Jad was stubborn and determined to keep up, to guard her back as she'd requested. Running up the gently sloping passage, she reached the door at the end of the tunnel only a few steps ahead of him.

They burst free of the underground tunnel and into what she

instantly recognized as the northern end of Magister Onathus's shipyards. As Athelas had reported previously, there were scores of carriages, wains, and hansoms patiently waiting for their noble passengers within the shipyards.

Or at least there had been a few minutes earlier.

No one was patiently doing anything. Pandemonium gripped the scene. Horses reared and snorted, kicking out with their hooves at anything that drew too close. Men and women ran, screaming, searching for any means of escape. They were likely terrified the cave-in would draw the attention of the Emperor's guards—or, worse, Thanagar. Horses charged left and right, stampeding over man, woman, and Orken alike, their traces snapped— or, as Natisse knew, cut by sharp knives.

The clash of steel and angry barks drew Natisse's attention to where three guards were locked in combat with two smaller, hooded opponents. Two of Magister Onathus's blue-and-green clad guardsmen were bleeding and down, but Natisse saw the battle was about to turn tides against those left standing. Indeed, a vicious slash of one guard tore open a ragged wound down one of the hooded men's sword arms, knocking the weapon from his grasp.

Natisse felt the sting in her own heart and cried out, "No!"

Before she could leap into the fray, Jad let out a furious roar and barreled through the clumped noblemen staring helplessly at their horseless vehicles. He hurled stunned men and women aside, then threw himself onto the guards from behind. His huge fists pumped and his spiked gloves tore chunks out of the armed men. Within seconds, the three guardsmen were down, unconscious, dead, or dying.

Wave after wave of guards kept coming, as if Branthe had hired anyone willing to hold a sword. Jad took it all in stride, but suffered more than a few glancing blows.

His cestuses drove outward, caving in skulls, shredding flesh, and cracking bones.

Natisse raced toward the two hooded men, having to dodge armored soldiers being hurled every which way by an enraged Jad. She'd never seen the man like this. Berserker rage swallowed him, devoured anything beyond the enemies before him.

Natisse couldn't watch. She arrived just in time to catch the man with the wounded arm.

"Haston, you idiot!" she snarled. "I told you to handle the caravan yard!"

His hood fell back, revealing Haston's golden blond hair. His face was pale and wan, pinched in pain.

"And leave Athelas to handle this alone?" he croaked. "Not a chance. Besides, Nalkin's crew got back in time to lend a hand "

Natisse turned toward the other hooded man. "Athelas, you hurt?"

"I'm good," the young man called, shaking his head. "Haston got here just in time. Some of the guards spotted me sneaking among the horses and cutting the reins. Had he not showed up when he did, I might not be here."

Natisse wanted to scold Haston—the fool had been badly wounded just a day earlier, and even Serrod's skill wouldn't restore him to full fighting strength in such a short time. But she hadn't the time. The gawking noblemen and women might get it in their heads to do something stupid like draw blades or try to attack the men who'd fought the guards set by the dead Magister Onathus—or, in truth, his master, Magister Branthe—to guard their carriages. They had to get themselves and their rescued captives away from the shipyards before the Imperial Scales or Orkenwatch blocked off the only exit.

"Uncle Ronan's bringing some prisoners out," she told the two men. "Help him keep them safe from these pricks." She gestured to the terrified, smoke-blackened, white-faced fops around them. "Anyone gets it in their heads to stop you, take them down. Hard."

"Will do!" Haston said. Despite his injuries, he rose, giving her an eager grin.

Natisse cautiously approached Jad.

The man was soaked in blood—his enemies' blood. He barely looked like himself, the calm, gentle giant she'd known for so long. Violence and pain had replaced those now as Jad tore through the last of the guards. She recognized the two she'd dubbed Red Cheeks and Flat Nose. The former streamed blood from half a dozen puncture wounds Jad's spikes had left in his face and along his jawline, while the latter's nose was now truly flattened, shattered by one of Jad's vicious punches.

From behind, a soldier leaped and landed on Jad's back. The big man let out a primal roar that shook Natisse's insides. As he flailed about, she spotted the dagger piercing her friend's shoulder. Jad reached back but missed the elusive assailant. He tried and missed again.

Natisse shouted, "I've got him!" and jumped. She grabbed hold of the guard and realized her mistake too late. The knife-wielder held tight to the hilt and her added weight dragged him down and the blade along with them, slicing a deep gash into Jad's back.

He bellowed deeply. Both of his huge hands reached back and seized Natisse and his attacker. Jad pulled them forward and his fingers closed around their throats. Red-hot fire filled his eyes, rage in the basest sense.

Natisse tried to scream, tried to cry out for her friend to stop, but this wasn't Jad any longer. The anger had a hold of him and refused to relent.

She heard a sickening crunch as Jad crushed the soldier in his left hand. He dropped the man to a crumpled heap on the ground and turned his full attention to Natisse.

She'd hoped that in the moment, the big man would recognize her, would immediately release his grip and beg forgiveness. But none of that happened. He bared his teeth, growling. Veins popped on the sides of his neck and forehead.

"Jad," Natisse managed, but that was all. A single syllable. She tried again, but got the same results. Then, finally, she said, "Jad, please!"

It didn't happen all at once, and not nearly as quickly as she'd have liked, but eventually, his fingers loosened and Natisse fell to her feet. She gasped, heaved, and scrambled away, unsure if Jad would pick up the attack again.

He didn't.

But he said nothing either. Just stood there, shoulders rising and falling, the rage inside of him almost tangible.

Seeing him like this pained her. She looked around at the death and mayhem surrounding her friend. Men were not just dead, but utterly ruined. Limbs missing. Blood pooling like a small pond in the shipyard.

She knew Jad's gentle soul would bear the stain of the night's events for a long while yet, and hated that she'd been forced to ask it of him. Yet she had, for Uncle Ronan's sake, and the sake of all the other prisoners who they had just freed. There hadn't been time to formulate any other plans. It was this or nothing.

Life returned to Jad's eyes and the realization of what he'd done seemed to settle in.

"I—" he started.

"Did what needed doing," Natisse offered.

Startled cries from among the nobility heralded the emergence of Uncle Ronan with the Orken captives in tow. One and all, the ornately dressed men and women fell back from prisoners so frail and weak they didn't even begin to resemble those that had chased her just days ago. The aristocrats' expressions were thick with revulsion, outrage, and shock.

Natisse's hatred for them roiled within. What heartless, vile people were they that would look upon such a pathetic bunch with anything other than compassion? Natisse had to wonder if the Emperor knew anything of this.

Her eyes were drawn upward, toward the pillar of smoke and fire that filled the night sky to the north. Leroshavé—with the help of a recently returned Tobin, L'yo, and Nalkin—had done fine work. Even now, Magister Perech's caravan yards burned. The giant pillar of fire and smoke rising into the air served not only as a fine distraction for Natisse's infiltration of the pits, but also might've put a final nail in the coffin of the Dimvein slave trade. At least for now. No doubt there would be more like Magisters Branthe, Perech, Onathus, and Taradan who would find ways to profit off of the misfortunes of others. But for now…

No one would miss the Crimson Fang's message tonight.

"Blood for blood," Natisse told Jad, but the big man just continued to stand there as if coming out of a trance.

"Let's go!" Uncle Ronan shouted as he herded the former prisoners through the yards.

Haston and Athelas had already joined in. The Orken women and children looked terrified, but they followed nonetheless.

"We still need you, Jad," Natisse said, placing a hand on his arm. He jerked away, but only for a second. "We need you."

Jad grunted and took a few lumbering steps to catch up with the crowd.

As they approached the front gate, Natisse nearly tripped over a body lying in the middle of the dirt path. The man was no aristocrat—he wore only ripped trousers, and his back bore the welts and mark left by a slaver's whip. But he groaned.

In the darkness, she knelt and brushed the hair from the man's face.

"Can you hear me?" she asked. "Can you move?"

The wounded man—and from what little she could tell, would barely fit that description—groaned again.

"Okay," Natisse said. "We're going to help you. It might hurt."

He bled from a deep wound in his side, and he was nearly passed out from blood loss.

"Jad, can you…"

Jad knelt beside the downed slave. "He's hurt bad. We don't get that wound bandaged, he'll die."

Natisse sucked in a breath. Then a thought struck her. "Gryphic Elixir! Uncle Ronan has half a vial left."

Jad's eyes widened. "Where—"

"The man in the dark cloak dropped it," she said, anticipating his question. "It'll be enough to get him back on his feet, right?"

"Right." Jad hauled the unconscious man up and slung him across his massive shoulders as if the limp body weighed nothing.

"Time to make ourselves scarce," Natisse said. "Before the whole palace shows up to investigate."

57

KULLEN

"Where is it?" Kullen demanded of the Magister's dead body while the tunnel collapsed around him. He rummaged through Branthe's pockets in search of the dragonblood vial the aristocrat had taken from Prince Jaylen. To his relief, he found it tucked into his front shirt pocket, within easy reach. Removing the vial, Kullen tucked it into the pouch to join Magister Deckard's vial for safekeeping.

Only to realize Deckard's was no longer there.

He sucked in a sharp breath, cursing the guard who'd cut his cloak—and the strings holding the pouch in place. It was gone. As was the Gryphic Elixir he'd been carrying.

Kullen swore and slid the prince's vial into another pocket, sealing it tightly.

A small stone crashed down onto his shoulder from above, reminding him of the need for haste. He quickly searched the remainder of Magister Branthe's pockets. He doubted he'd find the vials taken from Magisters Taradan, Perech, Taradan, and all the others on the aristocrat's person, but he had to be certain.

As he'd feared, the vials were nowhere to be found; no doubt already handed out to the noblemen Magister Branthe had convinced to join his conspiracy. His plan to strike against the Emperor—by eliminating Wymarc's heir—had failed, but there was no telling what other hidden traps lay in wait, what other daggers lurked in the dark ready to strike. Assidius and Turoc would have their hands full sussing out the rest of Magister Branthe's treacheries. Kullen suspected he'd be set by the Emperor to deal with the rest of Magister Branthe's co-conspirators.

He reached into the final pocket, and his fingertip brushed something. A mark? He pulled out a small circular silver object bearing the same runes found etched into every Orken leader's gold beard rings. *A Kharag?*

Kullen glared down at Branthe. The *Kharag* passed as a form of currency among the Orkenwatch. Possession of such a token was meant to gain unquestioned access to Tuskthorne Tower's uppermost levels where the gold bands were quartered.

But why? Kullen knew there was at least one Orken working with Branthe, but how many others were privy to this place and its festivities? Was the whole Tower in on it?

Kullen was about to stand, but a thought flashed through his mind. Leaning forward, he seized Magister Branthe's dragonblood vial, careful to keep his fingers away from the cap, and tore it free of the dead aristocrat's neck, snapping the gold-link chain from which it hung. He tucked it into his pouch alongside Prince Jaylen's vial. He could never let such power fall into the wrong hands. In a way, he was partly to blame for the other missing vials—he'd carried out his duty to the Emperor, but had failed to anticipate the possibility that someone would steal the magical artifacts from the slain noblemen. He'd never be guilty of overlooking such a thing again.

By this time, the noxious smoke had dissipated, leaving only the corpses and unconscious forms of Magister Branthe's guards. Kullen gave the whimpering man with the broken arm a wide berth, stepping over the other bodies on his hurried way back toward the fighting pits. Behind him, he could hear the steady clattering of stones as the tunnel continued its collapse.

Kullen picked his way down the blood-soaked, corpse-strewn stairs that led down into the sands. He spotted his purse lying where it had fallen after being cut away in the clash, but when he turned it over, he found it was empty. No sign of Magister Deckard's dragonblood vial or the Gryphic Elixir.

"Damn it to Shekoth's pits!"

There was any number of people who could have picked it up —one of Magister Branthe's guards, one of the fleeing slaves, even the red-haired woman and her comrades fighting to escape. That weathered but tough old man had been wounded badly—even half that vial of Gryphic Elixir would've gotten him back on his feet in no time.

It made sense, but only compounded Kullen's anger. Anger at himself, at the bastard who'd damaged Jarius's cloak, and, most of all, at Magister Branthe. Had it not been for the traitorous aristocrat, he wouldn't have had to come all the way down here to rescue Prince Jaylen.

The Prince!

Kullen's heartbeat quickened. He'd sent the prince out of the underground chamber along with the rest of the fleeing nobility, ordered him to get himself back to the Palace. But the young man was far too inexperienced in the ways of the world—at least the world outside the safety and security of the Palace's walls. There was no telling what sort of trouble he'd gotten himself dragged into over the minutes since they'd parted ways.

Kullen tore off through the sands and up the stairs toward the only exit that hadn't been cut off. His heart stopped as he spotted the body of a young man lying against the wall. For a moment, his blood turned to ice and his steps faltered. The man had been crushed in the stampede, the back of his skull caved in, his spine snapped, and his legs shattered.

His dark hair fell in a mop over his face. Kullen's heart may've stopped. His stomach definitely flipped. A faltering step brought him to the young man. He stretched out a shaking hand to grip one slim, bloodstained shoulder. But as his fingers closed on the torn shirt, a memory slammed into his mind. Prince Jaylen standing bloody and beaten in the fighting pit, his slim torso bare, his back marked by the lash of a whip.

Even as he turned the body over, relief flooded through him. The poor bastard was dead but it wasn't the Prince! He recognized the young man who'd been sitting next to Magister Branthe in his private box. His nephew, Baronet Ochrin. Kullen didn't know what his role in the slave trafficking and fighting pit had been, but if he'd been at his uncle's side watching the spectacle, he was complicit as far as the Emperor was concerned. His death was no tragedy—Kullen would call it grim justice.

Kullen let out a long breath, and the momentary tremor in his hands stilled. His respite was brief. The body may not have belonged to the Prince, but that didn't mean Jaylen was safe.

He charged up the incline, unsure where it would lead. However, light at the end of the tunnel spurred him onward. It opened up into the shipyard—Magister Onathus's shipyards.

Horses screamed and ran in all directions, while harried coachmen and their disheveled masters fought to regain control of the panicking beasts. The smell of smoke and dust hung thick in the air. The shipyards weren't burning but fires blazed to the north. The sight of it made Kullen sick once more. Dimvein was in flames again.

Terrified aristocrats were emptying into the streets, shell-shocked, covered in ash, many bearing alchemical burns or gushing wounds. Kullen wished he could chop them all down here and now. He wouldn't spare them a shred of pity. Indeed, his anger only mounted at the sight of their fearful expressions and pale faces. What they felt was only a fraction of what was to come. He made a mental list of each face he could identify, their house colors for those he couldn't. He'd deliver that list personally to the Emperor and make certain that everyone who'd been involved in the slave fighting—even as mere spectators—suffered harsh consequences. Arbiter Chuldok would soon have a fresh crop of aristocratic subjects upon which to practice his torturer's arts. If any of them could be tied to Magister Branthe's conspiracy, the Arbiter would uncover the link.

But what if Chuldok was in on it? What if all the Orken were? He pulled the rune-inscribed token from his pocket and glared at it.

He shook his head. That was a problem for later.

Scanning the crowd, he searched for any sign of Jaylen, but couldn't find the Prince's face anywhere. His worry mounted with every beat of his heart. Not even for a second did he believe Jaylen had made it safely to the Palace. The heir to the Empire had gotten himself captured, beaten, and thrown into a fighting pit already today—no telling what sort of trouble he'd find himself in next.

Kullen darted from alley to alley, looking behind every crate and barrel. There was no sign of Jaylen. However, there were bodies abundant. Guards mostly. Blood, gore. Death. It was as if war had come to Dimvein.

Branthe's words came crawling up Kullen's spine: "Chaos breeds war, even if that is civil war."

No one could be trusted, not even the Orkenwatch.

And now there was another dragonblood vial out in the world —Deckard's. One which the Emperor had trusted Kullen to keep safe.

Branthe was dead and as much as Kullen wanted to believe the man was the Red Claw, he had no proof. He'd come here for answers and was only left with more questions.

A sudden and blinding light broke through the darkness of the shipyards. Kullen turned toward the main gates. No less than two dozen Lumenators stood, globes glowing bright. Five times as many armored silhouettes stood beside them—the Imperial Scales. At the front, Kullen could just make out Captain Angban.

"Nobody move!" Angban shouted. "Every Ezrasil-damned one of you bastards is under arrest, by order of the Emperor himself!"

58

NATISSE

N atisse didn't stop running until she reached the welcoming darkness of the old theater from which the Crimson Fang had spent the last few days watching Magister Onathus's shipyards. They were far enough away from the scene of the chaos to be outside the search radius when the Orkenwatch and Imperial Scales finally showed up, but close enough that the man Jad carried over his shoulder wouldn't bleed out.

Still, there was a lot of blood staining Jad's black coat and arms when he finally lowered the unconscious man onto a cloak Natisse had Haston spread out on a relatively dust-free section of the theater's floor. While Jad bent over the man, Natisse turned back toward Uncle Ronan, who, with Athelas's help, were herding the freed Orken captives in. One by one, they took seats in the theater's pews.

Natisse hurried to where Uncle Ronan stood by the door, watching for any sign of pursuit. "That Elixir, you have any left?" She jerked a thumb over her shoulder at the unconscious man. "He's in bad shape. Between the whip marks on his back and the deep gouge in his torso, there's a chance he'll bleed out soon."

Uncle Ronan turned to her, his face drawn, tense with worry.

"No," he said sharply, shaking his head. "Used what I had left on Athelas. He took a nasty cut, and would have died without it."

Natisse's jaw muscles clenched, and not just from worry for the slave who might very well not live to see the morning. There was so much she wanted to ask Uncle Ronan—or General Andros—but his expression made it clear that pushing him for answers now wouldn't do either of them any good. There was a warning look in his eyes, a dark storm cloud hanging over him.

Natisse would ask him all the questions on her mind, when the time was right. At the moment, there were bigger fish to fry.

"You going tell me what they are?" she asked, her eyes darting toward the Orken huddling together. "And how you—"

"Not now." Uncle Ronan cut her off, his grizzled face stretching taut with warning. "Go, help Jad do what he can to stanch the bleeding. Send Haston over to help me."

"Help you what?" Natisse snapped. "I don't even know who you *are* anymore."

Uncle Ronan clenched his jaw. He might not be outright lying to her—that she could prove, at least—but the omission of so much made her angry enough that her temper flared.

"Just do it," Uncle Ronan barked in that tone of command. Then, without another word, he turned on his heel and marched toward the weakling Orken.

Natisse watched him go, suddenly keenly aware of the military precision in his posture and step, the air of authority that had always hung around him. The Crimson Fang had taken their orders from him with so little question—the way an army heeded their superior officer. Through it all, she couldn't help but wonder if it were true, that all this time they'd been following *the* General Andros.

It was a shame Baruch hadn't known.

And why hadn't Baruch known? Dammit, for all the lies!

If he wasn't going to fill her in on what she needed to know, she damned well wasn't going to stand around waiting for him to come to her. The Crimson Fang had finally succeeded in executing the mission for which they'd been trained. They'd put an end to the slave trafficking operations in Dimvein. They'd freed hundreds of captives and slaves tonight—not just humans, but these poor Orken as well.

Now, they just had to get back to the safety of the Burrow and lie low. Then she would have time to consider her next steps. And pry answers from Uncle Ronan, no matter how fiercely he tried to keep his secrets.

It would take some doing to sneak a few dozen Orken through the streets of Dimvein, even as skinny and frail as they were, even in the darkness of a cloudy night. Haston and Uncle Ronan would be the ones best suited to figuring out their path to freedom. Leroshavé had been given orders to return to base once he finished setting fire to the caravan yards—and he'd take Nalkin, L'yo, and Tobin with him.

"Haston!" Natisse shouted. "Uncle Ronan needs you."

The man responded quickly and rushed through the arched doorway, following Uncle Ronan out and into the next room.

Natisse looked across the theater at the man lying near Jad, blood leaking from a deep wound. She couldn't leave him to bleed out. And she knew Jad wouldn't, not even if Uncle Ronan ordered him to.

The man lay on his back, and though the night inside the theater was too dark to see his features clearly, his physicality made it clear that he was young. Too young, perhaps, to survive the wounds he'd sustained. He was no hardened warrior or soldier toughened by training and years of battle.

That realization made what Natisse had to say even harder.

"There's no more Elixir," she said quietly as she approached. "Uncle Ronan gave it to Athelas. Said he needed it."

Jad growled low in his throat.

"Damn it!" He pressed his hands harder against the long, deep wound in the young man's side. "We need to get this bleeding under control. He's already lost so much blood. Any more, and he won't wake up."

"What can I do?" she asked, kneeling at his side. "I'm no Sparrow, but tell me how I can help, and I'll do it."

Jad's bloodstained face twisted into a pensive frown. He remained silent for a long second, then spoke quickly. "We're going to need to cauterize his wound if he's going to have any chance of surviving. You got anything to heat a knife red-hot?"

Natisse thought about it, then shook her head. "No."

"Shite," Jad said.

Panic came over Natisse for long moments before she had an idea.

"Wait here," she said.

She found Haston and Uncle Ronan in the next room. Haston had a long tool pressed against the collar on Uncle Ronan's neck.

"He's going to bleed out," she said. "But you can stop it, can't you?"

Uncle Ronan gave her a hard glare, squeezed his lips shut and shook his head slowly.

"He's going to die," she repeated.

"People die," Uncle Ronan said, low.

"Who's gonna die?" Haston asked.

They both ignored him.

"You can keep lying all you want, but right now, that man needs you," she said. "He needs what only you can do."

"Let's finish this, Haston," Uncle Ronan said and turned his attention back to what he was doing.

"Baruch told me stories about you," Natisse said. "Said you were the bravest man to ever live. I guess that was a lie too."

Uncle Ronan didn't look up.

"He told me stories about Blackwater Bay—that was his favorite—about the Hudar and about when you tamed gryphons in the west and used them against the Southern Kingdoms. Were they all just stories? Tall tales about a has-been?"

"What's she talking about?" Haston asked.

"Fine," Natisse said. "Let him die. What's one more disappointment?"

She turned and left the room, returning to the bleeding young man.

"Did you find something?" Jad asked.

Natisse shook her head.

That was it. This slave was going to die just like so many others had. All because the Crimson Fang couldn't stop the evil that plagued this city. For years, they'd fought for people like this. Who else would? Someone needed to stand up for the downtrodden if the Emperor wouldn't.

They'd accomplished a lot tonight, but somehow the death of this one man seemed to encompass every shred of their mission. If this man died, their mission was a failure. She knew it wasn't reasonable, but—

"Move aside," came a voice from behind her.

Uncle Ronan pushed his way through. His neck was free of the collar, revealing the burn mark that had been there as long as she'd known him.

He bent beside the dying boy and pressed his hands to the wound. Bright blue-white light shone from his palms like daylight itself.

"What in Shekoth's…" Jad whispered.

A groan from the young man drew Natisse's attention to their rescued captive. In the light of Uncle Ronan's Lumenator's globe, she got a first look at his face.

Suddenly, it wasn't clear what Jad was exclaiming over: Uncle Ronan's use of magic, or the identity of the young man lying between them.

She'd never laid eyes on Prince Jaylen before this night, but there was no doubt about it. Magister Branthe had laughed as he promised Uncle Ronan would live if he killed the Prince, and the young man himself had attempted to order the aristocrat to desist his activities—"in the name of the Emperor, my grandfather," he'd said.

Natisse looked up at Uncle Ronan, then to Jad. Jad looked as stunned as her but Uncle Ronan just stood and walked away, his job done.

Of all the people to collapse in her path, of all the lives to save, why did it have to be Prince Jaylen? She hated the nobility and everything they represented: avarice, callous disdain for human life, misuse of wealth, seemingly endless lust for power, and every other nasty vice she could come up with. But their cruelty and depravity paled in comparison to Emperor Wymarc's. The man sat high in his Palace, behind strong walls that protected his luxury, feasting while his people starved. The enormous dragon perched at the highest point in the city was a daily reminder of the Emperor's power—and what he could do to any who opposed him.

Perhaps the only thing she detested more than the Emperor was dragons. Magister Branthe's men had killed her mother, but it was that terrible red dragon who had burned her father alive. She'd barely escaped with her life but lost her parents—and every memory of her life before that day—in the process.

She felt her hand moving toward her dagger. Temptation rose within her chest to kill the man Uncle Ronan had just saved.

"Uncle Ronan is a..." Jad's words hung in the air like flakes of snow.

Natisse looked up from her blade and into Jad's eyes. Gone was the berserker rage and in its place was that familiar, gentle look of concern. That was the Jad she knew, the soft-hearted, gentle healer. Despite the blood staining his hands, face, and clothing he would never let her harm a soul.

If he recognized Prince Jaylen from the fighting pit, his face betrayed no sign of it. And from what she knew of him, Natisse had no doubt that Jad wouldn't care who Prince Jaylen or his grandfather were. All Jad saw was a hurt man in need of his help. Nothing mattered to Jad in that moment except saving the man.

And Natisse knew he was right. Much as she despised the Emperor, she couldn't simply stand by and allow Prince Jaylen to die. She had taken lives, certainly, in the name of survival and the mission, but she was no cold-blooded killer.

Though it took every shred of willpower, she forced her hand to sheathe her blade.

"Uncle Ronan is a Lumenator?" Jad asked, this time getting the words out.

It was the first time she had confirmation that the others didn't know either. It was somehow comforting.

"There's much for us to discuss," Natisse said. "But for now..." She smiled. "We did it. We really did it."

The grin started small on Jad's face, then grew exponentially until it was all Natisse could see.

She thought of the burning flames within the fighting pits. The memories that had haunted her mind for her entire life had finally coalesced, and she had faced her past—and defeated it. She'd fought down her instinctive panic that threatened to paralyze her, had walked through the fire—not literally, but damned close enough—and slain her mother's murderer. The man who'd had her father killed, Magister Branthe with his silver dragon, had died, too, at the hands of that dark-cloaked man.

Thoughts of the man sent a shiver down her spine. Now that was a killer. She'd looked him in the eye and seen only death staring back at her. Perhaps not her death, at least not in that moment, but death all the same. She hadn't known it then, but there was no doubt in her mind now: if she had attacked him, he would have killed her.

Of course!

She cursed herself for a forgetful fool. She'd picked up two vials from the sand—the Gryphic Elixir had not been alone. She'd also pocketed a bottle that contained some strange red alchemical fluid.

"Jad, look," she said, digging into her pocket with a free hand, "do you recognize this?" She plucked out the vial and thrust it toward him. "Maybe it's some kind of alchemical remedy that can – ouch!" A sharp, pricking pain lanced her finger where it had pressed against the vial's golden cap.

"What happened?" Jad began to ask, but his words suddenly froze halfway out of her mouth. Everything around her slowed, the world grinding to a standstill.

Natisse tried to draw in a breath, but she couldn't. Even her heart refused to beat—everything had gone utterly motionless.

Then she felt the presence in her mind. It was enormous, seeming as vast as the ocean, emanating a terrible power the likes of which she could never imagine.

Fire burned inside of her, hotter than the dragonfire that had scorched her flesh. Hotter than anything she'd ever felt before. She felt it in her heart, her soul, her very being.

"*I see fire,*" came a deep, powerful voice—not in her ears, but somehow in her thoughts, as if from inside her own head. "*I hear the screams. You have known pain, so much pain. As have I. But it has made us strong. You are strong, mortal. As strong as any mortal I have known. But strong enough to endure the bond?*"

"*The bond?*" she thought.

She looked around, seeing nothing and no one but Jad, Prince Jaylen, and the Orken prisoners, most of whom were sleeping in the theater seats.

"*I will not be enslaved again!*" the voice roared in her mind, so loud Natisse wanted to cry out. But she couldn't. She couldn't even move, her body as motionless as the world around her. "*I will not be trapped by the weak-willed and cruel-minded. You wish to possess my loyalty, then let us see your strength!*"

Fire exploded from within her. She felt the heat of it on her skin, in her soul. She thought the theater would be consumed, it was so ferocious. But then, her vision cleared and she didn't see the theater at all. There was no Jad, no Orken, nothing. Just her and the now distant flames.

She stood in a stream of lava but it didn't burn her. She thought she heard the sounds of her mother screaming out, of Joakim laughing, but the moment she acknowledged it, the sounds dissipated, leaving her with just the roar of flames and the whistle of invisible wind.

"Hello?" she said, taking a few tentative steps. Despite the immense heat, she felt no pain. No fear, either. There was no threat to her here...wherever here was. Only a sense of over-whelming curiosity. But whose?

Behind her, she heard the flapping of wings. She spun quickly, but there was no sign of a dragon. It happened again. She turned. Empty space.

"Hello?" she called again, heart beating faster.

The ground shook and she whirled once more. There stood a magnificent red dragon. Its fiery eyes burned into hers. Two long horns rose almost straight upward from the top of its head. Their tips were nearly as sharp as the beast's claws. But both paled in comparison to its teeth. Long white fangs the size of Natisse's whole arm rose and fell like cave rock formations from its lips.

The dragon lowered its head. It sniffed, burning hot air gusting like gale winds from its nostrils as it sniffed her. It felt as if the creature was probing her very mind, reading her thoughts, judging her.

Natisse stared, frozen in place. Its lips parted, nearly touching her.

"*We are kindred, you and I,*" the creature spoke into her thoughts. "*You believe it's not so, but it is. You fear the flames. They consume your thoughts and dreams. That is good. A fearful mind is a careful mind. And a careful mind will not lightly unleash my power— nor seek to abuse it as others have in the past.*"

Natisse could do nothing but think back to her visions, her

dreams, of that horrible red dragon that had laid waste to her home, her world, had killed her parents."

"Those flames were not mine," the dragon said, making it clear that it did, indeed, read her mind. *"The one you hate was my mate, my lover."*

"Was?" Natisse said, barely getting the word out.

"I could not abide such wanton destruction," the dragon said. *"He will trouble this realm no more."*

Natisse stood, stunned. Could a dragon feel such remorse over something done by one of her fellows? Her mate? Natisse had spent the better part of her life despising these creatures, thinking them all cruel and callous. Had she been wrong?

"You were not wrong," the dragon said. *"I, too, have done terrible things. Your city still suffers for my actions."*

"The Embers... It was you?"

"The true fault lies with one who sought to control me, to force upon me the yoke of bloodsworn." The dragon's head sank toward the smoking lava-covered floor. *"But it was* my *flames that brought about such death and destruction. I wrestled with him, but I could not stop him from using my power. Long have I sought to be free. And yet, I sense in you great pain, but the desire to spare others such suffering. To use what power you have to free others from their burden of pain. Is that an accurate judgment?"*

"I... I don't know," Natisse admitted.

"But I do." The dragon lumbered closer, so close its enormous eyes stared directly into hers. *"And so, I offer you my bond."*

"You offer..." Natisse blinked. "Your *what?*"

The crimson dragon growled low in its throat. *"It is the night of the Dragon Cycle. The blood moon. And you have mixed your blood with mine."*

Natisse didn't understand. Then she looked down.

"The vial," she whispered. A small droplet of blood still bubbled from where the needle had pricked her.

"Yes. My old bloodsworn *is gone and I will spare him not another*

thought. But you... you are different. You are... good. I have been blood-sworn to vile men for longer than I care to remember. I long for something new, something better."

"Me?" Natisse asked, barely able to comprehend what was happening.

"You." The dragon lowered its neck, her head nearly touching the ground. To Natisse, it felt like she was bowing to royalty. *"I am Golgoth, Queen of the Ember Dragons, and if you will have me, I shall be your* bloodsworn."

Natisse was at a loss for words. This creature before her was nothing like she'd expected. It was gentle, and kind, and Natisse could almost *feel* the dragon's emotions. Golgoth was desperate for union with someone who would respect her and use her immense power for good.

And moreover, Natisse wanted to be that someone. She didn't understand it—she'd spent her entire adult life *hating* creatures like this, but now a desire beyond her understanding burned within her with such force she could not ignore it.

Turmoil stirred within Natisse's belly, but she acted as she'd been trained to, following her instincts. "Yes!" The words tore from her lips. "I will have you."

No sooner had she spoken than power sizzled within her. She felt the binding of their spirits like a thread of molten gold entwined around their very souls. A flood of emotions rushed through her, assaulted her mind. The memories of Golgoth's mate — Shahitz'ai, for that was his name Natisse now knew. She experienced within her mind the battle between them once Golgoth had heard of Shahitz'ai's destructive deeds. The pain Golgoth felt banishing to the Fire Realm—*this* realm—the one who had once held her heart. All connection to the Mortal Realm forever severed.

She felt pain, saw visions of searing flames pouring from her—Golgoth's open maw—as the Imperial Commons became the Embers, forever renamed for the damage that was done. She felt the disdain for the Magister who had tried to own her, to dominate her.

Most of all, she felt power. So much power. Enough to turn Dimvein and all the Karmian Empire to ash. Hand in hand came a desire for restraint. Control. An unshakeable will as mighty as the immense dragon standing before her.

"That is the bond," Golgoth said, rumbling low in its throat and loosing a snuff of hot air through its enormous nostrils. "We are bloodsworn, little human. I am at your command. Do *not* make me regret it."

Natisse went to reply, but darkness engulfed her, the surrounds—the Fire Realm—disappeared. Then, bright, blinding, orange light was all she could see. She heard a scream, a voice she was familiar with. Jad's voice.

He was calling her name.

"—tisse?" Jad was frowning up at her. "Are you—Ezrasil's bones!" His eyes flew wide and his face was pale in the firelight. "Nat!"

Firelight? Natisse frowned. Where was it coming from? Where was—

Then she looked down, and saw brilliant red flames wreathing her from head to toe.

She was the fire.

THANK YOU FOR READING BLACK TALON

We hope you enjoyed it as much as we enjoyed bringing it to you. We just wanted to take a moment to encourage you to review the book. Follow this link: *Black Talon* to be directed to the book's Amazon product page to leave your review.

Every review helps further the author's reach and, ultimately, helps them continue writing fantastic books for us all to enjoy.

Want to discuss our books with other readers and even the authors? Join our Discord server today and be a part of the Aethon community.

Facebook | Instagram | Twitter | Website

You can also join our non-spam mailing list by visiting www.subscribepage.com/AethonReadersGroup and never miss out on future releases. You'll also receive three full books completely Free as our thanks to you.

Did you love Black Talon? Get more books by the authors

In the West, there are worse things to fear than bandits and outlaws. Demons. Monsters. Witches. James Crowley's sacred duty as a Black Badge is to hunt them down and send them packing, banish them from the mortal realm for good. He didn't choose this life. No. He didn't choose life at all. Shot dead in a gunfight many years ago, now he's stuck in purgatory, serving the whims of the White Throne to avoid falling to hell. Not quite undead, though not alive either, the best he can hope for is to work off his penance and fade away. This time, the White Throne has sent him investigate a strange bank robbery in Lonely Hill. An outlaw with the ability to conjure ice has frozen and shattered open the bank vault and is now on a spree, robbing the region for all it's worth. In his quest to track down the ice-wielder and suss out which demon is behind granting a mortal such power, Crowley finds himself face-to-face with hellish beasts, shapeshifters, and, worse … temptation. But the truth behind the attacks is worse than he ever imagined … *The Witcher* meets *The Dresden Files* in this weird Western series by the Audible number-one bestselling duo behind *Dead Acre*.

GET COLD AS HELL NOW AND EXPERIENCE WHAT PUBLISHER'S WEEKLY CALLED PERFECT FOR FANS OF JIM BUTCHER AND MIKE CAREY.

Also available on audio, voiced by Red Dead Redemption 2's Roger Clark

(Arthur Morgan)

Nolan Garrett is Cerberus. A government assassin, tasked with fixing the galaxy's darkest, ugliest problems with a bullet to the brain. Armed with cutting-edge weapons and an AI-run cybernetic suit that controls his paralyzed legs, he is the fist in the shadows, the dagger to the heart of the Nyzarian Empire's enemies. Then he found Bex on his doorstep... A junkie, high on the drug he'd fought for years to avoid, and a former elite soldier like him. So he takes her in to help her get clean—Silverguards never leave their own behind. If only he'd known his actions would put him in the crosshairs of the most powerful cartel in New Avalon. Facing an army of gangbangers, drug pushers, and thugs, Nolan must fight to not only carry out his mission, but to prevent the escalating violence from destroying everything he loves.

Get Assassination Protocol Now!

For all our Aethon Books, visit our website.

Follow me on Amazon!

J aime Castle hails from the great nation of Texas where he lives with his wife and two children. A self-proclaimed comic book nerd and artist, he spends what little free time he can muster with his art tablet.

Jaime is a #1 Audible Bestseller, Audible Originals author (Dead Acre, The Luna Missile Crisis) and co-created and co-authored The Buried Goddess Saga, including the IPPY award-winning Web of Eyes.

All books below are available on eBook, Print, and Audiobook

The Buried Goddess Saga (Epic Fantasy)

Harrier (Superheroes)
Justice
The Trench
Invasion

Find out more at www.jaimecastle.com
https://www.facebook.com/authorjaimecastle

I am, first and foremost, a story-teller and an artist—words are my palette. Fantasy is my genre of choice, and I love to explore the darker side of human nature through the filter of fantasy heroes, villains, and everything in between. I'm also a freelance writer, a book lover, and a guy who just loves to meet new people and spend hours talking about my fascination for the worlds I encounter in the pages of fantasy novels.

Fantasy provides us with an escape, a way to forget about our mundane problems and step into worlds where anything is possible. It transcends age, gender, religion, race, or lifestyle--it is our way of believing what cannot be, delving into the unknowable, and discovering hidden truths about ourselves and our world in a brand new way. Fiction at its very best!

Join my Facebook Reader Group for updates, LIVE readings, exclusive content, and all-around fantasy fun.

Let's Get Social!

Be My Friend: https://www.facebook.com/andrew.peloquin.1

Facebook Author Page: https://www.facebook.com/andyqpeloquin

Twitter: https://twitter.com/AndyPeloquin

Printed in Great Britain
by Amazon